Praise for C. Hope Clark

Hope Clark's books have been honored as winners of the Epic Award, Silver Falchion Award, and the Daphne du Maurier Award.

"Her beloved protagonist, Callie, continues to delight readers as a strong, savvy, and a wee-bit-snarky police chief."
—Julie Cantrell *New York Times* and *USA Today* bestselling author on *Dying on Edisto*

"Award-winning writer C. Hope Clark delivers another one-two punch of intrigue with *Edisto Stranger*. . . . Clark really knows how to hook her readers with a fantastic story and characters that jump off the page with abandon. Un-put-downable from the get-go."
—Rachel Gladston, All Booked Up Reviews

"The scenery is rich, the characters interesting, and the mysteries complex."
—Bonnie Tharp, NetGalley Reviewer on *Edisto Tidings*

"Page-turning . . . [and] edge-of-your-seat action. . . . Prepare to be absorbed by Clark's crisp writing and compelling storytelling. This is one you don't want to miss!"
—Carolyn Haines, *USA Today* bestselling author on *Dying on Edisto*

The Novels of C. Hope Clark

The Carolina Slade Mysteries

Lowcountry Bribe

Tidewater Murder

Palmetto Poison

Newberry Sin

Salkehatchie Secret

The Edisto Island Mysteries

Murder on Edisto

Edisto Jinx

Echoes of Edisto

Edisto Stranger

Dying on Edisto

Edisto Tidings

Reunion on Edisto

Reunion on Edisto

Book 7 – Edisto Island Mysteries

by

C. Hope Clark

Bell Bridge Books

Bell Bridge Books
PO BOX 300921
Memphis, TN 38130
Print ISBN: 978-1-61194-996-4

Bell Bridge Books is an Imprint of BelleBooks, Inc.

We at BelleBooks enjoy hearing from readers.
Visit our websites
BelleBooks.com
BellBridgeBooks.com
ImaJinnBooks.com

10 9 8 7 6 5 4 3 2 1

Cover design: Debra Dixon
Interior design: Hank Smith
Photo/Art credits:
(manipulated): C. Hope Clark

:Lert:01:

Dedication

This tale of fiction is dedicated to the Summerville High School Class of 1974, Summerville, SC. They know why. Go *Green Wave*.

Prologue

JJ

JJ LOVELESS BROKE up her eight-hour drive from Nashville to Edisto Beach with an overnight stay in Atlanta, to see Antonio and run her thoughts by him for her next book. She was writing it whether he liked it or not. She'd already gone too far with it to alter her course anyway. She even had loose thoughts for a book after that, both ideas complete departures from those past. Unfortunately, her literary agent tended to freak at her wishes for change.

Twenty years ago she donned initials to hide her gender in the mystery world, and until the last five years had written from the dark, not making many appearances. Slowly but surely her talent evolved.

Her fan following *crept* into being, she liked to say, but finally the world embraced diverse authors and all they brought to the literary world. Her mother had been a product of Viet Nam with an Air Force father and Asian mother. Her father black from deep within the Carolina Lowcountry. The depth of her creative well was endless, no longer limited by genes.

Giddy at the concept spurred into being five years ago, the timing for this new book couldn't be more perfect. If the story came together as she hoped, it could be the masterpiece she'd be remembered for.

She made good time south on I-75, and as she crossed I-285, which circled the city, she used voice command on her Audi to check on Antonio.

"Hello, my sweetness. Where are you?" he answered. Low-level music in the background along with the tinkling of glassware. Totally predictable.

"Crossing into the city," she said, "and I expect a vodka rocks as tall as I am when I arrive."

He gave his signature tsk and subsequent sigh. "How you can drink those things is beyond my comprehension." He was there already, he said, eager to oblige, and she could meet him at the Lockhart for dinner.

Predictable, that man. No point in her coming to New York when he could just as easily fly to Georgia, he'd said. After all, he had arrangements to make for her latest mystery, the one coming out in November, but JJ knew better. His current beau served as chef for a well-known restaurant in the heart of the Peachtree City.

Once she arrived they shared gossip, compared her to other authors, him to other agents, but then over crab fritters she broke the news. Over grilled grouper in a scuppernong sauce, she opened the plot. And since he hadn't yet dismissed the book, she allowed him insight into her plan over the fig soufflé.

"I love it," he said. "Absolutely love it, girl. And the personal touch . . . we'll worry about legalities later, but this, my friend, could work."

But then the chef arrived, and Antonio knew better than to mix business and pleasure. The food had been foreplay, and the three of them knew it. After coffee, they retired to the chef's high-rise apartment where the gentleman routinely put them both up. The lemon ricotta pancakes the next morning always made the couple's love noises worth the trouble.

By noon JJ left energized, eager to make up the remaining five hours to Edisto Beach. She had a tale to spin, research to do, and clues to drop into place, water, and grow.

Chapter 1

THE SUN RICOCHETED off the incoming tide of the Dawhoo River. Over it, traffic snaked across the McKinley Washington Bridge, escaping the mainland like the plague. March winds followed the brackish creeks, licking up whitecaps and making sixty-six degrees feel ten degrees cooler, but enthusiastic beachgoers poured onto Edisto Island regardless, like goose-bump sunbathing was a rite of passage. Had to be warmer on the sand, right?

Ten a.m., Police Chief Callie Jean Morgan parked her cruiser at the corner of Portia Street and Palmetto Boulevard, judiciously still in long sleeves. From behind shades she scanned zealous drivers jockeying for places to park. Half-naked, cream-skinned folk on feet not yet calloused, high-stepped across the street, scurrying to stake their claims. Winter bellies out. Bikinis too new for tan lines.

Callie had just completed her second circuit around the tourist town, judging whether the lower temp had intimidated visitors. No such luck.

Easter came in March this year, plus this was the first Friday of the first spring break in South Carolina, and while the commercial side of Edisto welcomed the early horde, the year-round natives sighed with resignation. Nevertheless, Callie and her officers would juggle the car mishaps, trespassing complaints, and illegal parking, the latter having a raised fine of fifty dollars per the last town council meeting.

Beach season had arrived.

"First fender bender of the year," came a voice across her radio. "I won the pot."

Callie grinned into her mic at the enthusiasm of her youngest officer. "Can you handle it?"

"At Jungle Road and 174. Could use some help."

"Be right there," she replied and flipped on her light. A family of four with fifty pounds of beach gear scampered back up on the curb, letting her turn past them onto Palmetto.

June, barely two months away, would be two years since she'd planted permanent roots. Her childhood vacations on Edisto Beach left indelible memories, but none like those that came with year-round living . . . or policing these blocks. She could name each house and resident, and with the help of her admin queen, Marie, could recite skeletons of each.

Appointed by the town council, Callie's indoctrination into beach politics had come with wounds, lessons, and ultimate wisdom. They needed her now, and through thick and thin she guessed she needed them, too.

She rounded Palmetto at the Pavilion and hit a wall of cars and trucks. With a few *whoop-whoops*, she managed to reach the entrance of the State Park, left her lights on, and, eyes on drivers, zig-zagged her way on foot to Officer Thomas Gage.

Always a favorite with the ladies, the dark-headed officer stood fit and tanned amongst the melee, rerouting cars, hat low on his brow and arms snapping attention to drivers. He'd parked the two accident victims at the entrance of the Bi-Lo, soon to be Food Lion, not long ago having been a Piggly Wiggly.

Guess Pig-Lo would soon be Pig-Lion.

Callie and Thomas untied the worst of the traffic knot, and with the bottleneck eased she turned to her officer. "Want to handle the accident or the traffic? Shouldn't take long with the both of us."

"Traffic." Abruptly he stared over her head, his height a ten-inch advantage. "Watch it!" He leaped quickly beside her to pop a palm hard on the hood of a small Honda that veered too close. The car dipped, the woman behind the wheel wide-eyed and afraid to move until he pointed at her then down the road, telling her to proceed.

"How did these idiots get licenses?" he said, falling back into his conversation. His head tilted toward the parking lot. "Those two over there claim they know you. Asked for you by name."

She stared up at him, sunglasses to sunglasses. "And you believed them?"

He shrugged. "Both of them said it."

She gave Thomas the traffic and headed toward the men.

Her name wasn't foreign after the Pine Landing shoot-out incident, then the Indigo Plantation case, both of which gained her undesired statewide notoriety. These guys wouldn't be the first to name-drop and expect her to be flattered . . . or waive a ticket.

The men didn't act injured, but she asked anyway, "You guys okay? Nothing hurt?"

Both shook their heads, the sportier one grinning like a Cheshire cat. The other, however, carried a sour pout. She had no time to contemplate the whys.

Taking a stroll around the cars, she saw little more than a small dent and shared paint, nothing that justified filing a claim unless they just enjoyed paying a deductible. The driver in back, though, warranted a ticket. She pulled her pad from the back of her waistband where she'd slid it before leaving her cruiser.

"You're seriously writing me a ticket," said the sourpuss.

She pointed to the car in back. "Is this one yours?"

Lips tight, he nodded.

"Then you rear-ended that car," she said, and turned to the grinning guy. "Which is yours?"

As if he could, he grinned bigger. "Yeah. You don't remember me, do you?"

His skin hinted tanning bed, his teeth whitened in a dental chair. The sunglasses hid his eyes, and in an afterthought, he jerked them off. "That better?"

"Butch?" Then she caught herself. "Wait. That high school reunion committee thing is this weekend?" Damn, of course it was. She kept the word *shit* to herself.

A tad paunchy, yet he effortlessly swept her up in an armful. "You're still not big as a bug," he said, setting her back down.

Sheepish, she glanced at Thomas who snatched his attention back to traffic.

Brandon Ives, aka Butch, star baseball player and team captain at Middleton High School. He'd been scouted for the pros after playing for the University of South Carolina. Callie had no idea what washed him out, but he'd bounced back as a sports commentator for WLSC, a local station out of Charleston. She hadn't liked him in high school, didn't watch him on the news, and disliked journalists period.

Most of all, she wasn't into reliving high school history. Not with her memories.

She couldn't remember the other gentleman, though, the one she'd about decided could do without the ticket.

"Clearly I don't ring a bell," he said. "But then I'm not a television celebrity."

She tried not to squint too hard while picturing rows of desks and who'd been in her classes. Tall, black, attractive . . . just couldn't place him at all. Had the size to have played football, but she drew a blank.

"I wasn't memorable, or at least in a popular way," he said and reached out his hand. "Reuben Douglas."

Reuben, Reuben . . . then she took in a gasp. "Oh my God, you're Reuben?"

Which elicited a reserved smile from him. He didn't seem to be a man big on open expression. "President of the Science Club, which you weren't a part of," he said. "Graduated second in our class."

"The Perv, remember?" Butch added with a laugh too loud. "Skinny, kept to himself, hung out in the chemistry lab sucking up to Dr. Lynch. Watched the girls a little too hard, in my opinion, but never spoke."

Yet ol' Butch had owned a reputation for keeping a score card on his dates. Nope, still not a fan.

"Wendy spoke with him, though," she said, a slight smile at the slighted man. Reuben's eye connection showed he appreciated the mention.

Not the lead cheer and not the most popular, but, most profoundly, Wendy had been the sweetest on the squad.

And Callie had found Wendy's body after the football playoff against Berkeley High School.

After that night, senior year consisted of a unique and painful mixture of reporters, crazed parents, finger-pointing, and class gossip. Callie crossed that graduation stage, never looking back, and had missed every reunion since.

Butch guffawed. "Wendy just felt sorry for him. Look where that got her."

Reuben remained hushed except for a whispered afterthought. "Knew I shouldn't have come."

Callie would do her damnedest to avoid the bloody lot of them, too.

She tucked away her ticket pad. "If y'all are good about the fender tap, I am as well. We can—"

"Ca-a-a-l-l-l-i-e!"

The men pivoted toward the Pig-Lo. Didn't take Callie two seconds to spot the flurry of peach and white from the liquor store next door. In a fluttering layered, gauzy cotton dress, a blond woman their age scuttered awkwardly in low white summer sandals across the lot. Callie expected her to face-plant at any time, especially hefting two bags of liquor bottles.

Callie rushed toward the burst of personality in Bvlgari sunglasses and took one of the bags. The woman had to be freezing in that strappy dress.

Georgia Walker Stilmack owned a house out here, but was someone Callie had seen little of her entire two years on Edisto. Nothing in common except the same high school. They'd traveled in entirely opposite worlds back then, but the present-day distancing was mainly attributed to the particular beach house she owned, the infamous beach house titled *Water Spout*. Not many rental histories involved a tenant killed in the living room.

This particular one at Callie's hand. With a broken bottle.

Georgia shoved the other bag in Butch's hands to allow her to smack a kiss on Callie's cheek. "God, I never see you. Aren't you excited, girl? I ran out to get just a few more mixers and chasers for the committee meeting." She turned to the men. "Butch, be a doll and carry that in your car, will you? Damn, you look better than on television." Then to Reuben, as she took his hand and reared back, not hiding her inspection of his physique, "Honey, damn if you didn't fill out well. If you'd looked this good in high school, my children might've been darker complected. Um, um, um."

Callie pivoted Georgia around with a gentle escort toward the parking lot. "Georgia, it's too busy out here, so take your groceries on back to *Water Spout*." She spoke over her shoulder at the guys. "Twenty blocks down Palmetto on the water side. The house is about the color of her dress and, trust me, unmistakable."

Quite unmistakable. Three stories on prime sand. Used to be blue. Callie hadn't been inside since she'd killed Georgia's tenant, the man who'd kidnapped Callie's son. Callie poured herself into gin bottles for months after that experience.

Memories of *Water Spout*, memories of high school, memories of specific classmates—like this reunion planning committee—were anything but a catalyst for additional nightmares.

They reached their respective vehicles, pinched their ways into the stream of other cars, and headed down Palmetto. Callie returned to her cruiser but took Jungle Road instead, dominated by a sudden urge to see if her son's Jeep was in the drive.

Jeb was finishing up his second year at the College of Charleston. Spring break meant he had to visit at least a couple days, she hoped. The house didn't seem empty until she expected him home, but she found nothing parked there but her little Escape, and drove on. She took Jungle all the way down, left on Lybrand to come out on Palmetto. *Water Spout* rose tall and masterful, two short blocks ahead to her left.

Though repainted and re-landscaped to shed the dead body

reputation, the house remained ominous to Callie, and her pulse spiked in its shadow.

Butch and Reuben unloaded suitcases and Georgia's groceries, with Georgia already on the porch, empty-handed, unlocking the door. Men doing her bidding. Georgia wasn't nearly as bubble-headed as she let on. In addition to being lead cheerleader, she'd been in the Honor Society in high school and created the real estate business her husband ran in Savannah.

Callie, seeing each arrived okay, tried to slip past without stopping, but damn it, Butch waved. She made a U-turn and parked. She helped them tote belongings up the tall flight of stairs required of most houses for hurricane season water surges, with Butch huffing the most at the top.

While the others strolled in, in awe of the venue, Callie pulled up short at the door. No level of interior decorating could disguise those massive glass doors across the back of the house, reminding her of those deep, roiling gray clouds that night. Her gaze darted across the open floor plan and memories of that party, over a hundred people back then having no clue of the criminal element present.

That might be a different, bigger, softer color sofa, but it rested where the other had been, before Callie had fought her captor and soaked the furnishings in his blood.

She had to get out of there. "So who's coming?" Callie asked, setting a bag on the counter and remaining near the exit.

"Didn't you read your notice?" Georgia replied with her cute scold before speaking out to the group. "One of y'all want to turn on the heat? It's frigid in here!" Reuben searched walls for a thermostat, and Georgia leaned over to Callie. "Can you believe how awesome he looks? Damn, gives me little chills."

"The chills are from that dress, Georgia. Put some clothes on. Who else is coming?" Callie was eager to gain intel and leave. Reliving high school was a cliché on this beach, exponentially raising the odds of a disturbance call.

"Twelve," Georgia replied. "Figured the brightest and finest could come up with the best spring reunion so I invited the senior superlative people listed in the yearbook. Best of this, best of that. You were best of something. We all were."

Yeah, they dubbed Callie Most Political, thanks to her parents and the occasional cause she championed. One in particular about did her in . . . that she cared not to relive with this group.

Her father had been a fifth-generation mayor, her mother the political science mastermind behind his campaigns. Her mother's attempt
to blueprint Callie's life was part of what drove Callie to marry a federal
agent in Boston, and break the family chain of politicians.

Georgia opened a bag of something, tasted it, and poured it in a
bowl. "Y'all get chips for the time being. The hot appetizers go out at
four when the last are supposed to arrive. I have an entire agenda
planned!"

"I'll try to make it, but—"

Georgia pressed hands to her chest. "Awww, Callie, you promised.
Everyone promised!"

Actually, Callie hadn't promised a damn thing. "I'll do my level best,
but police work comes first."

The lie seemed to appease the hostess, so Callie moved toward the
door. But as she stepped onto the porch, two more cars drove in,
blocking her cruiser, and before she reached the bottom of the stairs, yet
another. On the ground, after brief handshakes and a couple hugs, she
directed musical cars to enable her escape before the whole bloody lot of
them showed up.

The trailing car turned out to be Jessie Jane Loveless, turned JJ
Loveless, bestselling author and former yearbook editor. Callie
motioned her to the far left of the drive, then held her door open.
"How're you doing, Jessie? Or is it JJ?"

"JJ," she said, hoisting over her laptop case to Callie as if she served
as bellboy.

Far from any sort of slick New York image, JJ rose casual in jeans,
turtleneck, and cardigan, though Callie estimated their value to exceed
her week's salary if she included the boots. A slight spread across the
rear end, but that's what hours at a computer did to a person. Nobody,
however, could deny her success. She'd always possessed a natural
beauty of sort, and Callie seemed to recall Asian in the author's
background. With the area's military history, mixed marriages weren't
uncommon.

"Did you ask Edisto Bookstore to stock your books while you're
here?" she asked the author. "They might appreciate a signing. The
crowd's pretty strong this weekend."

She got out and let Callie shut the door. "We'll see."

Guess her words were more meant for paper. "Suitcase?" Callie
asked.

"Rented my own place," she said, then headed toward the stairs.

"Carry that laptop up for me, will you?"

Okay, she'd tried. Yeah, Callie would work forty-eight hours straight if it meant missing this, but she'd be polite and tote the laptop and maybe stick around a few minutes longer. She might taste the appetizers if they looked good.

Six people had arrived, counting Callie, with six to go. After introductions all around, the amazements said and done about age and looks, Georgia brought out the mixers, the glasses, and finally the booze. These people would be snockered early if the proportion of alcohol to chips was an indicator.

JJ made her way to a barstool, ordered a fizzy water from Georgia, and seemed to analyze the others while they snacked, fixed drinks, and strolled the home, most collecting at the three sets of glass doors facing the Atlantic. Poised like a grand matron, JJ seemed forced to endure the noise of the irritating progeny around her.

Butch propped at the bar a few feet away with a straight whiskey, chin in his hand, studying her. He'd already asked how much she made, how many sales, how many proposals of marriage compared to his since, after all, they were both celebrities.

Callie moved toward the door again. "Later, y'all. When everyone arrives, maybe I'll drop in—"

"Everyone's here," JJ said.

Georgia chuckled. "No, they're not." She patted a notebook. "I have my organizer right here. Once the others—"

"I said everyone's here," the author stated, firm and loud enough to silence the group.

But then Butch jeered. "What, are you a fortuneteller or something? You dress like a bit of a snob, if you don't mind my saying, JJ. For God's sake, let Georgia find something with life in it for you to wear. Have fun."

Unsure how to behave at the announcement, Georgia stood motionless in the kitchen, peering over at Callie, as if the token cop needed to do something about plans already going astray.

"JJ," Callie said, "you headed up the yearbook, so you ought to know. There were twelve of us."

"And I *uninvited* the ones not here," she said.

"What?" Georgia yelled. "You didn't!"

"I did," she replied.

A half smile from Butch who enjoyed the theatrics. "Let the games begin."

Quietly, however, Reuben returned to his stoic look displayed at the accident. The one that hinted at distrust and commanded space. The others stopped dead, not sure what they weren't understanding.

Not surprised but not happy at how easily the event had turned on its head, Callie had to admit she was intrigued. Which classmates warranted acceptance versus those dismissed?

Georgia's fretting escalated, bouncing her focus from JJ to Callie, to each of the others. "This cannot be happening! How embarrassing! Why didn't they call me?"

"I told them not to," JJ said.

"You bitch," the hostess said. "You hijacked my weekend."

JJ ignored her. "Look around, people. What do we all have in common?"

Everyone exchanged tense glances, nobody having a clue. Yet Callie felt the bait-and-switch tactic taking place.

"Each of you was present the night of Wendy's death, weren't you?" JJ said.

The crew rose in an uproar of explanations.

"I hadn't even spoken to her that day."

"What the hell does that mean?"

"Who the hell do you think you—"

JJ abruptly raised a hand, which surprisingly stopped the ruckus. "I'm writing a true crime about what happened to our classmate. You can cooperate with me, or I can take your classmates' word for your involvement, but each of you is going in the book. Curse me, yell at me, or sue me; trust me, I'm girded for it, but that girl's death was an abomination, and you each know your involvement."

Heat rose up Callie's neck, and she agreed with Georgia. JJ Loveless was a first-class bitch. Opportunistic, callous, and cruel. Whether the author wrote for Random House or grocery store rags, she'd just fallen into the same category as journalists, and Callie shot one of those just last year.

The stunning announcement gave Callie just enough pause not to leave . . . and to scan the participants. To see if any of them looked half as guilty about Wendy as she felt.

Chapter 2

WENDY ASHTON had been Callie's first brush with death.

Middleton football had just overtaken the Berkeley High School Stags in an unexpectedly tight contest of sixteen to fourteen. A long game of tight defense on an October night expected to coat the area in its first frost of the season. Breaths hung cloudy in the air with nobody feeling the cold as students poured onto the field screeching, leaping, and claiming victory. Ball players and cheerleaders, band members and coaches intertwined with hugs and slaps to the back.

Wendy had been blond. The light, pure blond of youth, with hair barely touching her shoulders. Her green and gold outfit allowed for plenty of leg, was tight enough to flaunt abs, the skirt flouncy enough to depict innocence until a cartwheel gave a flash of beneath. Always smiling. A B-minus student, but a joy to be around. The town assumed she'd marry well and maybe teach school.

Not one to enjoy throngs, Callie told her date that she'd be right back and headed to the bathroom, cutting behind the bleachers since screaming enthusiasts blocked the normal paths. What she thought was an errant sneaker, upon closer inspection, came affixed to a leg, twisted unnaturally.

Callie remembered thinking how horrible to misstep and fall off the bleachers, expecting the person to start talking, moaning, grateful to have someone find them to offer help. Then she saw the cheer outfit. Then she saw it was Wendy, her eyes fixed wide. Her green cheerleading panties discarded six feet off to the right beside a soft drink cup.

Then Wendy blinked.

Callie blurted a scream, but clipped it short, stupidly embarrassed.

Her first instinct was to not touch the body. No, it wasn't a body because it blinked . . . *she* blinked. "Wendy?" she said, inching closer. She couldn't quite tell if the cheerleader still breathed, but her eyes remained open . . . *blink, damn it. Wait, did she?*

Call Daddy.

Her father the mayor fished with the police chief, but for some reason, she didn't want to report this to anyone but Daddy first. He ran the town. He ran the world.

She called him, and he called 911, telling her to stay where she was. He showed up out of nowhere, took over, and Callie only remembered feeling privileged . . . and guilty that she hadn't made the call herself.

A KNOCK SOUNDED on the door to *Water Spout*, and with Callie's hand already on the knob, it fell to her to open it. She didn't recognize the man standing there with a gym bag in his hand, and he seemed shocked, scanning a police chief in full regalia greeting him.

"Tony Tyler," he said, making his last name a question mark. In his mid-forties, he'd blend into most crowds with his dark hair, brown skin, upscale sneakers and khakis . . . except for his shock.

Georgia scurried over, snagging his hand as if she feared he'd change his mind. "Tony, thank God. Come on in."

Unmoving, Callie watched them retreat to the massive living room. Who the hell was Tony?

JJ likewise studied him.

Georgia took the reins. "For those who don't recognize this gentleman, Tony was a first-year teacher of sophomore history the year we graduated. He's currently principal of Middleton High School. As a courtesy, I invited him to join us since we'll be using school property for much of our festivities." She stared at JJ. "And he wasn't on your list to *uninvite.*"

Callie remembered. The young male African American teacher the girls ogled . . . the man off limits but hot enough to dream about. Looking at him approaching middle age, she couldn't recall why.

One of the late arrivals made her way forward. A short stumpy woman, but not so much overweight as stocky. A dyed brunette with a soccer-mom hairdo in jeans and a floral, cotton smock, Libby Lane left Middleton High just long enough to earn her education degree before returning to stay for good to teach junior and senior English, per the email each received from Georgia. The email didn't mention she'd married and divorced another senior superlative member, Peter Yeo, a British exchange student and star pitcher on the baseball team, Butch's old bestie. Libby had been cute back then. Tiny. And interested in way more than diagramming sentences and Shakespeare.

"Come on in, Tony," Libby said. "You seem to have stumbled into an awkward conversation. You're lucky your golden ticket wasn't cancelled."

JJ pointed toward the refrigerator while pushing her half-empty bottled water away. "You have any wine chilled in there, Georgia?"

Each stared at the principal, failing to place him. Reuben stretched out a hand in greeting. "Sorry, man, don't recall you, but welcome to the group."

Deftly, Libby handed off his bag to Georgia and led him not just to the massive back windows but through one of the three sets of double doors to the vista overlooking the Atlantic.

With their attentions occupied in the opposite direction, Callie darted to leave, thanking the heavens for the *interloper* stealing the attention.

Halfway down the steps, however, Georgia called out, "Callie. What are we supposed to do? JJ has ruined everything."

Callie stepped up a few stairs so as not to yell. "You're made of sterner stuff than this. Go back in there and throw your weight around. Or let the principal do it, but you still have enough Scarlet O'Hara in you to corral that group."

Georgia looked pained.

"Pull out your pot stash, why don't you? Loosen everyone up," Callie added, smirking. She'd caught the woman high on more than one occasion, just at other people's parties—once at Sophie's, Callie's next-door neighbor no less. She'd had to promptly bust up and disband the gathering under threat of arrest.

"I gave that up, Callie."

"You keep telling yourself that, Georgia," Callie said, hurrying down the remaining stairs.

Thomas couldn't handle this beach alone, especially on a day like this, and Callie was surprised she hadn't received another call to assist.

Her prediction was true. A call came across her radio as she reached her cruiser. "Callie here. What is it, Marie?"

"Another fender bender, this time in front of El Marko's. Thomas has a situation on Dock Site Road, so he's tied up."

"I got it," Callie said, clicked off, then, "You got this," she yelled up to Georgia. Relieved and released, Callie preferred encountering a thousand beach fanatics and all their quirks rather than these senior superlatives plus one.

"Brunch is tomorrow at ten," Georgia hollered back.

"Enjoy yourselves," Callie said out of earshot as she left.

The sun beamed, the sky a cornflower blue with wisps of thick clouds. Gulls dipped and soared in force with more than enough patsies willing to throw food to them.

Two miles to El Marko's, slower than usual thanks to folks darting across the street and the beach house gawkers driving slow, trying to justify in their minds how to move there. No drunks yet, but the day was early.

She reached the Jungle Road block where a mini-strip mall housed a candy store, pizza place, and assorted shops of clothing, art, and souvenirs. On the west end of the property, El Marko's had opened four months earlier, in December of all times, but Mark Dupree had jump-started his enterprise remarkably well in the off-season. Callie looked forward to seeing how he handled the summer crowds. Success for one business begat success for all.

His past experience as an agent with the State Law Enforcement Division, SLED, South Carolina's version of the FBI, had her asking for his viewpoint here and there, giving her a chance to drop in. He seemed to welcome those drop-ins.

She parked on the road's edge, lights flashing, and took a moment to marvel at the mishap.

A Mini Cooper had rear-ended Mark's Taco Taxi, a delivery golf cart custom-painted in red, green, and yellow with matching upholstery. The one and only. Thank goodness for the car's size or the taco driver might've been hurt, but the little cart's taco carrier on the back was crushed.

As usual, a crowd gathered.

Mark stood well off the road, speaking to the person Callie assumed to be the Mini Coop driver, from the panic of the girl. Late twenties, no makeup, baggy linen clothes, arms across her front, shivering. He'd had someone bring her a coffee.

Yep, this ticket would stick.

"Mark," Callie said with a nod.

"Chief," he replied. He'd retired from SLED, and with policing in common, they'd developed a decent friendship.

Callie looked to the girl, waiting for her name, but she didn't get the message. Callie finally had to ask, "Your name, ma'am?"

The routine took close to an hour. The El Marko Taco Taxi had pulled out in front of the Mini Coop. The Coop driver slowed, but admitted she underestimated the acceleration of the cart, and there might've been the distraction of a text. Once hit, the cart rolled onto the mall's landscaping out of traffic, thank goodness, but the driver bolted on foot before it came to a complete stop. He hadn't been seen since.

Callie took notes, clicked photos, and wrote the ticket. Once she was assured the Mini was functional, she let the girl go. Mark saw her off with a sack of free tacos.

Callie slid the ticket book back in her waistband. "Please tell me your guy had a driver's license, Mark."

"Yes, he had one," said the owner. "Can't guarantee he doesn't have any outstanding tickets, though. He's from the island, so he won't go far. Today was his first day."

"And his last, I hope. He'll have a ticket waiting for him, too. Fleeing the scene of an accident. So what're you going to do about deliveries?"

If she weren't so concerned about being on call, she'd deliver a few orders for him. Based on the day's events and the time stolen by the reunion crowd, she was afraid to, though. "Call Stan. Get him to deliver for you."

Having visited Edisto to aid Callie through a rough patch in her early days, her captain from Boston had divorced, retired, and relocated to Pompano Drive only a couple blocks from her, and a half mile from El Marko's. Stan had struck up a strong camaraderie with Mark and could often be found on his favorite stool at the end of Mark's bar sharing war stories . . . when he wasn't attempting to pair his two friends into more than a platonic relationship.

"He's off-island today," Mark said. "Errands. Some for me since I can't leave El Marko's with this crowd. And speaking of crowds, I need to go."

As did she.

He paused a split second longer than one would expect, and she sensed something, but then he smiled, winked, and left toward his restaurant. His limp wasn't as noticeable today, not that it was overly remarkable any other. Downstream maybe she'd find the opportune moment to ask how he got it. She'd asked before but received the strong impression he kept that secret pretty close to home.

Sort of like the burn scar on her own forearm, covered by long sleeves today. She didn't like reliving the night her husband died, either.

She returned to her patrol car and continued to cruise her streets, taking time to lower her window and speak to repeat visitors and everyday residents, but the rest of her day proved rather uneventful. She let Thomas answer what few calls they had, often involving the fresh crop of college girls, ever his pleasure . . . and theirs.

Around seven, she pulled into her drive, after a quick radio call to ensure that the night shift, mainly Officer LaRoache, had assumed his duties. Living on Jungle Road, she served as the perpetual backup.

As always, she glanced around ground level before exiting her cruiser, then observed the houses around her. A habit and an entrenched routine to surveil her surroundings for threat, but her past had proven the routine useful.

Next door, from the foreign car in the drive, Sophie Bianchi entertained a guest. The make and model gave Callie a chuckle. Guess Georgia already sought a reprieve.

Sophie, a self-professed yogi and spiritually connected goddess, in all her other-worldliness-spiritual-wisdom, would sage the heck out of her place before the night was through. She adored gossip, and Georgia would definitely suit her fancy, but Sophie preferred such conversation not happen under her roof. Negativity required smudging, and Sophie maintained an ample supply of sage. She'd even been known to pull out a stick and smudge other places, too. She'd cleansed Callie's house on more than one occasion, and once saged Callie herself.

Inside, Callie shed uniform and donned old sweatpants and a sweatshirt with teeny holes in the underarm seams. Too soft to give up. Then while eating dinner at her bar, Callie watched her house's recorded cam footage, a routine she'd fallen into, having been stalked in the past, then she did dishes.

The ravenous hordes of cedar waxwings had been entertaining in the early evenings of March, but they'd stripped her Palmetto trees of berries and moved on. So she came outside a bit later in the evening these days, often after a Brit movie, but she hadn't found one to her liking tonight.

Ginger ale in hand, she assumed her seat on the front porch to watch traffic go by in the cloak of night. She'd learned a while back that she craved gin less while outside listening to the tide several blocks over. She never lost it, though . . . that craving.

Her rattan rocker moved so it barely missed the wall, and with the porch light off, few would see her. When Georgia exited Sophie's place around ten, she would assume she left unnoticed. Sophie, however, knew Callie's drill. After waving Georgia off, she peered over and up to the porch. Callie said nothing. Sophie tiptoed over nonetheless.

Callie's motion spot flicked on. In tights and a loose weave sweater off one shoulder, Sophie held a hand over her eyes. "You up there?"

"Yep. You want one of my ginger ales?"

"No." The voice got closer. "I'll get my carrot juice." Callie kept a bottle of it in her fridge for times just like these. Not that Sophie offered to do the reverse at her abode with ginger ale. Sophie preferred to come over, not invite, especially if you were a cop and your day job involved bad things. Too much saging, you know.

Sophie parked her tiny butt in a neighboring chair, twisting the top off her juice, and a waft of marijuana reached Callie on the evening breeze. Guess Georgia took Callie's suggestion, just not in her own home.

"So," Sophie said with a dramatic pause, "why have I never heard about you finding a body in high school?"

"Never came up, I guess," Callie replied, rocking, teasing Sophie with short answers, knowing full well that she desired lengthy epistles of scandal.

"Don't make me dig it out of you," she said, tsking once, then twice when Callie didn't immediately respond.

"I found a classmate murdered," she said.

"Ooh, so that's why you're a policewoman."

"Not exactly. It was quite the shocker though. I liked the girl. Imagine finding a body when you're just a kid."

Sophie smacked Callie on the leg. "Our babies found a body as teenagers. They're all right."

True that. Their son and daughter dated regularly these days, and right after Callie became chief, they'd kayaked and run up on a body in Big Bay Creek. They weren't exactly scarred for life, but then they had pretty impressive mothers to carry them through it. Or so she liked to think.

"You never told me you went to high school with Georgia Stilmack, either," Sophie said.

Callie didn't hear a question and continued rocking, halting a moment as a car sped by. She waited . . . but LaRoache's blue light made its appearance. The whole force, a grand total of six, tended to police the chief's road a bit more than the others, accepting the boss often watched from her dark porch. The unspoken pastime originated back when Thomas kept a cautious eye on her before ginger ale replaced the gin.

"Well," Sophie started, and Callie predicted a long run-on sentence coming. "Georgia is beside herself because she had all these plans for you super special senior people, whatever those are, to spend the weekend making plans for this big shindig of a reunion next year, but one of them, some writer, told some of them not to come and seized control after Georgia ordered all this food and set an agenda and had the house scrubbed within an inch of its life."

Finally a breath, but not for long.

"Some of the people who came are threatening to leave while the writer is interrogating others so Georgia lied and said she had to run to the store but came to my house instead, bless her. I believe she's calmer though. So . . . why aren't you over there?"

Callie finished off the last of her bottle. "Would you want to be in the middle of all that?"

Sophie sat back. "Guess not."

"Precisely," Callie replied.

"Well, don't arrest them."

Which made Callie cease rocking. "Why would I arrest them?" Unless they killed each other, in which case, Callie'd be more than happy to go back over there. Then remembering the scene with the Russian, maybe not. She could give it to Thomas.

"I gave Georgia the rest of my stash," Sophie explained. "She said you said you'd look the other way if she taught them all how to properly chill."

Callie popped forward in her seat trying to see her friend in the dark. "What?"

Sophie shrugged. "Kinda makes me want to go over there and help."

Chapter 3

JJ
Friday night, just before midnight.

JJ WALKED IN THE door of the private rental Georgia had arranged for her. Bigger than any hotel accommodation, dusted and once-over cleaned but in sore need of a deep sanitizing. The *Flirty Flamingo*. Great touch to name these houses, as if they became characters in their own right. She'd be sure to use that.

Georgia had been indignant that the famous author could not share her roof with the others. Part of the attraction of the trip was spending time with JJ Loveless, but those people would've never behaved as she needed them to. And her plan would've lost its steam.

Their faces! Good heavens, JJ enjoyed those faces . . . those incredibly priceless expressions. Those naïve yet disturbed faces of denial, of concern that the bestselling author could read their minds and decipher the lies. These descriptions would be absolutely delicious to tell.

Their denials so forced. Innocent people didn't protest like that, and the guilty who thought they'd escaped connection were stunned at their past slapping them in the ass.

Every damn one of them mulled over how they fit in to Wendy's murder and JJ's book. To include the police chief. Especially the police chief. A cop wasn't the only profession who could read people. JJ had gotten pretty damn good at it herself.

She'd been fairly awesome at it back in high school, too.

She hadn't planned to stay long after dropping the bomb, but their reactions had been so luscious she couldn't resist staying longer.

Authors saw plots and subplots nobody else did. Couldn't that mean they could solve crimes? See through facades? Weave stories of gold out of the plain straw of normal existence?

Even Callie Cantrell was intrigued. Or Morgan, that's right. No longer the bigshot in Boston. Demoted to chief of a tiny, four-mile-long stretch of island. JJ could only hope the chief still owned the prowess for this.

But Georgia, bless her, that woman should've been an actress. Butch predictably proved an older version of his idiot teenage self. Libby flaunted her pretense that teachers were above condemnation. And that principal, planned but not planned, but who cared. He'd been there when Wendy died, too. She wished she'd thought of him herself.

All it took was her announcing the book to propel them into worrying all night. They'd awaken tomorrow behaving differently.

Except for Reuben. The anomaly. The quiet teenager now the silent adult, unwilling to let people read him.

She hoped he didn't get bored and leave. There was always the risk of any of them leaving . . . but would they? Wouldn't they want to try to understand how big a role they'd play in a *New York Times* bestselling book so they could get in front of it? They'd be begging her to return, yet afraid to ask questions, hoping one of the others would ask instead.

The trick would be eavesdropping on them when she wasn't around.

But she had that taken care of.

She dropped her suitcase on her bed, her purse containing her phone on the dresser. The urge to stop this moment and record a few words nagged her, as they were so incredibly fresh in her mind, even this late in the night. Her fingers literally itched with longing. So she seized the moment.

Her laptop was in her suitcase, and she lifted it out, letting the craving crawl through and consume her and bar her from sleep. She quickly checked the computer's charge and studied the rental for an appropriate place to write. No desk. The dinette table too high. The coffee table too low.

She inspected outside, the porch overlooking a lagoon of sorts. Dark, almost black, the air thick. Yes, a jungle feel. The sounds of wildlife. The nocturnal death of one species by another.

This would suit her purpose just fine.

She typed her first words, unable to contain the smile.

Chapter 4

EARLY SATURDAY morning, surprised at the decent night's sleep, Callie exited her house and assumed her tour of duty at seven, same as Thomas.

Callie easily looked the other way about Sophie's reference to pot last night, and a group high at *Water Spout*. The more chill they were, the better, anyway. Maybe they'd even come together as a team. Maybe JJ would learn to party instead of pissing people off.

Time for work. She liked working in tandem with Thomas, juggling issues in a natural sort of way. After sharing trauma, mistakes, and losses, they'd developed an in-step routine. Not old enough to be his mother, she was still of an age to mentor. He was a good officer who listened, with both his personality and his looks cute as hell.

He took the east end of older homes, where she lived, and she policed the west, toward the Wyndham community. Her end enabled her to leave the car and do some foot patrol around the marina. A five-foot-two mini-police chief tended to draw tourist eyes, and inevitably people asked questions. Property owners often came out for a chat. Community outreach went a long way toward preserving the peace on this short stretch of sand and marsh.

She'd just finished explaining leash laws to an Ohio couple with dachshunds, one of which almost took a head-first stumble off the marina dock. The dog, not the owners. A call came in from Thomas. Instinctively she checked the time. Nine thirty. She hadn't decided if she would make the ten o'clock brunch or not. "Callie here. What's up?"

"Odd situation on Thistle," he said.

Thistle Street ran perpendicular to Palmetto, six or so blocks from *Water Spout*. The road wasn't traveled much and crossed a part of the inland lagoon. The area had a quiet and uneventful history.

"I cruised by *Flirty Flamingo* around eight," he continued. "Took note of the car door open, assuming someone was unloading their stuff. But just now I went by and saw it still open, so I stopped. Expected the person to come out and ask what was up, but they never did. An Audi Q5, white."

The car description gave Callie pause but not the open door. Lots of people forgot to give the car door a last shove with their hands full. "Go on."

"I'm standing inside. The front door was not only unlocked but ajar. Bed's made like nobody slept there. Suitcase on it . . . still packed. Nothing in the bathroom. A phone and a purse on the bed. Just doesn't feel right."

Callie walked faster, nodding with a smile at a half-dozen tourists and passing a couple of work staff headed to prep seafood lunches at Pressley's. "Be right there. In the meantime, run the tag."

Her suspicion niggled her a bit, but she wasn't quite ready to go all APB. Callie clearly recalled JJ driving in behind the wheel of a white Audi. She was the only guest who expressed intentions of staying anyplace other than Georgia's house.

When she arrived, Thomas strolled around outside, canvassing the grounds. He met her as she got out. "Car belongs to a Jessie Loveless per the registration."

She nodded slowly, gnawing on her lip in thought.

"What?" he said. "You know her?"

"I do," she said. "Arrived yesterday along with a crew of people I went to high school with. They're planning next year's reunion."

Nothing more to add except how odd it seemed that JJ never unpacked. Had she gone to the beach? Having had one too many, forgotten to close her car door, then later went out for a walk? Slept at Georgia's before coming here drunk in the wee dawn hours? Convoluted, but still, stranger things could happen.

Callie walked through the house, spotting details Thomas listed over the phone. No sign of settling in whatsoever, yet leaving without taking her phone and keys. No used glass in the sink or food stocked yet in the fridge.

Odd as hell.

She peeked in the bathroom and then opened the medicine chest for one last look. Nothing except complimentary soaps and a mini-shampoo, but in turning, something snared her attention. She hesitated, her gut instincts waiting for her senses to catch up.

The toilet seat was up. And the little paper sleeve that had been on the seat lay ripped off and tossed in the waste can in the back corner between toilet and wall. Surely Thomas hadn't—

"Thomas? Did you use the toilet in here?"

His steps squeaked quickly on the tiled floor until he reached the bathroom door. "No way, Chief. I wouldn't do that. Not checking out a questionable scene. I'd hope you'd think I wouldn't—"

"Just no is fine," she said, giving it all another once-over for anything else. "Look around again, will you?"

She knew Thomas. He would scour the place to prove his worth, and he was worth a fortune in her opinion, but neither of them found a clue to point them in any direction.

"Not sure what we ought to do here," he said.

"Let's lock up the house and the car. I'll take the keys and her purse." She opened the purse for a cursory glance, taking serious note of the phone inside. Callie needed to check the reunion roster for the phone number JJ gave as a contact. Surely this wasn't it.

Callie shut the purse. "If the woman reappears, she'll come to me, I imagine. In the meantime, here, take her license so you have what she looks like. Keep an eye out, and I'll go on over to *Water Spout*," she said.

When he looked puzzled, she added, "Where I saw her yesterday with the others. We all went to high school together."

"Oh, geez, sorry, Chief."

She arched her brow once. "Haven't seen these people in years, Thomas, so nothing to be sorry about. She might be hanging with them, though. I'll touch base on what I find."

Her watch read five after ten. She could show up for brunch and not make anyone the wiser . . . until she had to.

This made no sense. But neither did JJ wanting to sabotage a beach reunion . . . at least to do so and not expect repercussions. It was those repercussions that had Callie concerned. When she'd left *Water Spout* last night, the topic had centered around a dead girl from their younger days and a subsequent book of the experience.

Took Callie two minutes to drive from point A to B, and that included parking. *Water Spout*'s door was unlocked, a habit that set Callie's teeth to grinding so often on this beach. She let herself in, like any burglar would, after nobody heeded her knock . . . which a burglar wouldn't do.

Nobody in sight. She'd prayed to find JJ here maybe looped out on mimosas or hungover from the pot, because if she was indeed missing, there were too many suspects to count.

The back double-glass doors were open, cooling the massive spread of living space. She went to the bar, made herself some coffee, snagged a bagel in afterthought and smothered it with pepper jelly and butter. With nobody noting her presence, she made her way to the back porch, a creepiness worming its way up her spine as she avoided the place where the man she killed way back when bled out.

On the back porch, again underdressed in a short-sleeve lacy top, Georgia wore a lap throw, captured in thought, a visor keeping the rays out of eyes staring out to sea. Part of the area was shaded, part wide open under the sun, the breeze still cool and brisk.

Libby, the teacher, sat next to Tony, the principal. The hint of body language said she cared for this man. Reuben hung over the railing, watching pelicans several hundred yards out where their dives and splashes indicated a school of bait fish. Callie half-expected a dolphin or two to make an appearance.

Sprawled on a chaise chair, Butch lay, head back with sunglasses, mouth slightly agape, and Callie bet a hundred dollars he nursed a hangover. If these people hung around after today, she'd be surprised. She wasn't too enthralled with the idea of aiding JJ in her research any more than they would be. One would think they'd get the reunion planned, over and done with.

No sign of JJ, though.

"Y'all barely touched all that food in there," Callie said, taking another bite of bagel.

Butch raised his shades. "Do you wear that uniform to bed?"

"The law never sleeps, Butch. Where's JJ?"

"She has her own accommodations," Libby drawled, in attempt to mimic the author's voice. "To soothe her muse."

Callie made herself comfortable in a deck chair, setting her cup on the table beside her. "Can't believe you guys are letting her mess up your weekend. What else happened? You look miserable."

Reuben turned his back to the water, leaning on the rail. "She pulled out her laptop and started asking questions is what happened. Georgia tried controlling the resulting animosity, but yelling commenced. I'm surprised nobody walked out."

Um, Georgia kinda did, but Callie kept that quiet. "When did JJ leave?"

"Not until after dinner," Reuben replied.

"I had pizza delivered," Georgia said, her sigh heavy and despondent. "Couldn't risk taking this crowd in public."

Tony got up, pointing his empty cup toward Georgia. "A bit dramatic don't you think? I'm getting more coffee. Anyone else need something? Then I suggest we do what we came here to do . . . plan a reunion unless we want to toss in the towel and cancel the thing." Motioning his cup toward each person, he left with no takers on refills. Everyone tried to give the impression the water occupied their attention.

"This is not what I planned," Georgia said, then stopped with that.

Callie waited for Tony to return. When he did, his coffee refill had turned into a plate piled high enough for two. Libby filched a strawberry, and Callie now could see they may be sharing other things.

"I heard y'all got rather fussy last night," Callie said. "What time did JJ leave?" she repeated.

Butch cupped a hand over his eyes. "After midnight, I think."

Reuben clipped a laugh. "Dumb shit. She was gone by eleven thirty. You and I stayed up until after one talking, after the rest went to bed."

Butch let out a guffaw. "Shows how interesting you are. What'd we talk about?"

"You, you, and oh yeah, you. Except you asked about how I made my money again."

"So why'd you talk to me if I'm not interesting?" Butch asked, then gave a challenging scowl. "Just how *did* you make your money?"

Reuben ignored him.

"She did leave after eleven," Georgia said to Callie, disgusted with the entire business.

Callie played nonchalant. "Yes, you would've been back here by then. How long were you gone?"

Georgia started to reply then caught herself. "How could you tell I was gone?"

Motioning around the deck, Callie noted each one. "I'm pretty sure one of you mentioned it?"

They hadn't, but Georgia second-guessed herself into acceptance. "I was gone over an hour but not two. JJ was here when I left, and she left shortly after I came back."

Reuben nodded. "We finally learned to keep our mouths shut. After that, didn't take long for her to leave."

"Thank God," Libby said. "We couldn't say a thing without her stirring shit."

"Is that how my teachers talk?" Tony said with a half grin.

She grinned shyly back. "Anyway, she quit interrogating us. Just sat back with her vodka and listened. Those slanted, mousy eyes watching us, like we didn't sense what she was doing. Straight vodka! Who drinks like that?"

They all glanced at Butch.

"A serious boozer, that's who," he said. "I'm more of a bourbon man, myself. With a splash of water, of course."

"A drop of water is more like it," Georgia said, and laid her head back against her chair.

Nobody mentioned Sophie's marijuana contribution, and Callie had no real reason to bring it up, but she did need to make these people aware of JJ's odd disappearance. Thus far the casual banter did nothing but show they were oblivious, or trying to be.

"Anyone aware if JJ is married?" she asked. The toilet seat had her curious, and could've been no more than JJ meeting her husband at *Flirty Flamingo*, wanting to keep him there and out of her business of milking the reunion members for intel.

Blank expressions all around.

"Don't think so," Georgia said.

Butch grimaced. "Why would anyone want to sleep with that?"

Callie continued. "Did she wear a ring?"

Nobody could answer. Callie didn't recall one. She tried again. "Anyone know which house she rented?"

Nobody said.

"Anyone go over there with her?"

Reuben began to sense a problem. "What's going on, Callie? You make it sound like she's done something."

She eased back in her chair, coffee in both hands. "Let's start with you, Reuben. Are you married? Divorced?"

"No to both."

"What do you do for a living?"

"Nothing at the moment. Sold a patent for a food additive which enables me to travel. Why does that matter?"

Butch sat up. "Damn, he's rich. Ought to make you buy me a new Lexus for rear-ending me yesterday." He turned to Callie. "What do you think, Chief?"

She ignored him. These people needed interviewing. Not immediately but soon. "Anyone keep up with her? Was her announcement about Wendy a total bomb on all of you or did anyone have a clue?"

All turned to Georgia.

"I had zero idea she'd hijack my affair! All I did was call the twelve senior superlatives and Tony. She's the bitch who re-contacted the other six and made them cancel." But instead of falling into a pout, she shook herself and stood. "But their loss, I say. We can decide without their help. And they miss out on a lovely beach weekend . . . on my dime.

We'll dump the pissant tasks on them."

"Not their fault that JJ misrouted them," Reuben said.

"It's their fault for not calling *me*! I originated everything."

"Damn straight," Libby said. "We'll mold this affair into something incredible, with or without them."

Libby had sure livened up. Callie wondered what she was drinking.

"Language, Ms. Lane." Mr. Principal seemed serious this time.

"Hush, Tony," she replied. "Or you can sleep in your own bed tonight."

Butch sat up and laughed. "Oooh. Now we're talking. Musical beds."

Callie remembered why she never attended one of the earlier reunions. She got up to deliver a last message when Reuben strode over and took her elbow, escorting her inside.

"What's going on, Callie?" he said, with a quick peek over his shoulder to ensure nobody followed. "The real deal, not the show for those morons out there."

This was good. He'd pass the word along to the others, and in her building a trust with him, he'd keep her informed. She'd hoped someone would step up like this.

"Her house and car were found open, her belongings not unpacked," she said.

His eyes widened.

"Nothing to get upset about yet," she said. "She could be flighty, you never know. Peddling on a bicycle touring the town. Walking the beach. Maybe she slipped off to write without interruption. Too early to panic."

He pointed at the bar against the wall. "But isn't that her laptop?"

Callie walked over. She found the laptop seemingly out of power, making her wonder if JJ hadn't charged it or if she'd left it recording conversations once she left. Wouldn't put it past her. The group said she'd been using it last night. She might even have a backup, which supported the idea that she could be off in some sort of self-imposed seclusion crafting the material she collected last night before hitting them up again today with information gathered on the sly.

In the case on the floor, Callie found a notebook with scribbles that appeared to be a log with times and codes, abbreviated notes, along with two of her own books, dog-eared and marked. All JJ's property. Callie couldn't check the laptop at the moment without plugging it in and waiting a few minutes, and doing so in front of this crew wasn't smart.

Callie zipped the case closed and took possession. Too early for this to be treated as evidence in a missing person's case, but better safe than sorry. And better in her possession than this crew's.

"Is that how you knew I'd gone out?" Georgia had slipped inside and apparently listened long enough. "Was her computer monitoring us? I don't even allow Alexa in my house, so I'll be pissed if we were recorded without permission."

Callie didn't bother to mention the state allowed recordings as long as the person recording was involved in the conversation—except once JJ left, she'd crossed the line. But they were taking huge leaps in logic here. Nobody had confirmed JJ recorded anything. "I've not checked the computer, Georgia. It's out of juice. So no, this isn't how I knew about you stepping out."

"Then one of us is a snitch!" she said, her voice rising high on the end.

Reuben slowly shook his head at the woman.

"Makes sense to me," said Libby, coming in. Tony trailed behind her. "Who says this whole reunion thing isn't a ruse for JJ?"

"Wait a minute," Georgia said, almost shouting. "I set up this weekend. In my house, out of my pocket, to reconnect and plan a reunion to top all reunions. It's why I chose the seniors from the superlative list. They were all accomplished in one way or another. Solid individuals."

"With money, you mean." Butch walked around them to the refrigerator, filling a glass with ice. "Last night we got off track, but don't tell me you didn't intend to hit us all up to fund this gala of yours."

"Of *ours*," Georgia said. "And every alumnus should donate. That's how it's done, meathead. Or are you too cheap?"

Callie couldn't have pitted these alums against each other any better, in hopes for a snitch or two to float to the top. She weighed whether JJ thought along those same lines, too, but playing people came with risks, and sometimes resulted in the unexpected.

They were premature in all this. Way too soon to report a crime.

"Georgia," Callie said, motioning to the hostess's infamous notebook of plans. "I assume you have everyone's phone, email, and address in there. Mind opening it up for me?"

"Why?" she asked.

"Yeah," Libby added. "Why?"

"Because it saves me from digging them up on my own," Callie said, in as nice a tone as she could muster. "And I'd appreciate it if you kept an eye out for JJ." She passed her business cards around. "Regardless of how much you wish she wouldn't come back, call if you see her."

"Wait," Georgia said, somewhat stunned. "JJ's missing?"

Chapter 5

JJ
Dawn Saturday morning.

WRITING FURIOUSLY while the images were crystal from Georgia's house, JJ ultimately discarded sleep. She adored gushes of creativity like this. To make things better, *Flirty Flamingo* sat at the tippy end of Thistle Street, its porch wrapping around the back to front an inland lagoon, providing the perfect buffer from the world. So perfect that she managed two thousand words into her draft before looking up at the sound of birdsong. The navy of night suddenly offered shades of color and the beginnings of dawn.

Crap. Her ride was to arrive at five thirty. What time was it?

In a flurry, she slapped the computer shut, hustled to the kitchen, and peered outside. Waiting in the drive was her scheduled pickup, the exhaust pipe in the back sending thin plumes of fog, the driver not willing to be get cold in the wait.

"Stupid, stupid," JJ muttered, half to herself for missing the time, half to the driver for possibly bringing attention to the vehicle.

She glanced at her phone. Four attempted calls. She texted the driver to sit tight.

"Damn it!" She pressed the sound through her teeth, this time accusing herself since the driver's orders had been to not leave the car and reveal themselves.

She stood in the middle of the kitchen, spinning a couple times, going through her beach plans. Leave this. Take that. Goddamnit, she hated to be rushed.

She glanced outside once more at the waiting ride, checked through the list of to-dos on her phone, and deemed herself ready.

Computer in hand, she fast-stepped downstairs, popped her Audi's trunk and grabbed a suitcase, then slid into the waiting car . . . not noticing the pair of eyes watching on the other side of the shrubs dividing *Flirty Flamingo* from the house next door.

Chapter 6

"THOMAS, YOU THERE?"

"Here, Chief."

Callie drove past Stan's house on Pompano, eager to inform her old boss about this new development on her beach, but his car wasn't home. She had a nervous feeling about JJ's disappearance, and if Mark weren't so inundated with tourists at his restaurant, she'd chat him up.

"Loveless wasn't at *Water Spout*," she said over her mic, "but I found her laptop there. I'm headed to *Flirty Flamingo* for another look. Maybe play with this computer while I'm there. I'm giving her until tonight before getting serious."

"Ten four, Chief."

"And hey, start canvassing the restaurants and showing her driver's license. Might be premature, but good to have more than our eyes on this."

"Ten four again. Thomas out."

His informal sign off brought a slight grin. Nothing got too terribly formal on Edisto Beach, including the policing . . . until matters turned sober. Edisto had seen its share of dark crime. The public just hadn't heard about all of it, and the entrepreneurs and residents were more than happy to keep anything they'd heard under their hats. Tourism revenue and property values had a way of controlling certain behaviors.

She soon parked at the *Flirty Flamingo*, making a family of five on bikes cross to the other side of the road, nervous as if the patrol car might suck them into some kind of ticket. Vacationers preferred unmarred fun and zero responsibility. She didn't blame them, and her job was to ensure they spent their week as close to that expectation as possible.

Before leaving the car, she opened JJ's purse, pulled out JJ's phone, and in her own phone typed in JJ's phone number from Georgia's alumni roster. JJ's phone lit up and rang. So that answered that. The author had another phone or she was missing, because who existed without a phone?

She dumped the purse's contents in her passenger seat, hoping for some sign of JJ's literary agent. Any author of her caliber would have one helping to run things behind the scenes, coordinating the next book at least. Business cards weren't the norm any longer with smart phones, but someone like a literary agent might still function old school or cover all bases.

A tri-fold wallet contained a whopping forty-seven dollars, the driver's license she'd already given Thomas, two VISAs, and a health insurance card. Within a zippered pocket of the purse, Callie located a checkbook and an assortment of business cards, flipping to an agent from New York City. Bingo.

Since it was business hours, she called the office first, but a recording asked her which agent she needed, then after hitting a number, she could leave a message. She hung up and phoned the cell. Mr. Antonio Galvin's voice mail answered, then so did she. "This is Edisto Beach Police Chief Callie Morgan in South Carolina. Please return my call. We found your business card in the belongings of one JJ Loveless."

Yeah, he'd return that call.

Inside the rental, Callie plugged in the laptop and left it on the kitchen table to charge. Then she called Georgia.

"You find her?" Georgia asked without salutation.

"Give me any other phone number you've got on JJ."

"I, um, I don't think I have but one number for each person."

"You think or you know?"

"I don't have another number." A hint of disgust in the reply.

"I'm not insulting you, Georgia. Just doing my job. Scroll through calls made to her and see if any of them are different than this main number. Then email her and copy me on it. Say we need her to check in."

"Um, I don't have your email."

"I'm one of your reunion committee members, Georgia. It's on your list."

Georgia had compartmentalized Callie in the role of cop, not alumnus. "Oh, sorry. Duh! So you've opened a case?" she asked. "Y'all, I think they're opening a missing person's case on JJ," she added to whoever stood nearby.

"No case. No missing person. Not yet."

"Oh." Georgia sounded disappointed. "Well, keep us up to speed."

"Call me if she shows."

"Will do!" she said, not worried in the least. "We're having a planning meeting at four, by the way, then going to El Marko's for dinner. Join us, if you don't mind. Without JJ and without the other six, we need all the planning power we can marshal."

Callie replied, "I'll be in touch." But once she hung up, she thought she just might make that dinner. In the name of the investigation . . . to see what Mark Dupree might think about this situation, and how the alums were coping with one of their own missing.

She dropped Mark a text. *A group from my high school is eating there this evening. Keep an eye and ear out on them, please. Anything about a missing person. Will explain later.*

She hadn't decided whether to be pissed or genuinely concerned about the author. JJ had orchestrated a coup of sorts taking over Georgia's weekend. Add to that she wrote mysteries. She would scheme more than the average person. If she had the time, Callie would read one of those books in the laptop case, to see how this woman's mind worked, but if JJ had fallen into legitimate trouble, there wasn't time.

She double-checked the linings of the purse then launched into the suitcase. Zippers, pockets, more linings. If she found cocaine or stolen diamonds, she'd regroup about not having a warrant, but for the moment she'd be fine. She simply hunted for someone inconveniently lost.

She didn't have to look through the contents very hard. Just beneath clothes lay a large envelope tied with a string around a brad at the top. Callie undid the string and lifted it by the bottom corner to shake out the contents on the bed.

Photographs.

The memories took Callie aback. Pictures of the dead girl, Wendy. Anything from a smiling close-up, beautifully organic, most likely from the yearbook, to an autopsy photo that Callie quickly turned over. Photos of Wendy with her parents. One with Georgia, a fellow cheerleader back in the day. Another with Libby and a couple of guys who looked vaguely familiar. In baseball uniform and cheerleading garb, Butch and Wendy laughed big and bold after a game. With Reuben in the chem lab, him showing her how to deal with a Bunsen burner, obviously staged for the yearbook. Four of the six invited to *Water Spout.*

Callie braced herself. Had to be one of her somewhere in the stack.

After all, wasn't this research material for the true crime? Weren't these individuals the ones JJ had accused of somehow being involved in Wendy's demise?

Which Callie understood perfectly well had included her.

Tentatively, she flipped over the photo closest to her left hand on the bed, her right holding the ones she'd already seen.

She first noticed the resemblance to Jeb, though these days he grew more into his father's likeness. Her photo-self stood outside Middleton High School in senior park with dozens of others, probably waiting for some sort of assembly, or the bell to bring them in after lunch. The photographer caught Callie carrying on a conversation with a guy she couldn't remember other than he led the Young Republicans Club. No telling what they debated, but that wasn't the point. In the background, Wendy watched, absorbed, listening with what could be interpreted as a longing to engage.

Callie couldn't recall Wendy at any sort of political or current event gathering. She belonged to the cheer squad. Then with guilty admission, Callie wondered why she'd thought that, as if wearing a cheerleading outfit disqualified her from having a serious opinion.

A black-and-white showed JJ, or Jessie Jane as they called her back then, operating in her typical mother hen mode, even at seventeen, trying to intently explain something to Wendy and another cheerleader . . . Georgia, maybe? Hard to tell from the angle. The blonds appeared lost. Inherently stereotypical. Yearbook editor-slash-honor-student instructing the bimbos. Most likely staged by JJ as well.

Did JJ consider herself one of those culpable in Wendy's death? Or did this picture fall under the Georgia column? Did JJ label herself blameless and purely seek a bestseller, or did she see herself as part of the problem and in search of redemption?

Callie left the four larger photos till last, and used the end of the one of JJ to turn the first eight-by-ten on the bedspread. As if uncovering a snake, she pulled her hand back. A funeral service.

Those unending days of agony rushed back, unchecked. Callie had attended Wendy's viewing, church service, and graveside at the push of her parents, Mayor Lawton and Beverly Cantrell. As the mayor's daughter, Callie was expected to make certain appearances. She almost tasted the vomit from throwing up breakfast the day of the graveside service, having nursed peppermints through it all. She remembered going to bed early with no supper, her parents too busy to check on her after such a fright.

Truth was, the girl's death had stirred the town so badly that the mayor, the police chief, the school district's superintendent, and the high school principal found themselves at every Wendy event as well as behind the scenes attempting to manage the fear coursing through the town. Callie was the last of her parents' concerns. Wendy Ashton and Stratton Winningham dominated Middleton's existence for a couple of months. Stratton had died a little over a month later, right before Christmas.

Callie sank to the bed with so many details again crisp. Family, friends, dodgy reporters, and the police chief who cut his chief-teeth on the case. Squinting, Callie canvassed the crowd at her first funeral, her first exposure to paying respects to a stiff replica of a person. With Wendy being popular as well as young, the entire town turned out along with cheer squads from six other schools. Several hundred strong. So much crying one couldn't not cry.

She moved on to the other pics. *Oh dear God.* Two of these were of Stratton's service.

And she hated JJ for exhuming this history.

Struggling to identify people, Callie blinked, then blinked again . . . then realized she struggled seeing through tears. Stratton Winningham.

She hadn't forgotten him, how could she, but she'd struggled so hard to tuck this boy on the back shelf of her mind. But after seeing his service again, especially compared with Wendy's, along with the sadness and shame came the fury.

No, Wendy hadn't been her motivation to go into law enforcement. Stratton had. Callie had cursed Middleton's Chief Warren for all he was worth back then, not talking to him for at least a decade after, both of them reaching a mutual unsaid agreement to not bring up the subject. He'd been nice enough when her father passed away a couple years ago, but some history never died.

They'd suspected Stratton of murdering Wendy, interrogating him relentlessly because he was Wendy's ex-boyfriend. He'd been Callie's date at the infamous ballgame. Wasn't until they'd leaned on him that Callie learned when he took a break in the fourth quarter, he'd also met Wendy. He'd returned, no mention of Wendy, but then the crowd noise had been intense as the last quarter ended. Callie took her bathroom break while he joined the kids on the field in celebration.

By the end of the next day, the whole town had turned on the boy. She sensed in her bones he hadn't killed the girl. He'd cried in her arms, so bruised and wounded at not only Wendy's death, but the pressure put on him to confess to something he didn't do. So she'd royally embarrassed her parents using what clout she possessed as a member of the town's "first family" to prove Stratton's innocence. She had connections to the police with her father being tight with the chief, and she'd used her father's name in vain to enter offices and homes to ask questions. Her father put the word out to city venues to block his daughter's inquisitions, so Callie grabbed people in parking lots. Ultimately Stratton's parents refused her to visit Stratton, their attorney saying Callie was making matters worse.

The investigation seemed to drag forever, but to angst-ridden seventeen-and eighteen-year-olds, six weeks was an eternity.

The authorities caved to the court of public opinion, knowing the citizens needed someone to blame. The long drawn-out effort to gather enough facts for an indictment led to an ending no one saw coming—Stratton's suicide. Then the sons of bitches sighed relief at the ordeal being over.

The pressure led Stratton to hang himself under the very bleachers where Wendy died, found by a Middleton town cop when his parents demanded a search because he didn't show up to school.

During that search, Callie's father called her out of class, asking if she'd seen the boy, and she then cut school and drove around hunting him herself. She'd checked the bleachers first thing, but he hadn't been there. The police began searching harder, after the Winninghams threatened to go to the press.

Stratton was still warm when they cut him down. Callie missed him by an hour, they said.

The Winninghams went to the press anyway, but the hanging only convinced the town that the boy couldn't handle the guilt.

With the butt of her palm, Callie wiped her eyes, taken aback at the wave of emotion. She thought she'd put all this to bed, and with all she'd witnessed in law enforcement, she figured these feelings scabbed over and scarred thick. And she hated JJ for digging this shit out for personal gain.

What else was in this damn suitcase?

A list of the twelve alumni, with six crossed out. No mention of the principal. Then a separate sheet on each person showing JJ had excavated each of their lives. Relationships with each other, with Wendy. Professions, marriages, divorces, and a timeline of it all. Then at the bottom of each page, summarized comments about why the individual hadn't done enough, had done too much, or aided in ruining Wendy's life.

So where was a page about Stratton Winningham? Did JJ peg him innocent? He should have a file. He was too big a part of this story not to. The file had to be elsewhere, maybe with her, or left at home with the emphasis for this weekend being the parties who still had a pulse.

Callie found a second envelope hidden under clothes on the other side of the suitcase. The autopsy report, or rather its detailed summary, and the police report for Wendy. Unredacted. JJ had connections with authorities.

Inhaling deeply, Callie held it, thinking before blowing out and deciding that packet of information could wait until she was home. As a kid she'd heard what it said, but then she'd been a kid, protected by parents who only hit the high points. Today, trained and seasoned, she'd acquired the ability to read details and interpret better, see more in the terminology. She understood how easily the medical examiner could have aided the chief in his accusations of Stratton . . . or how much the chief had embellished the facts and suppositions.

A struggle, bruises, a fall over the bleacher rigging, a broken leg, attempted rape but nothing consummated. A discovered pregnancy. These details she knew.

She reined in her thoughts. She had time for this later. She inhaled deeply to regroup.

Her watch noted she'd been lost in the Middleton High School time warp for over an hour. Bless Thomas for handling the beach. Bless the visitors for behaving. With one swipe at her cheeks, she returned to the kitchen table, finding enough power in the computer to have a go at it.

Before she could debate broaching legal restrictions of her search, the locked password blocked her from crossing that line. On television, detectives took locked laptops and phones to their highly specialized IT experts, cracking codes and bypassing passwords in a matter of seconds. In reality, devices weren't that simple to breach. In an even bigger reality, Edisto Beach had nowhere near that level of talent, and her buddies at SLED and even the FBI would take days or even weeks to assist and would make her open a missing person's case, something she wasn't quite primed to do. Guess she'd take it to Marie, the best IT talent on the island, and see if she could figure anything out. At least lock it up in the evidence cabinet for safekeeping. The paper notepad in the laptop case, however, would come home with Callie, along with the photos . . . along with the autopsy report. One of JJ's books, too. She left the suitcase. If JJ showed, she'd feel burgled, and the first place she'd come would be Callie.

What she wished she had, however, was some sort of manuscript to see what direction JJ was taking Wendy's death. Paper or hard drive, she yearned to read the draft. The nastier the story, the more motive for someone to stop the book.

Her phone rang, the number familiar. "Chief Morgan."

"Antonio Galvin, Chief Morgan. What is this about? Your message referenced *the belongings of one JJ Loveless?* What are you saying?"

"Mr. Galvin, Ms. Loveless is visiting our little island here in South Carolina, and she left her laptop at someone's beach house. Her phone and other belongings were found in her rental, but we've not located her. Without her phone on her, we've been unable to raise her, and the friends she rendezvoused with here are a bit worried . . . you heard she's down here for a school reunion, right?"

The hesitation said enough. He had to be aware of her trip.

"Is she still, um, missing?"

"Affirmative, sir. Would you happen to know where she is?"

His laugh rang hollow. "I'm miles away. Her deadline isn't for months. I can honestly say I have no idea where she is at this moment, but my client has displayed eccentricities before, especially when researching. She's worse than eccentric if she's slaving over a first draft."

"Has she checked in within the last two days?"

"She called as she was crossing some big bridge onto an island," he replied. "She was excited about interviewing people for the next book, but this particular book is in infant stages, Chief. Not much more than concept, to be honest. I told her to have a good vacation while she was there."

Selective in his word choice and cookbook-ish in his reply. JJ Loveless was his commodity, an investment to protect, and until Callie showed concern for whether JJ still lived, he wasn't divulging a thing.

"When you catch up with her, how about telling her to call me?" Callie replied, calm, no rush and no hurry.

"Absolutely," he said, hanging up with a good-bye, not worried in the least that Callie said JJ didn't have her phone.

Chapter 7

LAPTOP DROPPED off at the station for Marie to tinker with, Callie went home early making Thomas aware she remained on call. The town of Edisto Beach barely exceeded two square miles, if one didn't count the lagoon and inlets, so *on call* meant a minute or two from anything, anyone, at any time. One of the job's perks . . . and burdens. The police chief being available twenty-four/seven was a given. When she couldn't sleep, she cruised the streets at night.

After locking up the notepad, envelopes, and JJ's book in the closet safe at home—her afternoon skip down Memory Lane too recent and raw to leap into the evidence for the moment—Callie changed clothes. The almighty reunion committee was geared to meet in a half hour at El Marko's.

But first she'd detour past the office of Janet Wainwright, real estate broker extraordinaire, who controlled the majority of sales and rentals in the town. Judging from the permanent yellow and red sign on JJ's house, her rental was one of them. Wainwright handled Georgia's house as well when vacant.

This being the end of March, the red roses and gold lantana had leafed but not bloomed along the walkway to the Wainwright Realty stairs. Too early for red geraniums or yellow petunias hanging on the porch, so instead she had bunting, draped like Fourth of July across her bannister, in the U.S. Marine Corps colors. Janet clearly took her Parris Island past seriously, by her real estate branding. Once a Marine, always a Marine.

A new young girl manned the receptionist desk. Rarely did one last more than a season. Heaven help the office minion who let the toner run out in the copier or the hanging plants go dry. Janet liked her office in top order, which meant she checked, which then meant the staff better have checked before she did.

She scared people out of their shoes when she wanted to, but rental owners loved her reliability, and property sellers loved how vicious she could be at the negotiation table.

"I'm here to see Miss Janet," Callie said to the girl in a summery floral dress, two colors of which were yellow and red. Her yellow sweater accented the Corps brand, truly demonstrating the young lady under-stood the code.

Off season, especially during the dry months of January and February, Callie often let herself in, knocking on Janet's door, but not these days. Not when allowing an uninvited guest into the inner sanctum could get staff fired.

After an intercom message, the girl hung up and smiled from behind her desk with every paper, pad, pen, and assorted stationary item in clean, synchronized lines. "She'll see you, Chief Morgan."

Callie smiled at her. "You're doing great, even if she doesn't say so."

The girl smiled a little bigger. "I'm trying."

I see you are. Still, Callie guessed her *tour* would last no longer than the first of August.

She tapped on Janet's door.

"Enter," came the command.

"Bet you're busy this week," Callie said, taking seat in one of the leather chairs facing Janet's massive mahogany desk.

The close-cropped head of white hair was bowed, the realtor taking a moment to finish whatever she was writing before peering up. "I don't have time for chit-chat. What's your issue?"

Small talk wasn't in the Wainwright vocabulary. A retired drill ser-geant, Janet carried her military habits into civilian life. She'd com-mandeered the real estate industry on the beach, taking a business previously shared amongst three others and making it hers. Two of the old realties remained, but only as shells of what they used to be. They wouldn't exist at all if Janet hadn't allowed them to.

"You rented *Flirty Flamingo* to JJ Loveless, right?"

"Apparently you already know that. And?"

"How long is she renting it?"

"Three days."

"When did she make the reservation?"

Janet typed on her screen a second. "Three months ago."

Which coincided with the time Georgia was emailing the people about the when, where, and all on the "reunion planning" gathering. Callie wondered whether that was when JJ had her lightbulb moment, or whether she'd been the catalyst for the reunion, asking Georgia to organize such an affair. Then there was always the chance JJ was already working on the book, and Georgia's emails prompted the author to seize control in her own special way.

"Aren't your houses rented well ahead of schedule? With this being spring break, how did she grab *Flirty Flamingo* on such short notice?"

"She paid me twenty percent more to bump the other renter." No discomfort at all in the admission that money talked.

"How many people in the house?" Realties were required to ask, not that people spoke the truth. Word spread amongst families and friends that Aunt or Cousin So-and-so had a house at the beach for a week. A place on the water became incredibly affordable when a house designed for, say, eight wound up with sixteen. That's when parties got raucous.

"Two. She said a husband would arrive a day later, which often happens."

"Well, he didn't," Callie said.

"That happens, too," Janet replied. "Not my business."

"But you gave her two sets of keys?"

Janet gave a clipped nod.

"Seen her since she arrived?"

"No."

"You get where I'm going with this?" Callie asked.

"Call if I see or hear from her," Janet said.

"Correct." Callie opened her phone and showed the number Georgia'd given to her for JJ. "Is this the same number you have?"

Janet checked her screen again. "Yes, it is."

Callie put the device away. "Then that's all the questions I have. Wasn't too painful, was it?"

"Pain is character building, Chief."

"Indeed. Well, you know how to find me." Callie rose and left with one glance back. Janet had her head back into her work, driving on as only Janet knew how to do.

Two couples waited in front of the clerk's desk, and by the time Callie reached her cruiser, two more drove up. Janet would be showing houses like crazy this week.

Carefully driving around people on golf carts, bikes, and foot, Callie made it to Palmetto and headed down the main stretch. When she arrived at *Water Spout* at four straight up, she found the crew where she'd left them that morning, lazed across the back porch, exemplifying anything but *superlative*.

"Y'all heard from JJ?" she asked, coming through the double doors. The sun set on the opposite side of the island, so the brightness wasn't as intense on the water. The moon made the most memorable appearance on this side.

Sunglasses on their heads, the collective had the personality of a wet rag. Some nodded. Others let the other nods suffice.

"Wow," she said. "Y'all are going to have to take it down a notch before the neighbors complain."

Georgia pulled out the familiar notebook. "Waiting for you!" Her bubbliness fell a bit flat.

"Sure you were." Callie hunted around for a cooler, because they sure didn't look motivated enough to make trips to the kitchen.

"I'll get you something," Butch said, rising from his chaise, his glass lifted high. "Besides, I'm empty."

"Water or soft drink," she said.

He snickered. "I'll surprise you."

"Bring me anything alcoholic and you'll wear it."

The smile left. "Damn. You weren't exactly slapstick in school, but I remember more fun than this." He disappeared inside.

Callie assumed a chair as far from Butch as possible, hoping he didn't change seats when he returned. "How are the plans going so far?"

Georgia waved up a blank page, her expression infused with sarcasm. "Can't get past the criticisms. JJ really got into people's heads."

"Damn sure did!" Pouting, Libby sat next to the principal, their relationship in the wide out and open from the way their bare feet crossed each other's. Callie wondered how that worked at school. "I was Wendy's best friend." Out came Libby's finger jabbing. "And I'll not tolerate accusations, so yes, I was pissed when Jessie Jane, oh, pardon me, JJ, dropped her stupid one-liners about each of us. How dare she? Who made her judge and jury over something solved over twenty years ago? If she writes about me, I'll sue her ass."

"Language," Tony said, droll.

"You liked it enough last night," she said, her nose up in a snit.

Callie thanked the heavens Butch wasn't back to pounce on that. "The venue is the high school auditorium?"

Tony nodded. "Yes. Along with the use of the kitchen, cafeteria, and gym. Any or all."

A lot of space. "Weren't there, like, three hundred people in the class? Attendance would be, what, a quarter of those? That's around seventy-five plus their plus-ones. A hundred fifty. What's the theme?" There, Callie had made her contribution to the cause.

"Aren't we forgetting the teachers?" Libby said.

Callie guessed so, but seriously, how many educators from twenty years ago were still alive, employed, or retired nearby? "Yes, of course. The teachers are important." Someone else could take the lead now.

But nobody spoke, and after Butch returned and handed water to Callie, she tried again. "What's the theme?"

Butch plopped back down and shrugged. "Spice Girls?"

Ughs released all around.

He shrugged. "Then y'all figure it out. Just saying they were pretty hot back then."

His bad idea triggered a dozen other assorted clichés, the *ughs* becoming the norm.

Georgia perked up. "I've got one. Let's make the theme Prom Night. Tuxes and formals. Boutonnieres and corsages. A band. You know . . . pretending we're eighteen again."

Not a bad idea, and Callie was about to say so.

"Someone is bound to come as Carrie," Tony said.

Libby clouded over at her guy. "No they wouldn't. Eww. Nobody would think of that except you."

"I say," Butch said, holding up his glass. "Who gets to be Wendy and Stratton?" He lowered his glass at the silence. "Or is that too tasteless even for me?"

"Butch," Georgia exclaimed, eyes narrowed. "How cruel!"

"That answers that," Butch said, taking a drink.

Reuben did a *tsk* thing loud enough to be heard over the waves. "And this is why we can't plan a reunion," he said. "Truth is nobody wants to go back and relive those days, mostly because of Wendy and Stratton. What's the big loss if we let this plan die a natural death and just eat and drink the rest of the weekend?"

Callie almost gave him an *amen* until she envisioned them packing up and going home. That did nothing toward finding JJ. On the other hand, JJ could show up once she heard the meeting adjourned.

Until Callie knew which, however, she'd keep them here and rally them around. For a day or two more, at least. She couldn't believe she was doing this. "Let's not get ahead of ourselves, folks." To Butch, she added, "Try to curtail the dark humor, please. It doesn't help."

"Says the woman afraid to drink. Wendy keep you awake at night? You found her. Some say you tried to alibi Stratton, too."

"You son of a bitch," she whispered, a split second before the rest released their tempers in a tussle of overbearing, crisscrossing slings and accusations.

Reuben let loose with a roar, his volume overriding the cacophony. "You'd think we were all guilty of something, wouldn't you?" he said, his foreign boisterous behavior shutting them down. "Who says JJ's wrong in what she's doing, huh? What does she know that we don't? Or rather what we don't want to say."

Even Callie's heart double-thumped at the sudden quiet.

She knew her regrets. Not fighting hard enough for Stratton. If her son had come to her burdened like that, she'd have told him a child shouldn't have to feel so burdened.

Stratton had been a convenient date for her, having split from Wendy a couple weeks back. Callie felt sorry for him flapping around so unattached. He was a good guy. However, she devoted herself more to Stratton once he was accused. Then she turned anxious when the autopsy report noted a pregnancy, but he owned the mistake. She lost sleep watching the ease with which so many people connected dots that weren't actually there. But her guilt took up permanent residence once her parents caved to public pressure and let Chief Warren ride the lone suspect into taking his own life.

If one were to listen to JJ, each person on this deck harbored twenty-plus years of some sort of regret in relation to that horrible time. Callie sure knew hers.

"Where the hell is JJ?" Callie said, releasing her jaw. She was supposed to be the adult on the porch.

"Not sure we care," said Libby.

Callie stood, having stupidly fallen prey to their juvenile tendencies. "Well, someone has to care, because if her body shows up, I'm looking at a serious line of suspects."

Tony came forward in his seat, cheeks reddening, talking like he would to a student. "Control your accusations, please. I wasn't in your class."

Callie turned on him. "You taught when Wendy and Stratton were there, so own it, mister. You're included."

"What about you?" Libby asked, protective of her man.

"I tell you what," Callie said, trying to avoid the tit-for-tat everyone yearned for. "Let's go eat and calm down. If you can't stop at one drink then don't drink at all. We don't want booze in the mix. Then let's come back here and hammer out what makes JJ label us as screw-ups. And if she's not here to defend herself, we'll cover her, too. Sound good?"

Hopefully in the conversation, she'd gain some backstory about why JJ disappeared.

Nobody argued, and Reuben ultimately agreed for them all.

"El Marko's?" she asked of Georgia.

"Yes," their hostess replied. "I told you I had a reservation."

"Good. You don't want to be late, because the place isn't that big. We'll lose our table. Who wants to ride with me?" When nobody stepped forward, she rolled with it. "Very well. I'll see you there."

She left without hesitation, without a second request for riders. Nobody had even appeared out front by the time she pulled away.

She went back past the Thistle Street rental, got out and tried the doors of house and vehicle. Inside she checked for signs of a visit. Nothing.

"Thomas?" she said back in her car, calling up her officer. "Get serious on that missing person. She hasn't shown and none of her friends have seen her." *Friends.* Not quite precise, but close enough. "Get information to Marie and the others, then canvas each establishment on the beach. Send an emergency text out on the system." The same texts used for hurricanes, shark sightings, abrupt closings, traffic accidents, and, of course, missing persons. The whole island would receive it. Then she called Deputy Raysor, her liaison with the Colleton County Sheriff's Office, leaving word with him to spread the missing person's report across the county.

She wouldn't start a grid search just yet. During dinner she'd take in behaviors, listen to innuendo, then bring them back to *Water Spout* for more talk.

Tomorrow, Sunday, she would head to Middleton at the crack of dawn. Time to meet with Beverly Cantrell, her mother and current mayor of the town, having assumed the role when Lawton died. She was elected in her own right a few months later, but when Lawton was mayor, she ran Middleton joined at the hip with her husband. Anything he knew, she knew.

Afterwards, lunch with Chief Warren. And if he tried to claim Sunday privilege and wriggle out of the meet, she'd have her mother deliver the order to make it happen. Callie wasn't a kid this time.

The incredibly scary message in all of this was that Wendy's killer never was caught. Nobody cared to recognize that, appeased by the logic that the dead guy must've done it. Because to think Stratton murdered Wendy, closed that door and made them sleep better at night.

Callie believed someone else did the deed, and that it was most likely a one-time deal by somebody Wendy knew. By blaming Stratton, by Stratton dying, the murderer could fade into the wallpaper of life.

And people wondered why she had a security system on her house . . . and a gun on her nightstand most nights, and under her pillow during the rest.

Chapter 8

EVEN AFTER STOPPING at JJ's house, Callie reached El Marko's just as Georgia turned into the parking lot with Libby and Tony. The other two guys followed in Reuben's more expensive vehicle, of course, but rather than wait for them outside, Callie scooted in, seeking Mark. She'd want to be warned if she were him. He might not have seen her text.

Good thing the group had a reservation with this Saturday evening crowd. Tourists formed a line on the covered sidewalk that ran the length of the tiny strip mall.

Sophie caught Callie first, the yoga lady serving as hostess and fill-in-waitress or bartender, as needed. Mark had jumped on her request for employment back in December, recognizing her personality tripled anyone else's on the island. She did yoga in the mornings and El Marko's in the evenings, driving folks on the beach crazy in between, but she was ridiculously good at adding to the atmosphere of the Mexican restaurant and coaxing people in.

Callie saw Mark behind the bar but couldn't get to him for his hostess. "I need to see your boss, Soph, but there's a group of five behind me with Georgia in charge. With a reservation, I believe. They're not in the best mood, so use your charm." Callie leaned in closer. "Don't think Georgia convinced them to use your stash."

"Probably kept it for herself," Sophie whispered back, then she winked. "But I got this, girl. You eating with them?"

"Unfortunately, yes," she replied. "Just save me a chair. Try not to let them drink too much."

"Gotcha."

Georgia entered, Sophie greeted her, and Callie took off to the bar.

Mark smiled down at his hands, busy, and by the time Callie assumed her stool, he placed an iced ginger ale on a napkin, a twisted slice of lime wedged on the lip.

"Here for dinner?" he asked. "My table's open."

In the back corner, between bar and kitchen entrance, he kept a small table reserved for him and anyone else he chose. Interviewees, town big-wigs, and friends. The moment he took a seat there, his staff knew the unspoken drill of supplying a plate of appetizers while asking for the guest's drink of choice.

She nodded over to a table for six, where Sophie laid out menus and the crew jockeyed who had to sit next to whom. "A planning committee from my high school graduating class," she explained.

"Oh," he said, attentive. "I'll throw in a couple appetizers. What else can I do?"

"Save me from them," she said, taking a long draw of her drink.

He'd taken to wearing Hawaiian shirts like Callie's old boss Stan, and somehow nobody noticed they weren't Mexican . . . just bright. He leaned in, his humor empathetic. "How long are you stuck with them?"

Setting the drink down, she centered it on the napkin. "Well, that's the thing. Probably until I find the missing member."

His smile dimmed. "Missing? Change-their-mind missing? Or mysteriously missing?"

"The latter." She filled him in about JJ Loveless, the abbreviated version. Famous writer. House open. Agent not concerned. The group hoping she stayed gone. Then finally the tell-all story in progress, and the fact it was linked to a high school murder. By the time she finished, he stood still, lasered on her.

"Need to run this past another law enforcement brain," she said. "Stan back?"

With mock indignation, he straightened. "Okay, not feeling slighted in the least."

"No, no," she said. "I need to pick your cop intellect, too."

"Agent," he corrected.

"Agent," she agreed and peered over at the group's table. Orders placed, each of them took turns popping their head up and glancing over at her like Whack-a-Moles, clearly wondering how long she'd be this rude. Or maybe whom she socialized with behind the bar.

"In the morning?" he asked. "I can let you in here as early as you like."

She hadn't been to Mark's house two blocks over without Stan being there, and she could count on one hand how many times he'd been to hers. Namely Christmas.

Their personalities fit . . . to a point . . . and neither seemed to want to be the one to take things further. Dinner dates, yes. *Come up to my place for a drink?* Not really.

She shook her head. "Morning won't work. Heading to Middleton to confront the mayor and chief of police about Ms. Loveless."

"Good thing you have connections in that direction, Chief."

True that. And she'd use them to their max, because one of them, if not both, had already entertained JJ Loveless's mission and supplied her with information to begin fleshing out the book. If they thought Callie was a pain in the butt at seventeen, wait until they dealt with her at forty-two with a badge. Beverly already had a taste of Callie's brawn in that regard. She'd hidden for almost forty years the fact she'd adopted Lawton Cantrell's love child as her own . . . and that Callie's real mother lived two houses down on Jungle Road.

"How about tonight then?" he asked.

She tore her eyes away from the ice in her empty glass. "Sorry, how about what?" Tomorrow's plans had distracted her.

He took her glass and wet napkin, replacing both fresh. "How about I come by after locking up?"

She shook her head. "I can't keep you up that late."

"I work late hours. Comes with the job. Besides, the restaurant doesn't open until eleven in the morning." He made a conscious scan of his place. "We can't talk here with people dining, and you're already busy in the morning. I'll come by your place, say, around ten tonight?"

She tried to take a brief glimpse of the committee's table but got caught. Georgia was staring her down.

"Ten it is," Callie said. "If I'm late, forgive me, because between now and then, I've got to try and press these people for answers without them realizing it."

THE GROUP OOHED and aahed over the free appetizers, though any one of them could spring for the entire dinner and not blink an eye. Except maybe the school teacher.

Cute little pinwheels on one plate and cheesy quesados on another. Each member sipped on something alcoholic. Butch sucked his down and asked for another. At least one and all seemed to feel better, but her concern was that waiting to discuss JJ after dinner would be for naught if the alcohol kept flowing. Better for Callie to open the conversation now, putting Butch at the top of the list before he started on his third drink.

She sat at the end of the table, Butch to her left and Reuben on the right. "How do you like those?" she asked, pointing to the quesados.

"Best thing about them is they go with tequila," Butch said, following a bite with a Cuervo chaser.

"Tell Mark thanks," Georgia said from the other side of Reuben. "I hear he's sweet on you, Callie."

"People say a lot of things on this beach." Then to switch gears, Callie told everyone, "Eat up. If you finish those, the next appetizer's on me."

"We'll finish these, all right," Butch said, so Callie motioned to Sophie. "Bring them out the three-dip sampler, please. On me." Then she turned to Butch. "Why would JJ drag you into all this? She must have had something particular in mind. I mean, Wendy was nice to anybody . . . even you, but—"

Libby chuckled, mouth full. "Makes you sound like a charity case."

As predicted, Butch puffed up. "Reuben was the charity case, but this boy," he jabbed a thumb at himself, "did not go lacking when it came to the ladies."

Just as Callie had hoped. "So you and Wendy consummated your friendship, so to speak, huh?"

"Maybe," he said, but when his classmates smirked, he tacked on, "of course. Twice."

"Did they interview you when Wendy died?" She looked around the table. "Like they did us?"

He didn't redden, but he ceased bragging. "Yes. Of course. Like everyone."

Callie slid a chip with queso on it to his plate. "Don't let the snacks get cold. They warm up those chips." She dipped one for herself. "Could the baby have been yours?"

"No, um, *no*."

Like who could prove different? Back then DNA was time-consuming and costly. With Wendy dead and Stratton close behind her, the police department hadn't wasted resources. Today they'd have narrowed down the baby daddy as a standard course of action.

Libby reached for the last quesado. "You brag too much, Butch, plus Wendy had better taste. She'd have turned you down."

"There you're wrong, teacher. She fucked everybody," he said a tad too loud, "and I got my fair share!"

The group hushed, except Reuben who looked ready to come across the table. Callie glanced at the diners behind Butch, one man particularly stiff. She leaned closer to Butch on one elbow and lowered her voice. "How many times?"

He leaned in to her, ire in his glower. "I told them we had sex our junior year, then again our senior."

"Do you smell a story here, Butch?" she said, taking her voice even lower. "Is that why you're tolerating the way Libby and Reuben berate you? At the end of all of this, you're no different than JJ in that you hope to capitalize on this gathering."

"Stories are everywhere, Chief," he said, accepting her dare to fluster him. "Including about you and a certain reporter you killed because he shot your boyfriend. I covered that for our station, by the way, but you were so out of it you probably don't remember seeing me at the funeral."

The world was at that funeral. People filled every seat in Edisto Presbyterian and lined the walls, pouring out onto the grounds. They opened the windows for all to hear. Uniforms from across the state both paid respects for Michael Seabrook and respected her for the quality of a eulogy that about did her in.

Callie inched even closer, which made him do the same. "Don't take me on, Butch. Better men have tried, and as you just articulated, have died in the attempt. Did you kill Wendy?"

"No."

She leaned back with a big smile. "Nice chat, Butch. Thanks." She turned attentive to Libby, at the opposite end of the table. "As Wendy's best friend, you probably heard all about her social life, including who'd had their way with her . . . or maybe who she claimed as trophies."

"I'm not doing this here," she said, avoiding eye contact. "You don't have the right to interrogate me."

Callie moved her appetizer plate away a few inches and crossed both forearms on her placemat. "Actually, I do. With JJ missing, I have the right to ask all sorts of questions. Like why did JJ think you did wrong by Wendy?"

"Never," she attested. "Never did I betray my best friend."

"Not even the night she was found?" Callie said, but Libby dramatically shook her head.

"No, ma'am. I was in the stands with my sister and her friend who I can't remember. I recall watching Wendy, noting how tired she looked down there on the field."

"Where was Peter?" Georgia asked, catching Callie by surprise because it was only then she realized how quiet the hostess had been.

Peter . . . Butch's best friend from the baseball team, and currently Libby's ex. They'd been an item in high school . . . in between times when Butch and Peter weren't best friends. People had poked fun at the fact that Butch and Libby vied over Peter. Jokes ran rampant about how Peter's British accent had a way with people, male and female.

"Peter sat with Butch that night," Libby said, slinging Callie a look.

Which made sense without further explanation.

"So explain JJ," Callie said. "She thought you needed to be included in her plan, too, obviously."

"Who the hell can explain her? We haven't seen her in two decades. How can we figure out the who, what, when, where, why, and how of what's percolating in that woman's brain?" she said, falling back on her English theme paper teachings. "We were pawns, is all. She stirred us up to see what would float to the top. Probably didn't get the idea until receiving the notice from Georgia about a reunion committee."

Yet her chest heaved by the end. So simple to read.

"Think hard," Callie said. "What does she think she has on you?"

"God only knows what that bitch thinks, but nobody has a thing on me. There's nothing to have."

"Yet JJ wanted you here."

Butch gave a laugh. "Somebody bring me some hip boots, please. The crap's piling high."

Libby hard-stared him back. "Make that two pair."

Damn if the food didn't arrive at the most inopportune time.

Sophie assisted the waitress with bringing the entrees, attentive to her task until they were all laid out. "What else can I get you guys?"

"Another round of drinks," Butch said. "Somebody's gonna pull out a weapon and start dropping bodies if we don't mellow out." He looked at Libby first. "Whatcha want, Libby? My treat."

She planted a stare on him longer than one would call normal. "Martini, extra dry, three olives."

"You got it, sweetheart."

Callie waited for Libby's comeback at what she, of all people, would label a slur. But instead she gave Butch a frosty grin, and he took it with one of his own then spoke to the table, cajoling each member to give Sophie their order.

"Make mine a double," Georgia said, her sigh coming from a deep place.

Callie held up a hand. "Wait a minute. Two people drove here. Who're the designated drivers?"

Georgia sneered. "It's just down the road, Miss Police Chief. Give it a rest."

"I'll give you a rest . . . in the Colleton County jail," Callie replied. "Too many tourists on this beach for you to be driving drunk."

"Oh," Sophie said, livening at the prospect to help. "Our Taco Taxi is back running. It's available to take you home if you've had a few, and your cars are welcome to overnight in the lot."

What had she told Sophie when she came in the door? Hold back on the drinks?

"Then another round!" Butch shouted. "Our chief is a teetotaler, so it's the police car or the Taco Taxi. Either way we get back with a story to tell and isn't that what life's all about?"

Butch slapped the back of the nearest person, which happened to be Tony. The smack stung the way his grin turned to a grimace as he ordered a Tom Collins. Reuben a beer. And so it went around the group until people chowed down and drank, too occupied and tipsy to give Callie much of a second thought.

In hindsight, she should've ordered takeout and kept them at Georgia's.

Callie picked up a few crumbs in all this rowdiness, though. Like that exchange between Butch and Libby and the swapped glances after. Reuben's absolute silence. He of all of them could leave but hadn't. What was he waiting around for except to learn more?

And she'd forgotten about Peter Yeo. Who said the exchange student hadn't killed Wendy in some bet with the boys, and unable to make a marriage work with Libby, moved himself to the other side of the world thinking them all as clueless as they had always been? Had JJ forgotten him or just not gotten in touch? And why had he and Libby divorced?

Callie came to the conclusion that these people were too worried about what others thought, what JJ had in mind, to afford to leave. They'd stick around to avoid getting blindsided later. At least for a few days more.

Chapter 9

CALLIE GOT THE reunion crew home shortly after nine, escorted the ladies up the stairs and left the men to fend for themselves. They laid out on the back deck, in their inebriated sloppiness still finding the same chairs they'd claimed earlier when they were sober.

Her heart feeling pity while her head said she wasn't obligated to them, Callie studied these people telling old stories from high school while dodging the one they thought about most. They didn't talk about JJ, yet JJ was the reason they were there.

Maybe they spoke more intently of JJ when Callie wasn't around. But if they were so incensed about being accused of guilt for Wendy, then why not go home?

Sharing shame maybe. But shame for what?

The whole honor among thieves philosophy came to mind, and if they rallied because of past sins, who says they couldn't rally to confront JJ and her book? Only Libby spoke of legal action against the book, but while Callie wasn't an expert in intellectual law, she suspected JJ had already covered most of those bases with her own attorney.

True crime was fact, and who's to say JJ didn't have insight of her own? As the yearbook editor, she interviewed most students in the class for one purpose or another throughout their high school endeavors. For photo captions, for copy, to better understand which pictures made the most impact. Yearbook editors, newspaper editors, and the kiss-ups who worked in the front office heard all the student dirt, and JJ had done all three. Callie bet this story idea had been percolating in JJ's head for years.

"Y'all don't drink much more," she told the group, giving up asking them questions. Not in the state they were in. "I've got to go. With appointments tomorrow morning, I won't catch up with you until to-morrow afternoon. That doesn't mess up your agenda, does it, Georgia?"

"What agenda?" she said, and they all laughed themselves stupid. Even Reuben had gotten loopy.

"Good enough then," Callie said. "Please, nobody leave without calling me. And if JJ shows, notify me ASAP."

Which cranked up another round of laughter. She couldn't help but smile, the guffaws a bit contagious. Then glancing at her watch, she noted the time of quarter to ten. Before her visits to Middleton tomorrow, she had a visit with Mark tonight, and she could use some sane conversation, law enforcement insight, and someone who cared what she thought.

For a quick second, and with a hint of conscience, she welcomed that Jeb said he'd be coming through, but once school was out, he and Sophie's daughter Sprite might head to Jekyll Island instead of Edisto. The average person would find visiting a beach other than your own foolish, but Callie understood her son's intentions. He wanted to enjoy time alone with his girl, and doing so on Edisto Beach meant too much scrutiny when his mom was the chief of police and his girl's mother the island gossip queen.

The *sorceress* and the *commandant*. As if Callie hadn't overheard their jokes before.

The motion sensors flipped on as she left her car and rounded the end of the stairs to her house.

"I'm up here," said the voice, who understood better than most he needed to let his presence be known on the chief's property. He'd made that mistake before, making Callie almost reach for her weapon. Mark rose from one of her rockers, a bag in his arm.

She unlocked her door, deftly clicking off the alarm. "Sure you don't need to close the restaurant?"

"Nah." He shut and locked the door behind him. He stood about nine inches taller than Callie, his hint of ethnicity being his Cajun ancestry. Callie found it comical he chose a Mexican restaurant. Like his Hawaiian shirts, he didn't precisely match who he was with the brand, but he pulled it off nicely.

And he'd easily slid into her house.

"Between Sophie and Wesley, they'll close up fine," he said. "Thought you'd appreciate your next-door neighbor being occupied while I was here anyway."

Callie threw keys in the bowl and set her weapon on the end of her bar. She tended to keep it where she was, in the open area during her waking hours and on her nightstand at night, with the exception being when she hid it during Sophie's visits, for the woman's peace of mind. Callie had come to hate the smell of sage.

Grateful for having changed into civvies earlier, she reached for the refrigerator then hesitated. "Did you bring us drinks or shall I pour you something out of here?"

"Water's fine," he said. Bless him, he never touched alcohol in front of her, explaining during one of their outings a couple months ago that he could take or leave it, and since Callie abstained, he could leave it. "This"—he lifted the bag—"is your dinner, because you ate almost nothing in front of that band of fools. You actually grew up with that team of . . . never mind. They might be old chums, for all I know."

"Not to worry there," she said, exchanging his paper bag for a glass of water with ice. "And this," she said, emphasizing the bag, "is much appreciated. I nibbled but had my mind on other matters." She opened it and the waft of enchiladas set her stomach growling. He'd remembered her favorite.

Positioned at her kitchen bar, she spoke between bites, him listening to Callie's past and present. He needed to understand the foundation before she asked his opinion on addressing these people. On whether or not to get seriously involved in a search for JJ.

"Not a soul is concerned about her missing?" he said.

"Just me," she replied, "and she'd have been gone another whole day if Thomas hadn't noticed her car door open. Even her agent wasn't concerned. I've got nobody but myself to file a missing person's report."

She made quick work of the meal, equally grateful for the disposable containers and Mark letting her eat in peace. After she'd finished, Mark moved to the sofa, and she stacked a couple of her vinyls on the turntable. The beach house had a music repertoire dating to around the 70s, thanks to Callie's mother, the illustrious Beverly Cantrell. While one would think the music would remind Callie of the clashes between herself and her adopted mom, the albums instead soothed her, reminding her of times with her dad, weekends on Edisto, and Papa Beach, the deceased old man who used to live next door. An unburdened pocket of time when nothing was wrong with the world.

She preferred music to television all day long, too. She got enough reality on the job.

The kitchen windows open, sans screens, briny breezes entered unimpeded, making their way over the bar, through the living area and out the back windows to the marsh. She turned out all the lights except for the two lamps on either end of the sofa to wind down the night. She never would sit this open alone in the house, but with company, particularly Mark, she relished the occasion. There was a comfortable feel about the man.

"I can't help but feel JJ baiting us," she said, positioning herself cross-legged on the right end of the couch, her favorite spot. Mark already sat on the other end, the sofa not a long one. "Nobody cares enough that she's lost, but there's something definitely amiss. I could be jumping the gun, though. JJ is a squirrelly type. I might let it lay until another twelve hours have passed."

He blew out an exhale, weighing his answer. "Not a simple call, for sure."

She'd had a say in hiring four of her current officers, and they were no doubt diligent, but most were young and none had serious experience in investigations. With her background as a merited detective serving big-city Boston, she single-handedly addressed the few complicated issues on Edisto. When these incidents tested her, she went to her two friends, Mark and Stan. Retired SLED and retired Boston PD with ample experience between them. While she loved her officers, they hadn't a fraction of the experience of these guys.

"Do you have any sort of plan for tomorrow?" he asked.

"Had hoped to have more from these yahoos before I went, but regardless, I need to drive to Middleton." Her sip took her ginger ale to half gone. "The police chief is still there. My mother is mayor and had a front-row seat to the town scandal. I want to see what I can pull out of them, not only from back then, but recently as well. Find out if JJ has been there, and what information she coaxed out of them. The fact that neither called me says either JJ hasn't been by yet, or they're afraid I'll get involved."

He laughed, a head back laugh that referenced the absurdity of the comment.

Callie sheepishly grinned.

"Not laughing at you," he said, ending on another chuckle. "Laughing at the stupidity that they'd talk with JJ and not think to read you in. You'd find out sooner or later, one would think."

She got up. "Hold on a second." In the bedroom, she opened her closet safe and took out JJ's paperwork she'd safely tucked away. Better to lay two sets of eyes on them. Best to have someone there with enough professional insight to spot if she overread or emotionalized the memories.

"Here," she said, throwing the autopsy report lightly in his lap.

"What's that?" he asked of the papers still in her hands.

"The police report. You read what the ME said, then we'll swap."

Neil Diamond finished playing, and Callie looked up expectedly as the *Touching You, Touching Me* album dropped into place, an older vinyl. The arm assumed its rightful duty playing *Everybody's Talkin'*, and she returned attention to the police report.

The investigation homed in on Stratton almost from the start. He'd been the most recent beau. He'd admitted to fathering the pregnancy, and his parents had demanded a paternity test which somehow never occurred. Authorities interviewed fifteen assorted students, teachers, and parents, which fell far short of what Callie might've done in Chief Warren's shoes. Callie didn't have the interviews themselves, making her wonder if JJ had them or had been denied them. Another question to add to tomorrow's mission.

But the list of those interviewed was there. Reading her own name caught in her throat, though she knew good and well she'd be there. *Callie Jean Cantrell.*

She remembered the room they put her in at the Middleton police station. Her parents demanded to be present with her being a minor, as if the chief would ever deny the mayor and first lady. The simple pressure of others present had gripped her. She remembered thinking her life was permanently scarred. Would enough time pass for this incident to become one she could live with, or would it gnaw her in two? At the time she was too close to what happened to have perspective to answer that, but today, almost twenty-five years later she could. Life quit being simple that year.

In essence, nobody saw who killed Wendy Ashton, but Stratton was the last person she'd argued with—as far as anyone knew, and with him claiming fatherhood, well, what else was there to say? The suicide closed the case.

Callie still found the case horribly handled. The killer not found.

Neil Diamond hammered out *Holly Holy*, and she couldn't take his constant "yeah, yeah." Leaping off the sofa, she lifted the arm and shut the turntable off.

"You were eighteen?" Mark asked to her back.

She pulled herself to the present and turned around. "Pardon?"

"You were only eighteen," he said.

"Seventeen," she corrected, stepping toward him to switch reports, then returning to her spot.

Instead of curling up against the arm of the sofa, she put her back against it, stretching her short legs out lengthwise on the cushion, half to change positions and half to watch Mark over the top of her reading, hoping to glean his impression.

But he showed no reaction.

Reluctantly, she read the autopsy.

Wendy struggled with her assailant. When the panties came off—before or after—wasn't clear, but no semen found anywhere. The killer faced her to strangle her. The coroner said permanent damage had been done regardless of any involuntary eye movements. She died on the ground behind the bleachers.

Callie saw it.

For many weeks after, Callie languished over whether her hesitation cost Wendy her life with a constant, looping, mental debate over calling her father in lieu of 911. She lived endless nights of seeing Wendy's eyes blink once, or was it twice, then never again. She criticized her own inability to tell if she was breathing . . . Callie's inability to make herself touch the girl to tell.

"Callie."

She lowered her paper, almost ashamed, as if Mark might be seeing her thoughts about how she'd failed.

"Come look at this."

"I read it already," she said, frustrated at how affected she was, her pulse up.

But when she didn't come to him, he rose, lifted her outstretched legs, and slid closer, laying them across his lap. Reminded her of Christmas, when exhausted after three days of running a case, she'd fallen asleep on the police station sofa and awoken with her legs draped just like this.

He set his report on the cushion, pushing it away from sight, and rubbed the tops of her shins. "All this opening old wounds?" he asked.

She nodded. "I've seen so much worse. It shouldn't."

He continued to stroke. "Of course it should," he replied, serious-ness in his eyes. "That's way too young to experience murder."

"Is there a good age?" she asked.

"Let me change that. There are better ages."

She reached over and pushed the autopsy report atop the coffee table with the tips of her fingers. Then she lifted her legs off Mark's and sat up, moving closer. "I've seen a lot in my career. This shouldn't both-er me."

"Damn, girl. You've seen enough for any ten careers. You've had more than your share of . . . well, your share."

Of death, she finished in her head. On one hand she'd become calloused to it, but on the other, she ran continually gun-shy as well. Expecting death more often than the average person . . . even the average cop. And she had few people to relate that feeling with.

He reached over and drew her toward him. Shoulder tucked under his, she let him pull her to his side. He smelled clean. He'd showered off the restaurant odors before coming over. The scent was nothing special, but the smell traveled over her skin and made it tingle.

"That seventeen-year-old isn't responsible for a damn thing," he said.

"Stratton didn't do it," she said.

"Maybe not."

"Definitely not."

"And you can't stand the cold case being associated with you."

"Because of me . . . maybe."

With the slightest hug, he kissed the top of her head.

A shiver traveled her top to bottom. *Oh Jesus.* Like Seabrook used to do.

But the association to her old lover didn't repel her as she expected. Instead, the connection comforted. Maybe she was moving on.

From where she was up against him, she kissed his chest through his shirt, a sort of thanks . . . a recognition that she appreciated being appreciated.

She snuggled in deeper, not for him, but for herself. Living alone amongst the ghosts of so many, most of them the result of her involvement in their lives, was instilling a deep loneliness in her, which fought desperately with her sobriety.

Her mind went to the lone bottle of gin hidden in her closet safe.

"Stay," she told him.

He didn't force her to look up. Instead he answered, "I've been waiting to hear that. But if you want to talk the case, which is sort of why I came over . . ."

She untangled from their embrace and reached a hand behind his neck, kissing him to shut him up.

Chapter 10

JJ
Saturday afternoon.

AT A DIFFERENT rental, on an entirely different part of the island, JJ slept her Saturday away.

She'd stayed up all Friday night back at *Flirty Flamingo* causing her not to awaken at her new place until after two in the afternoon. She showered and shuffled to the kitchen. She'd pulled all-nighters more times than she could count, but maybe the drive on top of the party on top of the drinks at Georgia's had pushed her past her stamina.

But the new setting, the fresh spill of words, and the plan underway aroused her. This method of orchestrating a book thrilled her to her bones.

A tale within a tale. A la Anthony Horowitz, her mystery would match the likes of *Magpie Murders*, maybe more *Moonflower Murders* . . . solving a crime within a crime. One character rising from the fray to carry the new crime through, and therefore solve the old.

Leaving her extra laptop, her phone, the suitcase at *Water Spout*, would send Callie on a tangent. The raised toilet lid, a last-minute light-bulb moment, was a nice touch, pointing to a man. A stranger. An abductor.

Callie would redirect all her energies now.

And all JJ had to do was sit here and create while the others wove the chapters.

She wandered her new place, too tired to have done so earlier. This house was about the same size as the other but felt more like a residence. Cleaner. Better quality sheets. A toilet that didn't speculate on whether it was supposed to flush. She was glad she waited to arrive here to catch up on sleep. No name on the house, but the mattress slept well enough.

She'd risen noting the temperature a few degrees on the low side for her to remain in her silk robe, so she slid on slacks and a baggy, cotton sweater, thin socks, and her favorite flats too worn for public appearances.

She mussed through the pantry. Shame, these people didn't do tea, so coffee in hand she moved to a swing on the porch. She'd forgotten how these people believed in their porches. This one had two . . . one on which you could hold a party for thirty. She chose the smaller, to contain her thoughts and force them to hover around her and not scatter into the oaks draping the acreage.

She was blessed to find a plug close enough to park her laptop on a shabby chic table salvaged from someplace, or refinished to appear so. She had to double the cushions in the seat to reach the right height. She shifted, stretched her arms out for measure, and deemed the location suitable.

But instead of immediately typing, she reared back, crossed a leg, took another sip of the chicory she'd accidentally found and deemed delightful, and with her free hand lifted a file sleeve containing the old interviews.

Stratton first. Keen in several sports, attractive without being a class idol, Stratton appeared the boy any parent would want their daughter to find. What didn't make sense to JJ, however, was his attachment to Wendy. Her cuteness registered off the chart, but she wasn't the brightest, and being a cheerleader only served to affix an empty-headed stereotype to her, with her biggest potential being making pretty babies.

JJ never liked her, and didn't like Stratton having fallen for her with all he had going for him. Look where it got him. Lives needed structure to reach any level of success. Risk was one thing. Letting one's emotions kidnap that structure was grounds for disaster.

Yes, she liked that. She jotted down that thought.

But Wendy had owned enough charisma to draw the boys and make teachers look the other way. Girls adored her friendship and overlooked jealousy. An R-rated Disney character. A whore in Cinderella garb.

JJ never believed Stratton killed her, though, which made this story all the more worth the telling. Because the real killer got off, and JJ wasn't ready to label some random stranger as the felon. No, this was someone Wendy probably knew.

Her phone rang. The burner. No doubt, the chief had collected the original phone along with the purse and suitcase and the doppelganger laptop on which they'd find little to nothing. Just some loose notes of an outline, and a recording app that JJ planted for fun, understanding full well she wouldn't get it back.

"All good?" she asked the caller.

"They're pissed."

"Excellent," she said.

"How long do we do this?"

"Depends on everyone there. Especially Callie," JJ replied, reading Stratton's interview. "She's driving this now. Take notes, record what you can, and do what we agreed. Twice a day, I said. No more." JJ hung up.

Business as planned.

Callie Jean Cantrell, now Morgan, had been quiet in high school but all knew she was full of herself. The lone progeny of the town kingpins was presumed to be the next mayor once she returned with a degree and maybe a man on her arm with a pedigree of his own. JJ had waffled between liking her and not. Morgan wasn't one to let people in, which planted seeds of doubt with JJ.

Plus, the future detective had found Wendy.

Who knew what went down behind those bleachers?

Who would dare suspect or blame the mayor's daughter anyway?

An aroma of marsh brine made its way to the porch, then the chicory captured her nose. A wisp of cool breeze made her draw her sweater tighter.

Let's see how good a cop she is.

At this moment, while JJ studied twenty-year-old interviews, Callie probably studied the autopsy and police reports JJ had left behind for her. Callie would be wondering what happened to their famous author classmate. Assuming she was worth a damn, she'd wonder where the interviews got off to. Why just the report and not the interrogations?

Callie would be furious at being played.

Back to Stratton's interview. Per this record, the kid had totally lost his shit. An All-American boy at his wits' end, having earned decent grades, acquired first string status in basketball, and carved out a fast-track route to college. His worst flaw was falling for the girl every boy wanted, and her liking him back. For a while.

This was the tricky part, and Antonio had said the approach was her choice—fiction or nonfiction. Take the facts and weave them into the best make-believe? Or report them in all their ugliness and attempt to solve the crime.

But she drooled over the latter. Imagine the mystery novelist solving a true crime she'd had a direct relationship to. She'd record her own audio book. Speak to criminal justice academies instead of library book clubs.

Readers might wonder where her novels started and stopped when it came to reality or imagination, which would sell her backlist that much more.

Only time would tell. This was the first book she'd penned without an outline and without a solid roadmap to follow. She didn't want her creativity stifled by any tool or literary lesson.

And God, she loved the names on these beach houses.

SATURDAY NIGHT, JJ's protégé dropped off a seafood combo from a place called Pressley's. After the barest of an update, they scooted back to the beach. Amazing how easily one could bribe someone into being your assistant. The promise of a mention in the book's credits. The hope of fame in a bestseller if things went well . . . the looming threat of being painted as dark and devious if things didn't.

After having run the meal under a broiler for a couple minutes to reheat it, JJ ate on the porch, beginning to understand why each home-owner had one. Thank God for the bottle of Riesling she'd ordered with her platter.

Insects and creatures she couldn't begin to name screamed, chirped, and clicked, but far off enough not to irritate. The shrubbery and trees turned pitch black once she looked twenty feet out from the house. If the moon hadn't been almost full, she might have missed the marsh two hundred yards across the street and behind the neighboring house fronting it.

Sprinkled diamonds, she thought. Guess the tide was up. She didn't understand those things, but she could damn sure describe them. She jotted a few words on her notepad, put down her pen, and sat back with wineglass resting on her thigh.

She wasn't lonely eating alone, or living alone, for that matter. On the contrary. Except for two years with a partner who struggled competing with her story characters, JJ had lived solo and socialized with people at her leisure. Authors lived more in their heads than in reality, with characters offering enough company to chase off the negative of solitude. And if one was in need of company, there were always bookstore owners all too eager to talk the business. And when she longed for more sophisticated conversation, she left Nashville and flew to New York. Antonio never failed to replenish her creative well with all the city had to offer.

But tonight her meal was solitary. She'd eaten half the seafood, dumbfounded at the size of the portions, and saved the rest in the fridge. The wine, however, would return to the porch with her. She had accomplished a satisfying number of words today, and again was willing to work deeper into the night.

She fleshed out Stratton today, mainly because the others were still *evolving*, so to speak. Too much of the long weekend still ahead for her to fully capture them yet. They were still creating themselves, trying to decide how to behave about JJ's planned book, wondering how they'd be depicted, which made them act all the weirder around each other. Who was more guilty than whom? Curiosity eating them up as to the why of each. Each afraid to escape and go home.

Anyway, as for Stratton, they'd label him the usual suspect with suicide only confirming the verdict. Any normal person wouldn't want to think too deeply about a murder, such violence not welcome into their lives. As each Middleton inhabitant had adopted that line of reasoning so long ago, the high schoolers did the same. Silly, silly classmates.

JJ recalled how Callie fought for Stratton way back when.

She truly believed that Callie believed in Stratton's innocence, and JJ had given her, through the author's mysterious disappearance, a chance to prove it. And since she denied her legacy of politics for the much harder pursuit of justice, JJ fully expected Callie to accept the challenge.

Callie . . . widowed, lost an infant child, burned, shot, stalked. Dethroned from her decorated position in Boston. Lost two officers under her watch at Edisto. Alcoholic per some. She was a remarkably colorful chapter in the making.

Chapter 11

SHE NEVER SLEPT nude, so when Callie's leg brushed against another, not hers, the jolt in her chest almost had her reaching for her weapon until she recalled the night's events. Peering at her nightstand clock, she correlated the time with the fact it wasn't light yet. Sunday. A little after five. She had a few more moments until she had to rise and head toward Middleton, and she wasn't sure what to do with them.

God, how long had it been . . . but before she could languish in the enjoyment, thoughts poured into her head. The logic, the sanity, the common sense flooded in, advising her of the problems that grew from a bond with a native. Even more so with a cop.

Mark made his home on Edisto Beach, a home she policed, making a relationship complicated. If they fell out, that relationship would fall under serious public scrutiny.

Look at the county councilman Brice LeGrand and his wife . . . ex-wife. However, Aberdeen had been incredibly stupid slinging Twitter slurs which had gained her an insane number of fans, but cost her in alimony. One didn't pine over the death of who you had an affair with, then expect divorce court to pity you for the loss.

Then Seabrook sprang to mind. When she'd worked alongside him, Callie feared a conflict of interest and refused to act on her attraction to him. At least until she couldn't. At first she'd compared him to her deceased husband, then pushed off Seabrook to arm's length for fear anything serious would backfire, or interfere, or simply make her life complicated. Plus, any turn toward the negative sent her to the bottle.

She'd so screwed up with Seabrook.

However, Mark wasn't Seabrook. Callie was stronger, and she hadn't had a drink in ten months. But her loneliness had gone nowhere.

"You're thinking too hard," Mark said, reaching for her. "One night isn't a lifetime commitment, Chief."

She allowed him to ease her over such that she spooned into him, and the warmth oozed her into a pleasant calm she hadn't felt in ages. His scent was different, but soothing. She'd found it so easy to fall asleep feeling kisses on the back of her neck. Could find it so easy to skip Middleton until later in the day.

"I can read you like a book," he said, slowly rolling her over.

She grinned back. "You've barely read the first page."

"Oh, but I read fast." He kissed her. A peck at first, then sliding into a smile, he wrapped her tighter, pressing her lips harder to his. A kiss became more, and Callie decided Beverly Cantrell could wait an hour longer than planned.

It wasn't like Callie had told her mother she was coming.

Afterwards, the shower wasn't nearly long enough.

"I've got to go," she said, drying fast. Minimal makeup, not that she used much for any occasion, then a dart into her closet. Slacks, blouse, and a lightweight jacket. The slacks went on in the closet, the rest thrown on the bed.

This was Sunday, and she'd be snaring Beverly right after church, assuming she still attended early service, going home right after for a quiche breakfast she'd usually picked up from Emerson's the evening before. Gave them bragging rights to use her name in advertising. Callie would find her in the courtyard behind the Cantrell manor, perusing the Sunday paper, a black coffee hooked in a finger. Callie knew the drill. The timing couldn't be more perfect.

Mark's impromptu visit had only kept Callie from showing up in church.

"Wish I could fix you breakfast," he said, tucking in his shirt. He sat on an upholstered chair in the corner to put on shoes. The bed was too high; Callie used a stepstool to climb into it at night. The tall rice bed was the same her parents had used on beach weekends, before *Chelsea Morning* became hers.

Callie slid in some simple earring posts. "Never been a huevos rancheros kind of girl." Back in her closet, she grabbed her go-to purse to hold her weapon when she played civilian. "Onions and peppers for breakfast just don't cut it. Avocados either. Like ketchup on eggs, I can't make that work."

"Surely you can handle eggs, cheese, and bacon in a burrito."

She passed him to grab her jacket laying on the bed. "What's with you and Mexican food? You're Cajun."

"I don't like Cajun food," he said.

The banter proved amazingly effortless. Almost scary how simple. He fell into her humor just as she fell into his. She couldn't label one regrettable minute from the evening with him, but surely one would reveal itself once she slowed down, left his presence, and thought straight.

"Quit overthinking this," he said, and strode over to sweep her in and plant what had to be his fiftieth kiss of the morning. "Your brain is churning. Don't let yourself mess this up."

She smiled and shook her head. "You have no idea my luck."

"You have no idea mine," he replied. "And look how neither mattered last night."

She got assertive with the kiss this time, willing to accept his point.

The whole evening had been about the lovemaking and the appreciation of each other. He hadn't asked about the ugly, ropy burn on her forearm, and she'd forgotten to inquire about the scar on his leg. War wounds. Law enforcement usually got off on sharing stories how they acquired them, but after setting Wendy Ashton's reports aside, they'd forgotten they were cops.

Exposing their battle scars didn't open up conversation. Instead they represented a willingness to open up without explanation of the journey. Just the sight of old wounds told each other that they'd been broken and healed, and they silently respected each other more for the simple fact that they had pasts that didn't need discussion. Like war veterans. Once they stated the branch of service, the connection was made.

What she'd planned as a six o'clock a.m. exit had turned into eight. That still gave her a comfortable hour to reach Middleton.

"Sure you don't want breakfast at SeaCow before you leave?" he asked, going outside to the front porch as Callie set the alarm.

She locked the door, calculating. Skipping church had no doubt bought her time. "If we make it fast. No lollygagging."

"Hey, y'all!"

That unmistakable voice from next door. Sophie. "Y'all are up early."

"Heading to Middleton," Callie said from the porch. Sophie reached the bottom of Callie's stairs by the time she and Mark made it down. "Meeting with my mother." All Sophie needed to hear.

"Definitely not one of my favorite people," she said, taking in the head-to-toe visual of Mark, then Callie. "What y'all been up to?"

"We're about to be up to breakfast," Callie said. "Want to join us?"

Sophie perked up. "As a matter of fact I will! Let me get my purse." She skittered off.

"And so we re-enter the world," Mark said.

Callie stepped in front of him. "Before she returns, I have to say last night was . . . nice. Thanks."

"We never did discuss your reunion people, or JJ," he said.

"I realized that when I woke up," she said. "Makes me feel rather irresponsible."

He chuckled a couple times from down deep. "Giving us another reason to get together, don't you think?"

BREAKFAST CONSISTED more of Sophie chirping at those coming and going from SeaCow than speaking with Callie and Mark, allowing the two to eat faster. Ultimately, they left Sophie with a wave, her talking with the cashier. She'd ridden with Callie, but she could walk home or to El Marko's not a half block away. She never sat in one place long anyway, and could trot the length of the beach and back and rattle a conversation the entire way.

Regardless of the public exposure, from SeaCow's diners to nearby strollers, Mark wrapped an arm around Callie and walked her to her car. Going to the mainland, she always drove her personal vehicle and dressed civilian to keep appearances low-key. Unlike the final kiss he left her with.

Instinctively, Callie glanced around, to find Sophie pressed against a window watching along with several of the SeaCow staff.

Mark got into his car, laughing.

He could laugh, but they'd both hear about that kiss later. Sophie had once had hopes of courting the restauranteur. When he'd made no advances toward her, she moved on. Still, Mark might get an earful from his hostess this morning, and Callie would hear soon enough. Sophie'd make sure of it.

Callie left the beach via Highway 174 which wasn't busy in the direction she headed. From the other way, however, coming from the mainland, cars hurried from local towns and counties to spend a day in the sun. She'd left two officers on duty, with a reminder she was unavailable for most of the day, then informed Deputy Raysor, on loan from the county, that he would serve as backup if anything went haywire.

Before SeaCow, she'd almost left the autopsy and police reports in her living room after her guest's distraction, and had to run back to retrieve JJ's photos and notepad in case she needed them in Middleton. She'd fully meant to dissect that notepad, which from first scan, served as the average person's smart phone calendar. Those pages could hold secrets.

She sure wished JJ would call, asking what happened to her stuff in the house. Hopefully she would. But the writer was twenty-four hours missing.

Time to push Mark to the back of her mind. Nobody braced Mayor Beverly Cantrell without a plan.

Callie had presumed Beverly her biological mother until a little over a year ago, and had often assumed she just favored her father. Lawton came from a long lineage of Middleton politicians, and in an open sort of marriage had wound up with Callie via his long-time love. To save the Cantrell image, Beverly claimed the child as hers, not telling a soul until decades later when the real mother decided it was time to come clean. Both mothers sat across a desk in Callie's office and spilled reality. Took Callie a while to speak to either of them.

She'd become closer to her real mom, Sarah, and less connected to Beverly. Their relationship these days seemed to boil down to a love for Lawton Cantrell, French gin, and a recipe for the most exquisite martini known to man.

Unfortunately, Lawton was dead and Callie fought hard to stay on the wagon. Not much left in common anymore, which explained why she hadn't visited Middleton since a short afternoon between Christmas and New Year's, done mostly for Jeb's sake. He considered Beverly his real grandmother, giving Sarah the stiff hugs and minimal visits suitable for a distant relative.

Callie reached Ravenel and took a left on state road 165, halfway through the fifty-minute ride.

In Middleton, she reached Summer Downs United Methodist with parking lot packed and nobody outside. By the time she found a place across the street and down a block, and had walked back to her mother's BMW in its unofficial-yet-appointed space beside the handicapped slots, the minister had opened the double doors and taken his position to shake hands.

Took Beverly twenty minutes to appear. She waved but took her time with the meet and greet. Not that Callie wasn't busy herself with a meet and greet, being the last mayor's daughter, the current mayor's daughter, and the granddaughter and great-grand of others past. Middleton knew the mayor's child was a chief of police and had actually killed a few people in her legendary career. A reputation that Beverly ever addressed with some sort of irreverent remark, even more prompted since Callie had no intention of succeeding her mother on the throne.

Callie wouldn't put it past her to one day backdoor coax Jeb into assuming the family legacy.

After hugs from teachers and handshakes from councilmen and their wives, Callie managed to look up and find her mother waiting. "Callie," she said. "Coming by the house?"

"Yes, ma'am. Had a little time and thought we'd have a chat."

Through her wizened stare, however, Beverly smiled and motioned for her daughter to move aside from the car door. "See you at the house, then. You're lucky I have no appointments for a couple hours."

Callie knew there were no appointments. Beverly set her agenda in granite, and heaven help the poor soul who violated it. The woman's Sundays were always free between church and late afternoon, with only the most urgent of events earning her evenings.

Along the way Callie marveled, pined, and rued the changes on this thoroughfare or that. Middleton existed too close to Charleston to not be affected by growth. The ride took her by Georgia's old home, or at least that of her parents. If she cared, Callie could look at the list Georgia created and find where Libby lived. Where Tony lived. She knew where Butch and Reuben used to live.

Callie showed at the manor just as the garage door had closed. By the time she parked in the drive and took the walk that meandered between all those old heirloom azaleas she'd been made to prune for allowance, Beverly met her at the door.

"Gin or coffee?" she asked.

And there stood the foundation of Callie's love for alcohol.

"Coffee, Mother, it's not even noon," she said, coming inside. Once leaving the plush white rug by the door, they crossed the white Italian marble floors of the large foyer. "You remember I quit drinking."

Her mother shook her head upon entering the kitchen and switched on the coffee pot. "It's mind control, dear. You drink if you want. It's that straightforward. Mind over matter."

Whatever. A highly functioning alcoholic, Beverly Cantrell couldn't have lunch without a gin and tonic. Dinner without a martini. And if the day was appreciably horrid, three more of either before bedtime. Gin was delivered to the manor by the case . . . every two weeks.

To prove she could indeed not drink, or because quiche didn't exactly marry well with gin, even if it was from Emerson's, Beverly poured two coffees, cut two slices of the pie, and set all on a tray only to hand it to Callie to take outside. With the Sunday paper in hand, she threw open the French doors to the courtyard, and Callie laid out their dishes in proper fashion.

Before long, they sat with cups in hand, giving each other a chance to own their thoughts, which could be misconstrued by some as suiting up in armor. A jockeying for position before they opened up a dialogue that rarely ended in anything other than derision.

Chapter 12

CALLIE SAT IN THE Cantrell courtyard and another world. She caught the birdsong in the dogwoods and pines, whiffed the jasmine barrier across the back property line, and found herself assuming the stiff posture she'd been taught as a child. *Shoulders back, dear . . .* one of many habits of upbringing she'd attempted to shed in Edisto. It was frustrating how much power the past affixed to a person.

Focus. Callie had questions that needed answers. Her father might have been more approachable, definitely more honest, but he was gone. Callie continued to sorely miss him. Not that certain behavior of his learned after his death hadn't disappointed her, but as a whole he'd been a good man and an awesome father. She often called him Captain.

Beverly Cantrell, however, had always been the voice of the pair. Anything Lawton was involved in, she'd been as well. Only Beverly wielded the power of manipulation much more masterfully than her husband.

In her frustration at even being there, Callie shot straight over her mother's bow. "What closed door conversations did you have with Dad over Wendy Ashton's murder to make it go away?"

Having exchanged her low heels for gold lamé slippers, a brand she'd special ordered from Belk's as long as Callie could remember, her mother sat with legs suitably crossed. She still wore a powder-blue suit, but had shed the jacket to expose the tailored cream blouse tied at the neck. Pearls on her ears. She held the newspaper properly creased with her left, the coffee cup in her right, and at the question, she shook her head in her subtle, don't-move-a-silver-hair-on-her-head motion. "Don't believe I recall anything like that. Even at your age, you still love to exaggerate. We've talked about that."

"Yet we never managed to speak about you not being my real mother."

Beverly's attempt to smile faded. "That couldn't be helped."

Callie laughed, not facetiously but short and hard. The type of laugh to draw a disapproving scowl from a woman who believed life was a perpetual journey of etiquette. One either behaved properly to a person or ignored them altogether. The familial connection made Callie an anomaly. Beverly loved Callie. She just couldn't fathom how to behave around her. Her precious code of etiquette didn't seem to cover non-traditional daughters.

Which only made Callie bait her more.

Callie hated the nonsensical façade and social deceptions in her mother's toolbox, and she hated it more when the woman used them when they were alone like this. Beverly Cantrell had played this sport her entire life . . . so long she had no idea how to shut it off. "I never could get manners to stick with you for long," she told her daughter.

Callie remained silent and waited for an answer to her question.

"And I'm sure I don't know what you mean," Beverly concluded. "Of course your father and I discussed that horrendous situation, just as we discussed any other situation affecting this town. Nothing clandestine about it. Just a conversation about a sad happening and its aftermath."

"That murder was a slipshod investigation, Mother. Chief Warren fell far short of being thorough. I felt it then, but more importantly, I professionally see it now." She took a sip from her china cup, almost not wanting to, the formality interfering with the bluntness of her mission.

"To my chagrin," Callie said, using a word she'd never use except in Beverly's presence, "JJ Loveless has opened a can of worms about it with my graduating class. This murder will be published in a tell-all true crime, and I cannot stand by and let this injustice be amplified across the universe." She paused. "And don't tell me you don't know. She has research that brought me here."

Her mother had a queen-to-commoner quality to her speech. "The woman feels she has a wrong to right."

"So you have met with her."

"We spoke."

"When?"

Beverly gave a long exhale, peering down her nose at the rose bed that had absolutely nothing to admire in March. "I'd have to consult my calendar. Two weeks, maybe?" She gave a soft wave of her coffee cup. "Maybe longer. She asked for copies of things I didn't have, so I sent her to Town Hall. And to Warren."

Blew JJ off, she meant, by sending JJ to others, probably under the pretext Beverly wasn't mayor during that time, as if Mr. Mayor Cantrell hadn't shared everything with his wife.

But then her mother sat forward. "Why does this involve you? Let the woman write what she wants and ignore her. If you engage, you'll only make matters worse."

"She's engaged the class reunion committee," Callie said. "So that horse is out of the barn. They're reliving that incident over and over out at my beach instead of planning next year's reunion."

"Then your friends are fools," she said. "Tell them to hush. Then Ms. Loveless will go away."

"The woman has a publishing contract. She intends to write this book."

Cutting her eyes at her daughter, then finding Callie's gaze meeting hers already, she locked in. "So let her write the book. We're familiar with how the story ends. I imagine she'll try to interview Wendy's parents, who've moved to Florida, by the way. Then Stratton's family, whose mother died of breast cancer fifteen years ago."

That caught Callie off guard. She'd loved Stratton's mother, a common-sense lady who worked in a bank and baked bread as a hobby. God, the aroma of that house rushed to mind, then the permanence of it being gone. "What about Mr. Winningham? And Stratton's sister?"

"He took a transfer to Massachusetts." She did this arced pointy thing with her finger. "Boston, I believe." Then eyes widening, she seemed to have a revelation. "I swear, I just realized that you were probably working there on your police force when he moved. Dear, if I'd thought about it, I would've told you."

"Jesus, Mother. It's me sitting here, not the town council. You didn't tell me on purpose. Not that I would've connected with him, but you didn't want me to."

Beverly mashed her lips, her lipstick gone, her habit of mashing those lips having instilled certain wrinkles around her mouth. "Only for your best interest. That whole situation weighed horribly on you. Much too much for a young girl, and as a mother, I did my best to protect you."

They could carry on like this for ages. Beverly touting her incredible accomplishments as a mother. Callie remembering only the arguments, public grandstanding, and creative imagery painted of the first family of Middleton. Beverly dodged her questioning, and Callie steeled herself for the back-and-forth passive aggression. Truth be told, she hadn't realized the stress of having such a mother until she'd left home. Their inability to get along during her teenage years made so much more sense now. Amazing the awareness one achieves with hindsight and separation.

"You've taken her bait," Beverly said. "She'll write about whatever you react about, talk about, giving her a variety of personal slants. With you," and she nodded toward her daughter, "giving the most ammunition of all. You'll give her a chance to dig up details she hadn't access to, maybe even tell alternate endings based on your results. Mythical endings that you, as someone wearing a badge, breathe life into. You're making this woman ridiculously happy, Callie."

"JJ has no idea what I think, or what I'm doing."

"I'm telling you, she's milking the lot of you."

A thought Callie admitted contained grand potential, but not if JJ was missing, unable to capitalize on how her presence had riled up the reunion group.

"Has JJ been back, or was there just the one visit?" Callie asked.

"Just the once," Beverly replied.

No need for her mother to be aware of JJ's disappearance, so she came back around to the issue that itched her the most. "You prematurely closed that case."

With her slow shake again, Beverly denied. "The mayor closes no cases, dear." A nod at her daughter. "You are chief of police. Does the mayor tell you how to do your job?"

"We discuss impact. We discuss damage control. We talk about how to corral the public's impression of crime in the town. So don't you dare tell me, with as repulsive a crime as Wendy's murder was . . . attempted rape, a face-to-face strangling, and murder . . . that you, meaning you and Daddy, didn't hold closed-door meetings to determine how to direct the press and the community outrage."

Callie set her cup in its saucer a little too hard, tiring of the tea party, but more tired of the smoke screen. Saying Callie was too young to understand did little to assuage the guilt that she should've done more. She tumbled headlong into being incensed at the fact politics had played into making Stratton guilty for something that boy never would've done.

"Stratton was pressured because he was easy to pressure," she said. "He happened to be Wendy's latest. He worried he'd caused the pregnancy. Having him named openly as the prime suspect killed him and solved all your problems."

"Exaggeration, dear." A scoff again. "The boy had problems."

"That the town piled on top of him!" Callie said, making her mother's brow raise. "Then after he died, what did you do? You shut things down . . . after the parents of a dozen kids told you to shut it down. They had their patsy. Their sons could escape scrutiny. Blame the dead guy. Jesus, Mother, that's the oldest ploy in the book, and you and all this town shamelessly used it."

Beverly stiffened. "I will not have you sully the reputation of this town."

"Try this then . . . the killer got off!"

"Says you."

The childish comeback gave Callie pause, and she lowered her tone. "This town harbored a fugitive, Mother. You could still be harboring him. Imagine that . . . the man who strangled a seventeen-year-old girl sitting three pews over from you at church or attending the Christmas tree lighting in town square. Directing someone's choir or spectating high school sports, reliving his deed, watching for another chance."

Beverly studied the paper on the table.

"Which parents of other boys petitioned you to shut this case down?"

That raised her mother's eyes.

"Hah, someone did."

"Dozens of families begged us to wrap it up quickly. Not just parents of boys."

This time Callie shook her head. "Ever dancing in circles, Mother. Ever the politician. Do people even seem real to you?" Then in a sweeping motion of her hand toward the house, "When you ramble in this big place at night, on Sundays like this after church, before you rise out of bed in the morning and touch your phone, do you ever envision yourself *serving* the people?"

The glare was penetrating. "How dare you. Of course I do. Always. The nature of this family is public service." She jabbed a bony finger at Callie. "Though you prefer to think this family hasn't enhanced who you are, you serve the public. Where do you think you derived that desire to serve?"

"No doubt from this household," Callie said, her heart thumping. "But I believe in transparency. I believe in truth. I believe in getting to the bottom of problems so they do not recur under my watch. Can you own that?"

For a long minute, they stared, Callie preparing for another of her mother's scathing comebacks, but Beverly broke the look first. "I have duties to tend to. You're welcome to sit out here and finish your coffee, even have another cup. But I must cut this short."

Callie could've written this script, but she'd told herself she had to try and pry out of the mayor what happened behind the scenes at the time. Maybe Callie wouldn't have gone public with everything either, but she damn sure wouldn't have pushed Chief Warren to end the case so soon. Most of all she would've cleared Stratton's name and given his father some peace. She liked his father.

"One more thing before you go," Callie said, resigned.

Beverly had stood but waited to hear the favor.

"Call Chief Warren. While I'm in town, see if he'll see me. A heartfelt request from you might get me in. Might even allow me an invitation to dinner. Mrs. Warren used to have a Sunday spread at noon straight up." She smiled like her mother taught her. Besides, she always hated leaving this house with a fight hanging in the air.

Beverly said nothing but lifted her phone, hitting one button to reach her police chief. In those few short rings, the metamorphosis took place. Mayor Cantrell painted on the smile, reached inside for her manners, and in her best, pleasant, so-lovely-to-talk-to-you tone, asked about the family, the sermon that morning, and what was for dinner. Oh, did he know Callie was in town? She had a professional question and wondered if the chief would save a place for her at dinner. "Pot roast? Oh, I'm sure she'll be delighted. Your company is what's important. You've been such a role model for her."

Slick and oh-so-politically savvy. While Chief Warren had been around a while, he'd served at the pleasure of the Cantrells long enough to realize that a favor was an order and that dinner could be anything but a simple meal.

Callie was being passed off to the chief, just like JJ, and the mayor could continue to claim she was none the wiser about any of this. With the old mayor now deceased, Beverly Cantrell could claim no definitive knowledge of what exactly happened and why, and certainly didn't want to hear about it.

But the lady mayor had piqued Callie's interest about one thing. What if JJ had stirred trouble amongst Wendy's and Stratton's friends, hoping that the one with the badge would use her talents to reignite the embers of a cold case. What if Callie *had* taken the proverbial bait?

Imagine the appeal of that story.

Imagine an author conning a police chief, Stratton's old girlfriend, into writing a different tale? Making JJ the heroine. Making Callie simply a pawn.

Chapter 13

BEVERLY GAVE CALLIE a light, brief, formal hug. An ocean liner could've slid to the floor between them. Then she saw Callie off, standing cross-armed in the doorway as her daughter took the winding walk between the ready-to-pop azaleas. But when Callie reached her car in the drive, threw on her sunglasses and looked back, the door had closed.

Quarter to eleven. Chief Warren's house wasn't but ten blocks away, on the other side of the railroad. He'd inherited his parents' home like the Cantrells had theirs. He was sort of the duke in the Middleton hierarchy with Beverly wearing the crown.

Not much traffic since late church hadn't let out yet, and Callie arrived quickly at the wrought-iron mailbox clearly stating "Warren." She turned in the asphalt drive which wound amongst hundred-year-old loblolly pines and fifty-year-old camellias to a circular drive at the wide, paneled front door.

Middleton had been a haven for politicians and the well-heeled in the 1800s, to dissociate themselves from the malaria-ridden marshes of Charleston. Those historic homes remained, always white with black roofs and shutters, some with columns and others with massive wrap-around porches, passed from politician to politician, not always in the same family.

The Warrens had held town council, state representative, and various other public seats for several generations, with the chief taking a detour to choose law enforcement. Before Wendy's murder, Callie had admired the man without reservation. She still appreciated his desire to pursue law enforcement, because like she had, he'd turned his back on politics, choosing to serve in another, more satisfying role.

Like an uncle to her, he was a lifesaving hulk of a man who deftly handled her father's funeral that brought people in as high up as the Lieutenant Governor, but Callie couldn't help but think that politics had skewed his decision-making when it came to Wendy and Stratton. After all, he'd been young then, too.

She parked in front of the double stairway leading to a porch, the door displayed between two long accent windows. Anyone unaware that the chief had inherited the house would wonder how a cop could afford such a place on a four-acre spread in town limits.

He opened the door as she reached the top step. "Haven't seen much of you, girl. What's it been, a year?"

"About that," she said, smiling, accepting his bear hug. "How you doing? How's the family?"

They shared the back-and-forth niceties while heading across polished wood floors through the long, high-ceiling hall to the back porch, with him putting a tea in her hand on the way. The aromas of roast, potatoes, and something sweet coated the air. She spoke to Mrs. Warren as they passed the kitchen, but Callie had manners enough not to interrupt since she was in the deep concentrated efforts of bringing a meal to completion.

"None of the kids home?" Callie asked, accepting the wooden rocker he motioned to. The one next to that was definitely his from the flattened cushion in the seat, the faded one behind the head. A short table stood at the side with an ashtray, a Zippo lighter with his initials, and the paint worn on the armrests.

"What brings you here?" he asked, before lighting a pipe. The lighter clicked shut, and he reared back, assuming his rhythm. "Have to believe it's work-related since Beverly didn't offer to come with you." He stared off into the dense growth of pines and natural underbrush. He'd let the back half of his place go native.

"Heard that Jessie Jane came by here," she said, falling into the familiar name she thought he might remember better. She didn't see Warren as much of a female mystery author fan.

His brows were bushy and would've touched his bangs if he had any on his half-bald dome. "Who?"

"JJ Loveless," she said. "She graduated with me. She's an author."

The brows lowered, but Callie read his eyes. They sharpened, preparing, wondering like Beverly had.

"What's any of that got to do with you?" he said.

"Like you have to ask," she replied and rocked a few seconds before continuing. "As you're aware, she's writing a true-crime story. Already has a contract with a New York publishing house per her agent. She came through here and spoke to Mother, who passed the buck to you."

"I remember," he said.

Callie smiled. "And Beverly's done the same with me. Averted answers, claimed ignorance, and pushed me out the door in your direction."

He pulled the pipe away and blew out. "How lovely of her."

"She is sweet that way," Callie said.

He examined his pipe. "You did live here through all of that."

She nodded though he wasn't watching. "Well, I've read both the police and autopsy reports. JJ's copies, which I assume you made available to her, minus the interviews, I see."

"I included the interviews," he said.

Hmm, so JJ took them with her or someone stole them. Why take one part and leave the other?

He waited, like any decent law enforcement official, letting the party needing information fill in the empty space of a conversation.

"Petechial hemorrhage," she said. "Bruising on the neck from medium-sized hands. No skin cells under her nails. No rape but probable attempt per your police report."

Warren went back to rocking, and Callie guessed he gauged her. Leaning forward, she made the leap from the facts of the reports to her professional analysis.

"A cold weather rape is uncommon," she said. "As is wearing gloves, because someone calculating to do the deed wants to feel the goods and enjoy the sensation of touch."

With a half grin he assessed her. "Look at little Miss Callie."

"I learned a thing or two over the years."

"Over the years," and he laughed, which made her laugh as well. "Like how many can that be?"

"Two decades, Chief," she said. "Time's flying."

He chuckled and set his pipe in the ashtray.

Callie guessed she passed scrutiny.

"Okay," he said. "The body gave us no evidence. Face, neck, genitalia, no DNA. Nothing under her nails. Still, we surmised this a crime of opportunity by someone she knew, maybe in an argument that went south. Then something spooked him away." He nodded at her. "Possibly you."

Not a new thought for her. As a teenager, she was too shocked to think the culprit could've been nearby. She'd been too occupied at the sight to even look for him, too confused about what to do. "Yeah. Wish I knew then what I know now."

"Don't we all," he said.

"So," she started in. "What was your initial pool of suspects?"

"Besides every man in town?" he replied.

"I believe you did better than that."

He raised his pipe again, checking it once for life. "Realistically, any student or male at the game."

"That's still a major chunk of the town. Those games were sellouts. We were headed toward state champs, and that one against Berkeley was a predictable cliff-hanger. The place was jam-packed, the reason I didn't go to the restroom until the game was over and people poured onto the field."

"Which made the surveillance footage challenging," he said. "We went through footage from the gates, the concessions stands, and the parking lot. Just . . . too much. Of course, no cameras under the bleachers. But there are now."

Those cams went up before the next season; actually, the summer before she took off to college. Her father made sure those funds were raised.

"We even nabbed footage from local TV crews," he said. "All their raw footage of the night. Not productive. If that girl had been attacked today, we would've had a hundred cell phones covering something pertinent."

Very true. Callie wasn't a strong advocate of a camera on every person, always at the ready, but in this case, they might've narrowed the suspect pool if not caught the guy. And Stratton would be alive.

Mrs. Warren poked her head out the door. "Dinner'll be ready in about fifteen minutes."

The chief looked at his watch. "She's running late."

"Giving us time to talk, probably," Callie said. "Were you aware how sexually active Wendy was?" Of course he was. She'd read the report. Then before he could answer she added, "As in incredibly active?"

Funny how nobody thought of Wendy as the class slut. She didn't brag. She didn't date everybody, but her selectees numbered on the high side. Yet the world loved her personality, with few holding her sex life against her.

"Of course," the chief said, going with the flow, appearing to take no offense to Callie's line of basic questioning. "We asked her friends, and it didn't take us long to gather the string of names and establish a timeline of partners. The most recent being Stratton Winningham."

"How many?" she asked, almost afraid to hear the reality of Wendy's reputation. "How large was that pool?"

He laughed. "Let's see . . . the football team, the baseball team, some basketball guys." He laughed again. "But we accounted for the football team. All on the field, confirmed by coaches and hours of footage review."

"Seriously?" she said.

A minor chuckle disappeared in his throat. "No, but we spoke to every boy who identified as a former boyfriend, going back eighteen months. Which coincided with when she went on the pill. No HIPAA laws in place yet. Easier to get records."

Thorough enough. "How many boys did you interview?"

"Eight so-called boyfriends. Not as excessive as you might think, huh?"

Reputations, gossip, hearsay. With Wendy being likeable, no telling how many guys used her name as some sort of claim to fame, and with her wanting to be liked so much, she'd let them. Looking back, Callie recalled liking the girl, but also disliking how naïve she could be, hiding everything behind a smiling, blond veneer. Or at least Callie hoped it was a pretense. If she was really loose, her reputation was even sadder.

Warren's pipe smoke had turned from an aroma to an odor, a bit sickly of a smell. She tried not to show it, but if she didn't eat something soon, she'd be unable to. Her tea was gone, no real time to refill before the wife called them in to dinner. "Chief, the pipe?"

"Oh, um, sure." He placed a finger over the bowl and snuffed out the tobacco. "The porch is kind of my smoking cave. Sorry."

The air sure moved much better through her porch at the beach. "Can you name the boys?"

He stared up, toward a wind chime showing no movement. Thank God it wasn't July. "Not sure I can. It's in the report. Three football players, who were ruled out, remember. Anson, Baughman, and Stratton from basketball. Butch and Pete and that shortstop from the baseball team."

"All athletes," she said.

"Believe so."

She sucked down the melted ice in her glass, her stomach settling, the smoke about gone. "What about guys who never got to be her boyfriend? The frustrated wannabes?"

"No indication of any of those," he said. "Besides, like you said, everybody liked her. Damnedest thing I ever saw. But we found no information reflective of some discarded, broken-hearted loner. At least nobody mentioned one. It wasn't like she was that secretive of a person."

"Yet someone didn't like her," Callie said. "She was murdered. What about faculty? Male teachers ogled girls, especially cheerleaders on pep rally days when they were in uniform."

He shook his head.

"Her girlfriends?" she asked.

He winked. "Okay, there we had rub. Some of the cheerleaders thought Wendy was a little looser than she needed to be, but she never came on to *their* boyfriends, so they gave her a pass. The advisor repeated what the cheerleaders said, just adding she constantly worried about the girl getting pregnant."

Which segued into a specific name. Two, really. "Recall speaking to Georgia Walker?"

"One of the cheerleaders, nothing memorable. She's rich in real estate, what I heard."

"And Libby Lane," she added.

"Wendy's friend. We pushed her a bit harder, but she was clueless. Poor kid was broken up bad. Isn't she one of our teachers?"

"Yes, sir. What about Callie Cantrell?"

He reared back in his chair. "We talked to you."

He hadn't even served a full term back then, and Wendy's murder was the biggest case he'd ever seen. Callie recalled her interview. Two, actually, since the chief kept thinking of more to ask. She'd been asked how she happened to find Wendy, how Wendy had looked, and had Callie seen anyone around the scene. Nothing else.

"I had classes with Wendy," she said. "We shared a lab. Hell, Chief, I'd gone to the ballgame that night with her ex, the purported killer, yet you barely got a timeline out of me. Just how much influence did my father have on you? Who, if anyone else, encouraged your swift, we'll say, conclusion and the settling on Stratton being the offender?"

Mrs. Warren called from inside. "Y'all, it's on the table. Don't make me work doing all this for it to get cold. Stop your crime solving and come in. You can finish up over dessert."

His mouth flatlining, Chief Warren put palms on the arms of his chair, prepping to rise. "Don't come here making accusations, girl."

Callie tried not to be insulted. He'd called her *girl* on the doorstep, but this time his tone carried a slightly different meaning. But dinner was ready, the wife gracious, and the man had welcomed Callie into his home. She'd give him latitude because she was a guest . . . that and she had more questions.

"Let's eat, Chief, but after dinner, I still need clarity. I have the autopsy as well as the police report. What I need is the unsaid."

"Girl . . ."

And she tried not to cringe.

"Don't make me regret having invited you to dinner," he said.

"Don't make me regret having come," she replied.

Chapter 14

"HOW'S BEVERLY?" Mrs. Warren asked, starting the bowls around the table.

"Good, ma'am," Callie said, suddenly hungry. No wonder the chief stayed as robust as he was if he had a wife serving four course meals on a regular basis to only the two of them. Maybe her habit from being the wife of a town official, always prepared for guests.

The wife took the potatoes from Callie and handed her the field peas, no doubt grown locally from the smell of them. "Was this a social visit or something work related?" the wife asked, as if she hadn't deduced.

"Work," the chief said before Callie could.

"Oh," Mrs. Warren replied. "Then I'll change the subject. Nothing can turn an appetite faster than opinions and nastiness spoken over a fine meal. Did you get a herd of people at the beach this week, Callie?"

The missus rolled into nonconfrontational talk like a pro. She praised Callie, talked about the old days, actually recalling a formal dress Beverly made Callie wear to an inaugural ball. Callie had forgotten that evening, and recalled looking atrocious, but Mrs. Warren claimed that it proclaimed the teenage Ms. Cantrell as a lovely debutante. Sage green with cream lace.

The gracious woman made dinner its own event, dodging verbal skirmishes. Three decades of politics and law enforcement had made the chief's wife a savvy partner.

"Okay, y'all," the wife said. "Take your dessert out on the porch, and I'll clean up the dishes."

So they did. And in silence, Callie and the chief ate their caramel pound cake.

Callie finished first, setting her fork and saucer on a table a few feet away and against the wall. "Back to business. Yes, you interviewed me back then, but it was quite an abridged version," she said, picking up right where she'd left off. "Nothing about how I knew Wendy or Stratton's whereabouts. I had classes with her. I had dates with him."

"I knew all that."

"Yet you gave me a complete pass. Dad got to you."

"Wouldn't have mattered," he said. "You weren't pivotal to anything."

She shifted in her rocker to see him better. "I found the body. And that's not how you run an investigation, but I don't have to tell you that." She had her answer though. While Callie had little to offer the investigation other than finding Wendy and seeing no perpetrator, it was up to Chief Warren to confirm she hadn't seen the killer, aided the killer, or even done the deed herself. Her family, at least one of the two, extracted Callie from the situation which made her wonder what else had they used their pressure to accomplish.

Politics was such a powerful addiction. Those endowed with it used the tool in every aspect of their lives, and it wasn't surprising the profession ran in families. Like mobsters . . . like Sam Walton's progeny and Walmart. Once in your system, power was difficult to live without.

"Forget my family," she said. "And answer me this."

He went back to his dessert, mashing the crumbs with a moistened finger and licking them off before setting down his plate. "I'm listening."

"Did you never get close to having enough evidence for an indictment? I mean, a file doesn't necessarily contain all the information."

Not having the cake any longer, he studied the chimes again.

"You didn't actually believe you had enough evidence for an indictment, did you?" she said again.

Clearing his throat, he sat back and rocked. Callie read his dour expression and had her answers which only served to fuel her biggest concern. The concern she'd voiced in her childish way back then, one that she still felt strongly about today. "You still haven't said how you eliminated everyone but Stratton."

"Didn't need to. We had the current boyfriend, his obvious shame, his admission he was the father of the pregnancy," Warren said. "His alibi not a hundred percent. You couldn't alibi him for a little while at the game yourself."

"He was Wendy's ex-boyfriend," she corrected. "And did you do DNA to determine the father?"

"DNA took longer back then, plus he confessed. Callie, what are we doing here?" Apparently he tired of reliving the past, but Callie was not about to pull up stakes and go home, not yet, not this close to the end.

"*We* are giving me peace of mind," she said. "*We* are also trying to determine what the hell JJ intends to write about. I cannot let her mar that boy's reputation, regardless how long ago he died, regardless that he is dead."

Her tone had acquired a little iron, and he didn't argue. Just saying those words also made her wonder if JJ had manipulated Callie into doing just this, unearthing the corpses and reanalyzing the case. However, while Callie didn't appreciate being used, she fell on the side of truth. She hadn't realized what an unhealed wound Stratton had been until JJ scratched off the scab.

"I'm going to educate you on what happened, Chief, like I should have demanded to do then, and which you should have asked for." She tapped her fingernail on the arm of his chair. "And you *have* to listen."

Again, the chief didn't argue.

Callie thought back those twenty-four years. "Stratton hadn't quite rebounded from Wendy, but he was trying to. I wasn't looking for a steady guy, so when he asked me to the game, I said sure. I recognized a lonely kid with a broken heart. Made him nothing more than company sitting on a cold bleacher cheering our team. In the middle of the fourth quarter, he left before the concession stand closed to bring me a drink, probably to go to the restroom himself. He stayed gone ten minutes. Fifteen minutes after he returned, when the game ended, when the stadium was pure pandemonium from the score, I then went, caring nothing about piling onto the field like the rest. That's when I found Wendy. So . . ." and she inhaled and paused for his sake, as well as her own. "This guy kills Wendy, a girl nobody seemed to miss for the entire fourth quarter, and then Stratton comes back to sit next to me perfectly contained. No shakes, no pale skin, no fear in his eyes. Nothing disheveled. Just a guy enjoying an evening with his date."

"He wasn't with you the whole time, Callie."

"That's a miniscule window you're hanging your hat on, Chief," she replied. "Especially for a kid showing no change in behavior. Ever think that Stratton's suicide was regret he'd lost not only his girlfriend but a child? That he'd been watching a damn ballgame while they both were murdered? What if he hadn't broken up with Wendy?" She sped up talking, that emotion carried for so long creeping into her words. "Seventeen-year-olds don't think straight, and then you take that guilt and thrust him into the public's eye? Teenagers have killed themselves for much less, Chief Warren."

"Or he killed himself for killing them," he said in a level tone.

She shook her head slowly. "You can't have both," she said. "He coldly murdered without hesitation. Then you say he hanged himself with remorse? He was devastated when he found out, Chief. I was there. You were, too, if I remember correctly. Did you read his cries as an act?"

By the end of all that, she realized she was preaching. Tough. As a kid she'd been given an aspirin and told to go to her room. Today she could contest what had happened, and contest it wisely as both a witness and authority.

"Everything all right out here? Can I clear your plates?" Mrs. Warren had taken up residence in the doorway, consternation in her expression.

"We're fine, Mrs. Warren," Callie said, handing over her plate. "Did you make that pound cake?"

"Yes, I did," though she wasn't as sweet as before. Without a doubt she'd overheard. She'd lived through that period in Middleton's history as well, and though she had gathered the dishes, she didn't leave. "It's not his fault, Callie. It bothers him some, too, so don't go painting him as irresponsible or heartless. I won't have that."

"Mary, it's okay," said the chief. "The girl has to have some satisfaction."

Mrs. Warren stacked the plates in one hand and opened the screen door. "Do you know how the phone rang in this house?" she said, door propped on her hip. "How many people knocked on our door? At all hours of the day and night. Every child involved had a parent come over here wringing their hands over coffee or tea . . . bourbon or wine. Some left crying . . . others angry . . . one slammed a door. I had a child still at home then, too, and she locked herself upstairs when the Ives came around."

Callie wasn't interrupting. No way. Mrs. Warren stopped for a breath, and with the pause her thoughts caught up and she remembered her manners. "I'm sorry, but he did the best he could, Callie. That's all I wanted to say."

She disappeared inside.

The chief went back to rocking, staring off in those trees, and Callie obliged him and did the same. Maybe they all needed to slow down a minute.

"Not trying to pick a fight," she said.

He scrunched up his cheek. "Well, I halfway think you were prepared to, but I'm not necessarily opposed to that."

"But let's not fight," she replied. "Just tell—"

"Instead of this back and forth, avoiding each other's feelings, let's throw it all out on the table. Suit you?" He picked up his pipe, studied it, then changed his mind and put it back in the ashtray. "For a change, listen to me."

"Yes, sir."

He scratched the side of his jaw, as if he needed to shave, yet he didn't. Not at a quarter after one.

"The whole town wanted closure," he said. "Angry parents of boys the loudest. If they had a son anywhere near y'all's age, they begged me to make this case go away. The thought of anyone blaming a Middleton High School senior had all these families in an uproar, mostly because they worried the culprit was theirs. But your father," and he pointed a beefy finger at her. "He did not tell me to shut it down. I thoroughly briefed him. I admit I told him the Winningham boy looked better for it than most, but I had nothing conclusive."

His exhale carried a growl with it. "We exhausted all avenues of inquiry, Callie. You've been in law enforcement for, what, fifteen years? Twenty?"

She nodded. "Closer to the latter."

He seemed more tired with this two-hour recant of the worst crime in Middleton's history, taking a toll on a man approaching retirement. "Have you never had a case you couldn't solve?"

"Of course. They stick with you." She hesitated before saying the next. "However, Stratton did not do this. This is my teenage gut and my professional gut talking. He didn't deserve this. His family didn't deserve this. And Wendy's parents need to hear what really happened."

The bear of a man reared back, making his girth ominous. "What would you have me do?"

"It's a cold case, not a closed case," she said.

"Yes."

"Then tell me, who were the loudest of the angry parents?" Callie said. "Or can you remember?"

"No," and he was shaking his head. "I couldn't forget any of this if I tried. There were three in particular, but it involved four boys. All parents of athletes."

Callie pondered who fit that math. Someone with maybe a junior and a senior as sons? "There were no twins, so brothers?"

"No," he said. "An exchange student was staying with the Ives and their kid."

Butch Ives, and Libby's ex-husband Peter Yeo.

He mentioned the other two family names, and she remembered them, but they weren't the names currently gathered at Edisto. They weren't part of who JJ had orchestrated to gather at the beach and assist in her tell-all. But Callie wouldn't have pegged them either, though hopefully they had alibis.

And while Peter hadn't come to Edisto, Libby did, which made Callie wonder if JJ considered Libby a surrogate for Peter. Or was Libby supposed to be a performer all by herself?

"I've got to go," Callie said, and extended a hand. "Sorry if I ruined your afternoon, but bless you for tolerating my questions." Then she said something she'd wanted to say for a long time, and be able to say it truthfully. "You're a good man, Chief Warren."

He took her hand and drew her in for a hug instead. "Wish your daddy could see you."

They parted with melancholy smiles, and she left through the house, stopping long enough to give a thank-you to the wife.

Callie had an urge to return to the beach. For the first time since the reunion committee had arrived, Callie wondered if the real killer just might be staying at Georgia's, and JJ might be more on the ball than Callie thought.

Chapter 15

CALLIE PULLED away from Chief Warren's home, appetite sated by roast and field peas, and an extra piece of caramel pound cake sat waiting, wrapped in foil on the passenger seat.

Originally, the Middleton High School reunion group had committed to meet through tomorrow, Monday. Being at Georgia's house, a free stay at one of the biggest, poshest houses on Edisto Beach, nobody would be forced to leave, but they could. She doubted they cared if the reunion belly-flopped anyway.

And they'd damn sure appreciate never seeing or hearing from JJ again.

Trouble was, JJ *had* disappeared, which sort of made her Callie's business, regardless of the reunion.

Took her just under an hour to return to her beach town. Crossing the big bridge, her first thought was of Mark. Having pushed Mark to the back of her mind to deal with Beverly and Chief Warren, which hadn't been easy, being on Edisto ground brought his presence back.

A sleepover. God, she hadn't expected that, but she didn't fight it either. Her last had been Seabrook, the one time, the night before he died. A time that crushed her, and an experience she never thought she'd recover from.

Two-plus years prior to Seabrook was her husband, murdered by the Russian mob in Boston to get back at her.

Both of her men in law enforcement killed by someone she pursued on the job, and it made her feel no better that she'd taken down both parties. Her heart calloused over, making her wary about having another go at any sort of long-term relationship.

Both losses drove her deeply into her love for gin. Nobody was worth her sacrificing sobriety.

Mark needed to hear about what he'd walked into. He said their one night wasn't a lifetime commitment, but he'd sure plunged into their evening, their night, and the next morning with the fervor indicative of someone seeking something serious.

Not to mention she was lonely.

Not to mention he was awfully easy to like.

Did that make her appear needy? She'd known him for four months. Was that fast or slow to crawl into bed with a guy?

How badly was she going to regret a relationship? Or would she more regret not giving it a chance?

Her thoughts continued to chase themselves in circles as she crossed Scott's Creek and entered town limits, the time being almost four. Early enough to check JJ's rental, go by Georgia's, and possibly slip by El Marko's for a tonic at the bar.

Was she really trying to start doing this? Dating? Starting a fling? So alien to her.

So much talk for the beach inhabitants.

She followed Palmetto to Thistle Street and *Flirty Flamingo*. JJ's car remained in the drive. Pulling in, Callie left her vehicle and got halfway up the stairs before reaching for her phone . . . then her weapon.

"Thomas," she said low. "Have you been watching *Flirty Flamingo*?"

"LaRoache's job today, Chief. Why're you calling on the phone?"

She eased to the porch, stealthy on the balls of her feet, and backed against the wall. "Day off. Decided to come by. Glad I did. One of you get over here."

He quit with the conversation and hung up.

The door was left ajar. Not wide open such that you could see from the street, but partway up the stairs, enough for Callie to spot a six-inch-wide, long strip of blackness of the inside.

She eased along the wall, and upon reaching the doorway, called out, "JJ? It's Callie."

Nothing.

With her toe she pushed the door wider. Someone used a tool to force the lock, damaging the latch bolt and bending the plate. Old and worn like most rental locks on the beach, popping it wouldn't take much strength.

A patrol car came in faster than normal, and Thomas rolled out of the vehicle and headed up the stairs, light on his feet. Callie waved for him to get behind her, happy to see him in lieu of LaRoache. Thomas already knew the floorplan.

Together they breached the entrance. All lights remained off. They canvassed the rental, finding nobody.

The suitcase remained on the bed, but someone had tossed it. Callie had already taken the papers found in the lining but had left the suitcase orderly and closed.

"Look around once more," she said. "Anything used, out of order, moved. Then get your kit out of the car and dust the suitcase and that entry doorknob and anything else that strikes your fancy." Janet would be pissed, but she'd have to get over it.

Thomas got straight to work inspecting the house again, while she intensely studied the bedroom. What boggled her mind was who got in. They weren't happy from the state of the suitcase or the entry lock. Clearly the person wasn't JJ, who had a key, but someone hunting for her papers and photographs in Callie's possession, or someone just eager to find out what JJ was up to.

This person might or might not be the original suspect, assuming there was one. Could've grabbed JJ, unable to take the time to pilfer the suitcase, and returned. JJ wouldn't do this unless she was mentally off . . . or pretending to be her own abductor. Just savvy enough to keep Callie on edge, but not detailed enough to confirm anything.

What if Beverly was right that the author was playing if not testing Callie?

She returned to the door. Jimmied. Simple screwdriver from all appearances, which left the door unsecured upon leaving. Might have tried to pull it closed, from the fact she was almost on top of it before noticing it ajar.

"Thomas?" she called. "Did you check this place since we closed it up yesterday?"

"Twice," he hollered back. "Last time right before I ended my shift last night."

For a second she mused about bringing one of the cams from her place, rigging it up for whoever may come back, but they'd already realized there was nothing to be had. Callie had the purse, the phone, photos, autopsy report, and police report. The suitcase offered nothing of value and neither did the rental anymore.

Made Callie wonder what their next step would be, which was difficult to peg since it sort of depended on who was up to no good.

She came out and Thomas wandered over. "Maybe this woman really is missing after all."

Callie exhaled hard. "Can't tell. If she returned, she'd use her key. Wainwright Realty gave JJ two keys, so while I have the one we found in here yesterday, JJ should still possess the other. But this . . . this is a break-in."

Thomas did this twisted mouth thing.

Callie pulled out her phone and hit one of her favorites. "Janet? Callie. Have you heard from JJ Loveless today?"

The realtor's answer came back crisp, short, and sweet, like any Marine would deliver. "No."

"Well, you might want to get your handyman over here and fix the lock. It's been forced."

"What the hell is going on, Chief?" the Marine demanded.

"Your guess is as good as mine," Callie said. "Thomas will be here a little while collecting prints, so an hour or two maybe?"

If JJ had entered the place, say she forgot her key but didn't want to be found, she'd have not only wanted what was in her suitcase, but her purse, phone, and car keys as well. She'd have called Janet Wainwright upon not finding them. But she hadn't, so where could she be? And why?

JJ would also call Callie for assistance, or Georgia. Or if she was phoneless, she would go by either or both places.

"Do your fingerprints but don't leave until Janet's guy gets here to fix the lock, Thomas. Make sure it catches before you leave. Keep looking for this woman, and I mean look harder. I'll be over at *Water Spout*. Call me ASAP if you see her or if anyone reports having seen her. This is getting weird."

The situation was worrisome. JJ was either a serious manipulator, or someone had reacted rather strongly to her plan to write this book. Callie would gladly consider another option, but for the life of her, she couldn't name one. She wasn't accepting the fact the author just randomly disappeared by accident. It was a plan. Hers or someone else's.

Callie drove by her own home, just to put an eye on it and change to her patrol car. In and out, quickly. Nothing out of order, she headed toward the beachfront to hit *Water Spout*. She'd pulled into Georgia's drive about the time Thomas called her cell. Rather soon for him to do so.

"Chief?"

"FYI, I changed to my cruiser," she said. "What's up?"

"I haven't finished checking for prints, of course, but the trend is pretty clear. Wiped clean. I'll look closer on more surfaces, but the doorknob is spotless."

She let him go and sat there a moment. No, she wasn't comfortable with JJ's disappearance at all.

The time was just after five. She still had enough day left, and night, to delve into her concerns and ask more serious questions. The urgent matter at hand was, of course, JJ's whereabouts, but the Wendy Ashton cold case sort of segued into it. Timing couldn't be better with Chief Warren's recollection fresh in Callie's head. She knocked on Georgia's door, but when she found it unlocked, she let herself in.

She never understood people who didn't lock their doors.

Inside, she found Georgia in the kitchen, straightening up, as though relieved to be busy. Callie heard at least one shower going upstairs. "You need to start locking your doors, Georgia. Where is everybody?"

"Figured we'd do seafood tonight." Georgia threw away remnants of crackers and covered up a few bowls, putting some in the refrigerator. "Still have one left getting ready. Reuben was willing to take the cold shower."

Callie filched a grape before the bowl got put away. "Poor Reuben. Bet you'll be glad when these people are gone."

Georgia stopped and gave her a *you think?* look.

"Where are the others? I need to say something." Callie already headed toward the large back porch where classmates took up residence when they weren't sleeping or peeing. Butch probably slept in the open after a whiskey too many with the warming air just the right temperature to soothe a person to sleep. With the sun behind the house, the oceanic view mesmerized anyone with half a soul, the slow undulating water gray-blue and peaceful. The tide was out and its murmur soothing as the day closed. Callie longingly studied the beach. Anyone watching the chief would assume her protective and ever on guard, but finding oceanfront sparse with beachcombers, she wished her time was hers to stroll. Empty, just like she liked it. Might even ask Mark to accompany her sometime, then wondered how his limp would handle the sand.

Georgia followed Callie outside, her clip-clop mules announcing her arrival on the slatted porch. All but Reuben lounged outside, but he still ranked the lowest on Callie's list.

"Folks, JJ's absence has taken priority over the reunion," she said.

Butch laughed. "Can't get anything past that one."

She ignored him for the zillionth time. "We've had no credit card usage and no attempt to contact me or the rental agency. Her agent hasn't heard from her, and she hasn't been found after a cursory search of the marshes."

Not that she'd had anybody scan the marshes, but Callie painted a picture to capture attention and judge responses.

Libby gasped. Expected. Georgia frowned, worried. Tony kept his response in check, but Butch couldn't stand the heavy dramatic pause.

"No worries," he said. "This missing person thing is far more entertaining than this dumbass reunion nobody wants to go to anyway."

Georgia strutted across Callie's path, and for a second Callie expected to see Butch slapped. "I ought to throw your dumbass out of my house, you sorry piece of trash. I've about had my fill of you."

Butch only grinned, enjoying baiting a rise out of someone, but before he could speak, Callie did. "Folks, I'm sensing foul play, unfortunately, and I need your help. I'll be talking to each of you, one-on-one, to see if I can piece anything together. JJ takes precedence, I'm afraid. Nobody leaves the beach."

Reuben appeared in the doorway, freshly groomed in linen shorts and floral button-up summer garb. "I'm not sure anyone cares about JJ," he said. "She stirred us up for personal gain. Wouldn't be surprised if she hasn't put hidden cameras around here to watch how we react."

Georgia looked stunned. "In my house?"

Callie wouldn't be surprised. "When could she have done it, Georgia?"

Dazed, Georgia appeared stuck in place. "I . . . I don't know."

Georgia rented out *Water Spout* when she wasn't using it. There was always the slim chance JJ had somehow finagled maintenance to do so, but that would be some fancy finagling under Janet's nose.

So Callie went with no cams.

JJ had supposedly just arrived Friday evening, with Callie herself outside to welcome her in order to make sure her vehicle wasn't blocked in. Maybe the interviews would reveal otherwise. Interviews that needed to start immediately.

Libby scooted to the edge of her beach rocker. "I'm sorry, but I must protest to staying much longer. I've got to leave."

To which Tony turned to give her a hard glare, disapproving of this urgency. Callie could see him sticking around for however long this took, and his response made her think that Edisto had been the first chance they'd had to explore their relationship without the prying eyes of academia. Callie tried to discard images of meetings in school janitorial closets. Weren't they both single? Was it nothing more than the boss can't screw the employee? She'd learn soon enough.

"Libby," she said, pointing to the teacher.

Libby stiffened.

"Since you have the biggest desire to leave, let's interview you first."

"Um," she replied, backed into the proverbial corner. "Where do you want to go?"

"I've got plenty of privacy in this place," Georgia offered.

Butch watched, amused.

But Callie shook her head. "Has to be done at the station. Come on. We'll ride in my car."

Libby's stare stuck on Callie. "What?"

Callie reached out to her and helped her rise. "I don't bite, Libby. And I'll get you back in one piece."

"Wh-what about dinner?" Her gaze fell on each person, seeking rescue.

"Tell me what you like and we'll bring it back for you," Georgia said, ever aiming to smooth controversy. "Shrimp, flounder, scallops?"

Tony stepped up. "I'll order for you. Go on. We'll be here when you get back." Then to Callie, said, "I can leave tomorrow, right? I wasn't involved in this."

"What makes you think I was asking about back then, Tony?" A rather Freudian slip, in Callie's opinion.

"Well, I . . . I mean . . ."

"You need to stick around, too," she said. "This is about JJ being missing, not Wendy."

Libby's eyes widened round as silver dollars at her boyfriend. "You would leave me, Tony?"

"Oh, no," he said, backtracking, reaching out to his lady. "That did not come out like it sounded, babe. Of course, I would not leave you."

Again, Callie wondered how long they'd been together. "Let's go, Libby."

They all left Libby to fend for herself, and Callie loved it. That or they trusted Callie because she was one of them . . . one of the people JJ targeted to collect on Edisto Beach. She was as tainted as the rest of them per the author, which made her an ally. *The enemy of my enemy is my friend.* A trust that should make for wonderful interviews.

"Oh, something else, y'all," she said, halting. Libby paused in front of her. "No booze, okay? Drinking means I'll have to take longer interviewing you guys over the next day or two."

Butch looked about to burst with a grin, clearly having no intention of abstaining from a drink.

She headed toward the door with Libby.

"What about the reunion?" she heard Georgia ask behind them.

"Georgia," Butch said, then laughed. "When Libby gets back she'll be a basket case, and we'll want to hear what happened. Accept it. We don't give a damn about the reunion."

Callie pretended she didn't hear. Butch could laugh, but he'd be giving his own interview before this night was through. Drunk or not since it seemed impossible to catch the man sober.

Chapter 16

IN A SUNDRESS accented by a short sweater in primary colors, Libby sat across the desk from Callie in the Edisto police station, looking every bit the school teacher she was. Only needed her name tag on a lanyard. However, she glanced around as if gremlins waited behind furniture, or cameras hid in light fixtures. She scanned the desk's edge, the file rack, so Callie interrupted her anything-but-covert search and slapped a recorder right in front of her. The teacher stared as if suspecting spies clustered around the other end of the device.

Callie already spot-checked Libby's social media, consisting mostly of Facebook and Pinterest pictures of clothes and class decor, book titles, and a wish list of future travels. No kid pictures except those forwarded from the school's site for assorted awards and events. Some of her sister's children.

The social media bordered teenager-ish but showed nothing recent about JJ, the beach, or any of the other participants.

"Ready?" And Libby nodded okay.

Callie read in the introduction of those present, date, and time, then commenced with a timeline. A timeline was one of the easiest ways to trip up people, find inconsistencies, and learn which tangent was worth pursuit.

"When was the last time you saw JJ?"

Libby gave a puzzled expression. "You already know that, Callie. Or Chief. Which do I call you?"

"Whichever makes you comfortable, Libby."

That seemed to help lower her shoulders a bit. "Friday night."

Callie confirmed the date, then prompted her. "Go ahead. I left around four. Take it from there."

A nod, as if she better understood the rules. "Let's see. She'd dropped the bomb about writing the book and uninviting people by the time you left. All tried to ignore that for almost an hour, maybe more, letting food and drink sort of serve as the nucleus of things. Of course, nobody really wanted her there after that announcement. She started off quiet. Fielding questions from Butch, mostly. But then she'd drop a bomb of a comment, which made everyone stop and listen. Then someone would ask a question, and she'd answer with some off-the-wall sarcasm to get someone riled. Like that was her purpose for being there, to piss us off. Georgia attempted to pull out her notebook and talk reunion, but JJ continually found a way to interrupt and incense the group all over again. Georgia asked, *Should we have a king and queen?* And JJ asked, *Where were you when Wendy was murdered?* That type of thing."

As badly as Callie wanted to hear what was said, she didn't ask, because nobody likely gave JJ an honest answer. "So y'all never could get around to the reunion, huh?"

With a histrionic huff, Libby rolled her eyes again. Callie bet she taught theatre at the high school, too.

Libby's head did a side-to-side thing in sync with her words. "It was start and stop, until after the fourth or fifth time Georgia attempted to reel us in." Then she stopped, overly thinned brows rising high. "Then Georgia screamed, *I decide what we talk about!* That just dissolved everyone into hee-haws of laughter." Libby sniggered. "She got blood red. Even JJ laughed."

The spiteful merriment most likely enticed the author to stick around longer. "When did JJ leave?" Callie asked.

"Elevenish? Way before midnight."

"Did she leave alone?"

A surprised look. "Yes."

"When was the first time you saw JJ at the beach?"

"Why . . . when you did. When she got to Georgia's."

"Okay, slow down and think hard on this one," Callie said, coming over her desk just a hair, which made Libby come forward, too. "At any time since you arrived on this beach, have you left the group and gone out on your own?"

Libby leaned back. "What does that have to do with anything?"

"Why are you avoiding my question?" Callie replied.

Neck extended, eyes wide, she spouted back. "I . . . I'm not."

Callie continued. "Then answer. Have you been away from this group for any length of time?"

"This morning," she said. "Tony and I walked the beach. The first time we've left the house except to go out to eat like some babysat group."

Long after JJ disappeared Friday night or early Saturday morning.

"Since you arrived, who else ventured from the house, apart from the group?"

"Several of us this morning, actually. Tony and I sort of set the example. I think they all felt Georgia needed space, and to be truthful, she stayed behind, saying she'd have mimosas waiting for us when we returned."

Standard for most groups at a beach, frankly. Everyone's excited to be around each other, then a day or two later they need a break. Callie prompted her again. "Friday night, after JJ left . . ."

Libby seemed to hang on the words, as if to redeem herself for not answering properly before.

"Did anyone slip out when y'all were supposed to be sleeping?" Callie asked. Someone might've waited until all were in bed. For sure, the return visit to pilfer the suitcase took place after Thomas's last check Saturday night.

"I was asleep. How would I know?"

"Okay, when had you last seen JJ before y'all arrived Friday?"

Libby stared like Callie spoke Greek.

"Have you seen her since high school?" Callie said, giving Libby more context.

"She spoke to my AP English class five years ago, after her twelfth novel made the *New York Times* bestseller list. I threw her an invitation, and, surprise, she accepted. She spoke with one class. Fifty minutes. Then she was gone. Before that? High school."

Callie shifted back to the present. "Were there any one-on-one arguments with JJ or just roundtable general disgruntlement Friday night? Any animosity between you and her, for instance?"

Reserve dissipating, Libby had sunk back into the give and take with more ease. Posture rested further back in the chair, her head settled easier on her shoulders as she revisited the conversations of that night.

"Actually, we got along fine, replaying high school stories, catching up on what we do today until JJ tossed that turd into the punch bowl."

"The turd?" Callie almost asked which turd. There seemed so many.

"Wendy and Stratton," Libby said.

Turd was a decent metaphor. Just sounded odd coming from an English teacher, but then Tony'd been tempering her language since they arrived. "Did she seem to jump on anyone in particular?"

"Oh no," the teacher replied, instantly. "That bitch was an equal opportunity insult machine."

What was it about each of these alums that JJ had decided was worth this clandestine plan to get her suspects alone? "Explain the insults."

"That's just it," Libby replied. "It was maybes and what-ifs. *Sure that baby wasn't yours, Butch? Maybe you weren't the nerd everyone thought you were, Reuben. Everyone assumes you fucked students, Tony.*"

The F bomb. The English teacher was in fine form tonight.

Thus far, JJ's questions seemed directed at the men. "What about Georgia?"

"That's the thing," Libby said. "She lightened up on Georgia. Maybe because she owned the house and none of us would've shown up without her floozy beach mansion being free. But Georgia stayed busy with hostessing once JJ stole the evening anyway, her feelings sort of hurt." She tossed her hair. "People *think* Georgia was Wendy's best friend because she was also a cheerleader, but she wasn't. I was. We came to the game together and we expected to leave together." She sighed and stared at Callie, as though staring into a camera. "Her death destroyed me."

A zing of jealousy here. A taste of drama there. A complete change in subject.

"So JJ picked on you more than Georgia at the beach house," Callie surmised.

Libby blew out. "Sure did."

Callie paused questioning for just enough microseconds to indicate a change of direction. Over the years she'd developed a second sense of timing with interviewees. Sometimes she'd really change subjects. Other times, she'd let them think she had, then blindside them. "So what did you do to merit being in this group of honorees?"

She soured. "What did *you* do?"

Callie normally didn't answer questions in an interview. Her purpose was to ask them. But in this particular situation, she was part of the script. In a bigger department, she'd be taken out of the lead investigator slot for her familiarity to the players. On Edisto, however, she was it.

Truth was, JJ *had* included Callie in this motley crew. Callie had her assumptions, but it was too early to conclude whether JJ found Callie truly at fault, or if JJ planned to use her as a marketing piece to weave into the story.

So Callie answered, if for no reason than to buy trust. "I've asked myself that a hundred times, Libby. I discovered the body and called in the authorities. What about that was wrong in JJ's eyes? I have no idea why she invited me."

Libby gave a small grin. "You sure she doesn't think you did it? Or you waited until Wendy was dead to call anyone?" Libby had her facts wrong but said nothing Callie hadn't heard before. "Or maybe you covered for whoever did it, letting them get away first. Like Stratton, maybe? You dated him. We all believe that's what you did. After you left on Friday, it was all we talked about for a while, with JJ feeding the conversation."

A heat rose within Callie, and she quelled it. So the old scandalous tattle still lived amongst her high school peers. One of the myriad reasons she left Middleton and never moved back.

To a woman who wrote mystery novels for a living, JJ's suspicions, even if totally false, made for strong plot material. To affiliate that book with a current police chief, one who'd gained state notoriety in taking down former Police Chief Mike Seabrook's murderer, and one renowned for being a decorated Boston detective who'd confronted the Russian mob . . . well, who would argue against using that character? Think of the motivations to be explored. Had Wendy's murder enticed this child of the mayor to seek a badge? And if so, to assuage her conscience?

Yes, Chief Callie Jean Morgan would make for fine marketing material.

But Callie wasn't here to banter what-ifs about anyone but JJ, and hopefully about information that was more fact than what-if. "Guess we'll find out what JJ thinks when she writes it. Assuming we find JJ and she gets the chance to write it."

The teacher sucked in then whispered its release. "Do you really think she's dead?"

"The word is *missing*, not dead. What makes you think she's dead?"

Libby almost seemed to stroke. Eyes wide, fluttering, her mental faculties tangled. "I didn't say dead. Did I say dead?"

"Yes, ma'am, you did. Do you wish she were dead?"

"No . . . um, no! You know how missing people turn up dead, and with you being a cop and all, and it's been over twenty-four hours which is what they say is the magical time when the odds go down, but I don't wish anyone dead, Callie. Please don't tell people that." Then she thought about her choice of words. "Don't *think* that. That makes me a suspect, doesn't it? Oh shit, what am I supposed to do? This could cost me my job."

Yet she saw no repercussions from her affair with her boss.

Libby's chest rose and fell to the point Callie worried she'd hyperventilate. "Libby, shush a moment. Collect your wits. Breathe."

Callie grabbed herself a water, holding one out for Libby, who refused.

"Okay," Callie said after slowly taking her water break so Libby would calm down. "Why would JJ question you as a negative when it came to Wendy? She was your best friend. What about your story is worth writing about?"

A long exhale. "That's beyond me. I was watching football and then learned my best friend was dead." She shrugged. "How does that matter to JJ except for character development? Certainly nothing plot-related."

The teacher talking again. "Not even a hint of an idea?" Callie asked. "I suspect plot complication being more of JJ's interest in you."

Libby studied a photo on Callie's wall, to the left, as though bruised and hurt by the very thought of it all. Time to approach this from another angle. "You were there that night, right?"

A yes-or-no answer, but Libby was giving it thought. Before she could fabricate, Callie added, "I saw you."

Yes, Callie had, but only in glances. Couldn't recall who Libby sat with or how long she stayed in her seat. Just a memory of how far up and how far over in the stands.

Libby stiffened. "So?"

"Who were you with?"

She pooched out her bottom lip. "Depends on what part you're talking about. Peter and Butch were there, but Butch had to flit around, Peter tailing him. Damn it, keeping those two apart was a bitch. I was Peter's date, for God's sake, but no, there goes Butch then there goes Peter. Butch was chasing skirts, while I was the only skirt Peter was supposed to care about."

"Who was with you?" Callie repeated.

A shrug. "My little sister and her friends. My parents were nearby."

But Libby was still stung after all this time about being abandoned by her beau. Both her boyfriend and best friend too busy to keep her company.

"Who actually took you home?" Callie asked.

"Georgia," she said.

Callie studied her, caught off guard. "Not Peter? With a night as crazy as that, he stuck with Butch?"

The familiar pout was not as attractive on a forty-year-old woman as it had been on the seventeen-year-old girl, but Libby assumed it righteously. "Butch and Peter rode together." She pulled at her dress bodice, as if it clung uncomfortably. "I was hoping to leave with Peter.

Butch could always find a ride, but he was being his normal butt self, and apparently he grabbed Peter before I could."

That explanation was pretty much how Callie remembered their trio functioning. The boys were baseball stars, with Peter Yeo being an exchange student from the UK. The Ives family thought their son would appreciate a live-in buddy, and while the boys connected all right, the joke around school was who loved Peter most, Butch or Libby. Butch suddenly had someone to be mischievous with and took full advantage of him, often getting Peter to cover with the parents while Butch came in at three a.m.

"At Georgia's beach house, did anybody go off with JJ alone?" Callie asked. One of them could've confronted JJ in a more private manner. "Any odd behaviors between JJ and anyone?"

Libby denied with a shake of her head. Callie pointed to the recorder, and Libby replied, "No. Nobody I saw."

Callie paused, lifted her phone and shot a text to Thomas.

"So," she started, ending the text. "JJ left shortly after eleven. What did you do then?" Time was moving on, and Callie hoped to get one, if not two more interviews in.

"Had one more drink then crashed," Libby said. "Didn't expect such an exasperating damn day. Georgia painted this as a long weekend lolling with free food and the ocean and pleasant catch up about teenage years."

Hmm. Not how Callie recalled those years.

She jotted the occasional note, especially when it came to the timeline. "Did you *crash* alone or with Tony?"

"He talked with the guys for a while after I left. I didn't look at the time he came to bed."

"Any idea what they talked about?" Callie asked.

Libby gave a silly perplexing expression. "Sports maybe since Butch does what he does. Have no idea. I'd cracked the window to hear the surf, and I dropped off as soon as my head hit the pillow."

Callie sat back and acted as if she had a thought. "So tell me about your arrangement with Tony. Are y'all an official item?"

She could blush when asked about being a couple, but not about sleeping with the man? "Um, no. Not formally. Especially not at school."

What happens at Edisto stays on Edisto? "You think this won't get back to Middleton?"

"No. How would it? We're the only two people who are school employees, and these guys here this weekend won't care."

Sure, Libby. Nobody picks up a phone or posts a picture on Instagram. And nothing Butch learns ever turns up on the six o'clock news.

But Callie let her keep her sense of security. "Tony was the newest teacher back then, if I recall right. I never had him, but he was cute. Fresh out of college with the girls coming on to him."

A half smirk slipped into place on Libby. "They did. I wanted to check him out, but Peter was more within my reach. As many girls wanted him as Tony, but then you might not have seen that in your circle."

Whatever that meant.

Libby sighed. "There's something about that bloody British accent."

"I do recall," Callie said, leaving it at that.

Peter had been considered a catch, and Libby had latched ahold of him and clung on for the ride, which only made Butch compete against her harder. "Do you remember if Tony had a date that night?" Callie didn't see him at the event, but she had to assume he was there. The whole town attended that playoff.

"He was alone," Libby said. "Believe I'd have remembered a date, because it would've broken all our hearts to see him spoken for. He sat over and down a few rows from me, maybe twenty people between our seats and his. Kids took turns sitting near him."

Libby had indeed paid attention to Tony.

"Almost done." Callie jotted some more and then leaned on the desk. When she looked up, Libby had relaxed at the feeling she was about to leave. "Who do you think killed Wendy?"

Libby seemed to seize from the neck down. "I don't think about it."

"Think about it now."

"Could've been any of several, but Wendy particularly avoided Stratton."

"But he was with me," Callie said, though she skipped the part where he left in the fourth quarter to get them a soft drink.

"Don't care," Libby came back, sassing, willing to take the dare. "He got her pregnant and she was going to get an abortion before anyone knew."

"You knew she was pregnant?"

"Yes."

"Who else knew?"

"Nobody. She wanted it to just go away and nobody be the wiser," she said.

All made sense, and nothing about the teacher seemed deceptive. Paranoid, smug, and insecure, but nothing disingenuous.

"Okay, this time we're done," Callie said and formally ended the interview. "I really appreciate your cooperation." She'd attempted to build some trust with Libby, preserving a connection she might come back to with subsequent interviews.

She'd sort out fact from fiction later.

Libby did her blinking thing again. "I guess that wasn't too difficult." She rose when Callie did and waited at the door for Callie to open it, as though needing permission to leave.

The police station was small, the main lobby divided from a handful of shared desks by a counter, with Callie's office being the only private one. Libby came around the corner and stutter-stepped at the people waiting.

"It's all right," Callie said, passing her to the counter and holding open its swinging door. "Officer Gage is taking you home. Tony?" and she motioned to the high school principal. "Come on back. You're next."

The teacher and the principal almost fell over each other, their halting body language shouting the need to speak to each other without the officers hearing.

Her sweater slipped down one shoulder. He lifted it up for her. She eased over, kissed him on the cheek, and whispered something in his ear.

"This way, Tony," Callie interrupted, but not before Tony gave Libby a baffled look.

Callie led Tony away, not giving Libby a chance to say it again.

Chapter 17

JJ
Sunday.

JJ'S PHONE HAD LIT up with texts all day. So much so that she muted her phone and left it in the bedroom while she wrote into the night. The sender, her assistant, couldn't filter shit from gold. Full of gossip, trivialities, and personal affronts, JJ had miscalculated her assistant's worth.

The sender documented absolutely no redeeming qualities of anyone sleeping under that beach roof. Who cared how much they made or what car they drove, the women they'd bedded or the men they'd mastered into covering two-hundred-dollar dinners? One or two comments might define a person's immaturity or highlight their shortfalls, but JJ had no intention of penning a tell-all of soap opera paltriness instead of a true crime of failed justice.

She'd learned one person's meaning of juiciness wasn't necessarily hers.

Sunday started late, not unlike Saturday, after a night binge of writing, and the sun shined ten degrees warmer. She watched the house across the street, and upon deciding nobody occupied the place at present, she dared to cross to see the marsh before settling in to work. She forgot how beautiful the Lowcountry could be, and yes, it would receive its own attention in this book. The melancholy juxtaposition of danger and charm. Jungle growing right up to water with wildlife belonging to air, sea, or land at every turn. Location alone could be a selling point for this book. Again, true crime or fiction waited to be seen.

At the rate she was being fed intel, she leaned toward fiction. That was her strong suit, but she desperately longed for a bestseller in nonfiction.

She had an ace in the hole, though, and he'd confirmed his arrival. Damn if he hadn't been a hit-and-miss effort, but he would arrive late tonight. God, what she'd had to threaten that man with to get him on a plane.

She had yet to decide on the book's title. Sea Island . . . Lowcountry . . . Wetland . . . and something else. The word death, however, felt rather cliché. Maybe she'd bank off the small-town setting, but she had to be careful what she chose didn't evoke Hicksville or something from the Midwest. Titles were tricky bastards, she thought, coming back from the water.

After another coffee, she toasted a bagel and sat down to slip back into Callie Jean Morgan's mind. A wounded soul. After solving hundreds of cases, she still couldn't solve her first. Then here comes the author, JJ Loveless, master of mystery, exhuming ancient history and laying it out for Callie to tackle again.

Callie's character gave her the most joy. The juvenile one and the adult, which allowed JJ to define the thread that connected the child to the chief. The tortured heroine who called upon the proficiency of JJ Loveless to assist her in putting her demons to rest.

Damn it, she left her reading glasses back on the nightstand. Wearing her favorite flats, in the same clothes as the day before except for underthings, she scooted back inside. She was enjoying this. She might extend her stay another week.

She'd left her phone on the bed in light of all the texts, and she reached for the device, hoping for some crisp, luscious nugget of substance from her cohort's texts to jumpstart the afternoon. She froze at the other object on the quilt.

A bookmark. One of her own. She hadn't put that there.

She studied the front, but when she turned it over, someone had written *I'll be in touch.*

Chapter 18

TONY AND LIBBY couldn't have scrutinized each other harder, her heading out of the police station with Thomas, trying to telepathically deliver what she meant, Tony being led into Callie's private office, not getting the message. So comically obvious.

Ten after seven. With daylight savings dropping into place just two weeks before, the evenings extended longer. The view through the station's entrance was of the beach four blocks away. Even with the building positioned under oak canopies at the end of Murray Street, the sunlight still gave the impression there was ample time to collect shells before dark.

In other words, plenty of hours left in Callie's day.

"Sit right there," Callie said, closing the office door, thumb sifting quickly through the principal's social media as they both assumed their seats. He'd posted nothing since before Friday, not a surprise since posts would point people to the beach, and too many people at the beach could point to Libby. The man had gone dark, it seemed.

Tony took the chair, probably still warm from Libby, and he brought with him an aroma of seafood and what Callie thought was a whiff of beer.

"I didn't get to finish my meal," he said in his principal voice, as if Callie were a student needing to explain herself.

She reached down and broke loose a bottled water from a case behind her desk, setting it in front of him. "I've got granola bars if you're hungry."

"I'll pass," he said, his monotone defining.

Thank God she'd eaten a decent meal with Chief and Mrs. Warren or she'd peel open one of those bars herself. Supper would come and go without her this evening, and if Tony ate even half a meal, he'd be fine. Especially after the spreads Georgia doled out back at the house.

Callie made sure she had a new file on the recorder. "Are they packing up your leftovers for later? What'd you have?"

"Blackened sea bass with fries and slaw," he said, attitude caustic.

"Oh," she said, primed, her clean notepad at the ready, the other notepad from Libby's chat to the side of it. "Blackened fish heats up nicely. Better than fried. Now, let's get started," and without hesitation, she launched into the interview's formal introduction, Tony's mouth slightly parted at how quickly he'd been managed.

"Mr. Tony Tyler," she started. "Have you had anything to drink?"

He reached up and raked through his dark hair, dipping his head to avoid her stare. "Um, a beer."

After she'd told them not to drink.

"One or two?" she asked.

"Not even one," he replied. "Your officer interrupted our evening, so I drank maybe half of a perfectly good Guinness."

"I don't like wasting a drink, either, so my apologies. It's difficult to find a convenient time to interview someone about a missing person."

One slip of a nod, acquiescing. He'd drunk against her wishes but not over-indulged.

The principal had more edge to him tonight. Callie chalked it up to his position and a preference to being in charge.

Callie had begun the interviews with Libby who could speak on Butch and Tony. She'd been married to Peter. Chances were Wendy's killer was male, so Callie preferred to gain insight into the guys from the teacher before the guys spoke themselves. While JJ invited Reuben, he was never a concern of Chief Warren. Therefore, he could wait to be her last interview.

Libby first, for bearings, and Tony second because of her immediate relationship with him, timed such that they could not exchange stories, current or historical.

His story pretty much matched Libby's. They arrived on the beach at the same time, in separate cars, seconds ahead of JJ. He'd last seen JJ at the very presentation Libby described for her AP English class. JJ left for her own rental just after eleven, same accounting, and he hadn't seen her since.

Tony's mild nerves were apparent from the slight heel bopping motion in his right leg, not the laid-back administrator she'd seen at Georgia's. Otherwise Tony remained relatively stable, answering firmly to show he couldn't be dominated. Such a guy thing.

"What did Libby tell you on her way out?" she asked.

"Good luck," he lied.

"Try again."

"*Don't tell her anything,*" he said.

"Interesting," she replied, and took a second to make a conscious glance at the recorder. "So what do you know you are trying to keep secret from the law?"

He followed her eyes. "I . . . don't know." Then as if feeling he had to flesh that out, he added, "I was somewhat stunned at the remark, to tell you the truth."

Nope, she didn't believe him this time either. "Well, Libby is worried about something, someone, or worse, some secret she fears you'll tell me." Then she laid her gaze on him and went quiet.

He froze, then tried not to look so scared by moving his feet and studying them, as if they acted on their own.

She would come back around to that later, and she shifted gears to a topic he could answer freely. "What time did Libby go to bed Friday night?"

"Shortly after JJ left, maybe eleven thirty?" he replied, happy at mastering a question, academia clearly embedded in his pores.

"You joined her later?"

"Yes. After talking to the boys."

Callie poised her pen, watching him as if she already knew. "Talking about what?"

"Butch's job. What else are you going to talk about with Butch except Butch? Except sports."

Tony was a nice enough guy, a bit—maybe a lot—on the boring side. Soft but still slim, face long, cheeks inward almost skull-like. Commonplace in his khaki-pants-casual dress style and soap-and-water grooming. Nails clipped short, maybe manicured, and she bet he kept clippers in his pocket. No jewelry except for a college ring, and if someone had to guess his profession, they'd nail it within three tries. Not the sort that merited a lot of attention, but one never knew what any witness of any caliber could reveal.

Sometimes killers hid in plain sight.

"Did you step out any time that night?" she asked.

"For what?" This guy suddenly had a hint of something off about him she hadn't seen before he was cornered.

"The answer is yes or no, Tony."

"No."

Callie tapped her pen on her chin. "Not for a smoke, or a meditative stroll on the sand?"

A nervous laugh escaped him. "Libby and I hadn't been alone in three weeks. Why would I stroll the sand?"

"Libby said she remembers sleeping the whole night."

A louder laugh. "Libby remembers way more than that."

"Since you were awake," she said, "did you hear anyone else leave the house?"

"Not a soul," he replied.

A rumble rolled through Callie's stomach. Seriously, she might grab a granola bar at the end of this one, assuming she didn't go home. She quickly spoke to hide the noise. "To better understand why JJ might have disappeared, I'm attempting to define the uniqueness in each of us that would make JJ pick us yet tell others they weren't welcome."

Having survived talk of the affair, Tony waited to hear the next question, already turning the gears in preparation of solving and moving on. Too comfortable, in Callie's opinion. He needed his buttons pushed.

"The night that Wendy died, were you curious enough to go back there and see her body?"

His jaw dropped like clockwork, then closed just as quickly. "What?" The muscles in his neck protruded against his collar.

"You heard me. Did you slip back and take a peek at Wendy?"

She didn't recall him standing amidst the gawkers, the twenty or so high schoolers and staff acting stunned with hands over their mouths while still managing to whisper to each other to send a friend to tell another friend to get their butts over there. But he would not have stood front and center. Heavens, a teacher would not do such a thing.

"What did you think when you first saw her laid out under the bleachers like that, Tony?"

Instantly, Callie's own memory popped back crisp and detailed. The way Wendy's eyes stared. Popcorn aroma. Cold autumn air. A shiver rolled across her shoulders, and she shrugged as if to work out a kink.

Tony still hadn't answered, and Callie could see his brain sorting out the right response, the wrong, when the first and simplest answer was probably his best. She didn't have to hear him admit that he had eased down there to see the debauchery firsthand.

"I thought," he started, then cleared his throat. "I thought what a waste of a pretty girl."

"A *pretty* girl," she repeated. "What if she'd been an ugly girl?"

Mortification rode up his jaw and into his sunken cheeks. Poor thing. His political correctness had slipped. "I didn't mean that," he said.

"Yeah, you did. Own it. You were barely more than a kid yourself watching all those sleek-legged, tight-waisted girls saunter in and out of classes on pep rally days. Those uniforms weren't designed just to identify team colors, you know."

"You trying to make this about race?" he tried. "A black man wanting a young, beautiful white girl?"

"No," she said to the indignant man. He was not the first black man who saw her as law enforcement jumping to conclusions. "It's about sex and death."

He was unaware his glare shifted from Callie to the recorder. "Okay, I watched until the police came."

"Which wasn't long," she said. "You got there quick."

"I did, but I saw you."

The best defense is a good offense. "Other than Wendy, I was sort of the center of attention since I found her," Callie confirmed.

"I kept studying you," he said, seeking a higher vantage, emphasizing the *you*. "Wondered how you found her, what you did, whether you saw the guy who did it." His tight jaw softened. "Even for a flash thought you could've done it."

The poor guy was deflecting, probably for something he didn't even do. She felt a bit sorry for him. Principals were accustomed to being on top, not bested; however, their usual audience wasn't much of a contest.

He wasn't the first to think those words, though. *Did she do it?* People had mumbled the same that night as though Callie couldn't hear them. Stupid people. People who didn't realize that a person as tiny and as criminally inexperienced as teenaged Callie couldn't wring a neck and not be scruffy, scratched, or agitated. Wendy had ten or fifteen pounds on Callie, and was well-muscled from her cheering.

Callie silently endured the accusations and let the cops quickly rule her out, but that didn't stop Wendy's wide-eyed, barely conscious body from entering her dreams at night and catching Callie's thoughts unawares at odd moments of a day.

"Your daddy would've gotten you off if you did it," Tony said. "You were protected."

Why was he keeping on like this?

"There was nothing to get me off from, Tony."

The minute she spoke she regretted taking the bait. Not an original thought, but clearly one JJ could find a place for in her book.

She removed the emphasis from her role. "Did you take a date to the game?"

"No. I went alone."

"Who'd you sit with?"

"Nobody. Everybody. I was the new teacher, and yes, I was close to their ages, so that made me a magnet. People came and went all night long." He was puffed back up again.

"Name some," she said.

He rattled off last names without the first, and first names without the last, with Butch and Peter's names in the mix. Reuben's came up, though more in a passing hello than a sit-down conversation. She recalled him wandering, too, never in a seat, but some kids did that, especially on cold nights.

"Can you recall which quarter you saw Reuben go by?"

Tony shook his head. "Second half, is all I can remember. He was tall and paused in my line of sight of the field."

Callie asked Tony to elaborate further on what he could recall, trying to show no particular interest in one party or another. In other words, she let him tell his story his way.

"You claim to be more popular than I remembered," she said. "Everybody wanted attention from the new teacher, huh?"

Insult over his head, he grinned wide. "They even warned us in one of my senior classes about young male teachers in a high school crowd. Couldn't hardly watch the ballgame for the chatterboxes, boys and girls. Some wanted a date, like that was happening. Others begged for grades. A few asked for recommendations for colleges, thinking I'd be easy." He let loose a chortle. "Some asked me how I liked their clothes, their hair. One wanted me to buy his car."

"What about Butch?" she asked.

"What about him?"

"He ask you for anything?"

The brief laugh didn't roll out quite so jolly. "Rubbers," he said, laced with disbelief. "Said he forgot his."

Rubbers, as in more than one. Definitely fit Butch's reputation, but his self-professed sexual aptitude had proven a liability on that particular night. No wonder he made Chief Warren's short list of candidates. "Well?" she asked.

"Well, what?"

"Did you supply him?"

She made it sound like drugs. His eyes widened. "Hell, no. Seated there in front of hundreds of people, I'm supposed to reach into my pocket and equip that hormone-saturated brat so he can go for his personal best? Who do you think I am?"

He pushed palms against her desk like he'd reached his limit. As though he thought he was seriously going to walk out of a police interview because of bruised feelings.

She doubted he had the guts; though legally, he could because he was a witness, not a suspect. Mr. Principal had become quite the temperamental chap. "Sit down, Tony. Are you that sensitive?"

He sat, though the glower remained. "Just hate the insinuation that I carry rubbers in my pocket in case I get lucky."

She rolled on. "When did you see Butch?"

"Hunh!" he said. "Which time? Here and there, seated then gone. I swear he tailed at least five girls past me. The last time I saw him was in the third quarter. By then the game was hot, and I watched it intently with Peter who rode it out next to me." Again with the quick chuckle. "Butch rode it out in the backseat of his car, I imagine."

Just like she remembered, Butch never sitting still, more interested in collecting notches. Yet watching him at Georgia's, barely leaving his chair on the west end of the porch so the afternoon sun stayed out of his eyes, one would never match him with his teenage self. Eyes weighted half shut from dark liquor, behind five-hundred-dollar sunglasses and not nearly the stud he professed to be. Not that his quasi-fame reporting local sports didn't snare him enough groupies to satisfy his yearnings, she bet.

"Did Butch or Peter talk about post-game plans?" she asked.

"Don't remember."

"Did you ever suspect either of them killing Wendy?"

"Stop that!" he yelled, fisted hands pounding once on his knees. "Lobbing me easy questions to set me up for a hard one."

Look at this! "Settle down, Tony. I don't tell you how to do your job. Just respond."

Those fists did a drum beat a few times, while he blew out deep and hard. "This . . . finding ways to make me mad. It's got to stop."

"Or what, Tony?" She cross-armed herself on the desk. "Do you suspect either of those boys as Wendy's killer?" she finally said.

"Peter? No. Butch? Your guess is as good as mine. He was always on the fly. No depth, just shenanigans, and then he graduated and was gone."

Honest enough.

Once his hands unfisted, she downshifted to his comfort zone. "So, you're seeing Libby. Did you date her in high school?"

He scratched his head, some weariness in his movement. "No," and he dragged out the word. "I never dated a student."

"Did you talk to Libby that night?" she said.

He shook his head.

"For the recorder, please."

"Hardly knew who she was other than Peter's girl. I'm sure she was there if he was."

"You never saw her or spoke to her."

"No."

"So what did she whisper in your ear in my lobby?"

Which interrupted the string of easy questions again. His eyes narrowed. "She said to say she sat with her sister that night."

That sounded more truthful. "Did she?"

"I have no idea."

Miss Libby might need another chat. "Did you have Wendy in any of your classes?"

"I taught freshmen and sophomores," he replied. "So, no."

"Did Middleton PD interview you?"

"Of course. Just long enough to tick my name off their list."

"They ask you which kids you spoke to or suspected?"

He opened his water and took a long drink before answering. "No. Just asked me where I was and if I knew Wendy."

He took another swig. Wetting a dry mouth, a slight giveaway as to his nerves, but he overall sounded confident, mainly because Callie was again tossing him easy questions she already knew the answers to. "Did you see Wendy cheering?"

A scoff from him. "Who didn't?"

"Did you *like* watching Wendy cheering?"

"Of course, who did . . . n't?" And he caught himself.

Callie had halfway sucker punched him again. He contained himself this time, but subconsciously leaned forward in his urgency for that next question to take them away from this one. He'd turned an innocent question into something more foul.

"Ever imagine yourself with her?" she asked.

"Of course not," he yelled, but when Callie didn't flinch, he self-corrected by adjusting his shirt.

"You realize she was pregnant?"

"Not until she was the height of school gossip after. But let me set this record straight," he said, tilting forward to speak into the recorder, as if a closer proximity made him sound more honest. "I went as a teacher. I talked to students. I watched us barely win, anxious like the entire stadium. My conversations with students consisted of grades, sports, what was on the next test, and random discussions about soccer, baseball, and even one about tennis. Lots of jokes about wimps. Study hall talk." His respiration was up.

"You sure you never sat with Butch?"

He thought, his eyes straying up and right, which happened to also be toward the door. An indication of falsehood or need to escape. A recorder wouldn't capture that, but even on video, the behavior wouldn't serve as a precise measure of truth.

"No, I never sat with Butch."

"And you can vouch for Peter Yeo during the entire fourth quarter?"

"Yes," he replied.

A knock came at the door. "Come in," she called, knowing exactly who it was.

Thomas poked his head in. "We're out here waiting in the lobby."

"Thanks," she said. "We'll be done in a sec."

Thomas closed the door, and Callie turned back to Tony. "Anything else you want to add?"

"I shouldn't even be here," he said.

"Yet you are."

"Just because I run the venue where the reunion will be arranged."

She looked down her nose. "JJ had plans for you in her book from what she said. Controversy doesn't look good on principals. Any chance you had words with her before or after you came to the beach?"

"No." Commanding.

"Then I guess you have no concerns about JJ."

"I don't give a flying f—fig about the woman."

"Oh?" Callie said. "Even if her body floated up on the beach, you wouldn't care?"

He slid back like the distance protected him. "Honestly, I don't give a damn."

Callie reached for the recorder then waited to end the interview.

"We done?" he asked, already rising.

"Yep," she said. "This time. Need to give Butch his chance."

He eased back down. "This time? And chance for what?"

"To tell the truth. Not everybody does. Even when it would behoove them to spill the honest truth, people think too hard about what to say instead of just answering the questions. You've had your chance."

Callie could almost smell his brain churning about what he might've said wrong.

"I told the truth," he said.

"Didn't say you didn't."

"But you didn't say I did."

"I gather evidence at this stage, Mr. Tyler. The truth comes out down the road."

She gave her formal sign off on the recorder, rose, and went to the door, motioning for him to do the same. "Bring Butch on back, Officer Gage." Then she held the door open for Tony. "The officer will take you back to the beach house. I hope you enjoy that sea bass."

But Tony seemed uncertain whether it prudent to leave, gazing at the hallway then back to Callie. That is, until Thomas reached them with Butch.

"Come on in," she said.

Which made Tony reluctantly leave.

Chapter 19

BUTCH WOULD BE her last interview for the night. Legs crossed, he studied the office.

In Boston, Callie's interview record was eight in fifteen hours, in an inner-city neighborhood where everybody lived within three floors of each other. She'd started at eight in the morning and wrapped up at eleven at night, but being with a larger department meant some administrative person ensured she had coffee and something to eat, and uniforms watched over the interviewee while she hit the head.

On Edisto Beach she did the interviews in her personal office with a handheld recorder, and if she forgot to eat, she scrambled for bottled water and granola bars. This time Thomas played taxi service getting her interviewees to her as requested. Officer Gage might be over a decade younger than Callie, and inexperienced compared to officers his age in a city like Boston, but he had a deep well of common sense and desire to excel. She'd take him over many of the Bean Town uniforms she'd worked alongside in her past.

Her first text to Thomas, while Libby gave her interview, directed a time frame to bring Tony, then Butch. She almost dared to squeeze in another, but the estimated two hours per interview would take her past midnight. She could do it . . . they couldn't.

This day, though long, had instilled this slow burning, on and off feeling of concern about JJ. She'd stirred up crap and vanished. Seriously, something about this situation felt incredibly odd.

These people had been around each other the whole time, though, moving like a damn school of shad. Drink together, eat together, whine together. The only person who'd gone solo had been Georgia, as far as Callie could decipher, and that had been to visit Sophie, Callie's next-door neighbor.

Unless they slid out at night.

Who the hell could the offender be? Assuming one of them was the offender.

She held up her phone. "Had to mute this thing for a while, and I need to flip through it real quick. Give me a second."

"Fine," Butch said, and scanned the area before getting up to check out the two certificates on her wall.

She opened up Twitter first. Butch in the restaurant. Earlier on the porch. An awkward picture of his arm draped around JJ the first night, because he had to post about being a fellow alum with a famous author. A link back to the article he did five years earlier on her. Callie quickly glanced at Facebook, which he occasionally used for little more than promotion for his next high school sport appearance on behalf of the station. Instagram used the same pics on Twitter, and Pinterest was little more than repeats of Instagram. Truthfully, she bet someone at the station did much of that for him.

On the surface, Butch didn't appear to hold many secrets, but she wasn't banking on that being the end-all and be-all of Brandon "Butch" Ives.

She put away the phone. "Ready?"

Butch flopped into the chair before her. "What, no bright light over my head?"

"Saving on the energy bill," she said. As before, she arranged the recorder, but offered no frivolous banter to soften him up. Libby and Tony needed introductory prep. Butch, however, would suffer whatever happened on the fly. All a prologue would do was prime him for one-liners.

"Let's talk timeline, Butch."

"Whatever you say, Columbo. No, wait, how about Rizzoli? Ha, you used to work in Boston, too, right?"

Like that.

Yeah, this process would differ from the other two. This guy covered his flaws with humor and, when that didn't work, insults. He was her most logical suspect for Wendy's death on the surface, making him the same for JJ's disappearance since the first would make him much more likely to arrange the second.

But was he that smart?

"Okay," he said, re-sorting himself in his seat to show his readiness. "Timeline for what? My career? My love life?"

She allowed him her grin. "Let's start with your arrival here at the beach."

"Hah, easy," he said, cocking his grin up on one side. The man had an assortment of grins. Probably practiced in a mirror. "You were there," he said, "when Reuben hit my car coming in."

She remained unaffected. "How can I trust that's when you arrived on Edisto Beach?"

The test made him study her, wondering why the trick. "Guess you'll have to take my word for it."

"Hold onto that thought. Before you got here, however, when was the last time you saw JJ?"

"JJ," and he jeered a bit. "She'd have fared better sticking with her real name. Jessie Jane has a better ring to it, don't you think? Especially for a minority. How many races do you really think she is, anyway?"

"Says the guy named Brandon," she asked, using his real name and ignoring the racial remark.

He gave her a pistol shot with his fingers. "Touché, Chief. But to answer your questions, I interviewed JJ for the station when she came to Middleton to talk to the high school," he said. "Libby's class. She actually called me, asking if I needed a scoop. Hard to believe, huh?"

That was apparently the story Callie saw linked on social media. She didn't recall the story, but she would've still been in Boston. Five years ago . . . about the time she was suffering through her daughter's crib death. About the time her marriage started to unravel.

She forged back to the present. "Thought you only did sports, Butch. All the men think you're a walking encyclopedic cornucopia of athletics."

"I didn't get to this pinnacle overnight." He overestimated rearing back in his chair, the front legs coming up slightly off the floor from the sound of him dropping them back in place. He pretended nothing happened, pasting that grin back.

Butch alone wasn't quite the Butch with others. His brio seemed a bit off while he sought to find purchase for his humor and appreciation for his wit with such a small crowd.

Callie tapped her pen on her tablet. "Back to the beach house. JJ left Georgia's around when?"

"Eleven, I guess."

"Tony and Libby went to bed together about when?"

His brow popped up. "Nope. She went after JJ left, then he followed later. We guys talked for another hour, maybe longer. Reuben went to bed the same time as Tony. I slept on the chaise since it was so clement." He waited for her to not understand the word.

"Balmy," she replied. "And passed out was probably more like it than sleep. You'd tossed back a few before I even left."

"Says the woman who abstains. I recognize the urge. Kudos on riding that wagon. I prefer to drive."

Again, she didn't acknowledge the wit. But she acknowledged he could have slipped off the porch in the middle of the night and gone after JJ, with nobody being the wiser.

"Can anybody vouch for you the whole night?"

He twisted his mouth to the right in a comedic way. "Meaning, did anyone else sleep outside? Nope."

"Who woke you up?"

"Sun woke me, which meant I was up before the rest. But I barely made it to the refrigerator before Georgia showed to waitress us with breakfast."

No alibi for Friday night.

But same could be said for the others.

"Before she left, did you have any sort of altercation with JJ?" she asked.

"We sparred some."

"Alone? With witnesses?"

He did a coy, flirty thing with one eye. The man had a million expressions, his facial muscles elastic from practice. "Everybody there was a witness," he said.

She nodded. "I saw you picking at her at the bar, but she appeared to be holding her own. You aren't used to a woman jousting with you."

He gave her a *whatever* look.

"What did she say?"

"That I was her favorite for killing Wendy."

"Did she?" Callie sat up straighter. She hadn't seen that coming, but she gave him her reaction to make her appear an easy mark. "She explain why?"

"Textbook logic, she said. Scorned lover, which I wasn't." He lowered his voice an octave in an aside. "I had Wendy, then I had a dozen more after her. She wasn't anything special, and lesson learned, I moved on."

More like once conquered. Wendy was loose, making her an easy box to tick off his list in his hormonal quest for manhood.

"Names?" she asked.

He chuckled hungrily at the memory. "Like I want to tell you. There is no statute of limitation on statutory rape in this state." He pointed at her. "Not that anything wasn't consensual."

What the know-it-all didn't know was that sixteen, seventeen, and eighteen weren't statutory rape. Juniors and seniors experimenting with sex wasn't exactly a crime. In South Carolina, a girl had to be younger than sixteen for there to be a concern.

And Butch was proving a rather simple interviewee. Could be her personal experience gave her unique insight, but it likewise ran the risk of clouding her judgment. She had to be keenly aware of that risk, but she read Butch as too pompous to pull off too deep a deception.

"Nobody likes the book idea," he said, on his own. "I expect it to consist of lies and unproven ancient history, because nobody's going to cooperate with her. She better watch out for a libel suit."

"One would think you'd love the notoriety, Butch."

"Though I was eighteen at the time, people would only see this." He swept his hand up to down in front of himself. "I cannot afford to tarnish *this*."

"People would read yesterday's overactive libido as today's pervert," she said.

He clicked his tongue and winked. "Bingo."

"You could jeopardize your job at the station," she added.

"Or worse, any station," he countered.

"Which sort of indicates motive to get rid of JJ."

His smile shined less bright, though he painfully fought to keep it intact, unaware his fingernail tapped the chair at his side. "My movements have been in front of that beach crowd ever since I arrived."

"Like sleeping alone on the porch?"

The smile melted. "Callie, I seriously knew nothing about the damn book until after I arrived. Check her phone. Check her email. Don't y'all automatically do all this forensics stuff when someone goes missing?"

"This isn't some Brit mystery, Butch. It's Edisto. See a lab when you came through? She disappeared *after* you got here and after she showed her hand at Georgia's bar. One or more of you may have felt trapped, afraid of JJ's clear potential for success with this story, which you and I have to admit could create a great made-for-television movie."

Butch absorbed Callie's scenario, Callie's analysis, and seemed unable to slip back into his smiling persona. "Besides," he said, needing to chat instead of think. "The guy who did it couldn't live with the crime and offed himself. This isn't even an open case."

An easy enough mistake. Years had passed so he presumed that meant the case was closed. "It might be a cold case, Butch, but it's not closed. I spent this morning talking to Chief Warren in Middleton. Stratton killing himself wasn't proof he killed Wendy. JJ spoke to Warren, too."

From his stare, he wrestled with that.

"Where was JJ staying on the beach?" she asked.

His brow showed more worry. "No idea. I was disappointed that she wasn't with us, to tell you the truth. Wanted to ask her more about the book, and what the hell she thought she had on me."

Callie believed that.

"The police chief said you were pretty high on his suspect list," she began. "Might've been number one if your parents hadn't intervened and Peter alibied you."

The shock came and went quickly. "I alibied him, too. They spoke to him as well."

With her best suspecting look, she let a few seconds trickle between them. "I understand there's a question about whether everything was true. Whether Stratton killed Wendy. Whether your alibi was valid. Whether your parents fought to convince Chief Warren to quit studying you in particular. Maybe went through my father as an added effort since you and Peter had scholarships to protect. But JJ stirred up more than information for a book," she said. "She might've even convinced them to reopen the case. Think about it. If a famous author casts dispersions on an old case, still open, mind you, why wouldn't the police chief want to get in front of the potential blowback? Maybe use whatever she uncovers?"

In spite of his tan, Butch paled.

"Like you said, Butch, people confuse the past and the present."

She checked the recorder, as much for herself as to rattle Butch, and set it carefully back. At the same time she reached down and pulled out another bottle of water and set it before him, his stare taking in each of her moves as expected.

Why check the recorder, he'd wonder, unless she was preparing to say something that would prompt something he wouldn't want to say? Why put out the water unless she expected him to have a dry mouth from fear? Then he'd check his mouth, realizing he wanted the water badly, but didn't want to take it for fear of what that would reveal to her.

"That was too long ago," he said, clearing his throat when his words fell out meek. "No witnesses." Then he took an awkward breath. "This is nothing more than protecting your boyfriend," he said, then appeared to recognize how empty that accusation was.

"Nobody saw Stratton do anything either," she said, "but the town crucified him. Maybe JJ has a problem with a miscarriage of justice. A dead sweet girl and an innocent boy who killed himself from the pressure, leaving the killer to roam free. If JJ busts this mystery, you have to admit it would make for a great book."

Butch grabbed the water bottle, trying to open it with one hand, then switching to the other.

"Her inciting the lot of you was probably not her brightest move," Callie said. "It might have gotten her in trouble, and of course, those with the most to lose are the ones highest on her list to goad and draw out."

Like the cartoon figure he often appeared to be, his expression read concern. In a big way.

"You weren't with Peter that night," she said.

This was the time someone with half a brain would step up and ask for an attorney, but she bet Butch still thought of the case as too ancient to be relevant. What were the odds someone remembered as Jessie Jane, the high school yearbook editor who never wore makeup, had enough intelligence to unravel a cold case that an entire police force couldn't?

"Yes, I was," he countered.

"No, you weren't," she quickly replied. "I see your sweat and respiration. I can almost hear your heartbeat." She stared at his chest, and he snapped a glance down to see if his shirt moved and gave himself away.

"Sure you don't have something to get off your chest?" she asked.

He leapt up, one fist clenching the bottle, the plastic crunching. "Shut up, Callie. Or else—"

Callie stood. "Put yourself back down in that chair or you go to lockup, unless you want to try and take me, in which case you can go to the hospital."

The door cracked open. "Everything okay in here, Chief?" Thomas asked, though his stare lasered on Butch. "Need the ambulance yet?"

A bit overdone by Thomas, but the sportscaster sat back down.

Having done his job, Thomas backed out. "Call if you need me."

Callie let the door close, then pushed the obvious question. "Did you kill Wendy, Butch? You're covering something."

He quickly replaced his tell-tale humor with a steely push of fortitude. "Maybe I'm afraid something will get pinned on me like they tried to do before. They went after Stratton with little more than they had on me. And if they start looking at me about Wendy, they'll look at me about JJ. You even said that."

"If you did it, you need to own up, Butch. If you didn't, we need to catch who did."

"Since it's not me, go do your damn job and find who did."

"Finding Wendy's killer is not my job, Butch."

"But you . . . you said . . . you asked me . . .," he stammered, before Callie's words registered with him. "So what the hell are we doing here?"

"Trying to find JJ."

He left his seat, pacing to behind the chair, leaning on the back, his complexion tinged with red. "Am I under arrest?" he demanded.

Calmly she shook her head. "No, not at all, Butch."

"Then I'm leaving," he said, teeth so clenched she thought she heard the grind. "We don't speak again without me having my attorney."

There it was. The sign of a scared man. "You're not under arrest," she repeated, reaching for the recorder. "But stay on this side of Scott's Creek or I'll issue a bench warrant."

Butch stood stiff, eager to rebel at the order, but after a few seconds of indecision he slung open the door before Callie could stand. Thomas, however, waited a couple of steps down the hall. "Your chariot awaits, sir."

"I'll walk, Deputy Fife." Butch tried to yank the outer glass door open to leave, only to find it locked. "Do you mind?" he yelled.

Being past midnight, Thomas wouldn't leave until Callie did, holding Butch hostage at the exit until she turned off the lights and locked up. Then Thomas drove up Murray Street toward Palmetto and Georgia's place. He'd stick close to Butch until he found his way back. Callie cranked up and turned east up Myrtle to reach Jungle Road, toward her place.

Butch hadn't helped himself in that two-hour display. Said he'd been with Peter at the game, which wasn't entirely true. Not for the second half anyway . . . per two witnesses. Chief Warren's men had blown off Tony being a witness of substance and hadn't queried him very well, which hadn't exposed an issue with the alibi. In her interview with those same deputies, Libby had probably validated the Butch-Peter double alibi due to her relationship with them. Then she'd totally forgotten that in talking with Callie.

A fairly substantial clash in stories. That was the problem when a suspect locked down on a false alibi. They eliminate any possibility for a legitimate excuse, and suddenly they've lied to law enforcement. Such fabrication had put many an innocent party in jail by mistake, or like with the feds, got them locked up for the simple fact they lied. Ask Martha Stewart.

Tony would've blown Butch's cover if interviewed properly, and maybe Butch would've been scrutinized under that *bright light*, like he mentioned, instead of Stratton. Both would be alive today, because God knows she couldn't see Butch having the balls to off himself.

He'd been so predictable. He'd be even more predictable when she interviewed him again.

In her experience when the innocent lied, they did for two reasons. First, to conceal a moral wrong. An affair, for instance. Second, to hide another crime. In this case, however, this group of individuals from Middleton High School saw how the cops had hammered Stratton into suicide. They'd put all that behind them and would not want to support its resurrection.

Resistance to revisiting the trauma was part of why cold cases were so difficult to solve.

But in the midst of all that predictability and performance, an earlier thought came back to ride on her shoulder. A possibility that had to be considered.

What if JJ simply had issues that led to erratic behavior? Drugs or alcohol abuse. Something that her agent would hide for the sake of sales and royalties.

Callie started to call the literary agent again, but noticed the time. She dialed anyway. Instantly to voicemail, his phone was turned off for the night. Definitely on her to-do list for the morning.

Her day was done. A half mile from home, something nagged at her subconscious before it registered front and center, and instinctively she slowed. Eight houses from her own, she stopped.

On a dark street where everybody slept, *Chelsea Morning's* motion sensors had lit up the property like a carnival.

Chapter 20

NOBODY HAD A more secure house on Edisto Beach than the chief of police, and only then because she'd tired of criminals breaking in to prove they could. Said culprits being two. One dead and one in jail. After installing an assortment of devices, putting her back in charge, she developed a habit of watching camera footage in the evenings as entertainment. There was something intensely powerful about being aware of who set foot on her lot and porches in her absence and while she slept.

Her neighbor Sophie called her paranoid. Callie didn't care what you called it.

However, nobody should be at *Chelsea Morning* at twelve forty a.m. unless he lived there, yet her motion sensor lights shined insanely bright in contrast to the darkness of the surrounding properties. She slowly drove in, praying to catch sight of her son's Jeep, needing to accuse someone familiar. Maybe Jeb came home early to visit his dear old mother.

She pulled closer. A plain sedan, silver, parked in her oyster shell drive, off to the side as if as a courtesy to give Callie space.

A rental, if she guessed right. Had Mark put his car in the shop in Charleston? Or possibly her old boss Stan? They were the only souls with the audacity to visit this time of night, but both of them would have texted.

Which made her wonder if one of them might be delivering some sort of notice.

Jesus . . . Jeb.

She mashed the gas to pull in quicker, her cruiser tight behind her Ford SUV. She got out, instinctively eased the door silently closed, as was her way, but in the hushed darkness of the island, however, the click made itself known.

She approached the two levels of stairs required by homes in hurricane paths, knowing full well that walking up twenty-four steps— even avoiding the swollen risers that popped—she was exposed to whoever hovered above, or below, or in the copse of trees on the side of her lot. Wide open, especially under lights she'd designed to expose someone like her approaching. She reached for her weapon, released the snap, and rested her hand assuredly on the grip.

A man in his forties, a solid six-foot plus, stepped from the end of the porch. He moved with reservation, coming out of that shadow and into her automated porch light just as she reached the landing. His blondish-red hair swept across one brow and up over his ears in short waves, his wisp of a mustache matched, and to Callie he seemed an Irish stereotype. Legs and arms long, lean, and accustomed to the gym for toning, not bulk. Maybe a runner.

Stepping onto the porch, standing askance, fingers wrapped tight on the grip, she held out her other hand. "Don't come closer. Show me some identification, please."

As most do when approached by someone with the power to shoot you dead, he displayed his own hands, fingers splayed. "I mean no harm," he said, a keen worry in the accent. "It's Peter, Callie. Peter Yeo. May I reach in my back pocket? Please?"

She nodded for him to do so. "Open it and set it on the chair right there, then back up to the end of the porch."

He did as told, and as he moved backward, she stepped in, blindly reaching down for the ID, glare still frozen on him. She lifted it up so she could watch both man and ID. A blue passport, but when she flipped it, the name popped right out of a yearbook. "Good Lord, it is you, Peter."

"Yep," he said, the hitch in his shoulders smoothing down. "Wow, look at you, Callie. All badass and armed."

"Not cool you coming unannounced to my house in the middle of the night." Libby's ex. Butch's ex-best friend. All the way from London, with no announcement. "How are you?" she asked, imminently suspicious. Nobody mentioned he was coming.

How long had he been on her beach? And what was with the secrecy?

"Good, good," he replied. "You?"

"Okay. A lot of water under the bridge, but in a good place these days. What's the time difference," she said. "Six hours?"

He blew out a long, exhausting breath. "Five. Listen, I'm somewhat knackered after that long haul with the flight, renting a car, and driving out here. *Way* out here, by the way."

That brogue came back so familiar, only a couple tones deeper. That drive was an hour for someone familiar with driving through jungle and across marsh, so she understood the exhaustion. Chit-chat could wait. She wasn't sure he cared to catch up on much anyway since they hadn't been buds back in the day. She, however, had questions about why he came, and the nature of his communication with JJ or Georgia.

Either or both women sure kept this secret.

"Tried calling Jessie Jane, but she isn't answering," he said. "I asked a guy at the Mexican eatery if he knew where you lived, explaining we were high school friends, and here I am. Figured since I knew the top copper, I needed to inform her I was here, not have her accidentally find me." He clicked his tongue then winked. She wasn't sure she remembered him doing that, but the click sounded familiar.

"The lights were a bit of a fright," he continued, peering up to the eaves. "They went out when I sat in one of your chairs. Then I thought it not too brilliant to wait for you in the dark, so I kept pacing, keeping them on. Better to avoid a kerfuffle, I reasoned. You work rather late hours, don't you?"

While she was a common island presence, Callie was disappointed at an El Marko person telling a stranger where she lived, especially this late. She didn't take the time to ask Peter which *man* directed him here, but she'd damn sure query Mark tomorrow.

"And you make drop ins a little late as well, Peter. Jessie Jane goes by JJ, by the way. She called you to come this weekend?"

Callie didn't invite him inside. He was once an acquaintance, never really a friend, and with too many years between then and the present, she chose to err on the side of caution.

She motioned to the set of rattan rockers, a matching table between, and put the potted fern on the floor to clear her view of him. She'd just taken them out of their winter cover the week before, and they seemed to have enjoyed their days on the porch. While bent over, she extracted a notepad and pen from her purse. This wasn't the first time she'd regretted not having on the uniform where anything she needed waited in a habitual, easy-to-grasp spot. She sat back up and opened the pad. "Writing helps me remember."

"What's to remember?" he asked.

"Anything said I could forget." With a soft snort, she positioned her pad and studied him. "You have no idea what's going on, do you?"

Shaking his head, he then added a shrug for emphasis.

Callie preferred to collect information before passing it out, and she needed a couple of quick questions answered before she could let this go until tomorrow. "If you're clueless, how did JJ get you all this way?"

A bobble of his brow, like he understood. "She said she had something to discuss, but wanted to *read my eyes*. Like that doesn't sound dodgy. At first I told her she was full of rubbish." He sat sideways in the chair yet remained true to remarkable posture, but most of all he seemed to want to talk.

"Yet here you are," she said. "Probably paid a thousand, if not two, for that last-minute, cross-Atlantic ticket, so she must not be too full of rubbish. What'd she entice you with?"

He leaned elbows on those long knees, hunched and staring down.

"Or did she extort you?" she added at the delay.

He gave her a nod at that one. "There you go, mate."

"But she knew you were coming, right?"

"Right."

Callie peeked at her phone. Almost one o'clock.

She was extremely puzzled about how JJ handled getting Peter to the beach versus the others. Having the other prime suspect on Chief Warren's list could serve her purpose, and while she preferred her interviewees off-balance, even tired, Callie on the other hand preferred to be fresh. One didn't interview a cooperating witness on the fly. She needed thoughts and notes.

But she didn't need him talking to Libby, Tony, or Butch beforehand.

A creak. Peter shifted in his chair. "Not to be rude, but I'd be waking up in London about now, not hunting a bed."

Should she offer? "I have an extra bedroom." She wasn't especially fond of having him here, but he'd avoid the others. She doubted she'd sleep a wink, though. "Then we can pick this up tomorrow. You don't want to wake the others. They're at Georgia's beach house. I can show you where tomorrow."

He reared back. "Oh bollocks, no. Libby? Butch? Don't even need to know who else. I came to fulfill my promise to JJ then leave." He shook his head. "While your offer is most appreciated, I'm booked in a condo at some place called Wyndham?"

That was a relief.

Though somewhat wrinkled, Peter arrived remarkably attractive. Not the first time she wondered what caused his divorce from Libby. He sure beat Tony when it came to looks.

Had Libby been too tacky for Peter, had they simply outgrown each other? Or did they remind each other of too many high school secrets? Secrets that sent Peter back to dear old England once divorced. He yawned, making her want to do the same. "When can you meet tomorrow?" she asked.

"I really need to see JJ first," he said. "I should do what I came for then leave. Obligations back home, you understand. After her, why don't I ring you? She's at Georgia's, I assume."

Whatever leverage JJ had used against him had drawn him across an entire ocean, and to remove it so easily could send him right back, so no need to enlighten him about JJ's whereabouts, or lack thereof. "She's staying elsewhere," she said. "If she gets her grips into you first thing, I might not get you for hours. Tell you what, here's one of my cards. Call me if you don't hear from me by, say, nine, but promise you'll see me first. Call me *anytime* if you hear from her."

A short breeze lifted the fronds of the corner Palmetto tree, bringing a whiff of the marsh. Callie heard steps on the bottom flight well before Peter turned his head. Callie stood, which made Peter do the same.

The footfalls hinted at a gate slightly off. Peter tensed, but Callie relaxed as the intruder reached the halfway mark.

"Everything all right up there?" he asked.

Peter frowned, looking to Callie for direction.

No telling how long Mark Dupree had waited below. Callie suspected he parked behind her place on Jungle Shores Road, down a few houses, because she hadn't heard the car. The silt road enabled him to clandestinely approach and time his appearance.

"How long have you been down there?" she said, walking to meet the man with a paper bag in his hand like before.

But his attention remained on Peter. "Since my guy Wesley gave this *bloke* directions. I made the kid close up the restaurant for talking too much, so I could make sure of this guy's intentions."

"Just leaving, mate." Peter turned to Callie. "Right?"

"Sure. Get some rest, Peter."

The two men passed each other, Mark watching until Peter reached his vehicle, not waving when Peter did.

"I was fine," she said, "but I really appreciate the concern. He wasn't getting in, and he wasn't besting me." She'd never tell him that Peter declined the guest invitation.

Mark turned back from watching the vehicle leave. "He had a foot and eighty pounds on you, and for all I knew, you were in bed. Wesley will *not* be making that mistake again, trust me." His facial muscles softened. "You haven't eaten, have you? I'm learning that's what you do. Forget meals."

She retrieved her house key and opened up, disarming her security. "Is this how it's going to be? You bringing me dinner each night as an excuse to be invited in?"

"It worked well enough before."

"Huh." She grinned and walked in, throwing her keys in their bowl on the kitchen bar. "Then I don't have to tell you what to do or show you where everything is." Without stopping, she went to toss her purse on the bed . . . this time grateful she didn't have to unload all the gear of a uniform.

Quesadillas heated in the microwave, along with some Spanish rice, the aroma churning her stomach and making her happy she hadn't wasted calories on a granola bar. It took longer to heat the meal than it took her to eat it.

"It's late," he said, taking her plate.

"It is," she replied, loosely taking his hand once he returned to her side.

He squeezed her fingers. "You need your sleep."

She grinned. "Fella, you gotta quit bringing me food."

"Somebody has to look after you."

Brow provocative, she gripped his hand harder and took a step, pulling him away from the kitchen. "I've taken care of myself pretty well up to now."

Tucking her against him, he took her the rest of the way to the bedroom. "Then let's just say I'm here to give you some relief, Chief. Or backup. Whatever you want to call it."

But she halted at the doorway. "Can you talk clearheaded if we cross this threshold, or do we need to take this to the porch?"

The poor man's puzzlement took him aback. "Pardon?"

Sympathetically, she laid a hand on his chest. "I love it that you're here, but I'm tired. Since I have to hit the ground running tomorrow, and my energy can only last so long, I humbly request your feedback as a seasoned LEO with experience in investigations. Not exactly your mission tonight, but I could use your unjaundiced, yet cute, eye."

Which got a snort out of him. He bopped her on the nose with a finger. "The bedroom still works. Besides, saves time from having to relocate later."

Motioning for him to take the floral chintz chair in the corner, then sitting cross-legged on the bed, Callie rehashed the three interviews of the day, and the fraction of the one with Peter. Then she covered the details of JJ's rental and the literary agent's benign response. "I believe we need a search, Mark," she said. "Trouble is where to start? Is JJ mentally unbalanced or did someone take her? Did she go out for a stroll and have an accident, or catch a cab and set up a ploy for a book? What's worse is that I'm one of the people she sucked into this mess, which to an unjaundiced eye—"

"Regardless how cute," he added.

She grinned. "To that unbiased person, I could be deemed a suspect."

"Loosely," he said.

"I say more than loosely," she corrected. "I found Wendy's body. Some kids thought I might have done it."

"They were kids, and forensics negated that, I assume."

She nodded. "They did, but JJ writes fiction. She can take reality and turn it on its head, blaming my father and his control over town politics in handling the *forensics*. But what I have to be careful with here is that I don't let my opinions about her book, and her tasteless setup of these people, interfere with how I proceed. Jesus, Mark, I feel like she's watching with hidden cameras, studying how we are reacting, what we're saying, taking it all in as salacious material. Even if Wendy's murder investigation was complete and all was done that could be done, this subsequent . . ." She struggled for words. "This second story of the author's disappearance makes for a marketable—"

"Fairytale," Mark finished.

Wilting, she slowly shook her head. "Her book isn't just a silly thought, Mark. You haven't been on Edisto long enough to understand the ramifications."

He sat forward, his look consoling. "Imagine the rise in tourism. Doesn't that matter?"

"Or me losing my job."

Georgia was rich, not needing to work, and Reuben lived off of a patent, but Libby, Tony, or Butch could lose their jobs as well. "My mayor mother would save Chief Warren's job, unless he retired due to the publicity. But I don't need to be the famous lady chief who might have killed someone in high school. Been there in that spotlight . . . with . . . Seabrook."

Damn, why was it still so difficult to say his name?

For months people cruised past her house, hoping to glimpse the lady who shot a cold case killer at the sacrifice of her youngest officer and best friend. Took a month to recuperate physically, two to regain her sanity. "Do you not see the potential of what this book could do?"

At the mention of Seabrook, the restauranteur sobered. He'd been on Edisto long enough to hear that part of its history, and the toll that period took on Callie and so many others. "Tell me, what can I do?"

"Help me start a search of the island tomorrow. It's fruitless and too dangerous at night, plus we need a plan. First thing, can you talk to your staff and see if they and their friends and relations can search their own roads, marshes and inlets? I'll call Deputy Raysor and put him to work on it as well. He travels Edisto's jungle like his own backyard. My officers and I will handle the beach."

Mark lifted a slight shrug, as if he expected more. "Be happy to. I'll help myself. Maybe Stan can as well."

"You and Stan haven't walked these woods and marshes, Mark. Don't need for this hunt to change from one victim to three."

His droll look drew a tired grin out of her. "We're both retired cops, ma'am. We can handle the basics of a search."

"Just saying let Raysor coordinate you. But what about El Marko's?"

He stood, stretched, and slipped off his shoes, kicking them beneath the chair. "Sophie and Wesley can run El Marko's. It's a Tuesday, the slowest day of the week. Stop with this. You look beat."

She was fading, for sure.

Mark came toward her, then pressed against her so that she laid back. Item by item they undressed each other, making ready for bed. Yes, she was tired, but she could allow herself this moment, almost preferring the pillow of his warm chest and shoulder to what he most assuredly had otherwise on his mind.

Chapter 21

JJ
Late Sunday.

JJ EXAMINED THE handwriting on the bookmark. *I'll be in touch.* Her own bookmark, which she'd about decided came from the laptop case left at Georgia's on Friday night. She'd thrown some in a pocket as part of the pretense. The case most likely in Callie's possession now.

But who planted the bookmark? Her first consideration was Peter Yeo, but he wasn't due in until tonight, and, when here, her assistant hadn't been out of JJ's sight, much less in the house.

Damn. But damn in a cool way. The scare of being watched, even her home violated, came and went like a thought, quickly replaced by a thrill which set her creativity afire.

No, sir, or maybe *no, ma'am,* whoever they were. She'd not expected this at all. Kudos to them for providing the latest plot twist.

She repeatedly flipped the bookmark over in her fingers, staring out the window at a live oak whose tendrils of Spanish moss could brush the glass with enough breeze, but she wasn't really seeing it. Instead she saw prospects, and she accepted this change of plan.

The most worried classmate, the one with the most to lose, had found her. And they wanted to play.

She walked fast toward the porch, grabbing a water bottle on the way, and resumed her position at the small worn table. She wedged the bookmark into the corner of the window frame to her left, the message facing her, and she started to type. She had to record this moment, the zing of surprise . . . the satisfaction of a story taking new direction.

The average soul would be worried at a possible killer warning they'd *be in touch.* JJ had seen herself as the only proactive one, channeling, maybe somewhat directing the others. She never expected the most guilty would sleuth on their own and be adept at it.

She had half expected the bones of this story to be better adapted for fiction, but not any longer. Truth was she hadn't given any of her classmates this much credit.

Opening her research file, she went down the list, her program having automatically alphabetized her characters, which placed Butch at the top. Overbearing in his attempt to make everyone believe he was in charge of his destiny, he had the most to hide, in her opinion. Any sort of algorithm would label him Wendy's killer, and she had to address those odds. An author had to provide an obvious suspect in order to satisfy the more naïve reader, and Butch possessed all the criteria to wear his new senior superlative title: *Most Likely to Kill a Cheerleader.*

Son of a bitch. She had a title.

With a clipped squeak of a laugh she renamed her main file, admired it a few seconds, then returned to her list of characters. Next came Callie.

Callie was tiny, though, and without assistance from a co-conspirator or use of some debilitating drug, she could not have pulled off Wendy's murder alone. But with Callie's connections, she could have used either and the evidence conveniently mislaid. She dated Wendy's ex-boyfriend, and look at how hard she fought to clear his name. The career in law enforcement suggested guilt and payback to avoid karma.

The urge to write fiction tugged at her with a fierce intensity though. All these what-ifs. All these angles and choices.

Every single member of this group carried guilt. JJ could write this book eight different ways and still have a bestseller. With true crime one attempted to remain factual. With fiction she had literary license to take the what-ifs and flesh them in any direction.

She was giddy with the potential, but she'd remain true to the original purpose for now. Quite unusual to have this many facts at her disposal, with one of the primary suspects being a detective, rebuilding this case brick by brick, hour by hour, day by day for her.

She nodded to nobody but herself. Police Chief Callie Jean Morgan was all but the author of this story. JJ might as well take advantage of her services while available.

A COUPLE HOURS later, primed at her laptop, JJ couldn't stop watching the bookmark wedged in the window, then returned to her keyboard, pleased. Moments like these didn't come often.

What a catalyst. That tiny piece of cardboard had convinced her to write this book in first person instead of third.

That bookmark had also made things personal.

She was both adversary, as painted in the beginning of the book when all the players were dangled in front of the reader as potentially guilty, and victim, threatened by someone perceived as the killer. The audience would wonder if she could have stopped Wendy's murder or reported about it better. Then in a beautiful about-face, she'd be the target of the person who snuffed Wendy's life or sought justice for her. Either would work.

Frankly, the more this person hated her, the more exciting the narrative.

Not identifying the *who* behind all this shot crazy, racing inspiration through her. She'd even giggled, deleting and retyping one phrase. Never had she experienced this level of thrill. Her fingers shook at times. She had that level of a buzz.

The bookmark could be from someone, guilty or not, shaken up at having their life exposed in a tell-all . . . maybe angry enough to stalk her, or worse, shut down the voice telling the story. A principal, a teacher, a real estate broker, a television journalist, a patent genius, a police chief, and herself. Sounded like a children's nursery rhyme. She could not have created a more perfect diversity of characters. But there was even one more.

Peter Yeo took some convincing, but he flew in tonight. Or so she hoped. Those were his plans. Using her journalism past, JJ asked kindly, pleaded earnestly, then ultimately blackmailed the hell out of him to get his butt back to the States. She didn't care what he did for a living or how this case would impact it. If he ignored her, she'd rip that career of his apart at the seams simply through his connection to Butch. He'd lied about alibiing Butch, which of course meant Butch lied about alibiing Peter. Butch would lie about his own birthdate just because he could. He'd viewed himself as a Machiavellian exploiter in years past, so no telling the level of his manipulations now.

Any one of them could have done it or allowed it to happen or enabled the killer to get away. She'd been at that ballgame. She'd sat in a different place each quarter, like a lot of the kids, only while they did so to socialize, she sought stories for the two school publications from human interest to gossip pieces infused with enough fact to be credible.

Tying the jocks to their sexual tallies was how she got Butch to Edisto. He supposedly had kept a book, and coaches purportedly looked the other way. *Boys will be boys.*

She hinted at a secret system of some sort to Tony as well. A principal wouldn't want that smear against his school, regardless how long ago it happened. Assuming it wasn't a system that continued, albeit more sophisticated with technology.

They came, which said everything.

That sort of thing wasn't allowed in a yearbook, and the copy police, aka advisor, would've banned such mention. Reporting about the secret jock trysts would've brought in the police. Parents might have sued. Something in JJ's teenaged rationality told her to hold that ace to be played at a more opportune moment that didn't backfire on her own future. Kudos to the child version of herself for thinking so far ahead.

Going back to her characters, she looked at the thinnest file, Georgia. The head cheerleader who covered for her pregnant friend, allowing Wendy to miss the entire fourth quarter for feeling poorly. An entire quarter. Or had she set up the girl, telling any one of the others that Wendy would be in the vicinity of the restrooms, the shortcut route taking people behind the bleachers.

Nobody hated Georgia, but she ruled the cheer squad with a firm grip, and no doubt she disliked the shadow that a knocked-up cheerleader would cast on the entire squad. While popular, Wendy's social graces fell short, and Georgia had a reputation to protect. For the school, for the cheer team, and for herself.

The thought of the head cheerleader offing an errant team member bordered on the extreme, but teenagers overreacted when it came to impact on their future. The more industrious students felt their lives would be ruined by the slightest smear, making secrets pretty standard in their world.

Libby, for instance. She worried about her image as much or more than anyone. Had to date the British boy. Had to claim best friend status with Wendy. Had to befriend Butch while hating him to her core. Begrudging anyone who showed her up or passed her by, she wanted to be all things in all realms. Except maybe the beauty queen arena, but even then, she had to be a friend to whoever took the crown.

If she wasn't satisfied with her place in the grand scheme of classmates, grades mysteriously changed, weed was found in bookbags, and parents were notified of wayward behavior, true or not. Students earned detention for questionable reasons, earned zeros from misplaced term papers, and lost after-school jobs. Clothes disappeared from gym. Sugar found a way into gas tanks.

Libby was a bad girl who operated under the cloak of good. She had the intellect to grab academic accolades and the attention of teachers, some of whom relished having an easy-to-teach honor student, others who feared an accusation of sexual misbehavior with a student.

Yes, heaven help the person who got in the way of her goals. She called herself Wendy's bestie, but Wendy would've tested that friendship with her natural charisma and interaction with her peers. There could be no exclusivity status with Wendy, that was for sure . . . in complete violation of Libby's conventions.

Libby would kill her grandmother's dog to get what she wanted. She'd gone so far as to dictate to JJ that she be declared a senior superlative. And that it not be listed in alphabetical order, but instead in a ranking of accomplishment. She gave JJ the photo to use and the copy to go with it. When JJ ignored all but the photo, which was actually quite decent, she'd found blood poured over the computers in room 35, the yearbook office. Cops came, the blood identified as pig's blood, a la Carrie and Stephen King.

Putting her thoughts of Libby aside, JJ continued, fleshing out the character analyses, hoping that in doing so, she'd spot the holes, connect the dots, and label the incongruities that made one schoolmate *Most Likely to Kill a Cheerleader.*

Again, she cackled at that title.

That left Tony and Reuben. Libby suckered in Tony her senior year despite Peter's belief she stuck to him alone. After all, Libby couldn't be accused of having the second-best stud desired by all the girls, so she bedded them both to cover all her bases. What could Tony say? And poor Peter had fallen for Libby's assurance the teacher was no more than a professional educator. If Libby hadn't screwed that man before graduation, JJ couldn't spell CAT.

Reuben, bless him. The innocent in all of this, or not. Crushed on Wendy while she befriended him out of sympathy, but what if he'd hated his moniker as a poor, pitiful genius who didn't stand a chance with someone as cute and sexual as Wendy. The shy boy who sought revenge for his humiliation.

JJ hated Wendy for her treatment of Reuben more than any other stupid, haphazard decision she'd ever made. That boy didn't deserve to be jerked around like that, then forced to endure the mocking jeers and whispers of fellow students.

Remembering him all arms and legs, glasses and backpack, the soft-spoken boy tolerated more than his share of taunting. More than any ten other kids put together. But just look at him now. He'd tucked away his browbeaten days and replaced them with degrees, investors, and a bank account that left him comfortable. He had filled out muscles, donned contact lenses, and carried a charisma of his own.

But Friday night, at Georgia's beach house, JJ took in that image, that package, that man whom she adored even when he was all gangly and nerdy. A boy she had once felt an intellectual bond with. As a teen she'd been keen enough to forecast his potential, while more intimately feeling his pain from the bullies.

She got even with those bullies via the paper and yearbook by omitting certain accolades and emphasizing losses. She reported from angles that the average intellect couldn't deny but couldn't argue against. Nobody dared touch her for fear of how she'd report the incident. Words were indeed powerful.

She had wondered if Reuben would appear on Edisto. If his yesteryear had dissolved to nothing, he would not bother. However, he'd politely accepted, which made JJ wonder how did he exactly categorize his past. Routine childhood or a simple matter of weathering the storm? Maybe a scarring period in his life that merited retaliation. She hadn't been able to read him, but then someone like him might have learned to hold his feelings close.

Regardless, he came. And so did the others she chose.

All she had to do was be patient, write her thoughts, and wait for the details to reach her to better sculpt these people into their best *New York Times* bestselling best.

Chapter 22

CALLIE AWOKE TO an obnoxious amount of sun, her yellow drapes broadcasting an unfamiliar time of day against soft green walls. Yet her body begged for hours more rest.

She rolled over to squint at her clock on the nightstand. A quarter past eight? What the hell happened to her alarm!

"Get up, Mark," she said, throwing off covers. She sucked in at the splash of morning cold hitting her nakedness instead of her standard nightshirt.

He lifted his phone, adjusted eyes to read the time, then dropped the device on the quilt. "I have an hour. Come share it with me." But his eyelids were closed, any sort of come-hither beckoning lost behind them.

"The search for JJ?" she said, sliding off the high mattress.

"Mom? You here?"

Callie halted naked, standing on her braided rug. Mark's eyes widened. A thump hit the floor, a sound she knew well. Jeb's duffle bag. Then knuckles rapped on her door.

"Mom? Why are you still in bed?"

"Oh shit." Callie pointed to the chintz chair. "Throw some pants on."

Mark kicked at covers, untangling himself, and with his own thump, his feet hit the floor. "Get dressed," he whispered back.

"I need a shower first," she whispered harder.

Another knock. "Your cop car's outside. Aren't you supposed to be at work?" Jeb's voice lowered, becoming parental. "Mom, let me in. I have to see you."

"I'm all right, Jeb," she shouted up in the air, as if that would make him hear better. "About to get a shower."

"Throw on a robe. Talk to me first," he said, even deeper. "It's important."

Mark stopped his flurry, his pants one leg in. "That sounds ominous. He might be in trouble, which is way more important than us getting caught. Talk to the boy."

"You don't get it," she said. "I'm the one in trouble. Or that's what he thinks." She wrapped herself in her robe, ensured Mark was fully in his pants, then opened the door.

"This is a nice surprise, son," she said, knotting the sash.

"Wanted to check and see if you—" His rebuke stopped mid-sentence at the sight of Mark.

"Checking to see if I had a few drinks?" she asked. "The answer is no."

This young, blond clone of her deceased husband blushed. Callie sensed awkward sentences running through his head, but all he managed to say was, "Oh."

Mark came over with an outstretched hand. "How you doing, Jeb? Haven't seen you since New Year's. School going all right for you?"

Jeb returned the shake. "Good," he muttered.

With a smile, Callie proclaimed everything cool. "There, all's in the open. Jeb's school is going well, and I'm sleeping with Mark. We really need to get showered and going, son. I've got a missing woman and Mark's got the restaurant. Jeb, not sure your plans, but how about texting me so we can maybe get together for dinner. Sound good?" She reached up for a hug from this child almost a foot taller than she and scrunched him hard. "He's a good guy," she murmured in his ear.

"He's another cop," he murmured back.

"Used to be. Get over it." She kissed him on the cheek before backing away. When the door clicked shut, she fell back against it.

Mark softly laughed, but when she didn't fall into the comicalness, he stopped. "What's the problem—"

She snared his hand and dragged him into the bathroom to not be heard. Letting him loose, she rubbed a hand over her face and crossed her arms. "He'd be listening at the door."

He squeezed her shoulder and chuckled again. "The kid's twenty years old. With a steady girlfriend, I might add, so don't think they aren't—" He paused and let the image dissipate. "He'll be fine, Callie."

"He was making sure I wasn't hungover," she said in a hard whisper. She could feel grateful her son cared enough to check, but how could she not feel pissed that he did it spur-of-the-moment to catch her in the act?

"I really need a shower," she said, for what felt like the umpteenth time. "And I need to reach Peter before anyone else does while y'all start this search."

Mark could shower with her, and she wouldn't cast him out if he did, but the realities of her day wouldn't let her do more than get wet and get out. Work needed her, and she owned this niggling sense that she'd shirked it. And her son, who in two short phrases and a gaze that spoke volumes more, had taken issue with her new choice of man, making her feel even more irresponsible.

She turned the water hot, the sting a catalyst for getting her act together. Mark must've understood the change in dynamics because he didn't follow. She hollered from under the spray. "What if Peter went jogging on the beach by Georgia's place? He looks like a runner. I guess it's not the end of the world if he sees that crew, but I'd rather he not before I talk to him."

She shut off the water, drying as fast as humanly possible, and half damp, stepped into bra and panties she'd piled crumpled on the counter. Halfway through drying her short bob, a cut she often trimmed herself, she stopped. Listened.

"Mark?"

She put down the dryer and looked for him. The bed was made. Mark's clothes were gone from the chair in the corner, his shoes no longer under it.

She dug into her purse for her phone. *We'll talk later*, he'd texted.

Suddenly she missed the morning banter they might've had. The other morning had been so pleasant.

I'll have Raysor call you, she texted back.

Guilt already rode on her shoulder, having let her personal life interfere with JJ missing. Poor Mark had been cast aside. Was that an omen of sort?

She began throwing on the uniform.

If only Jeb hadn't knocked. She role-played it out in her head. She would've risen earlier than Mark would have, their morning schedules a bit off sync.

Share a few more minutes with me, he might've said.

I really can't, she'd have said, while contemplating how she could.

I take it when you're up everybody's up, he might've said, begrudgingly rising.

She'd have squeezed past him into the closet, not wanting to hear him pee . . . wondering if she was down to her last clean uniform or if she needed to pull out an iron for the one most clean. *I live alone, silly*, she'd have replied then maybe mentioned Jeb. She'd have acted as if solitude was her friend.

In reality, she was the loner who came home to British mysteries and something nuked for dinner, though a quick pot of boiled shrimp worked, too. The woman who studied her surveillance cameras, having nobody to eat with. The woman who used to drink gin and listen to her mother's vintage Neil Diamond albums, forgetting the nightmares. The woman who could barely do the latter anymore without pining for the former.

She loved Jeb on any day, at any time, but his impromptu arrivals saddened her. When he found her ride in the driveway, he had assumed his mother had binged the night before, a hangover making her late for work. Why not? She'd certainly worn that routine well in the past.

She should feel good about herself for that not being the case, but she didn't. Her baby boy had taken a gap year from college to babysit her because of that habit. Sophie still pulled spontaneous checks, and since Sophie's daughter was Jeb's steady, Callie had no doubt that her sobriety came up in conversation between them.

Guess she ought to be grateful for people who cared. A very bitter-sweet arrangement.

But seeing Jeb . . . and seeing him seeing her with a law enforcement guy . . . popped the top off a different Pandora's box. Her drinking had consumed her after losing her husband, losing her job in Boston, and losing Seabrook. A four-year stint of nightly drinking that Jeb connected to her badge.

For the last year, however, she hadn't touched a drop, and done so without the embarrassment of AA. No, AA wasn't an embarrassment. More like her heart fell at the memory of Seabrook forever prodding her to join AA.

Stop. Don't fall down that hole, Callie.

Forcing those memories aside, she buttoned up her shirt and made a note to take an evening to wash and iron uniforms . . . no dry cleaner on the island. If Stan was going to come and go so regularly to Charleston, however, she could ask him to take her uniforms. He'd tell them about starch and creases.

Which made her mind wander back, because Stan continually commended her for her almost a year's abstinence. Her old boss knew her better than her own son, who could only see his mother as loving but cracked in a few too many places. Stan had seen her at her absolute worst and her best, and understood Callie's talent and experience. Bless him, he watched over her at Jeb's request while giving her son a shoulder. She loved that, but hated the necessity of it.

She leaned against the closet wall. Her poor child. Could be Jeb saw Mark as a catalyst to her old ways, probably envisioning the relationship eventually going wrong.

Her utility belt hung exceptionally heavy today, but she took extra care to look good before leaving. She had a full day, but she had to get past Jeb first. She hoped to free his head to think only of spring break surf fishing, kayaking, and fun.

Without trying, bless him, he'd made her aware of a dilemma she'd let slip past her guard. Could she afford a Mark Dupree in her life?

Callie steadied herself, hand on the knob, then exited. In the kitchen, Jeb had already rummaged through the refrigerator. After finding the bananas she kept for Sophie, the yoga mistress who never ate bread, meat, or sugar, he'd sliced them into a small mixing bowl then topped them with half a box of cereal.

"Thought you had a meal plan?" she asked, pouring juice in a Tervis tumbler, no time for food.

"Too much trouble during spring break, plus I was sort of surprising you for an early lunch." He shoveled in a huge bite to match the huge bowl, his other thumb scrolling his phone. He mumbled, "I take it you'll work through it since you got a late start."

Not quite the level of passive aggression her mother, his grandmother, was capable of, but a nice stab at it. "I overslept, yes. Didn't get to bed until after two." She started to explain about having back-to-back interviews and discussing the case with Mark, but Jeb would only hear excuses. Plus, there was no denying she could've gotten more sleep if not for the overnight guest.

Butt against the counter, her ritual pose for morning breakfast, message checking, and the infrequent discussions with her son, she took a sip of orange juice and waited for the conversation. Apparently he didn't care to talk.

"Mark speak to you when he left?" she asked, trying again.

"Yep."

"You two okay?" she asked.

Jeb chewed and swallowed. "He asked how I was doing. Listen, it's your house, your rules, Mom. I think there's some sort of weird attraction between you and cop types, and it's not necessarily healthy, but who am I to say?"

"You realize you're talking about your father."

"Yes," he replied. "I do."

The first LEO in her life, besides the father figure of Chief Warren in her youth, was John Morgan, a deputy US marshal. Killed when Jeb was fifteen by the Russian mob after Callie arrested the family's don back in Boston.

"I wasn't drinking," she said.

"*That* I can get on board with," he replied, earning her a glance.

Which made her yearn for Stan. The only soul who understood the complexities of her life, and she was almost miffed he'd been so unavailable of late. She could hint he speak to Jeb, then Jeb could hint Stan speak to her.

But she was forty-two years old, for God's sake. She ought to be able to handle her social life without a handler.

Her phone rang. "Police Chief Morgan." Telemarketers usually hung up hearing that.

"What the hell, Callie? I never took you for a liar."

Peter. Crap. He'd learned something, and her late morning had likely factored in to the timing.

"What is it?" she asked, not arguing that she hadn't lied, only omitted.

He almost yelled. "I saw a missing person poster in the damn eatery is what it is. Shite. No wonder you told me to call if I heard from her. *Anytime*, you said."

"Let's meet so I can fill you in, Peter. I imagine you don't want to come to the station."

"You got that right," he said, exasperated.

She'd have to work some magic on the Brit to win him back over. "Text me your rental unit number." She heard the disconnect as Peter hung up.

Damn Mark for his bags of food and staying over. No, she couldn't blame him. The blame was totally on her.

She wrapped arms around Jeb from behind and kissed his hair, taking in the scent of him. "How long you staying?"

"School doesn't start back until Monday, but I'm on no schedule. Depends on the fishing or what Sprite wants to do."

She almost told him to check in periodically with her, an old habit hard to break. She'd demanded hourly check-ins once upon a difficult time. Guess twenty was a little old for that. So she kissed him on the top of the head again instead. "I'll update you on how my day goes," she said, the unspoken being that he might consider doing the same for her.

Kids growing up was not for the faint of heart. Especially for a control-freak parent.

She left, biting her tongue to not remind him to set the alarm. He would, because, after all, he'd no doubt noticed she hadn't last night because he'd been taught better than that.

Time to get herself in the car and her mind into the day.

En route to Peter's condo, she called Deputy Raysor. Temporarily assigned to the Edisto Beach PD almost two decades ago, the detail stuck as officers and chiefs rotated in and out of the town that could not afford much of a force. He should be on duty, on the beach. When it came to scouring the island that buffered the mainland from the town of Edisto Beach, however, nobody knew it better than Raysor.

"Missed you this morning," he answered on his radio. "Everything okay? Feeling all right?"

"All's good, Don. Promise."

Like Jeb, Raysor watched over Callie for the same reason. Thomas, too. Nope, no need for AA at all.

"A lot's happened over the weekend, and we need to fill you in, Don. You talked to Thomas?"

"In passing. Said you were onto something. Something sort of personal, sort of not."

Leave it to Thomas to say just enough without overstepping his bounds.

"Where are you?" she asked, idling at the T-bone end of Jungle Road. Right headed to Wyndham, left toward the police station.

"Just cruised past the marina," he replied.

"Stop in the Bay Creek parking lot," she said, taking the right. "I'm about to redirect your day."

A mile later, he sat waiting on her, and she maneuvered her car next to his, driver to driver with the windows down. Enough tourists goose-necked at them in passing to make her wait for a pack of eight to leave earshot before orienting the deputy.

She spoke a mile a minute. Raysor scowled, attempting to put the pieces together. She was glad she'd informed Mark in greater detail.

"So I'm hunting for an author who might be hiding or kidnapped or dead. Lovely," he said. "While I'm out scouring the island, where will you be?" Raysor respected authority. He just didn't know how to sound like it.

"Talking to a party of interest who flew in from London last night. Depending on what he says will dictate my day. Grab the normal volunteers who help us out on these things. I'm sure we can get Mark to throw in a free meal for them when it's over."

An arched, salt-and-pepper brow raised in Popeye fashion. "This Mark character is really entrenching himself into our little piece of the world, isn't he?"

"Edisto likes him. The restaurant seems to be doing well."

His grin slid up through chubby wrinkles. "Ain't the world I was talking about."

"He's a retired SLED investigator, Don. Why not use his expertise? It's not like we have a plethora of cop talent on this strip of sand. Case in point, I have to be at this interviewee's place, like yesterday, and you need to be scouting the island. I'll tell Marie to tell all the guys."

He laughed, slipping his SO cruiser into gear. "Still not the world I was referencing." More laughing. "All the diners in the SeaCow saw you, Callie. Ain't a better place to broadcast your business."

He pulled away, and Callie swore she still heard him laughing as he hit asphalt to catch Mark. Even with nobody around, she felt her neck redden into her collar.

Letting another visiting family pass in front of her, she entered the road, thumbing Janet Wainwright's number, then put it on speaker.

She had news to deliver to the realtor, and the Marine wouldn't take the news lightly. Wainwright Realty was practically next door to the SeaCow, unfortunately, and Callie hoped Janet didn't have some damn opinion about Mark.

Had she jumped into the sack too soon with the guy? She definitely could've concealed things better.

Damn if life wasn't a lot simpler alone.

Chapter 23

CALLIE PAUSED AT Wyndham's gate. "Hold on, Janet," she said into her phone. Then to the security guard, asked, "How's it going today, Dennis? Busy?"

"Not as bad as we expected," the guard answered, raising the arm. "Expect next week and the week after to be the busy ones."

"Well, you'll keep them in line, I'm sure," Callie cruised through. A dozen yards in, she returned attention to her phone call. "I'm back."

Driving one-handed at a slow creep, she took the curved asphalt with its carefully landscaped borders, lane dividers, and green areas, a whole different side of Edisto Beach, scanning for Peter Yeo's condo while Janet Wainwright screamed at her over her mobile.

"She leaves by tomorrow," the realtor ordered. "Agreement clearly dictates vacate by ten hundred hours."

Callie kept winding, believing Peter's address to be tucked back toward Driftwood Lane. "Janet, *Flirty Flamingo* might be a crime scene, so law trumps your agreement. Has JJ Loveless gotten in touch with you by any chance?"

"No, she hasn't." The Marine sucked in through her teeth, the seething heard clearly across the line. "I have another party coming in tomorrow for that rental, Chief. What the hell do I tell them?"

"Not my . . . decision to make." Callie started to say not her problem, but that would only send Janet into a worse tizzy. "Thought the Marines were trained to *improvise, adapt, and overcome.*"

"Lady, don't question my competence."

"Wouldn't dream of it." Callie found the condo. Couldn't miss the strawberry-blond hair of Peter, him leaning on the second-floor balcony railing, his expression none too happy. "You got this, Marine," she said. "Call me if you hear from JJ. I'll most definitely remind her of the lease agreement if I hear from her first."

"Damn right you will."

Callie took that as goodbye. Time to focus on the next storm on the horizon.

Last night, when she educated Mark on the case, past and present, he worried Peter might ignore Callie. Said he might hunt for JJ which might entice him to slip over to Georgia's. Callie had said no. Peter flew across the ocean to put something to rest, and he would not attempt to ruin that chance. He wasn't a rule breaker, and she trusted him to do as he said. Or at least that was her memory of him. Plus, he'd mentioned avoiding Libby and Butch.

Peter met her at the top of the balcony's stairs, taking a moment to look over her cop image. She liked it when someone took such a pause to understand what the uniform meant. "Inside or out?" he said.

"Depends on who can hear us."

Which he hadn't thought of. He opened the front door and allowed her to enter first, then led her to the living area of the tiny, studio condo.

He'd cleaned it up for her or was naturally a tidy fellow, leaving little sign of himself on tables, even in the kitchen. With minimal choice of seating, he let her choose first. She took the short sofa with its neat, straight lines and navy Scotch-guarded material. He then accepted the simple cushioned chair to her left which let him watch the small lagoon out back. A huge live oak sprawled all over the place, part overhanging the water, and while Callie would love sitting on that back balcony, one never could tell who might sit above, below, or to either side, just to hear what the neighbors had to say that day.

He smacked a flyer down on the coffee table. "Care to explain?" His impeccable manners from last night must've been left elsewhere.

"JJ is missing," she said, blunt and plain, not picking up the paper. Marie had printed and placed a few of these in the key restaurants yesterday. Just a few so as not to upset folks, in hope to possibly draw JJ out. "She arrived at Georgia's on Friday, left late that night, and hasn't been seen since."

"You could've told me that last night," he said, deadpan, staring as if she were the enemy.

"And you would've grabbed the next flight out." She retrieved her notebook. "When did you last speak to her?"

He sneered, the condescension crystal. "Again, you should've been up front. You'd have learned I spoke to her Saturday."

Callie did the math. Eleven or twelve Friday night would've been Saturday in the UK. "When exactly?" she asked.

"Had to have been almost midnight," he said.

Which would be five a.m. in the UK. "Got yanked out of bed early, huh?"

"Midnight *my* time," he corrected.

"So Friday *our* time?" she said, annoyed by what should be a simple calculation. East versus west coast time zones confounded her enough.

But when he shook his head she gathered she'd still failed at the math. He didn't have to say it. *Stupid American.*

"So illuminate me," she replied to the silent contempt.

"She called me at seven in the evening, Saturday your time, which would have been midnight my time. I stayed up until she did." He gave a quick scan of the place. "She made the arrangements for this place. I wouldn't have had a clue what was available. She paid for it."

What the hell? "Are you sure about that time?"

"Why would I lie?"

"But she'd been noted missing by then." Callie crossed through the two time mistakes on her pad. Then studying Peter, she hoped to catch his realization that he was the last link to a missing person.

She wasn't sure he'd recognized the dilemma.

"Show me her call on your phone," she said.

He rose and retrieved the device from the kitchen bar, and by the time he returned, he'd found the record. "There you go."

The time was right, but the number didn't belong to the phone retrieved from JJ's rental, the one Callie carried in her pocket in case somebody like the literary agent happened to call. The one she'd already called the service provider about yesterday, telling them to get her a list of calls and locations from between Friday and Saturday night. After that time frame, she'd been in possession of the device.

However, she hadn't asked Libby, Tony, Butch, or Reuben what JJ number they had, and now that there were two, she needed to know. She'd assumed Georgia had been the mouthpiece for the reunion getaway, but JJ had called others and cancelled them from coming, and apparently had orchestrated Peter.

She rang Georgia. "Tell everyone to give me the number they have for JJ."

"Um, I communicated with everyone," she said. "The number I have is the one on the list I emailed y'all."

"Get them, Georgia. I want to hear it from them."

Georgia walked out on the porch from the sound of the rollers and a few gulls. From the chatter, the team debated something with Libby's voice the loudest.

"Y'all, look at your contact list," Georgia interrupted. "And tell me what you have as a number for JJ. Read it aloud for Callie."

Amid the mockery, each managed to rattle off from their contact list, Butch waiting to deliver his in song, rising high on the last digit in a finale. Each, to include Georgia, gave the number of the original phone that Callie had in her possession. Not the number Peter had. She hung up on the laughter.

"Callie," Peter started, but she shushed him with a hand movement as she put in a radio call to her favorite officer.

"Take another hard look-see at *Flirty Flamingo,* Thomas. Yes, again. And make it a hard look-see, you hear? She may have been in and out of there after we were there yesterday."

She hung up the radio and scrolled her favorites on her cell. Then she stopped and pointed to Peter. "Call JJ. Put it on speaker."

He hit redial on the author's last call. After four rings the call defaulted to a canned recording about the person not being available. When the beep sounded, Callie motioned for him to leave a message.

"Jessie Jane," Peter said, falling back on his proper self. "I've arrived. Didn't call last night because of the hour, but we must talk. This is my third message, by the way. Don't tell me I flew all this way for a good laugh." He hung up.

"Excellent," Callie said, pleased at his performance and the confirmation that the number was a working one. "Sit there and wait a minute, if you don't mind."

Her next call went to Thomas again. "Call the law enforcement liaison at Verizon. We found another number for JJ, and it's been used since she went missing Saturday." She gave him the number. "Tell them the owner might be the subject of foul play, and everything is suspect since Friday night around eleven p.m. We need all phone activity and the location from which those calls were made."

"What if they aren't the provider?" he asked.

"They can tell you who is," she assured him. He hung up.

Then her next call went to Mark. An instinctive move. A surprise even to herself that the reaction hadn't been to Raysor first, but she justified it as Mark having been an investigator and most recently briefed on the case. He'd even met the reunion cast. She stopped with the excuses when he picked up.

"Just learned from our Brit gentleman that he spoke to JJ Saturday evening around seven p.m. That's twenty hours after we found her unpacked things abandoned in the rental, her car door open."

"What? Well, that certainly changes things."

"Rather ticks me off," she said. "JJ's playing us."

"Agreed. Are you calling off the search? I've got at least twenty guys about to start covering their areas of the island. I expect Raysor any moment. I'm riding with him." From the clink of ice, he took a drink of something.

"Stan helping?" she asked. His thirty-year career in a city as big as Boston wouldn't hurt as they worked this out. She hadn't seen the big, burly, buzz-cut boss man in, what, five days? Six?

"He's in Charleston again," Mark said.

Well, she couldn't blame the man for having a life outside of hanging around El Marko's bar, catching after-hours gossip about what Callie's people had done all day.

She wasn't quite sure how to proceed. Though the search felt less dire after Peter's revelation, a different emphasis remained . . . JJ had jerked people around in her make-believe crime. The charge might not stick, but her logic smelled off-balance, and one of Callie's notions suddenly carried more weight. What if JJ was not in her right mind? She might even be an at-risk party.

But then, she might be crazy enough to be a risk to other parties, too.

"No, don't call off the search, but tell your guys not to approach. Just report in if they see her. You understand why."

Raysor called Mark's name in the background. He'd arrived at the restaurant.

"I'll call them en route," Mark said. "On second thought, I'm taking my own car."

"Be careful," she replied. "Don't get lost. I would join you, but what I'm learning might impact y'all. Check in often, okay?"

"Will do."

She spoke to him like she did to her son. Like Mark mattered. Not that she didn't hold concern for every Edisto resident, but Mark had graduated to a different level of her worry. However, that wasn't a comfort to her. On the contrary, it made him a complication.

"My turn?" Peter asked.

She put away her phone. She hadn't interviewed either Georgia or Reuben, and time was running thin before they'd push to leave.

But Peter sat before her, front and center and full of intel. What little she'd gleaned from him had already altered her department's course of action and raised more concerns.

He hadn't wanted to come . . . yet he did, flying on his own nickel.

He hadn't wanted to meet the others . . . so JJ rented him his own place, on the sly.

He'd been the last alum to speak to JJ.

Why the special treatment?

She fished out her official recorder, having brought it home with her last night to listen to the previous interviews. "Oh, it's most definitely your turn, Mr. Yeo," she said, placing the device just so on the coffee table. "How about grabbing us a couple of waters, if you don't mind. I believe we're both going to need them before we're through."

The governing behavior he'd greeted her with had waned. He poured two glasses of water from the tap and set them on coasters next to JJ's missing person flyer, and settled into his chair that seemed unable to accommodate the athlete's long arms and legs.

He took a drink . . . winced and stared at the glass. Nobody drank tap water on the island. Not without a reverse osmosis system, and even then, a semblance of saltiness clung to the drink. Made for nasty sweet tea. Callie was used to it, and while Peter wasn't, in a little while he wouldn't care because his mind would be on spilling his soul to her. For all she knew, he was in on whatever JJ had orchestrated . . . might still be orchestrating . . . and he wouldn't give a damn what the water tasted like when his mouth went dry.

Chapter 24

JJ
Sunday evening.

JJ SAT IN HER porch chair on her double cushions, a flat dangling off the toes of her bare foot. A shawl covered her shoulders as JJ stared through the draping oaks toward the marsh. She couldn't see the water this time, but she could hear the subtle wildlife sounds. Another cup of chicory coffee warmed her hands.

There were facts and then there was how the facts were presented.

She couldn't focus though. The bookmark scared her a little. Just a little. Enough to double check her locks.

Otherwise, JJ could get used to this. She might have a new formula to writing her books to include secluding herself in the region, which meant she'd use actual settings, no fictional towns or made-up counties. Real places so that people felt what she wrote could be either truth or imagination, and it was up to the savvy of the reader to determine which. Definitely a plus for marketing.

Cup cooling, coffee half gone, she returned to her keyboard. She jumped as a bird flew into the screen wrapping the porch, her heart fluttering as much as the creature's. Then she wrote how that made her feel.

Night began to fall. She hadn't written a page. The bookmark silently screamed at her.

Her assistant had not visited last night, but they had texted. The schoolmates' temperaments had reached a fervor JJ had hoped for, and JJ's spy couldn't leave without being obvious. As expected, the alums queried each other, scrutinized each other, fussed and fumed with each other, and said things they had not meant to say.

It seemed everyone's emotions were running higher, faster.

Callie had begun interviewing them, raising irritability. Currently it was in the open that each attendee was a suspect in not only JJ's disappearance but Wendy's murder. Callie would not have looked at Wendy without JJ mysteriously vanishing.

All according to plan.

But the bookmark wasn't in the plan.

The occasional car traveled around the bend that curved in front of her residence. Good folks coming back from church. Third? Fourth vehicle, maybe? She wouldn't want her seclusion interrupted too terribly much. She'd been assured that this area would give her the isolation she desired.

Lack of food and three cups of coffee gave her stomach a churn. No, this wouldn't do at all. She saved her document, closed the program, and decided it time for a snack and maybe walk over to that marsh to see what the vista looked like with the water gone.

JJ had leftovers from last night and random stores supplied for her in the kitchen. Surely something was edible in the mix. She didn't eat much while creating anyway. The fullness impeded her thoughts.

She found crackers. In the refrigerator someone had placed an assortment of dips. Crab, pimento cheese, chicken salad, seafood . . . all from a place called King's Market. She could make that work.

As she doled a small spoonful of each onto a plate, a car door slammed. Hard to tell from where exactly but close enough. The first she'd heard. With her having arrived via someone else's transportation, again per plan, no vehicle sat in the drive so the house would appear unoccupied.

A knock sounded on the front door. Maybe her concierge. She stole a small spoonful of the chicken salad then wiped hands on a dishtowel. A neighbor, maybe. Surely not a marketer.

Approaching slowly, she tried to peer out a front window but could only make out the vehicle. Not her helper. With a glance out of the left sidelight window, she barely caught sight of a sleeve, an elbow wearing a soft gold sweater. Nothing cheap.

Back to the door, she waited. The person knocked again.

Oh, this was silly. "Hello?" she said, reaching to open.

About the time she wondered why they hadn't answered back, she turned the knob.

The door smashed into her face.

And as she went down, she thought . . . this was not according to the plan.

Chapter 25

CALLIE COVERED the timeline with Peter from when JJ had first contacted him to the current moment. Callie's strategic repetition of simple and easy-to-answer questions led to his cooperation, and he seemed to relax.

They always did, which was when they said things they didn't mean to say.

"You ignored JJ's original attempt to contact you," she said. "She persisted, and you finally took the call." Callie repeated the date, two months ago. "You refused to come to the reunion. She still persisted."

Head tilted, he waited for the statements to become questions.

"You finally agreed, yet you were handled with kid gloves and not thrown together with the rowdy group at Georgia's. Why's that?"

"I had no idea how she was *handling* the others, as you put it. Maybe they relished a free vacation. I didn't desire to open old scars. I told her I had no need to revisit those days."

Boy, could Callie understand that. "Did she even tell you about the others at first?" Peter's situation sounded so different from Butch, Libby, and Tony's.

"Yes, she did. It's what turned me off from coming."

"The reason she changed her strategy," Callie added.

He nodded in the affirmative.

"For the record, Mr. Yeo nodded," she said for the recording then continued. "Georgia managed the agenda. She might still have wanted to invite you to dinner, or a cookout. JJ wasn't staying at Georgia's, and she came over a while until she went missing. You confirmed she isn't missing or at least wasn't during the time frame in which the concern first arose."

He intently took each word in. "No. I made it clear I didn't want anyone to hear I was coming or see me once I got here. I assume the reunion social takes place on the opposite end of this island."

Not really. As the gull flew, the condo was barely a half mile from *Water Spout*, but with Wyndham being gated, the drive measured over a mile further. The chance of Peter's movements overlapping the group's was as slim as it could get on a small, four-mile beach.

"Frankly, I wouldn't have flown all this way for a reunion either," she said.

He snuffled a soft laugh. "At least somebody else in our lot had sense."

"Yet you came."

He no longer laughed.

"Your appearance and her disappearance smell oddly irregular, yet connected, Peter."

Not at first grasping her point, Peter gave a benign smile.

Callie let him think about that. She didn't respond, which made him rethink what she said, wondering what he'd fathomed wrong. Then she shifted her position a little, making her leather utility belt squeak a tad to remind him she was the police.

Making people second-guess their thought was an art form.

"I had nothing to do with JJ going missing," he finally said.

"Please retrieve your airline ticket, if you don't mind."

He leaped up, his willingness to oblige telling her the flight schedule would fall to his favor, but she had to check. He immediately lowered back into the seat. "Sorry, forgot it's on my phone." He scrolled and handed it over. He'd left London as stated.

"Show me your rental car receipt, please."

He scrolled and offered that as well.

Which meant Peter Yeo arrived as he stated, and unless he'd disposed of JJ in the middle of last night, he was in the clear of doing anything. Whether he knew about anyone else's actions was another story.

"Have you spoken to the other high school crowd here?"

"Not even sure who is here," he said, more shaken. Even when they got questions right, the repetition of having to account for behavior sucked confidence right out of people.

"JJ, of course, and Libby, Butch, Georgia, Tony, Reuben . . . and me," she said. "Apparently the senior superlative list from our senior year was the original basis for the invitations. I assume it began as a real effort to plan a reunion, but JJ hand-selected the ones she wanted and canceled the rest. Tony kind of happened last minute."

"Why us?" he asked.

"My next question to you."

He thought. "A connection to Wendy," he replied, almost a plea to be told he was right.

"Yes. And you could've avoided this altogether, yet again, here you are. Why?"

"She kept calling, kept baiting. Gave up on me for a few weeks, but she called back a week ago then daily, most demanding. Said she'd pay for this place if I covered the flight, then when I said no, she offered to pay for it all. I gave in and paid my own airfare. Couldn't let her own me like that."

"Sounds like she won regardless," Callie said.

Both of his palms went to the wooden chair arms, pushing himself forward. He reddened, so easy to read on the ginger. "I didn't care about the damn condo being paid for, okay! And I borrowed the money for the flight. Truth was she threatened me! I hung up on her. She called again, said the others had committed, and if I didn't show, she'd rat me out."

Sounded like he'd already heard who was coming.

Callie still saw Peter as a good guy, though. She'd always thought he got sucked into the wrong family for his foreign student program, and while he might've been high on Chief Warren's list of suspects, his association with Butch was what put him there. "Rat you out for what?"

"'*Protecting someone*,' she said."

Mashing her lips, Callie stared him down. "You said she wanted to see your eyes when you two spoke. She was going to accuse you of something, or either she wanted you to unveil a lie. Why?"

"Not sure."

"That's crap, Peter." Callie frowned at the avoidance. "Let's segue back to the word *blackmail*. What did she hold over your head to get you to Edisto?"

"High school," he said.

Sarcastic in her sigh, she pushed on. "You did something egregious enough to be used as extortion material? In high school? Wouldn't be murder, would it?"

Peter's British pallor turned pastier still. "I didn't kill Wendy, if that's the murder you mean."

"There's more than one murder?"

"No!"

"But you didn't do the actual deed?" Callie asked.

"No."

"Did you see who did?"

"No."

"Do you know who did?"

"Not sure," he said.

"What the hell *do* you know, Peter? I sure as hell haven't heard enough worthy of her paying for this condo for . . . how many days?"

"Until I leave, I guess. The sooner the better." With his hand clasping the water glass on one knee, which indeed the man had half-emptied, Peter tensed, with the exception of one leg that bobbed up and down.

Callie needed to change gears, get him to feel like she was on his side. She deduced JJ had pestered him, seeking threads to pick and unravel to later form into his own chapter for the damn book, making him believe she'd unearthed facts she hadn't. She had to have something of substance on him though, with all the trouble she went through.

Were the others not as important as Peter? Or were they easier to bribe?

Out of the group, neither Reuben nor Georgia was short on finances. Had JJ dug under their skin like she had with Peter, with Peter holding out longer, demanding more conditions? Or had she played to each of their personalities, promising each something different in exchange for their attendance?

Suddenly Callie had more questions for Butch, Libby, and Tony, and her upcoming two interviews with Reuben and Georgia took on more importance.

"How did JJ reel you in?" Callie asked yet again.

"Bragged she could frame us."

"Us?"

"Butch and me. Said she could prove Butch's whereabouts at the game."

"Butch hardly sat still," she said. "What did she mean?"

He shook his head. "She wouldn't say."

"I cannot believe you didn't tell her to take a flying leap. What else?"

"Said she could impact my career."

"Which is . . . ?"

He leaped up, those long arms spread wide. "Vicar of a large, rather affluent parsonage, if you must know," he said, releasing the secret with high frustration. He drained the glass and went back to the kitchen for more of that salty water. "With five children and a wife whose father was knighted by the queen," he shouted from the sink.

She waited for that last line to be a joke. Wait . . . he was serious. *Wow, how about that.*

Totally on edge, his back to her as he stood at the sink, she noted the flush of his ears and nape of his neck. Callie allowed him the break and spoke on the recording about him stepping away for a brief intermission though remaining in her sight.

Water filled the glass once, then a second time. She heard three deep gulps of air before he returned, calmer. "Sounds like she messed with your head," Callie said, her tone more gentle. "I'm gaining a newfound respect for this woman's talents, Peter. She's conniving. Truthfully, she might have nothing on you."

"Might have a ton of somethings, too," he said.

Which anybody innocent of secrets would not say.

Callie didn't respond, hoping he'd let her in on one or two of those mysteries. He'd denied the murder, but vicar or not, people lied.

"I'm not sure Butch didn't kill Wendy," he continued. "But that night was the most impressionable night of my life."

"That night seems to have changed a lot of lives," she said.

The others had adamantly denied anything to do with Wendy that evening, except Libby, who supposedly just rode with her. Peter didn't come with a gold-plated alibi, for himself or Butch. None she'd heard yet, anyway. She'd interviewed ministers before. They were as human as the next guy and lied just as often.

He seemed awful sure all this related back to the night Wendy was murdered, which meant his presence wasn't so damn innocent. "Talk about your whereabouts at the game, Peter. Did you stroll around, sitting with different people? Sit with, say, Libby? Pal around with Butch?"

"First half I hung with Butch, ever the scout for him, until I couldn't stomach his incessant need to stick his . . . property . . . in places it didn't belong. When the football team came back into the locker room at halftime, we baseball players couldn't afford be seen, so once we left, I took the liberty to divorce myself of Butch for the rest of the night."

She had to carefully choose her next direction. "Let's develop a timeline. Start earlier. Did you arrive with Libby or Butch?" she asked, though she'd already heard from the others.

He gave a tight shake of his head. "Went with Butch. He'd packed a case of beer on ice in the trunk. The weather being rather nippy, we wore longer, bigger coats, and between us probably hauled ten bottles in there. They didn't check as hard back then, plus we were jocks. Got in through the team locker room."

"Walk me through the evening."

He slumped awkwardly in the small chair, almost making her want to trade places with him. "Butch had arranged a *suite*. Had you heard of those?"

A suite? "No."

"Guess in your circles you wouldn't."

She let that go.

"They were predesigned locations on school property for when he, or any other jock, got lucky during a game. Another reason to enter via the locker room. A lot of the jocks did it. During football season the baseball guys used offices in the football locker room for their rendezvous. Then in baseball season, arrangements were granted for the football guys. Janitor closets, assistant coach offices, sometimes in a concession stand storage closet. Didn't need candles or goose down bedding for what was done, just something other than a concrete floor and out of the weather."

"The coaches?"

"Looked the other way, assuming they knew."

Callie had no idea, suddenly grateful jocks hadn't been her thing. Stratton ran track and played basketball, but he hadn't exactly been her thing either. He was just a friend. She was his buddy. He needed support and she supplied the shoulder. "Go on."

Peter's *humph* came out pitifully depressed, maybe at the absurdity of how that history sounded in the present or at the seriousness of it. Or both. "JJ'd heard about Butch and his setup that night. How? Beyond me. With that being a playoff, everybody but Butch and his girl of the moment would be in the stands or on the field."

Jesus. If she were Peter, she wouldn't have discussed any of this with JJ. Hell, she wouldn't be admitting this to anyone.

In all honesty, if she were Peter, the thought of doing away with JJ would've crossed her mind more than a few times. Might've even justified crossing *the pond*, as the Brits called it, in order to remove the problem altogether.

"And your role with Butch was what?" she asked.

"Retrieve the next girl he'd promised time with and stand on the lookout while they were at it."

"Jesus," she exclaimed, then wondered what he thought about that as a vicar. "How many times?"

"Enough. He collected the first girl. Afterwards, I bought her a Coke, while he collected the next. I handled three by halftime. When he told me who to get for the third quarter, I refused and left."

"Oh, Peter." His statement stunned her a tad. She'd been there and seen Butch bee-bopping around at least for the third quarter, jumping here and there, and could see he was collecting sex, while drinking one beer after another, likely refilling from his friend's coat pockets when his own stash ran out.

"Who was the third-quarter girl?" she asked.

"He was trying for Wendy."

What? "Thought he'd already . . . accessed Wendy before." She stumbled, avoiding *tapped, screwed,* and the ultimate *F* word in front of the minister.

"He had. Didn't live up to her reputation, he said. But he'd arranged for Wendy to meet us at the beginning of the third quarter . . . for me. Said he was tired of me being too goody-goody."

Chapter 26

LOOKING DISTRAUGHT over his high school admission about Butch, Peter Yeo sat across from Callie and rubbed his forehead, as if to dispel a headache. He'd just used his name, Butch's, and Wendy's in the same sentence, at the Berkeley High School football playoff, with fornication of multiple girls the focus.

If that didn't create suspicion about Wendy's murder, what did?

Seated in the studio condo rental to his right, Callie noted on the cable television box that it was going on eleven. With this interview, lunch would come and go like her son forecasted. *Smart aleck.*

Mark, Raysor, and the men searching the island for JJ had been out and about for over an hour. She had zero feel about how the search would go. Not knowing squat about the missing person factored into not asking the Colleton SO and Charleston SO to send in search parties of their own.

Professionally, Callie hoped she wouldn't hear a thing for a while, to give her a chance to dissect Peter's history, his knowledge of Butch, and anything in relation to JJ. Personally, she wished these high school oafs, including the author, would just pack up their things and head off Edisto Beach.

But a slow-growing suspicion had her concerned a killer had infiltrated their midst. This middle-of-the-road feel wasn't her norm. She was an all-in or all-out kind of girl.

She'd already reached one conclusion: having the police chief interviewing the alums, searching the island, connecting with Chief Warren . . . were tasks JJ had hoped would take place. The author had stirred things into a froth, vanished, and possibly, somehow, waited to see what revealed itself in the controversy.

To find the real killer? Or to pen a book in the name of making number one on some list?

Callie hated charades as much as she hated paparazzi and social media, but she was sucked in. Unfortunately, a small ember of fear also had her believing this insane performance could lead to tragedy. May have already.

She'd given Peter enough moments to collect himself, but instead he seemed to be sinking into misery which she couldn't waste minutes dragging him out of. "Peter. Back to the story. You declined to participate when Butch lined up Wendy for you for your physical entertainment. Am I clear that was supposed to take place during the third quarter?"

He sniffled, orienting himself. "That's right."

"But you declined to play."

"Correct."

"Did he step into your shoes with Wendy?" she asked.

"He didn't say, and I didn't ask."

"Hard to believe he didn't say, preacher. Butch's never held his tongue very well."

In a snap, a surge of anger swept over him. "I wasn't with him for the third and fourth quarters, okay? I kept away on purpose. I didn't want to be set up with a girl. I didn't want to see how many girls he achieved. Then once they found Wendy's body, I damn well didn't want to ask him if he followed through, Callie. Can you not make sense of that? Then on top of that . . ."

He shut his eyes and rubbed them, the interview physically impacting the man.

"You all right?" she asked.

Lids still closed, he nodded with reserve, as though to not disturb a headache further.

"Then continue," she said. "On top of what?"

"One of the girls was fourteen," he said. "Her parents were even there. Butch bragged about whisking her away right under their noses."

How in ever-loving hell did Chief Warren not march Butch to the front of the suspect line?

"Name of the girl," she ordered.

"It was so long ago," he replied.

Callie leaned so close their knees touched, her stare not a foot from his. "There is no statute of limitations in this state for rape. Give me her name."

"She was a damn freshman! We didn't ask those kids' names." Tired red eyes welled with tears.

"*Those* kids? How many minors were there?" Her heart flash-froze, then hardened. She might've once felt sorry for Peter, but minister or no minister, he let rape go silent for twenty-four years? How in the hell did he take his vows?

His fists pummeled his thighs. "Can't tell you," he yelled.

God help her, she bet this was the sort of depravity JJ hoped for. Damn it! She could hardly interview someone without wondering if this was what JJ wanted. "Who can vouch for you in the third and fourth quarters?"

"Tony."

"Is he aware of all this other business?"

Peter shrugged.

"Is Libby?"

To that he didn't respond, taking his attention out the doors to that huge moss-laden oak.

"Look at me," Callie ordered, not yelling but heartily wanting to. "Did she know?"

"Libby was only seventeen," he said. "Like the rest of us."

Her mouth fell open. "The freshman was fourteen! Libby hid that all this time, too?"

His tears spilled. "Libby knew her. She felt somehow the girl deserved it by hanging around Butch."

Meaning Peter could identify the child who probably lost her virginity to the sportscaster currently up the road, drinking all of Georgia's bourbon. Callie hadn't broken that son of a bitch when she interviewed him, but there'd be a reckoning now.

"You know more than you're saying, Peter. I want that name," she said.

Pain radiated off him in his repentance, but repentance for what? There were so many sins to choose from.

"You'll have to talk to Libby or Butch."

Jesus . . . she caught herself and thought it again. Jesus Christ. Yes, she was mad enough to take the Lord's name in vain, but the Brit before her had stood before his God and lied.

Her phone rang, caller ID Mark. She hoped he made this quick. No, she hoped he had JJ in cuffs. "Callie here."

"Sounds like your day isn't any better than ours," he said. "I got a call from one of Wesley's cousins who works cleaning pools. One of them is out in the Neck."

Wesley, Mark's right-hand worker at El Marko's, had cousins who ran the gamut in terms of trustworthiness, but at least this one worked. The Neck was filled with upper middle class to lower wealthy residents.

The community was built up with quality homes, half on two-to three-acre lots hugging the marsh, which inflated their value by thirty percent or more.

She heard several male voices, then Deputy Raysor took the phone. "We might have a problem, Chief."

He used *Chief* in lieu of *Doll*. Not good. "Shoot it to me, Don."

He gave the address. One of the smaller homes, a block farther inland from the real money. "Mark's guy told Wesley he thought the woman we're hunting for was staying in the house next to the one he cleans a pool at. It's frequently rented through one of those online sites. Nobody here when we arrived, but somebody has been staying here. Door kicked open. Blood at head level where it appears to have hit the person answering. A drink glass tossed and spilled on the porch. The bed disheveled. Got forensics coming to see what else."

So this business happened at wherever JJ spent the night? "The pool guy sure of the identification?"

"Pretty sure," he said. "Suitcase confirmed she stayed here. The purse had a couple credit cards."

Like the other house except for the bed. "What about a phone? A laptop? Any envelopes or papers that we could tie to her? After all, she was an author."

More voices in the background. "Mark says no sign of a phone or computer. Damn guy's already finishing your sentences?"

"Shut up, Don."

He did. She'd never told him to do so before.

Banter wasn't meshing well with her mood. "Check the marsh, note the tide, and search accordingly. You're the man in charge."

"It wasn't a house on the water."

"Who comes to this island and doesn't try to stand on the edge of the water? Call me as you need me."

"What? You're not heading straight out here?"

She looked over at Peter, who had miserably dropped his head. "Busy at the moment."

Callie wasn't ready to leave Middleton High School just yet, tethered to this fresh layer of her past. Her thoughts churned, and she was reluctant to turn the action loose. This baseball star, this once beautiful British boy the girls swooned over at his mention of their name, was not the tower of European honor as most remembered.

An old shame crept up in her. The shame that she'd been too straight-laced, too naïve, and maybe too reluctant to see her classmates as suspects. She'd been too incensed at the grown-ups simply because they were in charge and not handling things to her satisfaction, and subsequently too outraged at their incompetence when Stratton ended his life. She hadn't thought clearly.

Her jaw ached at the old familiar frustration filling her up again. "Doll? You there?"

Raysor's nickname for her, when nobody else could hear. "Yes."

"Your boyfriend here says to tell you—"

"We're on the job, Deputy Raysor. I'll be on Wyndham for a while longer doing mine. Then I'll be over at *Water Spout* in my official capacity, unless you can't handle things out there, in which case, I'll be happy to drop everything and come do your job, too."

He took his voice down an octave and clipped his words. "Not necessary, Chief." Then in a clumsy mumble, added, "What's your damn beef?"

Her deputy wasn't one for hierarchal formalities, and Callie rued her rudeness the second she gave it life, but this case had suddenly become about more than an irritating reunion.

"Later, Don," she said, and hung up. An explanation could wait for a better place and time.

She phoned Marie. "Take down this list of names," she said when her office queen answered. She gave the full names of each alum involved in this mess and their city of residence to the Edisto PD's master of data collection. "Not sure what you can find in London with the last one, but he was in the US for a good number of years. Criminal history check on each one."

Marie took her instructions without question.

Callie hung up. "When's your return flight, Peter?"

The man had done nothing but wilt further into his chair.

"Day after tomorrow."

"You might have to postpone it."

His sigh took his appearance down a whole shirt size. "Can't I give this statement and leave? I'll tell you all you want. All I can remember."

"Two days isn't going to cut it, Vicar. Don't make me go all international on you."

He didn't ask for explanation, probably because whatever he was afraid JJ could do to his career, he understood Callie could do as bad or worse. "Butch was an amoral bastard, but he never forced a girl, Callie."

"Fourteen-year-olds don't have choices, Peter. Did you tell him to talk to the authorities?" she chided. "No. Instead, you took that sorry,

172

infantile bucket of hormones home, discussed alibis, and convinced his parents that the jocks always get picked on."

His ruddiness crept like a rash down his cheeks. "No, I didn't."

She snorted, mocking. "Sure you did."

"No I didn't," he shouted. "I did make him go home. He was drunk. He was crying, for God's sake. I was scared."

"Scared he did it?"

"Scared to ask him if he did it."

"*Did* you ask him?"

He shook his head.

"Did he confess?"

"No," he said, pushing back. "We just went home."

But she kept him on task. "What else?"

"What?" he asked, brow creased deep.

"What else happened?" she demanded. "Did you call anybody? Order pizza? Play Nintendo. What the hell did you two do the rest of the evening?"

A shiver rolled through him. "Oh, God."

Sensing a crack in the door, she pushed through, harder. "Oh, God what, Peter?"

He stiffened, seeking enough guts to follow through.

"I screwed his brains out until he stopped crying," he screamed. "That's what I did. It's what I'd always wanted to do. There he was all . . . vulnerable. Crying. I held him like a friend is supposed to do. Until he needed more."

Tears dripped from his chin. With the secret out, he squinted his eyes shut, dropped his head to his knees, and unabashedly cried.

But she didn't want him to crawl inside his head and get lost there. Too much more needed to be said.

"In your liaison that night, did he confess to anything?"

He almost growled his response. "I told you he never confessed to me."

"Can the attitude, Vicar. If I have to ask the same question a dozen times, you'll answer it a dozen times. Did your physical relationship continue with Butch after that night?"

"No. He threw himself back into his swarthy, arrogant persona," he said, attempting to slow his sobs. "I returned to being his baseball buddy and pal-around dude. In other words, I honored his desire to stay straight."

"Is that what JJ is holding over you? How would she find out?"

"I have no idea."

"Are you straight?" she asked.

He took a second. "Wish I wasn't."

What a poor messed-up man. "Why'd you marry Libby?"

"She actually loved me once upon a time," he said. "She listened to me."

"Does she know about Butch and the *suite* business? About the two of you?"

He reserved his answer.

"I've already interviewed her," Callie reminded.

"She knows all of it. And she forgave me."

"She divorced you."

Both hands rubbed from brow to chin. "It was . . . too much history."

"You were only kids," she said.

He shrugged. "My God has forgiven me, too. He gave me some degree of peace."

Circling her finger in the air, she skeptically frowned. "That's what this is I'm seeing here? Peace?"

He sniffled once, twice. "Nothing will bring Wendy back, Callie. I did not kill her, and I do not believe Butch did either, so yes. Peace."

If standing, he would measure a couple inches over six feet, with her the same over five, but she abruptly rose, and she stepped into his space before he could stand. "You might tell yourself that at the pulpit or when you say your prayers at night, Peter, but your piety won't work on me. And between you and me, I don't think you've convinced yourself of that shit either." She backed away. "Don't leave my beach until I tell you to. I still have questions. And I'll need your passport."

She hid the disdain, not at his sexual experimenting but at his suppression of the truth . . . all the truths.

He rose to retrieve the passport.

Callie reached for the recorder to end the conversation.

"Am I a suspect?" he asked.

She left it running. "Won't know until we find JJ, will we?"

The puzzled shock pushed him back in his chair.

"Where's JJ, Peter?"

"I absolutely have no idea, Callie. She hasn't called me back."

With that she ended the recording. She repeated her order to him to remain on Edisto Beach. "If someone has taken JJ, in all probability, it's one of our group, so you should also keep a low profile from them."

She left the man still in his chair, his sovereign manners forgotten as she let herself out.

She hadn't enjoyed that. She'd confronted many a witness, many a target, many a cold-blooded criminal, but this one left her hollow. Not quite the right description. Unfulfilled maybe.

She got answers. She broke new ground, but this whole mess dredged up feelings.

He didn't hang over the railing upon her departure like he had when she arrived. Callie exited the drive and wound through the landscaped route back to the front gate, speed limit fifteen but gripped the wheel like she entered Charleston rush hour on the interstate, unable to shed the experience. She preferred her finger on the pulse of her emotions, control of any and all in her life.

She was angry, damn it. She was almost . . . hurt?

Her high school senior year represented her first loss, and her first sense of injustice. When she watched the father she worshipped play politics with a police chief, she'd convinced herself in her tender youth that even if she disagreed with the results, they knew better than she. They protected her from the ugliness of the truth.

She wanted to believe that Chief Warren ran the show, convincing her father the mayor that all was done that could be done. At yesterday's Sunday dinner, listening to Warren's spiel about dead-end investigations, she dared remember him as the uncle figure he once was. She had almost believed he'd worked around the clock to find Wendy's killer.

Not any longer.

Her father had been smarter than that, too.

God, she'd loved that man. He was what every little girl wished for in a father. But she learned more about Lawton Cantrell since he died than she cared to, and now she saw he'd fallen short of avenging Wendy.

She should've listened to her seventeen-year-old gut.

She passed through the security gate and reached Dock Site Road but pulled to the side to allow others to pass.

Wendy's murder and Stratton's senseless suicide were key in directing her toward law enforcement, but she'd compartmentalized high school into the furthest recesses of her mind.

She couldn't tuck away her two old classmates any longer.

Next stop, *Water Spout.* Revisit Libby? Check off Reuben? Grab Georgia to learn more about how this mess got started?

Not Butch though. Oh no, not yet. She'd save him till last, until she had all she could garner from the rest about then and now. His interview had to be well-designed, well-equipped, giving her full advantage, and while she had him, she'd savor every bloody second with him.

Damn JJ. Damn her all to hell.

Or maybe she should've asked Peter to do that for her.

The self-serving author had set one helluva stage for the truth to come out, but her style was nothing to admire.

The phone rang. Not her phone though. Some sort of movie ring tone.

Reaching into the pocket on the side of her cargo pants, Callie extracted JJ's phone. She'd held onto it just in case somebody in JJ's world would call. The caller ID, however, was only a number. Callie answered.

"JJ? It's me. Are you all right?" asked the caller, all mysterious and breathless. "Call when you need me. Call me anyway so I know you're okay. Things are getting weird." When Callie didn't reply, they hung up.

My, my, my. Guess who just climbed to the top of the interview list?

And Callie remembered the tone. The theme song from *Misery*.

Leave it to JJ to try and think like Stephen King.

Guess Callie'd have to think like Jack Reacher.

Chapter 27

CALLIE PARKED behind Libby's SUV, taking count of the cars at *Water Spout*. One, no, two vehicles missing, and one belonged to the person most prevalent on her mind.

It was mid-afternoon. The spring sun flickered bold and bright off passing cars, but especially off the churning water. The Atlantic's briny aroma hung more gently without the heavy humidity of summer. Peering through the house's stilts, she spotted roughly twenty heads between the property and the water, in assorted positions on towels. Prime lay-out-and-tan time. High tide crammed visitors closer to the beachfront homes, and the kicker of a breeze pushed the water hard, the rollers crashing making folks raise their voices to speak.

For these and other reasons, taxes and hurricanes included, Callie lived on Jungle Road four blocks over. A quiet, private, and much less costly way of life.

At the top of the stairs, she knocked while turning the knob, the door again unlatched. Butch messed around in the kitchen, his skin already dark from three days living on that chaise lounge, his cheek bones and nose sporting a deep-red tinge. With a floral shirt half buttoned to show his tanned chest sprinkled with salt-and-pepper hair, he looked every bit the plastic, quasi-famous television broadcaster he was.

He did a fake jolt of surprise, hand on his heart. "Do you always let yourself in to people's houses? Are you the beach Gestapo?"

"When nobody answers, I try the door," she said, hardly standing the sight of him after talking to Peter. "You're lucky it was me. Are the others on the porch?"

"Reuben ran to the grocery store. Something about needing drink other than booze and Coke." Butch emptied the last of the Jack Daniels, the bottle making a monster clunk against the beer cans in the trash.

Callie peeked out the window. Reuben's BMW was missing. "Go down the list for me, please."

"Actually, you and me are it, Rizzoli." He shot a flashy pearly grin.

"The two lovebirds are walking the beach."

Libby and Tony especially would milk this vacay as long as they could, enjoying the liberty of hearing the ocean's pulse morning, noon, and night. The feeling of affluence. Butch hadn't mentioned one person, though. "Where's Georgia?"

He twisted a lime into his drink, held up a finger for her to allow him a relished sip of approval. "Ahhh, the first nip is always the best." Another quick one for good measure.

"Butch, damn it. Where's Georgia?"

"Keep your panties on, Chief. Our fashionable, aristocratic hostess needed her daily *breath of fresh air*, she called it. She can only take so much of us. Honestly? Her dramatics only goad us more. Naïve as hell, that one."

Callie marched through the massive living space to the porch, unwilling to take anything Butch said as gospel. Truthfully, this whole Comedy Central collection of misfits would lie in a heartbeat, in her opinion, but like he said, nobody was out there.

Leaning over the railing, she scanned for anybody. At the beach, someone could easily hide in plain sight, but she was accustomed to scrutinizing masses of beachcombers.

She walked fast back to Butch, hanging at the bar. "Where did Georgia go?"

He shrugged and snared a handful of nacho chips.

His lackadaisical attitude clashed with her newfound wisdom of him. In an instant, out-of-body moment, she saw herself slinging him off that stool, across the kitchen table and into the wall. The itch to go another interview round with this idiot ran deep, and with nobody around, she could exorcise the demons right out of the bastard. She had the recorder in her pocket. Or maybe what she had in mind didn't need recording.

But the son of a bitch was drunk. Too easy and not worth her time . . . yet.

Georgia was more her target. She had kept them all in the dark as much or more than JJ, it seemed, and she'd shifted into Callie's top priority. Find Georgia and possibly find JJ.

Because when Callie pulled out of Wyndham, that had been Georgia on the other end of JJ's phone, asking for an update from a woman for whom the search team hunted. That call had detoured this whole case for Callie.

"Hey, Rizzoli," Butch started, then thought about what he really wanted to say. He wasn't smiling anymore. "Is JJ really missing or is this part of the plan?"

Like he'd read her mind.

She blistered him with a look. She wanted to tie him into a hundred knots, dive into that shallow brain of his and rip his psyche to shreds. Even if he didn't kill Wendy, he raped a young girl, took advantage of no telling how many more, and lied to God-knows-how-many people.

She didn't owe him a damn reply.

His perplexed expression only infuriated her more.

"Where did Georgia say she went to get this fresh air?" she demanded, telling herself she only shouted to be heard over the noise of the surf.

Butch just shrugged.

Georgia's Cadillac was the other car missing, and chances were that Georgia had the second rental address.

Callie got on her mic and put out a BOLO, be on the lookout, for Georgia Walker Stilmack and her champagne-colored Caddy. Then she called Raysor, to avoid giving the impression she favored Mark.

"She's misled me and this entire group of oddballs," she said. "She just tried to call JJ's cell that I happened to have in my pocket, and getting no answer, she left the beach house."

"Sure she wasn't just trying to locate her missing friend?" he asked.

"Maybe," she said. "But call me if she shows. Hold her if you can. One by one I'm picking the brains of this crew. I'm at *Water Spout* waiting on one guy in particular before he gets gone."

"Ten four," Raysor replied.

She signed off and turned to the kitchen. Pickings were sparse, but she managed some strawberries not totally spent and a tall glass of orange juice. She worried Reuben would soon slip away. He was smarter than the others and the least enthused by the retreat.

She wouldn't mind asking Libby if she wanted to rethink her story, too. It sounded innocent enough until she told Tony to cover for her and say she was seated with her sister. Which only screamed she wasn't. Then Callie would revisit Tony . . .

"You mad at me or something?" Butch asked.

"Or something," she said.

"What did I do?"

She motioned a strawberry at his glass. "How many is that today?"

His clownish look slid into a lazy smile. "I don't count. People who count want to brag or worry about how they look."

"You obviously aren't concerned about that. We'll talk about your past another time when you can remember it and aren't swimming in that booze."

He slid toward her along the bar, his elbows never leaving the granite. The sliding ceased when he bumped into her.

Which made her smell his bourbon . . . the earlier stuff, the fresh stuff, and the rancid smell of that he drank last night. Then he winked, too sluggish to give the effect he wanted. "You're single, I hear?" he said. When she didn't pay him any mind, he nudged her, from his shoulder to an unsteady hip which mashed her weapon into her.

She put down her glass. "Touch me one more time, and I'll find you another place to stay the night, Butch. They don't serve liquor and hors d'oeuvres."

She'd grown accustomed to men making attempts at her. Usually they knew better when she wore the uniform, but a touch of alcohol emboldened some to try anyway, to show her who was in charge. While she could control her temper, that domineering behavior never failed to make her want to prove them wrong.

"Don't touch me again, Butch."

He gave a gravely chuckle, the kind that broadcasted she didn't understand whom she was up against. The kind that put her properly on the balls of her feet.

With no discretion, his elbow left the bar, hand going down toward her ass. Problem was, it had to pass her firearm to get there.

"If I don't see that hand reappear on the bar by the time I finish my sentence, you'll wind up face down on the floor in cuffs, Butch."

The chuckle reduced to a grin, and to give him credit, he paused in that slurry of a brain to reconsider, but then his hand continued seeking a place to land on her person.

In a swish of a move, easily mastered on an inebriated dolt, the newscaster found his cheek on the tile and his ice and drink splashed across the walkway toward the living room. More ice than drink.

"What . . . shit . . . umph." He uttered assorted noises, some resembling words.

Having properly placed the promised cuffs, Callie got down on a knee and cocked her head so he could see her as clearly as a drunk could. "Bet you didn't see that coming, did you?"

"What the hell did you do that for?" Not Butch's words. Libby's.

She scurried over, awkwardly going to the floor. "Are you all right?" Then at Callie she gave her tortured woman tone. "How dare you?"

Callie's phone rang. She answered and heard traffic noise. "Mark?"

"I'm on 174 following your lady in the Caddy," he said. "She's on her way toward you. One of the guys at the scene spotted her as she came around the block, but she saw us and kept driving. I jumped in my vehicle and followed."

"Toward the beach?" Callie asked.

"Yeah. Want to stay on the phone so I can tell you where she lands?"

Tony had walked over by then, scrutinizing the attention Libby gave the drunk on the floor, no concern in his eyes.

"No point," Callie said. "Keep both hands on the wheel and follow her in. I have a strong suspicion where she's headed. I'll meet you there."

She hung up. After taking in the image of how overtly alarmed Libby was over Butch, she leaned down and uncuffed him. "Don't ever touch a person in uniform, Butch. Especially one with me in it."

On her chubby knees, Libby leered up with scorn as Callie rose to her feet. "And who exactly cleans up this mess?" she said, with a flamboyant wave toward the glass on its side.

"Not my problem," Callie said. "I've got a person of interest to corral. Just be glad it isn't one of you."

CALLIE PARKED HER cruiser under *Flirty Flamingo* as far back as she could, not wanting Georgia to spot it and flee. She discreetly hid under the stairs, behind an ancient eight-foot-tall pittosporum. She didn't have to wait long.

The Caddy turned onto Thistle, easing toward the rental like a tourist hunting for a potential dreamhouse they would never afford. The dead-end road had no walkers, thank goodness. Mark wasn't on her tail, but as Georgia reached the drive, he came around the corner.

Spotting the end of Callie's police car, Georgia braked and looked over her seat to back up. Mark, however, pushed the gas, closed the gap, and maneuvered to block her escape as Callie exited her hiding place. "Hey, Georgia. What's up?"

The ex-cheerleader peered behind at Mark then at Callie.

"I see what you're thinking. Don't," Callie said. "How about let's step inside?"

Mark got out and approached, waiting for cue from Callie. "Need me?"

Callie heard the question. Though she understood the simple request, in a crazy quirk of a mental blip she'd heard it framed as a query from a beau.

"I got her," she explained further. "I've taken you away from your restaurant enough already. Thanks." She avoided his name, worried she'd sound too informal in front of Georgia.

She imagined a hint of disappointment in his eyes, but his smile appeared quick enough to make her wonder if she read him wrong. He tipped an invisible hat. "Call if you need me." Then he returned to his car with that slight limp he avoided discussing.

"Well?" Georgia asked, throwing a hand on her hip, the boldness not matching the fret she tried to hide.

Callie motioned her to follow. "Come on inside. Let's see if JJ came back to her first house in the plan since she obviously isn't at the second."

The lady with the flighty manners and saccharin hostess skills blew out like a flustered deer, snatched up her purse, and slammed her door. A minute later, she stood in the dinette area of the small rental, peering around as if checking the quality of the last cleaning.

"Sit," Callie said, but once Georgia took her place at the dinette, Callie remained standing. "Where's JJ?"

"Why was a crime scene truck at the house?" she said instead.

"I ask the questions, Georgia." Callie pulled out her recorder and set it on the table, a quick intro thrown on record. "Where is JJ?"

"I . . . I thought she was at her house in the Neck."

"Which begs me to ask how you knew that?"

Callie watched Georgia let that sink in. The eye movement, the inability to keep hands still. "Start at the beginning."

The hostess weighed what to say and how to say it.

"Just tell the truth the best you can," Callie said. "If you don't talk, I can find ample to charge you with. If you lie, ditto. Start with when you first made contact with JJ, and I don't care how far back that goes."

Scared at the threat, Georgia glanced around as if she'd find allies. Callie didn't even offer her a glass of water.

"When JJ appeared in Libby's class five years ago, she asked to meet with me and Libby after."

Interesting, since Libby said JJ spoke to the students and left. She said nothing about a social hour. "Cover that meeting."

"She offered to be involved in a class reunion. As a sponsor, a presenter, whatever. But her schedule was too booked to do it that year or the year after. Her publisher had her traipsing the country, so she said she'd be in touch. We were told to keep it secret, but actually, we thought she'd forgotten until six months ago when she called."

Five years. Maybe she was busy . . . or she needed detachment from all the press from her Middleton visit so she wasn't connected to the plan. Or maybe a proper scheme took time to sculpt.

"Still have the call on your phone? And any messages," Callie added.

"I upgraded my phone . . ."

"We'll check later." Callie leaned against the wall, not eager to get comfortable at the small table. Even Georgia had height on her. Callie peering down possessed more power for encouraging better responses. "Go on. She got in touch when?"

"The end of September. She asked if we had a retreat place to plan the reunion. JJ suggested the senior superlative group as the coordinators, and Libby suggested we add Tony to acquire the school. I offered my beach house. From there on out she just spoke to me."

"Or so she says," Callie added, and Georgia blanched as if she hadn't thought of that. "Why that cast of characters?"

Georgia acted pained at her interrogator not understanding. "She was just writing a book, Callie. Come on. Scripting chapters. Creating a story that would sell. She analyzed us, measuring each of us as colorful enough, or suspicious enough. The best collection of people to tell the most enticing story. All centered around Wendy. Like a Netflix mystery."

Callie saw how she herself represented one of those colorful roles. The one having missed meting justice all those years ago, the melodrama incorporating the tormented righteousness-seeker.

"You have to admit it has potential," Georgia said.

"Not with the author gone," Callie replied. "But something doesn't set well with me, Georgia. Several somethings, actually."

Georgia waited.

"When JJ dropped her bombshell, saying she cancelled half the attendees, you flashed all disturbed and insulted. You knew."

Still wide-eyed, she looked caught.

"Okay," she replied. "I knew well in advance, but it was innocent enough."

"You cancelled the ones who didn't show," Callie said. "At JJ's direction."

Georgia gave quick mini-nods. "Yes, but not really. She made the selections. I just didn't invite the others at all. They never knew."

Callie rubbed her chin, with the appearance of contemplation. "Why leave out Peter?"

But Georgia shook her head. "He never confirmed."

"So he was invited?"

Her blinking showed confusion. "I sent him an email and he never replied." Then she gave a *whatever* shrug. "Besides, he was in England. Who'd fly all that way for this?"

"True." They almost spoke as fellow graduates. "But Reuben. Explain him."

"JJ crushed on him in high school."

Whoa. Callie hadn't seen that coming and didn't recall an inkling of that.

Wendy had treated the lab nerd with kindness, while others didn't treat him any way at all. Invisible. The unrequited love interest so easy to milk in a screenplay.

But JJ and Reuben? "I don't recall seeing sparks on Friday night. Or any sideline conversations."

"Too much arranging," Georgia said. "Too much stirring the pot."

"Time to ask the thousand-dollar question, my friend."

Georgia hesitantly smiled, more willing to please.

"Did JJ suspect who killed Wendy?"

Tucking her chin in surprise, Georgia feigned ignorance and shrugged with almost cartoon exaggeration. "Doesn't matter. I don't think she was solving a crime or creating a crime. This was a storytelling project."

"Tell me about JJ's con to disappear and fake a crime."

That smile slid like butter off a griddle. There it was, laid out bold and naked. Georgia had played the Igor to JJ's Frankenstein in setting something up, regardless of what she was told it was.

Her bottom lip pursed.

Callie finally pulled out a chair, tired of being on her feet. "Cut the acting."

"It's not acting. I'm scared."

"As you should be. Answer the question."

Georgia fished a tissue from her purse and dabbed femininely at her nose, then with a final sniffle, looked back up with genuine red around her eyes. "The beach event was supposed to be a dinner mystery. JJ would pretend something happened, to judge behavior. I was to watch, take notes, and keep her informed. If it got entertaining, she would plot a book. I saw the whole thing as the eccentricities of a creative spirit."

JJ had picked the right lacky, but Callie showed no mercy. "Go into the plan."

"I . . . she . . . we . . ."

"Start over."

Georgia repositioned herself and willed back her tears. "She was to drop the surprise about who was invited, the emphasis being they were connected to Wendy. For an hour or two, she'd watch everyone, then leave. From that point on, I checked in with her several times a day."

Callie motioned with curling fingers. "Show me the phone number."

Anxiously, the woman plowed through her purse. She pushed buttons on her phone and scrolled, turning it around to Callie, the cell shaking in her hand. A different number than what the others had.

"So when you called me, you called JJ's personal phone by accident?"

"Yes, we had a special number, but I forgot."

Callie took the phone and scrolled through the history. A dozen calls since Friday afternoon. Indeed, JJ had been alive through the weekend, at least until Peter arrived and couldn't reach her. The last Georgia call was Saturday afternoon, as with Peter, with neither able to connect.

"Lying to me was part of the plan?"

She started to shake her head, attempting to read Callie in hopes of remaining noncommittal.

"Talk, Georgia!" she said, firm. "I could have a body to look for."

The gasp choked the hostess. "A body?"

"Let's just say this," Callie said, growing impatient with this whole mess. "We found blood in the house at the Neck. The door left open. Signs of a kidnapping."

Georgia turned the color of her tissue. "What?"

"Who took her?"

She shrugged. "It was mystery theater, Callie. To get people looking at each other."

Stupid, stupid woman. "Did you ever think one of them might actually be the killer? And your good friend JJ left you living with them all stirred up like bees under your roof?"

Callie was already up and easing Georgia's head on the table before her eyes rolled back in her head.

Of course, she withheld that JJ could've planted that scene at the Neck, too, but the abduction story made for a much better reaction.

Chapter 28

JJ
Sunday . . . Monday . . .

ON HER BED. Tied to the headboard, the footboard. Gagged.

JJ drifted in and out of consciousness, but she wasn't sleepy. But she couldn't see anyway with the black whatever over her head. The heavy material draped down across her chest. What had they given her? Was she still in the same house? The same bed? On the same island?

Blinking, blinking. All she could see was black. Then a whiff of something chemical almost choked her.

He was pouring it on her face, straight on the fabric.

Smart, she thought, as she faded into oblivion again. He didn't even have to take her mask off.

JJ AWOKE IN THE trunk of a car, the wheels humming loudly on the pavement, her pulse accelerating at the realization of where she was . . . and the uncertainty of where she was bound.

Like before, she saw nothing except the cloth wrapped over her head. A bag, a jacket, a tablecloth, whatever it was, she could not tell other than all was black and she could barely suck in air. Thick material that draped over her shoulders and onto her chest. She was unable to tell because she could not touch it due to her hands taped behind her back.

And she could only use her nose. Tape covered her mouth in lieu of the gag. Thank God for that.

A dull ache gripped one side of her head, and slowly she worked her chin, jaw, shifting muscles around. That damn door had knocked her out cold, apparently, and whatever he used to keep her knocked out kept her from analyzing the damage. From the fat feel of the right side of her cheek and the copper taste of her lip, she'd suffered some. She couldn't open one eye all the way.

The intricacies of detail about her own injuries threw her back into one of her books. Her seventh novel placed the protagonist in the trunk of a car, though the car had been old, the chassis heavy with spots of rust. There had been worry of exhaust seeping into the trunk, and for a moment JJ feared the same. She could die from the fumes . . . until she sensed the vehicle modern. It would have a release handle for situations such as this, if she could see. If she could feel. If she could move.

Who did this?

Use your head, woman. Deduce. She couldn't tell the type of car, but damn it, she also hadn't made note of who drove what make and model when she arrived at Georgia's. Callie would have noticed.

She messed up. She'd underestimated the bad guy. She'd set herself up and ruined everything.

Slow down.

Her heart flipped in her chest, then again. Panic did that. She was better than panic. She tried to take a deep breath, but the air would not come in as fast as she needed, and even in the head cover, she closed her eyes and willed herself to be what she needed to be. *Be the author, JJ.* Be who the world thinks you are, incredibly instinctive.

She stretched her legs, but not far. She rolled back, hit the wall, and returned, then forward, with only inches in front of her. A deep trunk but not wide. Not much debris. Smelled clean.

Smell. Yes. Use all of the senses. She sniffed. Brine. General car odors. Newer rather than old. No chemicals. Nothing rotted. *Shit.* Nothing of note.

Think like your readers think you do.

Thinking like an author might actually get her out of this. Might allow her to deduce enough to tell the authorities when she got away. Or leave enough clues in case she didn't.

The last thought shot her pulse into overdrive again, this time drawing tears.

No. No! She wasn't doing this. Wasn't letting this demon tap into her fears. That was how they won. That was how they would beat down her will, turning her into nothing more than a minion cowering to please to avoid pain and horror. Like she wrote about in her mysteries.

Dear God, she was in a thriller of her own making, in a twist she never saw coming.

Chapter 29

GEORGIA DOWNED one glass of water and asked for another, almost at hyperventilation mode seated at the rental's dinette table. "I can't go back," she gasped, hand on her bosom. "Not with a killer under my roof."

"I didn't definitely say there was one," Callie said. "And it'll look odd if you don't return. Where will you hide out otherwise? Besides, isn't your home on the mailing list?"

A big gasp. Then tentative contemplation, and finally, the fear of having no answer made per speechless. Callie felt for the woman. She really did. She'd been used and made to think that misleading people could be grand fun. Nobody ever thinks of the criminal element entering their little bubble worlds. Callie couldn't imagine a world without it.

"After we get done here, go back to *Water Spout*."

"What if they can tell I spoke with you, Callie?"

"If you tell nobody, and I tell nobody, then how would they?" she replied, trying not to demean the frantic woman.

"But . . . but . . ." Georgia shook her hands before her.

"But what?" Callie asked calmly.

Nervously, Georgia uttered, "What if they figure it out on their own?"

Well, there was that. Anyone out of sight for any length of time would be suspect, and time was running out on the patience of these people.

JJ was proving herself a doozy of a manipulator, a trait she'd probably mastered from years of devouring plots and what-ifs to best the last she'd written. With eighteen books under her belt, she had to find each story more delectable yet difficult than the one before, and she appeared to have done well at climbing that hill. Callie wasn't enlightened about publishing, but she understood enough to realize that the idea of today became a book many years downstream. The writing, the publishing, the promotion came in long, slow stages.

Made sense that coming back to Middleton five years ago to speak to Libby's high school class could have sparked this story line. The place, the people, the ripping-off-the-scab sensation of such a life-altering moment left damage on all their young lives.

Akin to *Murder on the Orient Express*, JJ seemed to treat this beach vacation as if all could have been involved.

Like the others, Callie hadn't forgotten the night of Wendy's murder. The night had redirected her future. Each of them had to preserve a scar of some kind like that as well.

To JJ, returning to a school environment spawned the premise for a juicy conspiracy narrative. Maybe she owned a talent for sleuthing even as a teen. No doubt she loved to tell a story, being involved in the yearbook and the school paper. But was her interest from a big picture stance? Or did she nurse a personal grudge?

Did the writer hate the injustice or see one hell of a story that needed a better, more satisfying ending? Like Callie resented Chief Warren letting the case grow cold, like Peter couldn't close the door on his memories of those girls, like Libby felt the need to tell Tony to lie about who she'd sat with, JJ could harbor a secret of her own.

"Georgia . . . answer me this, and don't you dare lie," Callie said. "Do you hear me?"

"Promise," and she literally crossed her heart, finishing with her palm pressed over it.

As if such a promise held substance. Callie was really disappointed in this woman. She'd been smart in school, in personal finance, and adult success. Was her ignorance a ruse or had she truly been taken advantage of, stepping in crap she wasn't sure how to wipe off her shoes?

"Where is JJ?" Callie asked.

With exaggerated shakes of her head, Georgia replied. "If she isn't at the Neck, I have no idea." She curled fingers at Callie. "Keep them coming, Callie. The questions. I want to show I'm a good person. I didn't mean to break any laws. I wasn't trying to hurt anyone. I . . . I—"

"Next question . . . was an incident planned at the Neck like she did here, at *Flirty Flamingo*? Any sort of orchestrated abduction or violence?"

Hand up as if in a courtroom, she answered, "Absolutely not! I swear! If something happened to her, I'd die!"

Then came the tears again.

Callie wasn't feeling particularly sympathetic anymore.

Men's voices sounded outside. Callie had an ear for distances on Edisto, and she read two people, male, on this lot.

She stood to check it out when feet scrambled up the steps,

clumsy-like, as if chased. On cue another set ran up, steadier, pursuing the first.

Georgia got up and mashed herself into a corner behind the table. Callie motioned, and Georgia sank to the floor per command.

With a scuffle on the porch and a thunk against the outside wall, Callie retreated into the hall that led to the bedroom, not ten feet from the door, hand on her weapon.

Someone tried the knob, failed at his first effort, then tried again.

The door flew open, bouncing off the cheap rubber stopper on the baseboard.

Butch fell in . . . literally, his weight taking him to the floor onto his forearms. "I tell you she's here," he said.

Thomas peeked in and announced, "Police."

"I'm here, Thomas." Callie appeared, close enough Butch could reach out and touch her shoes, if he could find them. From his stillness and need to remain horizontal, he wasn't sure what had happened.

"Claims he got lost leaving the liquor store," Thomas said, bumping the man's leg with his boot while stepping over him. "Drove drunk as a skunk over here."

Georgia eased out of her hiding place. "Butch? I had more liquor in the bar."

"No, you didn't," he said into the throw rug bunched under his chin.

"Not sure he could find the bar," Callie said, stooping down. "Butch, sit up."

But he couldn't seem to make his arms and legs cooperate, and it took Thomas under an arm to get him to his feet. Georgia slid a chair behind his legs, and he still almost missed it. Ahold of Butch's shoulder, Thomas righted the man and gripped tight until he remained upright.

Georgia came around. The man had three humans in from of him, his alcohol-saturated brain fighting to make each one out. But after scanning the three, his gaze tried to remain on Georgia. "What the hell are you doing here? Were we supposed to meet you here?"

"I'm meeting Callie," she explained. "We're talking about JJ. It's all screwed up. Did you hear—"

Then with a look from Callie, she shut up, already forgetting her promise of silence. How she'd pulled this coup over the group was beyond Callie's comprehension. She looked to Thomas, about to ask what happened.

"I fucked her!" Butch yelled.

Thomas flinched, frowning at Callie for a clue. She gave him a subtle head shake to hold his thought.

Butch swayed, his balance off, his voice slurred but brazen. His clothes were awry, and a gold chain dangled weirdly, the St. Christopher's medal hung up under his wrinkled collar. "But I never hurt her. Don't a one of you say otherwise. I fucked four others that night, too, and didn't kill them neither." He pointed toward Callie, but not quite at her . . . probably at one of the several versions of her. "Your Chief Warren tried to kill my future, the dumb shit. I can look at you and see you think I killed Wendy. But I didn't!"

Callie had turned on the recorder after he yelled the F word. "But you don't have an alibi, Butch." Not that she'd be able to use the recording in court, but she'd use it to get him to repeat it again once he was sober. Nothing like hearing yourself spilling guilty thoughts to make you tell the truth.

Butch tipped forward and caught himself. Thomas stood primed for the drunk to swing, and Callie still took a step back. "You don't exactly have an alibi," she repeated.

"For what, killing Wendy?" He laughed a crazed, disturbed laugh. "I got plenty of alibis. Ask Peter."

"He no longer covers for you," she said.

Which drew Butch up short. Even Georgia checked herself. "You've spoken to Peter?" she said.

Callie nodded, matter-of-factly. "Oh, yes. I got an earful from him. He remembers that night much differently than he swore to as a teen."

"Did Peter kill Wendy?" Georgia almost whispered.

"No, that's not quite where I'd put my money. What do you think?" Callie nudged Butch's foot. He scowled and tried to move it, unable to do both at once. "My bet's fairly safe on you, Butch."

"I didn't kill her!" he yelled and swallowed hard after the effort, forcing something back down. Callie took another half step back.

"How are we supposed to believe that?" she said. "Not a one of your alumni can vouch for where you were. Is drinking how you try to forget, Butch? Can't get the look of her red, bulging eyes out of your dreams? Too much booze foiling your attempt to rape her?"

He stood, then fell back, missing the chair, and collapsed on the linoleum in ragdoll fashion. With a growl, he punched the chair away and flushed, his eyes pink and teary. "Yes, I fucked Wendy that night, but she left alive. After that I was with that little girl."

Georgia's mascara-loaded lashes about touched her bangs, and she covered her mouth. "Oh my God. What little girl? How little?"

Butch spun on the floor toward her, and she high-stepped back, knocking into the dinette. "I didn't kill Wendy, you dim-witted cow!" Then to Callie, "And I didn't rape the kid, either. She lost her shit and started screaming. She changed her mind about losing her virginity to me and started shaking. I bought her a Coke and calmed her down, and I talked to her friends like I was her older boyfriend or something, to make them jealous."

Something Peter might not be aware of. Not if Butch was hell-bent on being macho and lying. After all, Butch didn't do gentleman very well.

"Why didn't you tell Chief Warren?" Callie asked.

He leaned back on his hands, pushed his legs in front of him. "Why the hell would I do that?"

"To avoid being suspected of murder!"

His belch almost came out like a vomit.

Thomas waved his hand like a fan. "Christ, man."

After a cough and a slight gurgle, the newscaster took another confirmed swallow.

"Telling ya, he's gonna puke," whispered the officer.

Butch's glower moved from Thomas to Callie. "Sure, how's that sound telling the chief of police that my alibi was what he'd see as an attempt to rape a fourteen-year-old. Then tell him I screwed the dead girl before that. That pig would've locked me up without looking at anyone else."

"The girl was your alibi," Callie said, but no doubt he'd been between a rock and a hard place. The questioning would've embarrassed the girl and dumped an attempted rape accusation on Butch, not to mention the craziness the parents would've heaped on his head. Definitely made the horny boy a much more likely suspect than Stratton, though.

Besides, why admit to something when another boy already assumed the spotlight?

Time moved on and scared kids became nervous adults. Who could prove any of this today anyway?

Then along came JJ, hinting she could see in everybody's head.

Callie motioned for Thomas to lift the man to his feet. The officer understood that the rest of his day was obligated. Edisto had no lockup, meaning a forty-five-minute drive to Walterboro. "Once you test him and confirm he's over the limit, cart him to jail." Then to Butch, "Who at the house let you drive drunk?"

"Nobody," he said. "You left me alone there, so look in the mirror."

Like that made sense.

Georgia sniffed. "Oh my Lord. Did he just—"

Thomas did likewise and grimaced. "Crapped his pants? Damn sure did."

But Butch remained planted on the floor, unaware he'd soiled himself, mulling over thoughts nobody had a clue about.

Both mics went off from Marie back at the station. "A gator came out of the marsh behind Wainwright Realty. Traffic jam per Mark Dupree. He's trying to control the scene."

Callie answered. "Call DNR and put an ASAP on that. Both Thomas and I are on it."

"Damn it," Thomas moaned, gripping Butch. Callie gave him an assist on the other side. "I take it this shit waits in *my* car while we handle that call."

"Perks of being a chief," she said, letting loose once Butch appeared mobile.

Georgia scurried over at Callie's directive, and as Callie locked the door to the rental, her phone rang. Caller ID Janet Wainwright. Quite surprising she hadn't called before Marie.

"Need more than a damn Mexican directing traffic in front of my office," she yelled. "Someone come get this animal away from my property."

Callie hustled down the porch steps, past Georgia. "He's not Mexican, Janet, and we're on our way."

"All of you," Janet fussed.

"Thomas and me," Callie replied. "Do not get into that ruckus, and keep you and your people up on your porch. Understand?"

"Roger that."

One had to talk brass to brass to get through to that woman.

"Go home, Georgia," Callie hollered over her cruiser's roof.

The hostess snatched her Caddy's door open. "If you won't hunt for JJ, I will. This isn't how we planned."

"We'll get to JJ," Callie shouted. "Get your butt home."

If Georgia had long hair, it would've whipped over her shoulder with that head snap. "You already told me a killer might be sleeping in my house."

"You're safer at your house surrounded by witnesses than alone hunting for JJ. Or you can ride with Butch in Thomas's cruiser."

The pout got bigger.

Callie strode to the Caddy. "Where exactly would you look, Georgia? Was there a third backup house? How deep does this prank go?"

"There is no prank."

Callie hmphed. "You mean additional prank. Is there another house?"

"No."

"Do you have any idea where she is?"

Georgia dropped her shoulders. "No. I was going to ask the neighbors. I was . . ."

"Going to do what the police are already doing. You'll make matters worse."

More tears. Either her emotions were that fragile or she cried on cue, but Callie had no time to care. "Thomas? Want another passenger?"

"Okay, I'll be at the house," the hostess said and plopped into the seat of her car.

Callie jumped in her cruiser and snapped her belt.

Thomas had to situate Butch, so Callie pulled out and around the officer and dashed right on Atlantic to hit Palmetto. Left on Mary Street would've taken her close to the problem, but a block away people jogged toward the action, cars already blocking the sides. Her siren and lights parted the human sea, getting her somewhat closer, but ultimately she stopped in the middle of the road a half block away.

A roar of voices, like a wave in a stadium, reached her before she could see. She imagined the poor animal surrounded by phone-camera-frenzied tourists . . . and Mark attempting to control the fracas. Callie turned her fast walk into a trot.

Fifty people hovered, more coming from all directions. This was an all-available-men call. She shouted into her mic. "LaRoache? Need you at Wainwright's as fast as you can get here." Raysor had to remain at the Neck, processing that crime scene.

Another wave of voices lifted. Callie ran faster, waiting for someone to scream from underestimating the speed of an alligator on land. They weren't as slow as people thought.

The last thing she needed was for someone to think they could catch it and hold its mouth shut like they'd seen on a stupid YouTube video. Pushing through the crowd, she came out on Jungle Road. El Marko's was half a block down on her right and Wainwright Realty across the street.

An assortment of humanity lined both sides of the road and blocked it off to the right and left. With its tail in Wainwright's driveway and body on the asphalt, a six-foot alligator poised, mouth agape.

Mark tried to circle the beast, creating a perimeter with his bit of a limp scaring the bejesus out of Callie. What if he tripped? What if his gimpy leg, as minimally restrictive as it may be, gave out? He continued shouting to this person and that, "Get farther back. I'm telling you. This animal can move!"

But as soon as one cluster moved aside, another moved closer.

Callie ordered those in her path to leave the scene, rubberneckers treating her the same as Mark.

And Sophie made the rounds with appetizers from El Marko's, handing them out along with miniature menus.

"Get back," Callie shouted to college teens, mothers and dads, kids as she worked the crowd en route to Sophie. "Farther back, sir. Over there on the other side of the street." And upon reaching Sophie, she gripped her arm and yanked.

"Owww!"

Callie gave it another shake. "This isn't a carnival, Soph. If you want to help, divert these people inside the restaurant instead of fueling the entertainment. If you're giving away free food, lead people away from the danger. They're only scaring this animal and making matters worse."

Grinning, her turquoise contacts sparkling, dangling beaded earrings brushing her collarbone, Sophie kept up the appearance for the crowd. "Thanks. Check out El Marko's. We're right across the street here."

Callie gripped her upper arm again. "Sophie!"

"I heard you," she mumbled through a plastic smile.

"Now!"

In her pixie manner, Sophie Bianchi swished her broom skirt like only she could, and in loud sing-song began working the people. "Follow me for free appetizers."

A half dozen turned, then a couple more. At least that was something.

Callie turned back to Mark. He motioned around the animal, attempting to keep the gator affixed on him.

"Everyone move back!" came a voice over a bullhorn.

The crowd jumped. Callie jumped. Most of all the gator did a side twist of a jerk. The meaty tail caught Mark unawares in that split second he had instinctively looked for the source of the horn. He went down six feet from the butt end of the beast.

"Here, here!" Callie screamed, waving her hands, her heart coming out of her chest.

The crowd noise only swelled, a handful of them clapping. Two men part dragged, part lifted Mark to his feet.

"Shut up with the bullhorn!" she yelled, doing any sort of gyration she could to attract the gator's attention. "Just get these people back, Thomas! Those who don't listen, arrest them."

A few were suddenly convinced to move on. Sophie continued to funnel folks toward El Marko's, but there were still too many gawkers. A twenty-something stooped, aimed, seeking a money shot in the gator's face.

Callie snatched the phone camera from his hands. "This is mine until the gator's gone. So get off the road."

But the young man only stood . . . and stood his ground. "That is my property."

The gator growled, and Mark kicked the tail, redirecting it.

Callie pulled out her cuffs and slapped them on the man's left wrist. "What the hell?"

She had no more time for words, and with half the crowd cheering and the other booing, she dragged the gentleman to Janet's property. She attached the other end of the cuffs to a spindle and trotted back to the gator, the man swearing behind her.

Some of the tourists started taking pictures of him.

"Mom! Get out of there."

From the throng Callie recognized that voice, and it sounded too close for comfort.

Jeb appeared. Callie put herself between her son and the gator and pushed him back. "Don't add to this mess, son. Go."

"I can't leave you wrangling an alligator!"

"Callie!"

Suddenly an arm snatched her around the waist and off her feet.

Chapter 30

JJ
Monday afternoon.

THE CAR SLOWED way before she expected. The island wasn't monstrous and the beach was tiny, so JJ presumed her abductor would head toward the mainland with its vast choices of hiding places.

Assuming she would be hidden. Fear rippled through her that disposal would be easier on a remote island in one of its many marshes, or weighted down and dropped into one of its innumerable inlets. That didn't count the ocean and its huge creatures, but the marshes housed smaller denizen, more efficient at consuming bodies down to bones. She'd done her research before coming.

She tested her feet again, trying not to admit she felt for a weight to be used if they dropped her into the water. None there. Nothing around her she could tell.

Wait, no, they would delay that until she'd been taken to where she'd be disposed of, attach her to the anchor, then drop her in. Way less trouble.

Good God, but who? Who! Maybe how many whos?

For God's sake, she'd planned all of this only to die at the hands of the person she'd never identify? What kind of holy hell was that?

What kind of ironic twist to a story that would never be told?

Brilliant, actually.

She blinked back tears, her head covering sucking in with her sniffles to block her intake of oxygen. Slimy cool snot clung to the inside of the material.

Grasping she hadn't planned nearly as well as she should have, her weeping flowed anew. She should have guessed the malefactor in all this had spent many years keeping one eye on the horizon, waiting for some witness, some old friend, some unforeseen somebody to walk out of history and bring the past back to light. They had way more to lose than she, and therefore, would fight shrewder, harder, and more creatively to keep that history in the dark.

Which made her wonder if she was even the first. At least the first after Wendy.

She could hardly breathe.

Curled up in a fetal position, she hoped, no, prayed, for a swift ending. She wasn't a physical woman and had no idea how to fight. All she had were words.

Words. She had a way with them. Maybe she could use them with this person.

She inadvertently sniffled again, the material sticking to her nose. In an almost panic, she brushed the cloth against the floor to dislodge it and give her air. She had to quit crying.

The car slowed more, then turned . . . left. The smooth road changed to gravel, shells, something that popped beneath the tires . . . then they parked.

Scream or not scream?

Kick or not?

But her questions ceased at the sound of footsteps on the rock. One, two . . . five steps, each closer until she could sense the person outside the trunk lid. Her heart pounded hard and brisk up through her neck and into her ears, filling them so loudly that she was sure she wouldn't hear when the lid opened.

But she did hear. First the beep then the unlocking click.

Even stuffy headed, she smelled the ocean. Smelled rain. Heard it as small and infrequent. This was the beginnings of a shower, or a storm for all she knew.

She waited for a voice, then waited to be lifted out.

Waited to be stabbed.

Pressure covered her mouth. A cupped hand, a mask maybe . . . the sweet whiff of that same substance. Damn it! Her tensed shoulders melted first, then her back just a second before the rest of her body succumbed.

She jerked in final attempt to fight, but against her will she relaxed. Then against her wishes, she sank into that dark, dark place again, but not before thinking she might get wet from the rain she smelled.

Chapter 31

LITERALLY, MARK swept Callie off her feet, the gator's snap mere inches from their ankles.

In the momentum, Mark slung them both into the crowd, bouncing her off a couple in their forties which kept her from sprawling onto the ground, knocking the husband back into a palmetto. More picture snapping occurred around them. The wife fussed, "Hey, that was un-called for!"

Callie apologized and anxiously recalculated her bearings. "Get the hell away, people!" she yelled, as much for her own release of fear as their protection. "Go, go!" she shooed. "Thomas! Manage these people before someone gets eaten!"

The officer pulled out his pad and boomed an order. "Every person who isn't off this road in thirty seconds gets a ticket." People hustled toward the commercial venues on the El Marko's side of the road.

Callie wished she'd thought of that.

"That was stupid to get between Jeb and that animal," Mark said, leaning down to her, his respiration a little ragged, too.

Her chest hammering, Callie fought the shriek inching into her voice. "And you weren't? I swear I smelled its breath."

"I'm half Cajun. I read gator. And I saved your butt."

Jeb waved from the sidelines, motioning he was leaving. Grateful he understood she'd be better off not having to worry about him, she still worked to control her adrenaline at Mark. "Don't care if you're half unicorn, this thing is too big for us." She sucked in deeply, her thoughts needing more oxygen to think straight. "Maybe if we give it an escape route, it'll return from whence it came." She blew out, regaining control. "What do you suggest?"

"Actually, that's not a bad idea."

With the crowd thinned, they redirected the stragglers to the other side of Jungle Road, opening the way across the Wainwright parking lot back to the marsh.

Struggling to keep the alligator's attention, the two continued their gestures, flapping and clapping when the animal even thought about turning around, remaining ever in the corner of its eye. It moved toward the parking lot, but then found itself a safe spot between a truck and a sedan, frustrating the owners on the Wainwright porch.

A four-by-four and a van from the South Carolina Department of Natural Resources arrived, lights flashing, and the crowd waved at them, pointing toward Callie and Mark. Three guys and a gal poured out in olive cargo pants and long-sleeve polos with the department's insignia, laid eyes on the gator, and commenced to unloading their gear. The oldest came toward Callie, and she met him halfway. "We've done the best we can."

The officer pointed to her leg. "He do that?"

The three of them looked down. Her right pants leg sported a six-inch rip.

Mark took a quick look-see for anything deeper, and finding nothing, stood. "Told you," he said, taking hold of her arm just in case reality did a number on her.

She snatched her arm back, in defiance of being deemed any sort of damsel.

Thomas came over. "Couple things . . . first, want me to stick around and assist these DNR guys?"

"What about Butch?" she asked.

"That's sort of the second thing. Someone let him out."

Mark and Callie both gave him a hard stare. "Someone?" she asked.

"I bailed out to aid with crowd control. Left him in the back where he couldn't . . . get out."

"And you didn't lock the cruiser?" Mark said.

But Callie saw the situation more clearly than Mark. This was Edisto. They didn't put people in the back seat that often. Particularly island guests. Bad optics.

"He's on foot," Thomas said. "And too drunk to walk three feet without falling. Won't take long to find him. His scent alone . . ."

Callie tossed a nod toward the DNR team. "Go play with them. I'm sure you want to, but the second that's under control, you radio me back. We're not only chasing JJ but also Butch. I'll put out a BOLO for him."

Thomas took off, not eager to pursue the issue further. He'd messed up. He would go above and beyond not to do it again.

And as he had reminded her, Butch wouldn't feel too comfortable in his soiled clothing.

She got off the radio from the BOLO . . . six foot, tanned, very white teeth, dock shoes, no socks, and seriously intoxicated. Notify Edisto PD. She shot another brief update to Marie and a text to Jeb to remain inside. They had a lifetime of conflict over her protection of him.

An arm whirled her around, and she found herself against Mark's side, again. "Call if you need me, too," he said. "I mean, like Thomas."

"Hunh," she said, eying him over. "You're nothing like Thomas."

"I would hope not," he said, comically leering a second before sobering. "But seriously, I've come to rather like you, Police Chief Callie Jean Morgan. Do not walk into anything, please. While you might think you know these people from childhood, you don't."

"No more than they know me," she said, extracting herself from the hold. "I need to go."

"Where next?" he asked, and for some stupid reason, the question felt one too many.

It was innocent enough, and with him being retired SLED, a natural question. But he'd given it with a personal touch, and the professional interpretation had been lost in the personal, as if he had a right to know her movements.

"*Water Spout*," she said, moving off. "Where Butch could show up first, as well as the person who might've let him out."

He waved. She returned it. Then she put her back to him and trotted the half block to her cruiser, worried he'd read too much into the wave.

THE WIND HAD swung around from the St. Helena Sound direction, the house buffering it from her position on the front porch. No doubt the back porch caught the brunt of it, and Callie worried the crew would disband to other interests. She'd ordered them not to leave, but they hadn't shown much willingness to listen up to now.

The barometric pressure plummeted, from the mild sinus headache starting behind her eyes, and she expected a shower within the hour.

Again she walked right in. "Where's Butch?" she called in her crowd control voice, expecting it to be more effective rebounding off the high ceilings than it had with the alligator crowd.

Libby sliced fruit for some sort of Polynesian concoction. "Quit yelling, and we have no idea. He's not here."

Callie kept walking, not bothering with a woman her gut told her not to trust an inch. With the back doors anchored open, breezes pushed from the clouds rolling in, the twelve-foot sheers on either side undulating from the weather. Tony and Reuben sat on the porch. "Where's Butch?" she asked again.

They looked at each other.

"Let's make this simpler for you gentlemen. Have you seen Butch in the last hour?" She enunciated the sentence word for word.

They shook their heads.

"What about Georgia?"

"Georgia is right here," came the voice from behind her. "What, you had to check on me? See if I was good for my word?"

"In light of your recent lies, damn straight." Callie looked around at the lot of them, including Libby who came out with four drinks on a tray. A gust almost cost her the whole lot of them before Tony quickly grabbed two.

Callie tired of these people. "Each of you has told half-truths or hidden the unsaid since you hit this beach. To update everyone, in case Georgia hasn't come clean," which made the three scrutinize their hostess, "Butch was arrested . . . then escaped. As of this moment, a BOLO has been issued to the island."

"Why is that our problem?" Libby asked.

Callie had wondered which one would be the first to defy . . . or care the least. Libby won both categories.

"Because one of you let him out of my officer's patrol car."

They gasped, appeared insulted, and so on through the whole range of expressions, with Callie trusting nary a one. Each had already proven capable of distorting the truth. Except Reuben who'd more witnessed than participated the entire weekend. She still itched to get him aside, identify his purpose for being in this motley crew. It was as if his shy, naivete lurked, unable to completely disappear.

She scanned those seated. "At this moment that patrol car is being checked for prints." It wasn't but it could be. "We'll go easier on the person who let Butch out if they step up now. Otherwise, they get charged with aiding a fugitive to escape. Also, aiding and abetting a kidnapping and possibly murder."

"Murder?" Reuben spoke up, astonished. "Have you found JJ dead?"

"Not yet," she said. "But it's a reasonable expectation." Her phone rang. "Give me a sec," she said and left the porch to detour into a hallway . . . a hallway she remembered from that first Edisto case. Seemed this house was good for nothing but criminal behavior.

"Go ahead, Don."

"Prints on the glass we found in the front bushes are pretty fresh and belong to your man Brandon Ives," he said. "He's in the system from a prior DUI. Blood and DNA will take longer to process. Other prints, too, but we made those on the glass priority."

Butch. What a surprise. "Good," she said. "Keep feeding me what you find." With that she marched back onto the porch. "Give me Butch's comings and goings from the time he set foot on this beach, people."

Libby brought her offensive feelings to the edge of her chair cushion. "Don't tell us what to do. Butch is a grown man, and we are not accountable for him."

Callie slowly walked to stand almost touching the teacher's knees. "I'm not talking as your fellow classmate, Libby. And God knows I'm not speaking as your friend." She flicked her badge. "I'm speaking as the Town of Edisto Beach Police Chief, ma'am, and if you refuse to cooperate, we can take this conversation to a place other than my quaint office you experienced the other night, and give you the overnight version of an interview. Or a more long-term getaway, whichever suits your liking. Boyfriend or no boyfriend, your boss here might struggle overlooking the moral turpitude clause in your teacher's contract."

That shut Libby up. She looked to Tony for assistance. Instead he lifted the pineapple off his drink to sample the Hawaiian specialty, conceding to the cop in the room.

"Tony," she whined.

With his glass he motioned to Callie. "Answer the chief. I'm sure she'll get to me next."

Libby's reddened cheeks almost matched the hibiscus on her muumuu. Tony wore something equally floral. Callie only then recognized Libby's effort at going for a themed evening.

"We all got up within a half hour of each other," the teacher said. "Ate breakfast at the SeaCow. Once our meal settled, Tony and I left Butch alone in the kitchen, and we went to the beach. That's it."

Callie turned to Reuben. "I left him doing the same thing," he said.

"And you went where?"

"The Bi-Lo. Alone, but maybe the cashier can identify me. She was yay high." He hovered his hand out straight. "Fake eyelashes. Skin tone about as dark as mine. Not too long out of high school. Gone maybe forty minutes? I'm sure I have the receipt in the car unless I tossed it in the bag."

Thorough. Callie admitted he covered his bases. Next was Georgia, who studied the entire group was as if she were about to present a graduate thesis.

"I fed him breakfast, visited Sophie, visited the Neck, then went to *Flirty Flamingo* where . . . you, um, found me."

"Found you?" the teacher asked. "What were you doing there?" She inhaled quickly. "What aren't you telling us?"

Georgia flipped her nose up. "Shut up, Libby. None of your damn business."

Libby twisted around to Callie. "What was she up to?"

"Who can confirm you remained on the beach?" Callie asked instead. "How long were you strolling?"

"About an hour. Maybe more."

As unfit as she appeared to be, an hour steady walking would have the back of her calves quivering. People underestimated the impact of sand walking on untoned muscles. Libby appeared unaffected. "How far did you go? To which numbered access?"

"Um, access? We saw the clouds and turned around, or we would've walked the whole water line."

Bullshit. "Talk to anybody?" Callie asked, feeling the temperature drop a few degrees with the incoming front.

Tony quit sipping, his stare on his lady. His tendency to follow her lead had become obvious.

"A couple with a German Shepherd. A kid who hit me with his Frisbee," Libby said.

Callie noted it all. Nothing remarkable. Reuben's was simple enough. He'd described someone she knew worked at Bi-Lo. The academic duo not so much.

Georgia couldn't prove squat between the time she left the house and Callie caught her, except for Mark following her from the Neck. But she'd clearly hunted for JJ, having gone to where the police already searched. A pretty good alibi for part of the day.

Peter, however, hadn't been accounted for other than his time with Callie. She'd check in with him next, keeping his presence quiet. Still no point in mingling him with the others. No telling how contaminated all these stories would get hearing his version of everything.

Her phone rang, caller ID . . . Sophie?

"Soph?"

Yells and grunts sounded in the background. "Callie," Sophie yelled. "Get your ass over here! A drunk guy broke into my house. With us in it!"

"What do you mean *us?*"

"Me, Sprite, and Jeb." Then to someone else, she shouted, "Watch out, baby. Let Jeb handle him. We'll hold him for Callie."

Jeb? Callie's nerves ran a cold current. "I'm coming, but just let him go, Soph. Tell him to leave and don't get in his way."

"Y'all stay here," Callie told the porch crew then ran toward the door, keeping the phone live. "If y'all hear from JJ—"

"Call you," said several of them together.

"Same with Butch!" Callie added.

She took the stairs two at a time, random drops spitting from the first clouds, and she leaped into her cruiser, kicking up scrabble and shell backing out on Palmetto Boulevard. Thomas replied, on his way to rendezvous at Sophie's.

Of all places for a burglar to hit.

His mistake.

Yeah, Sophie knew calling Callie beat 911 by a mile.

Chapter 32

THE DAY'S SUNSHINE had given way to a band of clouds moving in from Beaufort, southwest down the coast, a deep-purple swath hugging the horizon. Callie coincidentally sped straight toward that wall of weather.

Damn it, she had already done battle with Sophie over locked doors and windows since the day they'd met. Locks invited bad spirits, Sophie said. Callie swore easy access invited bad guys. Sophie only put hands over her ears, later smudging both hers and Callie's houses with smoking sage to expunge them of the discussion.

Sage be damned this time. Jeb was involved, and Callie suspected who the dumb idiot was who'd stumbled into a house full of people.

While Callie didn't want to envision Butch as much of a threat, he was inebriated, and, in keeping with their high school theme, the person voted most likely to have killed Wendy Ashton. And that person, by connection, leaned toward being JJ's abductor . . . if not murderer.

There was no predicting his behavior, regardless how soft and silly he'd acted up to now.

Cornered animals reacted badly, but she'd kill anybody in her path to protect her boy. Jeb had suffered in the wake of her career too many times to count. Losing his father, grandfather . . . a year of college to nursemaid her . . . Mike Seabrook.

Callie piled out of her cruiser at the base of the hurricane stairs leading up to Sophie's house and took them in multiples as fast as her legs would allow. No holding back on the noise. Any distraction could prove useful.

The door gaped open. A crash inside shattered something. Butch screamed for someone to get off of him. Sophie's daughter shrieked for help.

Callie entered, hand on her weapon. "Police!"

In a tangle of arms and legs, Butch and Jeb grappled, oblivious to the cavalry's arrival.

"Damn it, Butch. Stop!"

Jeb lightened up, expecting his adversary to do the same at the order of his mother.

Which enabled Butch to shove the kid backwards, bowling him across a coffee table and over the sofa arm, sending a lamp into the window blinds. Sprite charged Butch, who shook her off as if she were no more than a grumpy cat. Her footing tangled in a shag throw rug, and the girl went down, sliding into the wall with a grunt.

"Stop!" Callie shouted, navigating the jumbled mess of smashed knickknacks and another lamp. Someone had thrown a coffee cup, which lay in pieces under Butch's feet.

Still soused, Butch tried to train his vision on her, but Jeb wasn't done. Call it temper, call it embarrassment in front of his girl, call it retaliation for the man not listening to his mom, Jeb leaped off the floor, booted the broken coffee table out of the way, then charged and side-kicked Butch. He went through the entryway into the kitchen, stopped only by a dinette table, its feet screeching the floor. Shells on a small curio table scattered.

Thomas charged in the front door.

Callie rushed in and shoved Jeb to the side, entering the kitchen before him, to come between the two men and bring this to an end.

But Butch grabbed a knife out of the sink.

He gripped it without a clue what to do with it, as though someone else put the blade in his hand, but she learned many years ago to never underestimate a drunk with a weapon. They were capable of anything.

Callie drew her Glock. Thomas did the same standing beside and a little behind her.

"Drop that knife or I drop you, Butch," she said.

The knife bounced, clattering on Sophie's tile floor. "I didn't mean it," he said, staring at his hand as if it had acted on its own.

"Thomas," Callie said, keeping her weapon at the ready, but her officer already had his cuffs out.

Butch turned and vomited toward the sink, the liquid and clumps not quite spanning the gap. The spew coated counter and cabinet before dripping to the floor.

Sophie let out an angry, "You bastard!"

Thomas lifted a leg, noting small spits of upchuck on his shoe and pants leg. "Son of a bitch."

"I ought to shoot you for good measure, you idiot," Callie said, watching Thomas snare the man up tight. "You went after my son."

Sophie appeared from behind Callie with her phone, taking pictures. "And I'm the police chief's best friend, moron. This is my house. Look what you've done! I'll never get the smell out. I'm sending the bill to your TV station, along with pictures."

Coughing, clearing his throat, Butch begged for a rag on the counter, but Thomas only cinched up the cuffs.

"Sorry, y'all," Butch said, spitting.

"Sorry? What do you think you did, crash a party?" Jeb's temper hadn't fully resolved, and he stood behind his mother, towering a foot taller, easily able to see the intruder. "You scared us to death. You hurt my girl, you bastard. I still ought to—"

"Jeb," Callie said, noting in her motherhood tone that the incident was over. Youth took longer to cool off.

"Good, he's tied up so I can whip his ass," Sophie spouted, bouncing forward ready to spar. "And nobody here would testify against me." She tried to squeeze around Callie, only for Sprite to hold her mom back.

Callie wouldn't mind throwing the idiot to these wolves. She made her directive clear. "Jail, Thomas."

"Jail?" Butch whined.

"Do not pass Go. Do not collect two hundred dollars," she said. "Jail."

"But that's a long ride, and he stinks," Thomas said.

"Hose him in the outside shower downstairs," she ordered. Every house had one, to clean sand off feet and fish blood off tables where the fishermen prepped a day's catch for the grill. "Sophie, give him a towel and a trash bag for the seat."

The adrenaline and blood surge of the fight must have sobered him some, because Butch made a jerky move toward Callie, his cheeks flamed. "You're taking advantage of your position. Way too much advantage. Wait until I tell this story." An idea seemed to fill his eyes. "Who says you aren't working for JJ?" He tried to move closer, but Thomas yanked him in check. "Who says this isn't part of her grand scheme, coordinated with you? You keep talking like this is your beach, so how can you not be aware what's going on around here?"

"Butch," Callie said, none too reserved. "We have your prints on one of your drink glasses where JJ went missing."

His sarcasm shriveled like paper in a fire. He canvassed his memory bank, probably too fuzzy-brained to deny her accusation, possibly questioning his own movements. "You planted that glass."

"Nope. A deputy found it at the address where JJ was hiding. I haven't been out there yet." She continued, watching pieces of Georgia's gracious hors d'oeuvres sliding down a cabinet door in Butch's vomit. "And I didn't have a thing to do with drunk and disorderly, escape from custody, disturbing the peace, trespassing and burglary, assault with a deadly weapon, and resisting arrest. Those you arranged all by yourself."

Butch tensed and Thomas gripped the cuffed wrists tighter.

"It's afternoon, Thomas," she said.

Thomas read what she meant and gave a nod.

"Tell them to make sure he doesn't make magistrate until late tomorrow," she said. "Gives me a chance to see if we need to add kidnapping . . . or murder."

Butch blanched, and Thomas moved his charge closer to the sink. "Murder?" said the sportscaster, voice wavering. "You found JJ?"

"Not yet," she said. "The reason we need a little time. But there's always Wendy."

"Too long ago," he argued.

"No statute of limitation on murder," she said back. "We covered this already."

"Still no proof it was me."

She motioned for Thomas to proceed. "You haven't heard what the others have said, Butch."

Suddenly he was ready to talk. "Wait. What others? Who said I did anything?" He refused to move, desperate for her answers, but Thomas pushed him on.

"You'll learn more when charges are made, Butch."

"What the hell is going on?" he yelled. "Talk to Peter!" he added. "He'll cover for me with Wendy."

She raised her voice as they reached the front porch. "How do you know I haven't?"

He tried to stop. "What'd he say?" Down two more steps. "Did he say he raped me?" he yelled.

"He tried to cover for you, you ingrate. Where's JJ?"

"Don't know!" Butch hollered on his way down the steps.

They heard the water turn on downstairs about the time a single clap of thunder noted the arrival of rain. Rain sputtered on and off, but a deluge was on its way. She would ordinarily wait for rain to let up, but time was not on her side and its arrival unpredictable. If JJ was hurt, assuming she was even alive, Callie needed to find her. She was already scolding herself for not having assumed the worst earlier than she had.

"Y'all okay?" she asked her people. "Jeb?"

"Good, Mom." Maybe sheepish for his mother assuming control. Maybe a little proud.

"And this coffee table, Sophie, I'm so sorry. We'll talk about replacing it later, but I've got to run." Then she remembered the kitchen vomit. "I'd stay, but seriously, this man is just the tip of the iceberg. Jeb? Help her clean this mess up?"

He raised a hand to acknowledge, more attentive to Sprite. The odor seemed more notable with the sudden humidity outside not allowing it to escape.

She apologized again, and meant it, but she couldn't help her departure. She couldn't delay heading back to *Water Spout* to update the crowd and continue this saga. While all arrows pointed to Butch, she was beginning to think too conveniently so. And while that smidgeon of doubt existed, she had no choice but to follow through, validate it or put it to rest. Stratton's memory clung to everything she did, and she wasn't pulling a Chief Warren here and pinning the crime on the guy it too easily stuck to first.

CALLIE HAD GRABBED a raincoat out of her trunk, but not before getting wet in the exercise. Now she stood dripping in Georgia's beach retreat, refusing to leave the kitchen tile and make a mess on the rest of the high-end décor.

The high school crowd had moved inside, the remaining four anyway, and truth be told, Butch's absence seemed to drain the life out of the party. Either that or the weather.

Libby had already exchanged the sleeveless muumuu for jeans and a long-sleeve shirt.

"Case solved then," Tony said.

"He's charged with a litany of things, but nothing about JJ, Tony," Callie said. "Regardless, he's in jail for the time being."

"Did he do Wendy?" Libby asked.

The use of the term *do* sounded like dialogue out of one of JJ's mysteries, and when Callie didn't honor the question with a reply, Libby went to the array of double glass doors as if she hadn't asked. The woman's mind seemed to be gnawing on something.

Outside, churning waves smacked the beach with a receding, sucking sound, as if intent on undermining the earth.

"This weekend is definitely not what I expected," Reuben said, his tall stature dominating a wide, upholstered chair. He drank sparkling water, resting the bottle on the chair's arm, uncaring about the condescension wicking into the material. The water was probably from his run to the store that morning; the attitude from being with these people too long.

"What exactly *did* you expect?" Georgia asked, her own attitude casting a hook for an argument. Callie was almost willing to take that bait, but she preferred to hear more from Reuben since she'd seen him the least, heard the least from him, and wondered what his frustration would have to say.

As if on cue, Reuben laughed at Georgia, hard and loud, so unlike the shy student. Flustered, Georgia stood to her feet. He only stowed back more laughter when she appeared to take him on.

"I expected boring chit chat about the color of crepe paper and cost of catered rubber chicken," he said. "Maybe some drunk evenings by people who couldn't let loose of their teenage years. Maybe even a drinking challenge that involved guessing if Stratton really killed Wendy, like it matters twenty-five years later. Instead, it's all just . . . pitiful."

Way more than he'd said at one time since he bumped Butch's car, and he immensely enjoyed saying his piece. He acted like the loner amongst these people, or the person with the least at stake. Or the kid who'd never been invited into the conversation in high school but suddenly had the most powerful words to say. For the first time since he'd arrived on the beach, to Callie's knowledge anyhow, he appeared to enjoy himself.

"Admit it, do any of you really care Butch did it? Or didn't do it?" he continued. "Y'all will all go home leaving him in trouble up to his neck and return to your routines." He nodded to Tony. "And your little secrets." This time attentive to Libby. "And you'll pretend you once again have nothing to worry about. You will have escaped yet another bullet in being accused of a crime."

Libby's glare tried to kill the man. "I hate you," she said. "Yes, I have nothing to worry about. Past or present. I'll sleep perfectly fine, you heartless geek."

"The arrogant dolt has no feelings," Georgia added, piling on. "Hadn't any in high school and none now. He lives alone. Never been married. Has all this money and nobody to spend it with. He's a sad human being, is what he is. Shouldn't even be here, I say."

Tony stared down and said nothing.

Callie just watched the dynamics.

Reuben, still in the best mood of them all, unfolded out of his chair and went to the kitchen and opened the refrigerator. "Out of Cokes," he said. "I assume you have a pantry or storage of some sort for this resort?"

"Under the house," Georgia spouted. "I ought to charge you once this is over, you rich son of a bitch."

His smirk remained. "And I'd gladly pay. This has indeed been entertaining." Looking over the interior in an overt demonstration of judgment, Reuben's gaze stopped on her. "My apologies, m'lady, but I've been negligent in admiring the accommodations. Your furnishings rate absolutely satisfactory for this rich son of a bitch. So how do I find your storage?"

"You condescending bastard." Georgia seethed through her teeth. "You don't even care about JJ! Get out of my house."

Callie'd seen enough. "Georgia, tolerate him for another day or two, because none of you is leaving quite yet."

Libby came shoulder-to-shoulder with her hostess, joining forces. "You have Butch. You no longer need us, and you cannot keep us."

"I'm the officer in charge, sweetheart. I haven't ruled out all of you. If it makes you happier, call for an attorney. To be honest, lawyers are easier to deal with, way less emotion."

Affronted, Libby returned to the windows and the roiling, fisting sea.

Reuben stepped in front of Georgia. "The storage, or shall I go back to that grocery store?" He lightly bowed to Callie. "For you, I promise to log in time, mileage, and any parties who cross my path."

No, not anything like what Callie expected from the reserved teen-age boy. Reuben had become rather haughty in his climb to affluence, and being around these grown-up kids who'd either snubbed or disregarded him had given him license to wield a piece of power he'd never had before.

Georgia snapped a motion toward the kitchen. "Through there. Key's hanging in the laundry area. It's huge, with an eight-inch piece of driftwood on it."

He disappeared, and Libby came back to utter her impatience with the inconveniences and slights of the man. She graduated to observations about the inadequacies and obvious criminal tendencies of Butch, then moved on to Callie and the entire entity of Edisto Beach being inept at safety. Callie decided this was one tourist not worth salvaging on behalf of the Chamber of Commerce.

She'd about decided to drive out to the Neck, and put her own eyes on the scene where JJ disappeared when Reuben returned. "No such key, madam."

"Yes, there is," and Georgia strutted off, prissy and pompous, only to return empty-handed. "Who went down there last?" she demanded.

Reuben went palms out. "I wasn't even aware of said storage."

Tony remained silent and only shrugged. Either Libby had completely neutered the man, or he'd given up trying to hold the talking stick with this group. Callie wouldn't play the odds on the couple remaining such upon return to the real world.

"Butch kept restocking things," Libby said.

Georgia frowned, exasperated. "I don't keep alcohol down there, you idiot."

Leaning into her space, Libby countered, "I'm talking other drinks, princess."

"Ladies," Callie said, interceding. "Butch didn't have it on him if it was that gawky."

Like gas station restroom keys, a lot of beach keys were chained to the most bizarre items. Alligator feet, flip-flops, crushed beer cans. Things got lost easily around sand and visitors.

Marching out, Georgia's peach and aqua mules clumped up the stairs to the bedrooms. She soon returned, dangling the keychain and its driftwood from the top level for all to see. "Butch's room. Figures." She sashayed back down and handed them to Reuben, who disappeared.

"Again, nobody leave," Callie said. "I'll be in touch later today, or tonight."

Libby scoffed. "Leaving us hanging, you mean, when we all have lives to get back to."

Callie had about had enough. "I could get back in touch at my own convenience, Libby, wake you up in the middle of the night, maybe?"

Thunder sounded outside. Nobody hated rain more than fishermen and beach bunnies. Rain became the time when renters put puzzles together, ate too much junk food, and stayed out of the police department's hair. What wouldn't Callie give for an afternoon and a drink watching that storm.

Feet clumped up the outside stairs, the footfalls so unlike the manner in which they went down. Reuben shoved the side exterior door open with his foot, his arms occupied but not with Coke.

He helped JJ enter first. "Look who I found in storage."

Chapter 33

JJ
Early Monday evening.

THE FIRST THING JJ noticed upon awakening was the cramped pain in her shoulder from lying on it, but at least she could stretch her legs. She lay on a blanket, doubled, no doubt on a cement floor, but before she dared sit up, she feigned her blackout a bit longer, hoping to tell if someone watched.

All she heard was rain, and then distinguished the surf from it. Both were muffled but right outside, their odors of ozone and salt seeping inside. She sensed herself close to the beach, on ground level, most likely in someone's storage. All the beach houses had them since code didn't allow people to live on ground level.

She tucked her head, listening harder. An older refrigerator hummed in the back corner about ten feet away. But as hard as she tried, she couldn't make out movement. No sound. None of that sixth sense of someone nearby that you could not see. Having used that angle in at least two of her books, she'd always wondered if it were true one could blindly sense molecules move in the air.

Opening her eyes, she hesitated, then with the black cloth stuck to her from her crying and runny nose, her mouth behind the tape, she made all sorts of contortions to loosen the material. Finally, she could breathe easier.

Flopping until she could get her weight to roll over and take her to her knees, she eased herself back onto her butt. Her hands still taped behind her, she felt for what might be there before leaning back. Shutters. Hurricane shutters maybe? Beside them, boxes. Sturdy. At least two.

Her cheek throbbed, her injured eye more swollen. No telling how long she'd been out since her unconsciousness was chemically induced. That sweet scent wasn't easily forgotten, and she'd look that up when she got out of here. Then she scolded herself for thinking about mysteries.

But she couldn't help herself. The mental exercise kept her sane and put alarm at bay. For instance, she wished she'd thought to keep up with tides. This current one was close from the resounding crashes, but she couldn't tell what that meant in terms of time of day. Note to self in case she ever pulled another stunt in the name of a novel . . . study the inherent nature of the area. She cursed herself for her other fault . . . not memorizing vehicles around her. If she had done so, she might have been able to narrow down the make and model of the car belonging to who grabbed her.

That is, assuming they were one of the high school crowd.

But who else knew she was on the island but her agent? She'd been assured the crime rate was minimal, and her presence kept secret, so the odds of a random crime were low. She left no car in her drive. No, she believed somebody came for her.

Maybe Georgia opened her damn mouth or turned against her.

JJ leaned toward a man being the perpetrator, unless one of the women had employed someone male. Just as forensics had sided on Wendy's killer being male, her own abduction smacked of it, too. Other than her face, which could have been accidental, she wasn't bruised or damaged. She'd been transported with some semblance of care which took strength. He also might not be a natural criminal. Otherwise, she'd be dead.

She bet one thing, though. He took her laptop, and she'd never see it again, because this whole orchestrated business gone awry had originated on the promise of a tell-all. As she'd hoped, one of them stepped up more than the others, probably with more to lose. They would dispose of her phone as well. Saving to the cloud would be her saving grace as to the manuscript and her research, but first things first. She had to live and come out of this healthy enough to continue writing the damn thing.

There, she felt somewhat better. She wasn't losing her mind.

Thirsty, she toyed with opening the refrigerator, but decided no point. Unable to see, unable to grope inside, and even if she managed the gymnastics, how was she to get it around to her mouth?

She sighed. All trussed up and nowhere to go. Again, thank God she wasn't dead. She had to keep telling herself that. Thank God she wasn't dead. Yet.

No, not yet. Never. This was just a major bump in her road.

Damn, who was she kidding?

Another sigh. They seemed to hold her together, too.

Yelling and shouting might draw help, but also draw her captor. The more of a burden she was, the higher her chances of being shut down permanently.

Thunder rumbled. Indeed, a storm had set in. Her captor may have locked her in an unoccupied rental. But he could also be standing outside the door.

This was so not like the movies. This was so unlike her books. Building up guts to pull MacGyver stunts didn't happen as easily as one would imagine. Building the nerve to shriek yourself hoarse was harder still. Everything had consequences.

Footfalls sounded, coming down steps. Someone *had* been upstairs.

Again with her speeding pulse. Her gasps turned choppy.

She died with dignity under the worst of circumstances.

For God's sake, was she really inventing headstone quotes in her final hour?

When the key went in the lock outside, her breathing stopped completely. She fought not to pee in panic. She wished herself invisible in spite of the fantasy of it.

And when the door opened, she shut her eyes and tried to crawl inside herself.

"JJ?" said the familiar voice.

Of all the people to find her.

In spite of herself, she cried. The kid she'd had the crush on in high school proved the knight to rescue her in her middle years.

Sobs escaped her, until Reuben rested hands on her shoulders, shushing her as he eased to her level. "Good heavens, JJ. How long have you been down here?" he asked, as he removed the cloth from her vision, then the tape off her mouth.

"I can't say," she said, blinking hard.

He was the most attractive man she'd ever seen. "Thank you," she whispered.

"I'm not believing this," he said, undoing the tape from her wrists before helping her to her feet. "Who did this to you?"

"Didn't see them," she said.

"Well, it's a good thing Callie's already upstairs," he said, collecting her against him. "Because if she doesn't find who did this, I'm having her badge."

She melted into him, so unlike any of the strong female characters she'd written about before.

Chapter 34

CALLIE RAN TOWARD JJ, ordering everyone to stay clear, just not for the reasons they'd expect.

"Don't. Touch. Her," she repeated. "She's wearing the clothes she was abducted in which could have transfer from her assailant."

Setting JJ on the nearest chair, a bar stool, she studied the split lip, the black eye, the mussed hair, and totally bedraggled look of the author. "I see the obvious, but are you hurt otherwise?"

JJ thought, taking inventory, then smiled. "I'm actually the crime scene, aren't I?"

Callie instantly took a dislike to the author persona dominating over the victim. "Answer me."

JJ stretched her left leg. "Think I went down on this knee," she said, then peering past Callie to the others huddling around, added, "Somebody take my picture."

Each ran for their phone . . . except Reuben. "I touched her," he said, reaching out then holding back. "I removed the hood, which is downstairs," he quickly added. "Then I cut her loose, helped her up . . . hugged her."

Nothing Callie didn't expect from the person who found her, but the unexpected was the enamored warmth melting in JJ's eyes. And Reuben smiling back.

Phones appeared, clicking. The author swiveled the chair for some to take a better look of her shiner. "Where's Butch?" she asked, puzzled.

"In jail," Georgia exclaimed.

"For what?"

"Later," Callie said, and while the crew took its pics, Callie called the fire station. "Get one of your EMTs to *Water Spout*, please. We found the missing woman, and it appears she's in need of medical attention. Might be in need of transport."

By the time she hung up, the circle of classmates spouted questions right and left. "Who did this? What happened? How long were you downstairs? Why didn't you scream?"

"Enough!" Callie shouted, then to Georgia, "Get her a bottle of water and a towel with ice in it for that eye."

Georgia scurried. The hostess quickly returned, and remembering Callie's order to remain distant, leaned, arm stretched, to hand over the bottle, the towel after that.

Giving JJ time to compose, Callie called Deputy Raysor to get himself to the house along with the forensics team already at his disposal. Hopefully they weren't going back to Walterboro from the Neck.

In the meantime, she needed to talk to JJ while her thoughts were fresh, at the same time keeping the schoolmates corralled. She was short of help and couldn't allow a one of them to bolt or collaborate, and someone needed ears and eyes on them all just in case.

"Don, on your way, before you leave, whenever, call one of your judge cousins in Walterboro for search warrants on all the cars belonging to these people. Hold on." She motioned to Libby. "Make, model, and color of your vehicle," Callie said in a tone not to be argued with. "Say it loud for the deputy on the other end."

Libby cocked a pose. "I don't have to—"

"Uncooperative. We'll arrest you in a minute. Okay, Tony. Make, model, and color of yours."

Tony rattled off the details of his Toyota.

"All right!" Libby hollered, and dictated the details of her Nissan, then as Callie pointed, Georgia next on her Caddie, and Reuben gave info on his BMW. Callie described Butch's as well, which she'd have them look at after tending to all those at the beach house. At this rate the team would be here the rest of the day.

"Tell forensics to especially see to the trunks first, Don. We're looking for JJ's fingerprints. Then have them go over the storeroom under the house where they kept her."

"Gotcha. Give me a hard half hour, Doll."

"Just don't dawdle," she said and hung up, immediately announcing to all, "All keys on the bar, please." She dug in her pocket for Butch's.

Raysor was right. It would take him a bit of time to talk to the judge and arrive from the Neck. Officer LaRoache was the lone officer manning the beach since Thomas was en route to the jail with Butch, so yet again, she put a call in to the handiest person she had at her disposal . . . Mark.

With it raining and it being mid-week, he just might be available.

"Be right there," he said, and hung up without asking why.

She wasn't sure how to take that, but she was damn grateful. She'd worry about feeling obligated later.

Remaining at guard status near JJ while eying each beach guest, she made yet another executive decision. Without saying his name, she called Peter to drive to *Water Spout* immediately, the news of finding JJ the urgency to prod him when he acted leery of seeing the characters.

Good. She was running out of officers to send one to force him to appear.

Exasperated at all the invitations Callie was making, Georgia waved a hand. "Excuse me. Who all is coming to my house?"

Callie didn't even try to hide her irritation. "A handful of folks I need, Georgia. Nonnegotiable."

She exhaled a pout. "Do I have to feed these people?"

Callie just tended to JJ. "When the medic gets here, we're going in the other room. We need to talk."

"Can't you tell us anything?" Libby asked.

Callie stared. "Just keep pushing my buttons, Libby."

The bottom seemed to fall out outside, and Reuben went to shut the glass doors. Closing them sucked a sense of vacuum into the space making voices lower, and after Callie's caustic reply to the teacher, they moved to the sofas and wide, tufted chairs.

"Pssst, Callie," JJ whispered.

Callie leaned in.

"I can't tell who took me," she said. "I'm completely in the dark."

"In a minute," Callie said.

But JJ wasn't used to being told what to do. "I sense you don't care for me at the moment."

Understatement of the decade. Callie tightened her mouth.

"I did spawn this little mystery in hopes of great fodder for a story. Can't deny I also had a thin hope of Wendy's killer making a move." She gently touched her injured eye. "Never expected this . . . actually not sure what I expected. Had hoped Georgia had a better handle on things so she'd call me if one of them flew off half-cocked."

"I gave you way more credit than that, JJ. Not sure I even want to read your books anymore."

"Ooh, ouch, Chief." JJ gave a sarcastic squint, feigning pain, then actually winced at the real deal.

"We could've been dragging you out of a hole somewhere," Callie said, too low for the others to hear. "Or fishing your gnawed and nibbled carcass from the water. There are always repercussions when you mess with people's lives, Jessie."

"But I'm seated right here, safe and sound."

"By your own design, I'm guessing."

But JJ lost her haughtiness, and her uncertainty spoke otherwise. "No, not by my design. Not by plan at all."

"Then why didn't they kill you?" Callie asked.

Which made JJ scrutinize the others. "Because I think they knew me," she said, though not sounding too assured. "There's a relationship amongst us, and I still think the person's someone here."

Callie couldn't argue with that. "How long were you downstairs?"

"Don't rightly know," she said, completely serious. "Yesterday, I assume . . . I sort of lost track of time . . . I answered the door. The person forced the door when I opened it, and I was out like a light before I saw him. I've thought hard about that. Had to be a him. To shove that hard to damage me this way. To carry me . . . twice. Just feels like a man."

Callie agreed. "And you woke up downstairs?"

"No. The first time I was tied on a bed, so doped I couldn't think straight. Then more clearly in a car trunk. I couldn't stretch out, and I could roll halfway over until I hit the back, and I was less than a foot from the front. But trust me, I touched everything I could to leave prints."

Okay, that Callie could give JJ credit for.

"Wasn't there long," she continued, "or at least the time I was conscious wasn't long. He probably brought me straight here from my rental, but he knocked me out with something when he went to take me out of the trunk."

"What?" Alarmed at potential head damage, Callie took hold of the stool. "Let me look. Turn around here. We've got to get you to the hospital."

"No, no." JJ pushed palm out, and Callie backed off. "He put something over my mouth and nose that smelled sweet and rendered me unconscious. He didn't really hurt me. I believe the door thing might have been an accident."

Doubtful about it being an accident, JJ was correct in that she hadn't been abducted for long. She had no idea what a blessing her abduction had been compared to most.

A knock sounded at the door. She waved Georgia off and answered. Mark entered with his forty caliber on his belt. "Tell me what you need," he said, discarding social politeness for perceived necessity.

The man was beginning to act like he'd be and do anything for Callie, and without a doubt he missed being on the job. She hadn't exactly told him not to, and he was licensed to carry. When it came to the blue line, retired was about as good as current in each other's eyes.

"First, take the key with that piece of wood on it and lock up the storage downstairs," she said.

All pairs of eyes watched, like children waiting for the teacher to name who was in trouble. "Then come back up and babysit them," she added. "Don't let them leave. They are all witnesses and persons of interest."

Tony stood. "Which of us is the person of interest? I think we're entitled."

"Actually, you're not," Callie said. "Not yet. Stay there until you are needed. This man acts under my authority to contain you if you attempt to leave."

"I may want my attorney," Libby said.

"Then call one," Callie retorted.

She ignored the fuming and under-their-breath utterings and reached for JJ. "Off the chair, my friend. We head to the nearest bedroom where the EMT will look you over and you'll answer a few questions."

With Callie taking a small light hold of one elbow, the author slid off the stool and clutched the bar's edge at the stiffness that had developed in the waiting.

Callie took a last glance back at the other occupants. In hindsight, she was glad Mark was armed. At least until Raysor got there.

She no longer believed Butch did it, either, making her all the more leery.

They hadn't gone two steps when another knock sounded. She wanted to hang just one more moment before questioning JJ if this arrival was who she thought it was. She needed to see their looks.

"Hold on, JJ." Callie answered the door. "Peter," she said as the Brit closed his umbrella, uncertain how much of this place he was allowed to get wet.

If only Butch were here.

Libby stood, stunned at seeing her ex from four thousand miles away. "Peter? Why would you—" She abruptly shut up and sat down, clearly containing herself.

Callie could smell her mind cooking from across the massive space. Why had her ex-husband made such a bold trip? Why was he a secret? What did JJ expect from him that she couldn't get on the phone? What would he tell that would conflict with what Libby had already said on the record?

Tony repositioned himself, not acknowledging Peter until the man stood almost within reach, hand outstretched in greeting. Peter reluctantly accepted the greeting. After visually connecting a second, Tony let loose and moved his attention to the porch and the weather commotion outside, his discomfort at this turn of events evident.

Georgia said hello and nothing else, angry. Reuben, however, stared him down. "Why are you here?"

"Not by choice, I assure you," he said, choosing a loveseat in a grouping not up underneath the others. "Where's Butch?"

"In jail," they all said in unison.

After a quick jolt of surprise, Peter sank in the cushion, one arm on a pillow. "So what are we doing here, mates?" He'd acted like he hadn't seen JJ at all.

JJ limped up, holding the ice pack to her eye. "This is great. Looks like an Agatha Christie mystery with all the usual suspects."

"Then make yourself at home, sugar," Georgia said. "Because you're one of us. Why didn't you tell me Peter was coming?"

"Need to know, sweetheart."

Squinting hard, Georgia spouted, "You're a complete bitch."

"Complete bitch," JJ echoed. "Not partial, not half, a complete and total bitch."

"Go to hell," said the hostess.

"You're crazy," Libby said. "Utterly."

JJ grinned. "More adverbs. Utterly. Love it. At least I go all the way. The question is why didn't one of you go all the way with me? Had the chance and couldn't follow through? Instead you hid me below to be found. Sneaked into my house and left your little bookmark on my bed as a supposed threat? I assume that was Peter."

But Peter was shaking his head. "No idea what you're talking about."

She looked for a place to rest. Tony kicked an ottoman in her direction. She positioned it and sat, ignoring his manners. Instead she homed in on the latest arrival. "What a surprise you finally made it, Brit Boy."

"Like I had a choice," he said. "And too late, love, on the façade. Callie already interviewed me." He gave her a wry grin and a slight cock of his head. "And we talked at great length about absolutely everything. No more skeletons in my closet."

"Bookmark?" Georgia repeated, as though trying to catch up.

JJ looked down her nose at the woman. "Yes, on my bed, Georgia. Could've just as easily been you."

"No, ma'am. And you can choke on that accusation."

But JJ cared little about insults. "The person who took me most likely tossed my laptop, I'm sure, but do you think I don't protect my creativity? The cloud is my friend . . . my friends."

Less shielded by her words and way less smug, JJ looked at Callie who remained expressionless.

"What skeletons?" Libby asked, the one most likely to have shared those skeletons.

Peter's smugness embraced a higher sense of classiness. "You really want to do that here, love?"

Tony slid forward. "I might want to . . . *love*."

Callie hung back, a wink at Mark to do so, too. Five of her classmates plus herself, all proof of that night so long ago. She would give this crew their moment, at least until the EMTs got there.

On one hand she wished Butch was here to participate, to stir the conversation if not boil the pot. On the other, if he wasn't a suspect any longer, the others couldn't hide behind his absurdities. With him arrested, they just might loosen up. Just like they were doing.

Chapter 35

GEORGIA SPOKE through her teeth at JJ. "I'm so pissed at you I could scratch your eyes out!" They sat in the huge living room, the wall of glass doors showing bouts of spray off the sheets of rain. "You used me. You used my house! I was told nothing about Peter, or about the kidnapping . . . what else don't I know? I kept my end of the deal!"

Reuben watched Georgia with a wary, yet intrigued, interest. "So you were the inside lady, huh. Co-conspirator? Is she giving you a byline by any chance?" He looked over at the other lady. "At least mention her in the acknowledgements, Jessie."

Callie twitched a brow. *Jessie*, huh? Said with the embodiment of suavity to boot.

She stood to the side a reach away from Mark, both watching the theatrics. "While you were . . . away," she said to the author, of course for the others to hear, "I performed a few interviews. Spoke to all but you, of course, and Reuben. Collected some interesting material, and to think I thought I knew all that went on at Wendy's last night. Turns out I didn't know squat."

Which shut up the entire group.

Their eyes moved, then they dared turn their heads. Though not a soul spoke, the air filled with unspoken questions, suspicion, and doubt. An array of secrets piled thick amongst this crew, with each wondering who ratted on whom, but Callie's question remained. Could anyone identify Wendy's killer?

Deputy Raysor called on her mic to let her know he'd arrived. She started to go into the kitchen, then felt it best this group hear. The more nervous they grew the better.

"I got Mark up here," she said to Raysor, glancing at Mark. "You tend to forensics. Come collect the car keys, and then have those cars gone over, particularly the trunks." She looked at Reuben. "Start with the BMW." Might as well start with the guy who found JJ and work back from there.

Reuben tried not to appear bothered, but he wasn't quite pulling it off. Nobody, innocent or guilty, liked being singled out by the police.

"Someone go through the storage downstairs where she was found," she continued. "She woke up on a blanket pallet with cloth on her head. Both should still be there."

Pretty soon Raysor stepped in, dripping. "They're having to set up canopies with the rain, so ain't nobody going anywhere."

"We understand, Don." She pointed to the bar, and he took the keys and left.

She left JJ in place. The EMTs were taking their time getting there.

"So, JJ, who do you think killed Wendy?" Libby said.

Good gracious, not a more volatile question to ask, and Callie wasn't sure this was the time to ask it. "This isn't the place to do this—"

"Butch," the author replied. "He was a total piece of garbage. He screwed girls, probably raped some, and he screwed Wendy at the game. In the fourth quarter, no less."

"No, he didn't," Peter said.

She pivoted, taking him in like he was a fool. "He damn sure did. I was moving around, looking for stories and taking pictures. Lots and lots of pictures, y'all. I can place people where they don't want to be placed, so keep that in mind." She leaned forward, like a librarian reading to a sea of kids. "And I have copies, so stealing my laptop means nothing, my friends. Nothing."

"We're telling you he didn't," Libby exclaimed, parroting her ex.

JJ studied Peter, as though her theory might have cracks in it. "I told you I had Butch at the suite with Wendy," she said.

"And you threatened him and me both with exposing that, too," he said.

Callie studied the author. "Were you extorting these people?"

Like a stadium crowd, they all spoke up with their accusations, animated with pointing.

Callie almost missed the knock at the door. Whoever would be standing in the rain, so she trotted to answer. Two EMTs, each with a case in their hand, entered and looked for a door mat to stomp their feet.

"Come in," she said. "Our victim is seated over here." Callie went over the situation with them, and they knelt on either side of JJ, asking if she wanted to go into the other room with so many eyes on them.

"No, we're holding court," she said, smiling. "I'm really fine, but do what you must." She pulled off her sweater, still eying the group. "I was not extorting. I was . . . offering options," she said. "I gave each of you opportunity to define how you wound up in my book."

The two medics sneaked glances at each other.

"This stays in this room, guys," Callie warned.

"Opportunity," Libby began. "Blackmail is more like it. And an incredible deception that cost us the money and time of coming out here."

"You're staying for free, you moocher," Georgia said, but to JJ, she added, "Granted we were *all* deceived."

"Damn right," started one person, and the round of complaints began anew.

Pulling out her recorder, unnoticed with her classmates so up in arms, Callie reached four feet over to the side and slipped it, live, atop a tall curio cabinet to the side of the sofa and loveseat combo where most of them still sat. Then back to the melee, she lifted her hands. "Stop," she said, voicing over the herd. "Tell you what. Let's go back to the *suites.*"

Not a soul claimed awareness of what she was talking about.

"Butch screwed Wendy in the third quarter," Peter said. "We met her, took her to the suite, then he tried to leave and make me screw her. I left and sat with Tony, and Butch kept Wendy for himself."

JJ seemed to internally self-correct. "Can you vouch for her the fourth quarter?"

A medic asked her a question and she responded, not taking her eyes off Peter.

"I was with Tony part of the fourth," he said.

Callie recalled him saying the entire quarter. "Where did you go if you weren't with him the whole time?" she asked, wanting to rectify her record.

"I didn't leave. I just didn't have Tony to vouch for me."

Which made the group turn to the principal. Upset at being outed, he stared at Peter. "Much obliged, bloke."

The ginger easily reddened. "It's twenty-four years later, you plonker. Be a man. Tell them."

Funny how Libby wasn't saying much.

"I was with Libby for part of the time," Tony said, trying not to look at his woman.

"Could've lost your job back then," JJ said. "Sorry I did not uncover that."

Georgia leaped in. "Or you would've used it against him, huh? Like you used against me that I had covered up for Wendy? I had no idea she was meeting Butch. She left in the third quarter, then came back, saying she had morning sickness while I knew she was pulling her usual stunt of meeting somebody . . . while friggin' pregnant? Damn girl was like a frickin' rabbit! Two minutes into the fourth quarter she leaves again and doesn't come back. How was I to contain her? At least I talked her into the abortion she was about to have the next day. And I was taking her!"

Everyone silenced.

"What," she asked, tweaking her head around to each one. "I call that being the responsible one. Look at all of you and tell me that ain't the truth. I was even paying for it."

"You were forcing her," Libby said with hard conviction. "Wendy wasn't the brightest bulb on the tree, Georgia. You were a Merit scholar and her mentor on the squad. She admired you and listened to you, and that's what you did with that trust? Told her that her only option was an abortion?"

Peter ran stiff fingers through his hair. "Butch is no doubt a cad, but damn, Georgia, he would not have pursued her if he'd known she was expecting."

Georgia stood. "What, this is all about me now? What about the teacher screwing the student! A minor!"

"Not exactly a minor in this state," Callie said, level, in attempt to remain the calm amidst this storm. "But most likely a terminating offense by the school district back then."

Tony only hung his head, with fear spreading across Libby. Their current-day relationship was nothing more than a giggling affair compared to this. Callie wouldn't report it. Neither Tony nor Libby would. It just depended on the others, but what a blade it was over their heads.

Reuben, always the quiet one, worked on the inside of his cheek. He normally saw no need to enter banter, further underlining his intelligence. Instead, he said, "That still leaves Butch unaccounted for in the fourth quarter, people."

Like a school of fish, they re-diverted.

"Like I originally said—" JJ started, but never got to complete the sentence.

"I said he was accounted for," Peter said. "Libby, we were married for three years. You hated Butch from the day you met him in middle school, but he doesn't deserve being hung with a murder. You can tell them or I can."

Callie saw this one coming, and the entire group held its collective breath. Like JJ said, damned if this wasn't an Agatha Christie novel.

"He was tending to my little sister," Libby said.

"Tending . . . how?" Georgia asked.

Glaring, Libby answered, "Took her to the *suite*. But—"

"But hell," Georgia shouted. "You crucify me for Wendy's abortion, but you let your, what"—she did the math—"thirteen-year-old sister get f'd by Butch?" She reared back, wearing a slick grin. "Honey, you hypocritical bitch."

Libby jumped to her feet, the men tucking in theirs, gawking and silent and waiting for a cat-fight. "He didn't go through with it, witch," Libby said. "He brought her back because she got scared and changed her mind."

Peter nodded.

"He bought her a drink and a snack from the concession stand then escorted her around to her friends, so she'd look like she had a hot-shot date for the night," she said, done with the screaming. "Gave her the whole quarter. Ask my sister. Ask her friends."

"Told you," Peter said, still tight in the jaw. "He's a bastard and an arrogant ass, but he isn't a rapist. And he's damn sure no killer. But Libby . . . you should have come forward back then."

"We've been through this."

More like a Baptist than the Anglican preacher he was, he spread out his lanky arms. "We might not be here, doing all of . . . this . . . if you and your family had spoken up. Butch had an alibi."

"I was protecting her reputation," she shouted. "Someone would think he did screw her. My parents would've lost their minds. I stand by what I did."

JJ was eating this up. "But who vouches for you, Peter? Not Tony, not Butch, not Libby." She turned to Callie. "Can you?"

Callie could vouch more for Stratton than Peter, but she didn't want to get caught up in this back-and-forth business. She wanted them talking and confessing. She needed them ticking each other off as all alibis took form. "He wasn't there when I found Wendy. He didn't show up when the crowd arrived."

"Because I took Butch home," Peter said. "We were kids. He was scared that his DNA might be found on her. He used a rubber . . . he always used a rubber . . . but—"

"Damn straight he used rubbers," Libby uttered. "Probably went through them by the case. Otherwise there'd be enough Butch juniors running all over Middleton to own the town."

Tony came out of his funk like a cannon. "Prove you took him home. You're covering for him. He killed that girl."

Yeahs came from all the others, even Reuben. Smug and elated, JJ basked in the story line spinning out.

"Butch isn't here, y'all," Callie said. "This is Stratton all over again where you're pinning the murder on the guy who can't defend himself. I don't know how any of you sleep at night because of Stratton."

They'd struck her nerve this time. Stratton Winningham was the first body to give her nightmares. Though only friends, they hadn't had time to develop anything further, and she hadn't made gentlemen friends easily.

And she wasn't about to out Peter to this mob, either.

"And where were you and Butch?" Georgia asked Peter.

But of course someone else would try.

Peter stared at her from under a very heavy brow. "We were teenage boys and a girl was raped. Butch had already screwed her. The last place we needed to be was hanging around. The second we heard, I took him home. Just him and me the rest of the night. Cowering, I might add. Losing a classmate is scary stuff."

Georgia was eerie when she turned snooty. "Cowering? Don't make me laugh. I'd heard rumors about you and your bunk buddy. Libby hated to compete with Butch for that hands-on time." With a click of a tongue she searched for looks of support, but received none. Even for this band of buffoons, from the glares she seemed to have hit below the belt.

The lull only made the storm outside seem louder, unless it was actually building intensity. A chair blew over and slid about ten feet in front of the glass doors. They'd passed supper time, and Callie turned to Mark. "You still okay being here?"

He'd stood solid, waiting to be needed, no doubt entertained by the show. "With this weather? El Marko's is dead."

"We're about done here," said the EMT. "She's fine. Though with her having been knocked out by the door, we suggest she have a hospital look at her."

"Not happening," JJ said with a snap. Then to herself, "I had believed it was Butch all this time. I thought y'all sharing like this would make the truth come out."

"Hah," Libby said. "You've been gnawing on that bone for twenty-four years only to come full circle to where you started. Serves you right."

The EMT leaned into Callie. "Can we hang for a few seconds to see if this storm passes? I mean, the one outside. Looks like the one inside might rage for a while."

Callie appreciated the humor. "Sure, but like I said, nothing you hear leaves this house."

"I have to pull out those photos," JJ said. "Every one of you is in them. Throughout the night of that ballgame."

"So why didn't you get a picture of the killer?" Tony asked.

"I'm sure I did," JJ replied, so sure of herself. "Just a matter of putting your stories together with the police report and the images with their date stamps."

Which disturbed all but Callie, who wished her the best of luck locking all those pieces together.

But it was Peter who noted the obvious. "Why is Reuben even here?"

True, he'd contributed nothing to the construct of that night.

"He's everywhere in my pictures," JJ said. "Never sat down for long."

Like clockwork, they looked to him. God, people loved talking themselves into group think. People so yearned being part of a collective even if the dialogue was wrong. It was how mobs were born. The reason Callie appreciated Mark being at her side.

"I had nobody to sit with," Reuben said. "I'd like a set of those pictures, though. I wasn't that popular back in the day, so I don't have many photographs of myself at that age. Surely we can get together, maybe even go over them so you can identify who I can't."

"Kind of creepy," Georgia said.

This time Libby sided with her hostess. "Yeah, but JJ was sweet on him if you remember. Bet she took loads of pictures of him."

Reuben turned to JJ, as though waiting for authentication of her feelings, which led her to blush.

"See? Look at her," Libby said. "He became hot and rich . . . and she's famous. That's why he's invited. To see if they can spark something."

JJ fought to hold her aloofness intact. "He was in a lot of pictures, I said. And he was a senior superlative. That's why he's here."

"Maybe the bookmark was a gift from him," Georgia said, still unhappy at the earlier accusation. "A lot of others were on that list, but you excluded them. No, this is personal. Our illustrious author thought she had a shot at kindling something, and who says he didn't feel the same?"

"The bookmark was a threat," JJ said.

Reuben sat stock still.

Callie's phone rang, in lieu of her mic. "What is it, Don?"

With her occupied, the group returned to their own chatter. The EMTs had moved toward the exit, peering out at the forensics going on below.

"This weather is shit," her deputy shouted over the wind. "Awnings are taking a beating with the wind blowing sideways. It's dark, it's wet. These guys really need to return in the morning."

But Callie was putting two and two together. It had been slow, it had almost been painful, but the tricklings and dregs were trying to take form.

"Really? A blood speck?" she said just loud enough. "In one of the trunks?"

Everyone silenced to hear. She scanned them then looked down, as if trying to hear herself. "How long before we can confirm it's JJ's?" she said.

Stunned, JJ touched her face, sore shoulder, probably wondering the source of the blood.

"Oh," Raysor said. "I see what we're doing. But I'm telling these guys to pack up. Call me when you can." He hung up.

"Which car?" Callie said into the empty line. "Gotcha. Yeah, keep at it. We'll be down in a sec." A pause. "Who? Reuben and me. We haven't done his interview yet, so your timing is perfect."

Suddenly the glass with prints at the Neck made more sense, and it didn't belong to Butch.

Chapter 36

CALLIE HUNG UP. "Reuben, we might need to go—"

"What did they find with the cars?" He obliged her and stood.

She shrugged. "They aren't done working, and with the weather . . ."

"Who says the killer even was one of us?" he said, stepping over Tony's legs. "Could've been a pervert dad with hots for young skirts for all we know."

Backing up, she created wider space between her and Mark in which Reuben could pass. "Not the issue," she said. "With you finding JJ and all, we really need to head to my office and do a long overdue interview. I put you until last on purpose, because—"

Reuben's wide hand caught her in the chest as he pushed her against the curio cabinet. Then in a football move, he pivoted, tucking a shoulder to plow his gym-built bulk into Mark. The retired SLED agent went down hard, sliding into a recliner. Reuben snatched Mark up and against him, using him as a shield, easily snaring the forty caliber from Mark's holster. "Don't think about it," he ordered, aiming at Callie.

Already in mid-draw, Callie clenched tight, and while she reserved pressure on the trigger, she kept the Glock's aim steady. "This is what I do, Reuben. Don't try to best me."

The EMTs dove behind the kitchen bar, and Callie prayed they'd relayed the change of events at *Water Spout,* getting the word to Raysor downstairs, or to LaRoache somewhere on the beach.

He shook Mark who gave a harsh shrug of a shake in return. Reuben tapped Mark with his weapon and resumed its sights back on Callie. "Hand me your gun, Callie, or I shoot people, beginning with you, then this one. Then any one of these flakes over there. If I do one, I might as well do them all, because how many times you pull the trigger doesn't matter once they give you the death sentence."

Georgia exploded a loud gasp, but Libby clapped a hand over her mouth. Libby clearly preferred Reuben's focus on Callie, as did she.

Damn it, Callie hadn't concluded fast enough, but she'd been on the right path. She absolutely understood better now.

"Drop the gun," Reuben repeated.

Mark stirred, but he wasn't fully alert.

"You can't take back killing someone," Callie said. "Especially a police officer."

She'd had some clues, and while they annoyed her, they hadn't fully taken hold.

For instance, Butch had said Reuben didn't like Cokes, yet he was the one who offered to go to the storage and replenish the fridge. He'd earlier commented that Reuben went out to find something to drink other than Coke.

Chloroform and ether were myths in terms of effectiveness, in spite of the movies, and who other than a wealthy, patent-wielding chemist would understand what to use to knock out JJ so efficiently and not kill her. Something sweet, JJ said, ruling out the two commonplace substances.

Callie remained homed in on Reuben, and he on her. "Slide it here," he said.

She shook her head.

He punched Mark upside the jaw, then regained his grip on the man. Mark's knees buckled, but Reuben was a big enough being to hold him up. "I can do this however many times you like, Callie, each worse than the last. Then there's always this," and he put the gun against Mark's temple.

The audience clustered on the sofa clipped cries and gasps while Callie reserved a pained moan of her own. JJ looked grieved, huddled in on herself on that ottoman in the wide open, afraid to get up and move.

"This time walk it over," Reuben said, "or I put a bullet in his head."

Clearly Reuben wasn't feeling vulnerable, and nowhere near needing to take stock of his future as to how it hinged on his actions.

"I'll set it on the floor," she offered.

"You'll place it on the table right here," he said, nodding toward it.

She did as told, ruefully taking in Mark.

"Now go back to where you were."

Reuben threw his hostage to the floor, collected the weapon, then kicked Mark in the ribs.

Mark . . . Oh God, where the hell was Raysor?

"So you've got two guns," she said, backing up to where she'd originally stood. "Where are you going? All these people in here and down below. You can't get to your car. I can't even get to mine."

"Reuben?" JJ asked.

What the hell, what did JJ think she could contribute to this? Callie couldn't shush her. Worried about not saying anything to aggravate, she couldn't say much of anything except, "Let me handle this, JJ."

But of course the author ignored the advice. "Nobody seriously thinks you killed Wendy, Reuben. Especially me."

Of course they did. Especially now.

Oh, how stupid, JJ.

"And thanks for the bookmark. It was motivational."

With the gun trained on Callie, Reuben lowered the other firearm, though he didn't put it away. His gaze moved back and forth between Callie and JJ, but his words definitely went to the author.

"Stop with the lovesick puppy routine, Jessie." He emphasized the old high school name but with no sense of nostalgia. "You're flat out embarrassing yourself. And you couldn't take a hint to give it up."

Not good.

"I invited you here to see you again," JJ said.

"You only wanted characters in a book."

"Reuben," Callie said, to recapture his attention.

"Shut up," he yelled to Callie, then took his voice back down. "I'm talking to the world-famous author. Who gets a chance like this?"

"There are prints in my car," he continued. "You put plenty of them there, on purpose. Left your blood for DNA."

"I didn't know it was your car," she replied in earnest, still not hearing how stupid she was.

"Stop playing with my intelligence, of which I'm well endowed, story lady. If you hadn't started this shit we'd all be a lot happier . . . some of you a hell of a lot safer." He swept the untrained firearm over their heads. The group flinched. "These people were bigger suspects. Twenty-four years, Jessie! That night was almost forgotten. I made something of my life. I donated hundreds of thousands of dollars to charity." Another swing of the weapon. Even Callie flinched. "You're fucking up my whole life over thirty seconds of detached misjudgment."

Then as if building up for the finale, he shouted, "I loved her, but I wasn't good enough."

Was JJ crying? Good lord, she was almost sobbing. "I invited you because I cared for you. Then . . . and now."

Callie worried each word led the author closer to earning Reuben's first shot.

And with two firearms he would keep firing. Rounds flying. God no, Callie couldn't afford for him to take that first shot, because in his fatalistic frame of mind, the beach house could become a massacre in a matter of a magazine.

Mark was awake. His eyes trained on her. Good. He knew better than to move . . . yet.

And in the front door window, she could make out the edge of Deputy Raysor's mug.

Reuben took a hard, deep mouthful of air, as if to let the universe hear his sorrow. "I killed the only girl I ever cared about," he said.

"But she didn't care," JJ shouted. "In my opinion, she deserved to die!"

"You and your book deserve to die," he yelled.

Callie dove as Reuben raised one weapon and shot at JJ, the other releasing a shot toward Callie . . . a miss.

Knocked off the ottoman, JJ went to the floor and didn't move.

Quickly rolling up, Mark went to grapple the big man, but Reuben caught him across the head with the butt of his own gun, then fired another shot in Callie's direction as he leaped away from Mark and headed for the closed doors . . . and the storm outside.

"Shots fired, shots fired," she yelled into her mic. "Officer needs assistance."

Reuben slung the back doors open and escaped into the sheeting rain, just as Raysor slammed in from the front.

Taking after Reuben, Callie leaped over the coffee table and into the massive pounding of weather, halting on the porch, eyes squinting. Reuben ran up the beach.

She bolted back in toward the deputy, shouting Reuben's description into her radio. "On the beach running toward the Pavilion. Armed and dangerous," she finished as she reached out to Raysor. "Your weapon."

"I can—"

"Your weapon, Don! You're too old and too fat to run in that sand. You have a backup piece. I've seen it!"

He handed over his nine mil. "LaRoache is on his way."

"Can't wait for that. Reuben's headed east, giving me eighteen blocks to catch him before he hits a populated area."

Taking a quick second to see that an EMT tended to JJ, she pointed also to Mark. "Check his ribs," she said. "And he was knocked out."

"Callie," Mark said, his lean crooked to protect his side, his voice gravelly. "You cannot go out there."

"Watch me," she said, and disappeared into the rain.

She couldn't let this man run loose on her island.

She was soaked in seconds. The tide ebbed, but just barely, high tide having peaked not an hour before. The jetties, however, remained covered except for the twenty to thirty yards on the beach. Edisto's beaches slanted incredibly steep, meaning the water at the end of each jetty could go fifteen feet deep. Some more.

She hit a hard stride, the sand familiar to her, and grateful for it being wet, she found the flat, hard area where she could get traction and gain speed. Each step faster. Each step made her grateful for her jogs and sobriety. Each step also reminded her of the twenty pounds of utility belt around her waist.

He had an edge on her, and with the darkness rushing in with the fog and the pummeling rain, she could barely make him out. He'd realized he had no place to go, she guessed, and his run had reduced to a jog. Regardless of his long legs and hers half the length of his, she imagined herself gaining ground.

She could hear nothing but rumbling thunder and the deafening resonance of the ocean's fists on the beach. Repeatedly, never ending, reaching for her as though to claim her. Oppressive clouds gunmetal gray and almost touching the water.

No advantage going for her except Reuben would run out of beach. Then even from this distance, Callie spotted a blue light in the parking lot beside the Pavilion. Had to be LaRoache.

Reuben was sandwiched in what had reduced from a two-mile to a one-mile stretch, and he was foolish to think he had any sort of way out.

A clap of thunder. Instinctively Callie hunkered, but barely a couple seconds. He probably did so, too. She returned to running, but the deluge hit harder. From above, from the side, from the ocean hurling its part in spits and splashes severed from the maddening waves. Every one of her senses was tested with the dominating storm.

She could barely see from the drops slapping her like tiny stones, and she ran almost blind, telling herself she didn't need to see well for at least a mile. But Reuben could stop, hide behind a jetty, and shoot. So she slowed.

Which made her feel the nature all the more. There was no mercy in the wind, the sea dark and unyielding. Rain poured furiously, drowning any clarity of sight.

Staring through the misty grayness and the torrent, brushing the rain from her vision in vain, she sought his shape, finding none.

She stopped and jerked around, probing through the dark toward the piers, especially the one closest.

The ninth access. Halfway between *Water Spout* and the Pavilion, she guessed, noting the shapes of houses. Then she recognized one of the more substantial jetties, a walkway wide enough to entice visitors to stand at the end and test their balance, and arms wide pretending they teetered on the edge of the world.

Reuben stood ten yards from the end.

"Reuben!" she yelled, but he could not hear . . . or acted as if he couldn't. The churning and growling of the sea's interference most likely not allowing her voice to carry.

She tried to time the waves better, shouting between crashes. "Reuben!"

He couldn't reach the end. However, where the jetty disappeared, he halted . . . then took two more steps to where the water covered his feet, the waves hitting his knees. A smaller person would have been swept under.

Callie had no chance to get near him. Not in this weather. Not with her size.

But she could get closer on the jetty than remaining on the sand, so she hoisted herself up and walked as far as she dared. This gave more chance for him to see her on his level, though they still stood twenty yards apart. She just prayed he wouldn't shoot.

"Thanks!" he yelled. "For trying for Stratton."

Surprisingly she heard. The wind pushed the words to her, while hers scattered in a hundred directions when she asked, "Come with me." So instead she motioned for him to walk to her instead. Likewise, he refused with his hands.

She dared walk closer. The good thing was that the tide was going out, which was also the bad. One slip meant being dashed on the rocks and pillars, concrete and embedded shells, and if one wasn't careful, the right combination of wave and undertow could carry a person out into that dark-gray tempest.

"Reuben, please!" she tried again. Short sentences. Too short. But anything longer was futile.

"Does not matter," he enunciated. "My life ends in prison . . . or ends now."

She'd put the weapon away when she struggled up. "Not shooting you," she said, hands out. "I refuse to shoot you."

"I killed JJ," he shouted, then raised his weapon, aimed directly at her. "Kill me or I kill you."

"No!" she yelled, wiping wet hair out of her way. Again she showed her hands empty. A particularly hard band of waves caught him. He side-stepped, leaned off on one side, but regained his balance. She had to crouch and grasp the top of a pier to re-center, then she rose back up.

He shot into the sand close to her right before she could return erect. She dropped back to the crouch.

Another gun sounded. Took her a split second to register it as different . . . from a different direction.

Reuben froze, his expression stunned. He lowered his weapon and stood as though debating a mild dilemma. Nothing deep, nothing fearful . . . then he cast himself into the sea.

"Reuben!" she screamed, unable to move forward without being grabbed by the angry water. She ran back and leaped down to the sand, running waist deep, hunting, cupping her sight with her hands to stop the rain.

Officer LaRoache ran up beside her. "Had to do it, Chief. Are you all right?"

"Call the Coast Guard," she ordered, taking a step forward then changing her mind as sand eroded beneath her feet, sucking her in, the whitecapped breakers reaching for her like hands. "Reuben!"

LaRoache walked to find shelter under someone's porch to make the call, leaving his chief in the weather where she stood watching the waves. In spite of the storm, he could still tell tears from rain.

CALLIE CALLED FOR her classmate, walking both sides of the jetty until the Coast Guard arrived which wasn't for over an hour due to the weather. Couldn't get a chopper in the air.

By then night had fallen pitch and stifling, clouds all low and ugly and changed to black. In spite of the squall declining to steady drizzle, Callie remained, watching, hoping that their overhead scan with hers on the shore would result in at least a body.

Lights lit up the beach houses, and as the rain subsided, a few ventured out in slickers, but Raysor and LaRoache ordered everyone off the beach, leaving Callie and her closest officers alone to walk the water's edge . . . plus one more.

Stan came up behind her and eased a burly hand on her shoulder. She turned and wrapped arms around that huge torso. "Where have you been?" she said into her old boss's windbreaker.

"Doesn't matter. I'm here tonight," he said, scrunching her hard.

"How's Mark?" she asked.

"He's the one who called me," he answered.

That's all they said in the miles they walked up and down the ocean's line, staying until the tide was completely out. The jetty stood stark, the sea calmed to swells, the rain no more than a soft and steady whisper.

Several hours later, wet to their bones, her spent legs quivering, she got the radio call. A mile out they found him. She didn't need to see him, though. She spoke with them about where to take his body, then she let Stan take her home.

Chapter 37

JJ
Tuesday.

GOD HELP HER, she'd been shot. Not in the plan at all.

JJ hung up the phone one-handed, tossed it on the bed, and threw her head back on the hospital pillow. Her arm remained in an elaborate contraption, her hand numb, her humerus shattered, her future a matter of whether or not she could keep the arm.

Her writing arm. The hand she kept her coffee in while mapping the next five hundred words of a chapter. The one that carried her laptop and handed off boarding passes during her cross-country book tours. On and on she listed the uses of that arm and what her limitations might mean for the next few months. Maybe forever.

She hadn't slept a wink despite the pain killers.

The ER doc passed off to the specialists, the specialists to those performing scans. Nurses dodged her questions, unwilling to explain the care plan for even that day. "The doctor will talk to you later, after all the results are back. But don't move the arm." Incessantly, with hard assurance they warned that movement would make matters worse, but nobody could tell her yet what might make matters better.

Only that they attempted to save the arm. They'd consider all options before the final choice. But the longer they waited . . .

No, so not in the plan.

She would not allow tears. She would not allow anger. No. This was *opportunity*. Or so Antonio had said. Thank God somebody informed him. She had neither of her phones, which became the justification she hung onto as to why nobody else had called.

"Flowers will be there soon, hon, and they'll put every other arrangement in that hospital to shame! Everyone in New York sends their best. But on the bright side look at this as the most exquisite ending to your book. His voice heightened to almost a squeal on the end. "What happened to your guy? God, you were so close to the action, Jessie.

Can't wait to read how you tie this up." Then his voice lowered. "How much of this did you really plan, hon? Is there any liability here?"

His exclaims of incredulity and disbelief, fret and flurry filled a half hour, ending with, "When can you get this to me?"

By dinner the flowers arrived, as promised. Over the top, as expected. "We love you, JJ," on the card, ordered by his admin clerk from the use of her author name.

Not that Antonio didn't care ... as long as she could type, or dictate, or punch keys with the end of her nose to spit out the story. Clearly he made no move to catch a flight to Charleston either, not with Edisto lacking in chefs offering overnight privileges.

And she knew what happened to the *guy*. That leant itself to a tear. For such a brief, beautiful moment, she thought Reuben her rescuer. Hearing him promise to find her abductor had raised new hope in her for the briefest of minutes, that all she'd planned would amount to not only a cracker jack of a story, but also the possibility of her reconnecting with the boy she'd never forgotten.

And all he'd done was use her back.

This wasn't the plan. Not at all.

Chapter 38

CALLIE HADN'T BEEN in bed three hours before rapping dragged her to her front door, her body still holding a sense of waterlog. Her security lights lit up the visitor in contrast to the pre-dawn hour, so she immediately recognized the tall, ginger figure before she got halfway down the hall.

"Peter? What's wrong?"

"Hate waking you, Callie, but I need my passport, please? Nobody was at your station, so I hoped . . ."

She crossed her arms, the early air a bit nippy for a cotton robe. "Why would you be needing it at this hour?" Though ordinarily she'd be up.

He looked tired as well, but he'd showered and spruced. "Sorry. Waited as long as I could. Catching the earliest flight I can to leave this place," he said.

These people, too, she guessed. She got it. Like Libby, Peter wasn't a tourist to salvage for a repeat visit. "Hold on."

She went to her closet safe and retrieved said passport. After handing it over, he delivered a brief "have a good day" and left. No regrets. No thanks. No wishes things had been different or goodbye. Just a man putting countries and miles between him and a horrible experience.

Too early to go to work and too late to go back to bed, she cranked up her own hot shower and stood under it until her shoulders throbbed red from too long running and rerunning the actions through her mind.

The twenty-four-year cloud was over, thank goodness. That was about the only good to come from this.

Last night, upon returning to *Water Spout* to deliver the sad news of their classmate, she learned that JJ and Mark had been taken to Charleston hospitals. While JJ would be there for a while, Mark was expected to be outpatient, back to his bed by morning, per Stan.

Drying off, she noted the dawn attempting to make its appearance, and in her underwear, unplugged her charging phone and found his number. She seriously owed Mark her first call of the day, hopefully before he went to bed to catch up on sleep and recuperate. Apparently Stan left her around one to stand by his buddy and bring him home from the ER, and bless him, he'd texted her about Mark's injuries.

Friends didn't get any better than Stan.

"Did I wake you?" she asked when Mark answered, hoping not, fully aware she probably did. He didn't do early when he was healthy, much less after getting in late from the hospital with two cracked ribs and a moderate concussion.

He'd volunteered to assist, come to her aid, and put himself in harm's way. Not requests she'd make of him again any time soon. The men in her life took a beating, and she had hoped this one might be different.

"Come over and see me," he mumbled. Still a sense of humor with a headache that had to be taking off the top of his head.

"Wasn't begging a visit," she said, suddenly guilty she called, seeing that she'd done so to assuage her guilt about him getting shot at, kicked, and pistol whipped under her watch. "Go back to sleep, Cajun. We'll talk once you've snoozed. Restaurant covered? Can I help?"

"All good," but the word trailed at the end.

"Get some sleep. Maybe I'll bring *you* dinner this time."

Which brought a sluggish chuckle out of him. She told him to take care and said goodbye, not letting him make the exertive effort to respond.

Something inside her hurt for him, cared for him, maybe wanted to make him fit in her universe. Maybe she'd have Ella & Ollie's fix him something special.

She put the reminder in her phone and instantly rolled into making her second most important call. And she would not mind waking this one up. "Chief," she said.

"Chief," Warren replied. He didn't sound tired at all.

"I solved your cold case."

He didn't ask which case. "Arrest him, kill him, already dead? What?"

"My officer killed him last night," she said. "After he shot at the rest of us and injured two civilians. He was about to shoot me."

A pause, then, "Everyone all right?"

"No. One in the hospital, another convalescing after a night in the ER, and an officer coming to grips with using his weapon on someone for the first time."

No badge wanted to put a bullet into someone. Callie doubted Warren ever had.

"Give your officer my deepest thanks for his work, Callie. Who did it?" he asked, a long second between the two thoughts. He'd already proven he recalled the names in that file.

"Reuben Douglas," she said.

"Wait, who?"

"Exactly. You never interviewed him, never met him, never had anyone else mention him, yet there he was with a crush on Wendy and nobody thought to question the quiet nerd who stood on the outside looking in."

"I'll be damned," he half-whispered.

He'd been the man in charge, but he hadn't been anywhere near the truth, relying on stereotypes instead of hunting for the right man . . . or boy. She wasn't quite comfortable with condemning him, but she wasn't into absolution either, and while she could, she didn't care to tell him that she might be more natural at this than he. And maybe he should've listened to her seventeen-year-old self back in the day.

They hung up awkwardly after an uncomfortable silence.

She dressed, unable to remove Reuben and Mark from her conscience. Each item she put on added more to the heaviness, the weight of the two men riding her like a wet wool cape.

Funny, though. Call it compartmentalizing, vengefulness, or a callousness from years of handling manipulative people, but she could not find one ounce of empathy for JJ. And she wasn't sure she could read a mystery again without wondering the motive of the author.

She moved into the kitchen, hit the button on her coffee pot, and unable to find anything palatable in the fridge, she leaned back on the counter, in her usual spot in the corner near the sink, and arms crossed, closed her eyes and waited.

"What you doing up so early?"

She jumped as Jeb strode in, still in baggy gym shorts, his hair askew. "I thought they'd cut you some slack after the craziness that went down on the beach." When she didn't quickly reply, he came over and wrapped arms around her, and she laid her cheek against the center of his naked chest.

"I'm the one who does the slack-cutting around here, son, which means there's no slack left over for me." She pulled away, noting the coffee pot done. This morning she needed that caffeine like air to breathe. God, what four days had done to rob her sanity.

Jeb helped himself to a cup after she filled her high octane, six-teen-ounce thermos. No cream, no sugar. The one she refilled once on a normal day, twice for overtime. Today might set a record with as little sleep as she got . . . her head still filled with rain, wind, and gunshots.

She leaned back on the counter, sipping the coffee hot. She loved it hottest when she was tired.

"Why don't you quit?" he said, seated at the table with a double bowl of cereal. "Find some peace, Mom. For God's sake you've done more than your share of civic duty."

Lowering her mug, she stared at him as if he'd asked her to skydive without a chute. He also sounded like someone's father, and in a brief flash of reality fathomed he was old enough to be one.

"I know, I know," he said, before she could reply, then he gave her his deep announcer voice. "It's who you are, Callie Morgan. So many windmills to challenge. So many dragons to slay. So many—"

Her expression stopped him.

She knew he hadn't meant to hurt her, but was that how he saw her? A fantasy creature trying to prove herself and never quite accomplishing the feat?

Leaping up he approached her expecting to hug her into another conversation, but she kept the thermos between them. He stared down at the barrier. "Mom, I'm sorry. I didn't mean it in a bad way. Just saying you don't have to work."

"No, I can *afford* not to work. There's a difference," she said, ig-noring his sting for no other reason than she knew her son loved her. A lot of parents could not say that.

He stared down at her, long enough to make her uncomfortable. "I worry about you," he finally said.

"I'm supposed to say that about you, kid."

"Well," and he laid his forearms across her shoulders, her height perfect for the propping. "We've never been the most normal family."

He needed a bath, and a swipe or two of deodorant with his arms propped like that, but she loved every scent of him. "I'm sorry you don't like me being in law enforcement."

He shrugged. "No, I don't like my mom getting shot at, but hey, I do so knowing you'll support me and my life's choices."

She waited for a revelation as to what those might be, but he left things unexplained, and she was glad. She wanted him to be whatever he wanted, not like her choosing to be a cop to exorcise demons like Stratton, or defy her parents' political aspirations.

Which brought back something her mother said. "You get it that I'm never running for Middleton office, right?"

"Duh, Mom." And he laughed.

"Your grandmother might skip a generation and come to you to continue the legacy."

He shrugged again, nonplussed. Not even flattered. Guess when five generations of Cantrells have run a town, the heirs are born with a sense of that responsibility, or a numbness to the idea. "We'll see," he said.

Her instinct was to tell him she hoped he wouldn't, but he'd just backed her into the corner with his sage remark about a mother's support for her son. But mayor sure beat him becoming a cop.

Her phone had buzzed three times since Jeb entered the kitchen. Leaving his mother to her business, he returned to his cereal only to twist his mouth unfavorably at the soggy remnants, so he poured it down the sink. He gave her a smile as he left.

The kid knew the power of hugs and smiles on her, used them strategically, and she savored them like the blessings they were. She hadn't grown up with too much of that. He, however, did it naturally. Maybe he was politician material.

She turned to her texts, the first from Marie. *Hope you come in late. Expect media.*

With a deep exhale, Callie anticipated that. Hated journalists with a passion, she did, but what did she expect with the famous, now infamous, JJ Loveless affected? Callie's only wish was, one, that JJ recuperated . . . just not anywhere close by, and second, that the author not capitalize on the whole affair, again, from Edisto. No press releases from her wheelchair on the sand. No signings at the bookstore, although, God help her, Karen at the Edisto Bookstore could sure cash in on JJ Loveless books for quite some time to come.

She tapped the next message. Janet Wainwright. *Can I rent the damn house yet or not?* Callie typed, *Yes you can,* and moved on.

The third text. She read, and a warm, grateful sense of belonging melted through her from the person who understood her best. *Meet me at the swing? I'll bring breakfast.* Sent by Stan twenty minutes ago.

Sure, she typed. *When?*

Walking in SeaCow. See you there in thirty.

The man could read her like nobody's business. Her boss, her friend, an almost lover, she respected him as much as anybody. She'd missed him so much in all of this.

Mark kept making excuses for him, referencing other interests in the man's life. Callie could not deny Stan that, but admittedly she was envious of whoever had captured his attention well enough to distract him from Edisto . . . and from her.

He was her touchstone. Through every relationship she ever had, through every job she tackled, he delivered the warnings and accolades, suggestions and orders that she could rarely argue with. He'd taught her to be hard on the job, and fair with the lower ranks.

Mostly, when she lost her way, he brought her home. That process usually started on *Windswept*'s porch . . . in that wide red swing.

Seabrook's old place.

She held her breath when it rented and treasured that porch when it wasn't.

Windswept was on Palmetto, only not as far down as *Water Spout*, but she detoured anyway to finalize things with the remaining class reunion crowd.

The door was still unlocked, but without Butch there, she wasn't as quick to enter and knocked on the glass. Georgia answered. "Oh, hey," she said, standing there uncertain, eyes making contact with anything but Callie.

Libby came up behind her, her curiosity quickly replaced with a shadow of what Callie registered as contrition.

"May I come in?" Callie asked when neither made the invitation.

The massive beach house felt like more of a cave without Reuben, without Butch . . . even without JJ. The good, the bad, and the ugly, she thought, only the three could have swapped nicknames from one day to the next.

"How y'all doing?" she asked the ladies, seeing Tony out on the porch by himself. She and the two remained standing in the foyer. The kitchen where Butch noshed and chugged bourbon was clean and tidy. No food. No drink. A vacation coming to a close.

"Peter's gone," Libby said. "Left once we heard about Reuben. He lit out to the airport, saying he'd rather wait there for the next available flight than hang with us."

Callie didn't say she knew. She presumed the man rather relieved at not having his past fully aired, especially his secret with Butch, and the less discussion about him the better. But he'd be the most nervous about JJ's future intentions. Callie didn't blame him a bit for escaping back across that pond as quickly as possible.

"JJ's arm is in a bad way," Callie said. "She's lucky that's all Reuben hit."

Georgia crossed her arms, recrossed them, weight shifting from foot to foot. "Why did he bring her here to shoot her? Why didn't he just do it at the Neck?"

"My gut, which is all I have to go on, is that he followed you during one of your visits to see JJ," Callie said. "Wanted to see what was being written about him. He came equipped with the anesthesia, but accidentally knocked her out with the door. When he found nothing incriminating on the laptop, he panicked. I believe he just couldn't make himself kill her."

"But he shot her!" she exclaimed.

"People strike back when you back them in a corner, Georgia."

Georgia stilled, struggling to take in that unpleasant reality.

Libby touched Callie's arm. "How's your man?"

"Home. His home," she corrected. "In bed. He'll be all right."

"He's nice," she added.

"That he is," Callie said, really meaning it.

Libby peeked back at her boyfriend. "Tony and I are leaving today."

"So I take it the reunion is cancelled?"

"Not funny," Georgia spat.

Callie had about had enough of these people, this one more than most after realizing her hand on aiding JJ. "None of this was funny, Georgia. Not a damn bit. You deceived every one of us and look at the results."

"But JJ—"

Callie moved toward her, closing their separation to inches. "You do not get to blame all this on JJ. Co-conspirator is what we call people like you."

The hostess went ashen. "Are you arresting me?"

Libby stepped back so whatever happened didn't splash on her. God, these people and their pretenses. Not a loyal one in the bloody lot, as Peter would say.

"No. Just saying it's over." Callie turned to leave but in afterthought peered back. "Next time you want to plan a reunion . . . leave my name off the list. And I'd really prefer you find another beach."

Georgia started to spout back, probably to dispute Callie's authority to dictate what she could do in her own beach house, but Libby gently took her by the arm, pulled her back, and closed the door.

Callie trudged down those long steps to her patrol car, but from behind the steering wheel stopped to study the tall profile of *Water Spout* against the slate-gray water and azure sky and a sun that glistened on gentle, rounded swells. This was the tallest house on Palmetto, popular for its parties in days past. Where she'd killed one man two years ago and basically killed another last night.

She never wanted to set foot in that place again.

She could almost see *Windswept* from where she pulled onto Palmetto, and Stan was a comforting sight waiting on that red swing when she parked. He was already setting out egg, cheese, and bacon biscuits, double the bacon, and cups of orange juice on a small rusted table he'd dragged over. The Yankee's favorite breakfast since he moved down.

"Figured you needed something other than coffee," he said, holding out his hand to present the spread. The big man slid over for her to take her seat within reach of the breakfast.

"I love it when you take care of me," she said, lifting one of the biscuits, suddenly feeling quite desirous of carbs and protein. In silence they ate, him finishing well before she did and easing back on the swing, his leg starting the motion once the table was empty, since Callie's feet barely touched the plank floor.

She balled up the biscuit wrapper and tossed it toward the bag, missing. "This is getting to be a habit of yours, tending me after . . ." But she couldn't finish.

"After a case," he offered. No use of the words *murder, death, kill,* or other applicable descriptors. "No different than in Boston. Me, captain . . . you, detective. We play the roles so well, no point not using the experience."

Out came the arm, and she leaned into it. "This job is wearing on me," she said. "Jeb suggested I retire."

"He's a kid," he said.

"I don't remember Boston being this taxing, except . . ." She started to mention her husband, but that could go unsaid. Stan had been there when Callie's professional and personal lives collided like two meteors, leaving nothing but remnants of destruction.

"You had the backup of an entire major city department," he said. "Here, you're it, Chicklet."

The old nickname he anointed her with back in the day, and he used it when teaching her or praising her performance. To her, he was just Stan. Ten years older, a thousand years wiser, but mostly, the voice that pulled her off the crags.

"This one feels like a loss," she said, falling into the sway.

"Hmmm." His foot kept the movement smooth. "From what I gathered, you solved an old cold case nobody expected to ever see the light of day again. And not too shabby figuring him out. That other chief owes you big time, I'd say."

Yes, but she wouldn't cash in that favor any time soon. She probably wouldn't go to Middleton any time soon. So much for having an old homeplace to visit your mother.

"The woman's probably all the more eager to write that book," she said.

"Won't see me buying it."

While she had no feelings for JJ, incredibly she did about Reuben. He'd shifted in just a brief matter of minutes from the reliable smart guy in her eyes to a killer. He'd been good in her mind way longer than bad, which had her interpretation of him sort of mangled.

"He killed himself, Chicklet."

"He was a kid who messed up," she said.

"Humph." He pumped the swing a tad harder. "You sort of cross over to the dark side when you squeeze off a girl's windpipe for not kissing you back."

Stan had a way of distilling things down to their most basic level.

"I told LaRoache that in essence JJ killed Reuben, not him," she said. While he was her most seasoned officer short of Raysor, he'd never had to use his weapon. "I hate he's got to go through all that officer shooting scrutiny. Glad he's got wife and kids." She looked up at Stan. "While he's out, might have to call on you more for traffic duty," she teased. He loved getting those calls. She often let him handle crowds in his Hawaiian shirts.

He and she had made a wonderful team. Still did . . . just not as often of late. "Where have you been these last few days?"

"Thought I had me a new lady friend," he said.

She pulled away from him. "What? You would do that to me?"

"Tried." He shrugged a tiny shrug. "The cop thing . . . too strong for her, she said."

"You need a lady cop," she teased again.

He turned rather plainspoken. "We tried that, Chicklet."

She didn't reply.

He was the one to change the subject. "You did fine this time, and I believe you know it. You're not a rookie, and you know that, too. I can't always be your security blanket, and frankly don't need to be."

"My what?"

He patted her on the leg. "I'm here when you need me. You just don't need me as much as you think."

They let that conversation slide into the cool morning air until it was gone.

He spoke up first. "So . . . you and Mark?"

She turned and studied the Atlantic across the road, blindly picking at the flecks of paint on the swing beside her.

"He sounds hopeful," he replied. "Question is, are you?"

"Don't ask me that, Stan. Look at what happened to him thanks to me. He's retired from it and I'm not. He might feel the need to protect, or worse, get jealous I'm still in the action."

"You're already overthinking it."

She looked back at her old boss. "That's just what he said."

Stan smiled. "He's already reading your mind."

She snapped back to the water. "Good Lord, that's what Raysor said."

"And Mark's law enforcement," he finished, like a period on a sentence.

"And that's what Jeb said," she said, wincing. "But not in a kind way."

Stan reached over and drew her back. "What does he know, Chicklet? He's just a kid."

The End

Acknowledgements

On the way to my mother's funeral in September 2019, I heard on the news about how one of my high school classmates had died at the hand of another. I remember it like it was hours ago. As a yearbook editor, I crossed paths with classmates probably more than the average person, and years later as an adult had lived down the street from the real-life murderer. Our children had played on the same t-ball team for which he'd coached. He had insomnia and a few times had seen me online late into the night, the time of day when I created my earlier books, and we'd talked about the old days.

The premise for this book came as the result of the tragic demise of Karen Simmons, whose murder rocked my graduating class. But I write fiction, not true crime, so instead of recording her story, I created a tale that touched upon the shock of knowing someone murdered and how the event can alter lives for a long time.

In that effort, I want to thank my husband, Gary, for walking me through how law enforcement handles cold cases, and correcting me in my interview techniques. Of course, always for being the patient stalwart support system I can count on when I need an ear to listen and tell me that I'm not bonkers in how I wrote a scene or tacked on some dialogue. I love you bunches.

Three particular people in my family read each and every book I write, and since this is book twelve, I must speak up about how appreciative I am for their steadfast loyalty. Thanks so much to my son Matthew Jerdan, my sister-in-law Angela Lane, and "the other grandmother" Phylis Weeks.

And of course I'd be remiss not thanking Edisto Beach for welcoming me each time I visit to sign books, interview people, and tuck myself into a beach house to research yet another tale. There's something incredibly recharging about going to bed with the sound of the tide and waking to bright sunlight beckoning me to breakfast on the porch, a walk on the beach, and a laptop in a rocker, recording all I see, hear, smell, and feel. Those visits infuse Edisto into the storytelling.

Also, I greatly appreciate the Edisto Beach Police Department for allowing me to take strong literary license with how law enforcement is actually handled. My depiction of Edisto PD is solely to make Callie Jean Morgan feel alive and look good. The real guys and ladies in uniform are highly efficient in how they protect natives and tourists alike on that island. I'm much obliged for their patience and understanding with me and my craft.

Finally, I continue to marvel at my readers. Bless you all for continuing to read these books. Your emails, texts, Facebook mentions, and even Christmas cards make me realize I could do this for all eternity.

About the Author

C. HOPE CLARK has a fascination with the mystery genre and is author of the Carolina Slade Mystery Series as well as the Edisto Island Series, both set in her home state of South Carolina. In her previous federal life, she performed administrative investigations and married the agent she met on a bribery investigation. She enjoys nothing more than editing her books on the back porch with him, overlooking the lake, with bourbons in hand. She can be found either on the banks of Lake Murray or Edisto Beach with one or two dachshunds in her lap. Hope is also editor of the award-winning FundsforWriters.com

C. Hope Clark

Website: chopeclark.com

Twitter: twitter.com/hopeclark

Facebook: facebook.com/chopeclark

Goodreads: goodreads.com/hopeclark

Bookbub: bookbub.com/authors/c-hope-clark

Editor, FundsforWriters: fundsforwriters.com

Made in United States
North Haven, CT
04 May 2023

36248425R00157